Finding Love in Positano

Finding Love in Positano

Lucy Coleman

First published in Great Britain in 2022 by

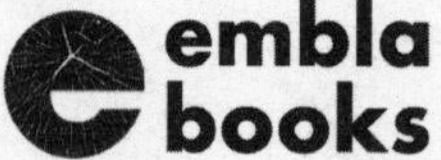

Bonnier Books UK Limited
4th Floor, Victoria House, Bloomsbury Square, London, WC1B 4DA
Owned by Bonnier Books
Sveavägen 56, Stockholm, Sweden

A CIP catalogue record for this book is available from the British Library.

Print ISBN: 9781471411601
eBook ISBN: 9781471411595
Audio ISBN: 9781471411618

This book is typeset using Atomik ePublisher

Embla Books is an imprint of Bonnier Books UK
www.bonnierbooks.co.uk

Dedicated to Abba, for those inspirational moments when I need to step away from the PC and dance wildly around the room before getting back to work . . .

Marci James

Prologue

As I stare down at the postcard on the table, the picture is mesmerising. Three small boats are tied to a large wooden stake on an otherwise deserted beach that most people would consider to be a vision of paradise. In the foreground, it's easy to imagine the photographer peering out from behind a clump of vibrant greenery, eager to frame the shot to perfection. Beyond the white sand, the turquoise-blue water is crystal clear and far off on the horizon, the sea appears to melt seamlessly into the sky.

My brother, Guy, slowly turns the card over. The handwriting is instantly recognisable, but I can hardly believe my eyes.

My dearest Marci and Guy

Surprise – I'm in Thailand! Your indomitable godfather is on his travels and sending a long-distance hug. I'm standing here looking at this view right now and life doesn't get any better.

Giving you both a heads-up that an important email will be winging its way to you shortly as I have some exciting news to share.

Hope you and the family are all well.
Sending much love – as always,
Richard

He finishes off with a smiley face drawn in the bottom right-hand corner, but neither of us are smiling. Richard has lived on the Amalfi Coast in southern Italy for the last eighteen years and when I last spoke with him, a mere fortnight ago, there was no mention of him heading off on his travels. What is going on?

May

1.

Drawing the Short Straw

'Un-be-liev-able,' Guy exclaims, exhaling slowly as he continues to stare at his phone. 'Has Richard lost his mind?'

I'm still reading through our beloved godfather's email, thinking much the same thing. Richard Havrington is one of the kindest, most thoughtful men I've ever met, but he's a man who – even he would admit – enjoys a quiet, simple life. Albeit his style is different to most. The words I would use to describe him are flamboyant, fun and grounded – someone who has never believed the grass is greener on the other side of the fence.

'He's married?' I gasp, staring across at Guy, who doesn't seem to have reached that part of the email yet.

'What?' he replies, his finger scrolling down quickly and when he resumes reading again his jaw drops. 'This is sheer madness, Marci. Why is this the first we're hearing about it?'

I shrug my shoulders. 'I have absolutely no idea why Richard decided to keep this a secret from us – it doesn't make any sense.'

With two failed romances behind me, Richard was always just a phone call away. He was my listening ear and helped me to put things into perspective – even when my heart was broken. And he was the one Guy turned to when he had some pre-wedding nerves last summer, so for Richard to go off and secretly marry someone without even mentioning it, is completely out of character.

Richard was at boarding school with Dad and after university they were both drawn into the world of antiques. They set up a business together in an old warehouse situated at Gloucester Quays. When Richard suddenly announced that he was moving to Italy, it's true to say that his decision came totally out of the blue. But it made sense because for two consecutive winters he'd ended up in hospital with pneumonia. The warmer climate was going to be beneficial for him and it paid off. At the time I was eleven years old, and Guy was about to turn sixteen. Saying goodbye to Richard was tough, he'd been around all of our lives, always present and supportive. As a bachelor, Richard had time for us when our parents were busy and sometimes he'd pick us up from school and treat us to a meal out.

Richard left a hole in our lives when he went, although the irony is that it drew Guy and Dad even closer together.

'I'm not abandoning you, poppet – I promise to come back to see you all at least twice a year,' Richard had stated quite firmly, the day before he flew out to begin his new life. 'Your mum and dad will visit for holidays, and we'll hire a couple of camper vans and meet up somewhere to discover the delights of Italy together.'

And, true to his word, every summer until Dad passed away just six years later, that's what we did. We met up during the summer holidays and for two glorious weeks we travelled around in a little convoy. We toured large areas of Northern Italy together before our lives were suddenly turned upside down.

Losing Dad was devastating for us all, but especially hard on Mum and Guy, who had to shoulder the responsibility of the business while dealing with their grief. And my dream of working at Anvil & Anchor Antiques with Dad never came true, as it was another four years until I gained my degree and joined the team. Naturally, Richard took losing his closest friend very hard, not least because he didn't get to say a final goodbye.

'I know it's a shock, and unexpected, Guy,' I reply, trying to sound composed. 'And I'm surprised he didn't drop any hints when he was here in January. But now I think about it, when I met up with Richard in Rome last year, he was a little preoccupied even back then. One of the contacts I was due to visit was based in Genzano, about twenty-five miles away, and when I mentioned that to Richard, he insisted on driving me. He'd always wanted to visit the town during the flower festival, and he told me it was on his bucket list. There were moments when I felt there was something he wanted to tell me but kept putting it off. Maybe he was already thinking of closing the shop before Angela even appeared in his life.'

'Hmm. And the bucket list? He's only sixty-two,' Guy points out.

'You can have a bucket list no matter what your age, Guy. I have one – whether I'll ever get to tick everything off is another matter entirely.'

'Aren't you a little young for that?' he quizzes me.

That remark makes me smile. Being five years older than me, at the age of thirty-four Guy pretty much still focuses on each day as it comes. Each to their own, as they say!

'He was really excited about visiting Genzano, though, and it was awesome. During the festival, the Main Street is entirely carpeted with flowers. The town is on the edge of a volcanic lake called Lago di Nemi, so the views are stunning. Among the tiny alleyways and cobbled streets, we discovered that wonderful haul of eighteenth-century wooden doors. Do you remember them?'

'I do. We could have sold them several times over, in fact.'

Despite the fond memories, I find myself biting my lip anxiously. Richard would say if his health was failing, wouldn't he? It's hard not to dwell on the years we didn't have with Dad. If he had known how little time he had left, would he have done something totally out of character? Like dragging us all off to Saint Lucia, for the holiday of a lifetime he'd always talked about?

'You think he's going through a bit of a . . . what would you call it? Late-life crisis?' Guy continues.

'It's easy for us to sit here and try to second-guess what's happening, but what if he's finally found the one, after all these years?'

'Fine, if he'd flown his lady love over to meet us all. But he's in Thailand. With his *wife*. And now he's asking one of us to head over to Positano to close his business down and sell off his things. It's bizarre and I refuse to be a party to it. What if this woman is simply after his money?'

'Her name is Angela, Guy, it says so in the email. Perhaps she was on holiday when they met and the attraction between them was instant, who knows?'

I can't help but stick up for Richard and hope that he has simply found happiness. Richard has been my go-to person ever since Dad died. Mum was distraught, but she had to keep the business going and I couldn't bother her with my woes. Then, when she met David Parker, I was glad to see her smiling again, but I was left in limbo feeling on the edge of things. Richard tries, even now, to avoid David on his trips back to the UK and I felt that he thought Mum could do better.

The truth is that I am shocked and a little hurt that Richard hasn't taken me into his confidence. Naturally, I noticed the contact with him has been patchy recently, which isn't entirely unusual when he's busy, but I'm struggling to understand why he didn't talk to me about this. My annual buying trips to Italy are extra special when Richard can make time to join me for a few days, but I guess I'll be going it alone in future.

'Leave it to me. I'll tell Richard straight that I don't intend on doing anything until he calls me, and we can talk it through in greater detail. What do you think?'

Guy shakes his head, frowning. 'Well, he's more likely to listen to you than he is to me. Look – if it does turn out that he's met the love of his life and they want to travel the world together, then good luck to them both. But I'd hate to see him turning his back on the great life he's made for himself, only to end up regretting what appears to me to be a hasty decision.'

'I promise I won't let him dodge my questions. But if he's serious about this, it's a huge favour he's asking.'

Guy puts his phone down on the desk and gets to his feet. 'That's for sure. Richard knows I'll have my reservations, so he's banking on you to sort him out. If you feel it's the right thing to do, Marci, then go for it. Last summer I left you in charge while I disappeared for two months to get married and take a leisurely honeymoon. If you're happy to be pulled into this, then Positano's a wonderful place to spend the summer. I can hold down the fort here. Anyway, I'm in need of a strong coffee – can I get you one?'

I nod, letting out a deflated sigh once Guy is out of earshot.

Oh Richard, you deserve to find a woman as kind and caring as you are, but I won't relax until I meet her face to face. You told me once that you fell in love at a young age and the woman of your dreams broke your heart. It's taken you forty years to get over it. And now you're throwing caution to the wind. I can only hope Angela's feelings for you are genuine. Guy is right, you'll talk me into doing this for you because what I want more than anything is to know you're no longer alone. Is that hopium? I don't like being on my own, either, but if you can find your soul mate out of the blue, then maybe there's hope for me, too. The problem is we're both hopeless romantics at heart, aren't we?

2.

Happiness is Infectious

'Marci, dear lady. Have you come to rescue me?' Anthony Montgomery is one of my favourite clients. His reputation is infamous, as are the prices he charges his wealthy clients. 'I'm in desperate need!' he declares dramatically.

I fall in alongside him and the two members of staff he was grilling melt into the background, grateful to be rescued.

'Tell me more,' I reply, trying hard to suppress a smile.

'Where do you keep the really *interesting* items?' Anthony demands, the corners of his mouth turning down.

My eyes widen and he looks back at me, shamefaced. 'I know,' he protests, 'I buy them up before they even reach the shop floor. But you must have something I haven't seen yet.'

'Only a few items from my recent trip to France. They're being worked on as we speak. You had the decorative wall panelling, didn't you? And that enormous stone urn?'

'I did. And what an eye you have! But I'm desperate. I can't sign off on my latest project without a few final, finishing touches. The client is big in the art world,' he leans in to whisper conspiratorially.

'Well, as it's you, you're welcome to come and take a look around the workshop.'

Anthony's beam is dazzling, the whiteness of his teeth in total contrast to his gorgeous tan. And it's real, as is everything else about him and his glamorous lifestyle. He follows me to the lift, and we head down to the basement. The minute the doors open he takes in a deep breath and groans. 'Oh, the smell of French polish and newly sawn wood. It's heavenly!'

I let him wander, as I stop to chat to two of the guys who are busy sanding layers of paint off an old armoire that I discovered in a dilapidated outbuilding in the Loire Valley.

'Marci!' The urgency in the tone of Anthony's voice makes me turn and walk briskly in his direction. He seems to be arguing with poor old Harry, who has stepped back from his work bench looking somewhat bewildered.

'I'm just gluing this pot back together, Marci. It was on my list for today.'

'Some things were meant to be broken, there's a fragile beauty to imperfection,' Anthony informs him with a level of seriousness that is genuine.

'It seems we have a customer who loves this piece just the way it is, Harry. Can we find a suitable packing case for the main part of the pot and pack the smaller pieces up separately?'

Harry lowers the brush in his hand as a small blob of glue is about to plop off the end of it. 'Of course, Marci.'

'Thanks so much. We'll um . . . leave you in peace, then.'

Anthony links arms with me, his day clearly made.

'You prefer an absolutely stunning French stoneware confit pot in two pieces?' I enquire, turning to look at him. With the entire neck and one of the handles sitting alongside the pot, I'm at a loss to understand Anthony's excitement. Harry would make the repair look invisible and the pot is a real treasure.

'The gallery I have in mind is full of oversized, colourful canvases. The background dressing should be eye-catching and a broken pot displayed on a pedestal is a statement. Knowing Kelvin, he'll probably end up selling it.'

'I hope so because broken pieces attract a premium,' I banter, jokingly.

'His pockets are deep. What else have you been keeping from me?'

My stomach rumbles hungrily, but who has time to eat when they're in such charming company?

Sitting down at my desk with a hearty bacon, lettuce and tomato sandwich, I start munching before checking my phone – only to discover two missed calls from Richard. Immediately pressing redial, I wait anxiously as the seconds tick by. Just as I fear it's about to go to voicemail, the sound of Richard's voice puts a huge smile on my face, and I turn on the speakerphone.

'You rogue, you! What time is it there?'

'Just after eight in the evening. And I know. I do feel badly, but I'm so darned happy!'

And I can hear that loud and clear. He sounds full of energy. 'Then you're forgiven. We're still in shock, you do know that?' I tease.

'Sometimes life forces you to grab the moment. I'm in the bar waiting for Angel. She's fussing with her hair, but I told her it's lovely just the way it is.'

Aww. My bottom lip wavers as I sit back in my chair. 'Angel?'

'I never call her Angela. You'll love her, too, Marci. She's a breath of fresh air. I learn something new every single day I'm around her – things that astound me. She's a chiropractor, and my back has never been in such good shape,' he enthuses. 'Angel also practises kinesiology and uses tapping, which is based on the principles of Chinese acupressure. She's practised in holistic centres all around the world.'

'That's incredible, Richard – I can't wait to meet Angel and find out more about her. She's spent a lot of her life travelling then?'

'She has, but now it's time to put down some roots, although we have a growing list of wonderful places we want to experience together.'

So the travels will be ongoing and I'm going to have to look up kinesiology, as I have absolutely no idea what that is.

'I'm assuming at some point before too long you'll be making a trip back to the UK?'

'Not you, too, Marci! I had a bit of a disgruntled text from Guy, but he did send his congratulations. And your mum wrote me a long email. Most of the sentences ended with a question mark, which is precisely why I decided to keep it a secret and tell everyone after the fact. You aren't going to interrogate me, too – are you?'

I sigh, softly. 'That's the price you pay when people love you, I'm afraid. What you forget is that video chats are all well and good, but it's the things you haven't been talking about that worry us.'

Richard chuckles and it feels like he's close by, instead of five thousand plus miles away.

'Duly noted. But there wasn't much to say, it was a whirlwind affair – literally!'

Uh-oh. 'So . . . how long have the two of you known each other?'

There's a pause and Richard clears his throat. 'Three months, one week and four days. And probably nine hours.'

I let out an exasperated 'Oh', unable to disguise a sense of apprehension. 'That's . . . um—'

'—enough time to know it isn't a fleeting thing,' he jumps in. 'I was the perfect gentleman and even though I bought the ring on the day of our one-week anniversary, I didn't ask her until we'd reached the one-month milestone.'

Richard might be a character, but no one would ever describe him as impetuous. One month is a *milestone* in a relationship?

'I'm pleased for you both. At least if I ever meet *the one*, I know I'll be able to count on your support when I run off and get married without telling the family.'

Richard dissolves into a fit of laughter because he knows I'm trying to make a point. 'Touché. Out of you, your mum, my sister and Guy, I knew the only person who would unreservedly forgive me was you, poppet.'

Hmm. Now he's tugging on my heartstrings. He hasn't called me that since I was a pre-teen.

'Us romantics need to stick together, Richard, but—'

'Stop right there. Just be happy for me, Marci, please.

Suddenly life is exciting again and I'm at that time in my life when I'm tuning into that inner voice. I don't want to live to regret the things I didn't do, that's all.'

'Inner voice?'

'Angel and I meditate each morning. It's cathartic.'

What's that old saying Gran used to use . . . something about being too late to shut the stable door after the horse has bolted?

'I'm impressed by the new *you*. What exactly do you want me to do?'

'I don't own the shop in Positano, or my accommodation above it which makes life a little easier. However, it's crammed full of stock – you know what I'm like. Collecting has become a bit of a hoarding habit over the years, I'm afraid. There are some fine pieces there, Marci, which I know you'll appreciate, as well as the usual things to catch the eye of tourists.'

I groan inwardly as he continues.

'My dear friend, Luca Romano, is expecting the keys to be handed back by the end of July, so everything must be gone by then. Obviously, I'm travelling light but Angel and I were so tied up organising the grand tour and our exotic beach wedding, that I didn't have time to go through my stuff.'

'Stuff?' I enquire.

'Personal effects. Everything in my office is a bit chaotic, I'm afraid, and will need a bit of a sort before it's all boxed up. Luca will store them for me. The big problem is the stock. I've been reaching out to my contacts to see if anyone is interested in buying it as a job lot but, so far, I haven't had any firm takers.'

I immediately picture Anthony Montgomery's reaction to a whole host of Italian treasures, hand-picked by one of the best dealers I know. He'd think he'd died and gone to antique heaven.

'I'm sure Guy would be delighted to have an influx of new stock if that's an easier option,' I offer. 'I know how excited he is when I return from a buying trip abroad.'

'I was hoping to have it all gone by the time you fly over, so that it was only my personal bits and pieces left for you to deal with.' Richard does sound extremely apologetic now. 'You can blame Angel for being such a tantalising distraction and keeping me otherwise occupied.'

If that means what I think it means, then my godfather is giving me way too much information. I give myself a mental shake to get that thought out of my head.

'I could send Guy photos of everything and get him to appraise it as a job lot, if you like?'

For a moment I think we've lost our connection, then I hear Richard exhale.

'You'd do that for me, just to get me out of a hole? I thought it might be asking a little too much of you both. I'll prod a few people about some of the big-ticket items, while you have a chat with Guy. Oh, a man like me doesn't deserve to have two angels in his life, but I'm blessed. When I emailed, we both know I was only speaking to one of you. My star, my little shining light of happiness and the one person with whom I'd entrust my worldly goods!'

I start to giggle. 'And the only person who is fool enough to help you unpick what has been a wonderful life for you on the Amalfi coast.'

'Luca and his English wife, Celia, also own a local hotel – Il Posto di Luca, home of the extremely popular Ristorante Sul Mare. They've both told me there will always be a room waiting for me if I ever return. But I won't need it. I've waited a long time to find a woman like Angel and, to be frank, I'd given up looking a long time ago – as you know. Ironically, she rather reminds me of you. Strong, intuitive, caring.'

'Ah, so you mean a person who is able to get things done out of sheer determination, and not always in their own best interests?'

'That's something Guy would say, not me – and you know it.'

'Okay. I'm in.'

'In for a delightful summer in Positano! And afterwards you'll thank me because they're going to love having you there. I guarantee it will be fun. Have you ever waited tables?'

'No. Why?'

'Just wondering. Anyway, let me know when you plan to fly out and I'll let Luca, Celia and the family know you're coming. I owe you, poppet – big time! But I wouldn't ask if I didn't think . . . well, this could be your summer of happiness. Regretfully, while I adore talking to my favourite goddaughter, a vision of loveliness is walking towards me and she's threatening to render me speechless. I'll be in touch by email, as we're on the road early tomorrow morning. As for you, it's time to dig out some summery things and put the stuffy suits away on the hangers, Marci – you're in for a treat!'

* * *

'Well, what did Richard have to say for himself?' Mum and Guy are staring at me intently.

'He's on a high. Angel has literally given him a new lease of life. In my opinion we should let things settle down and . . . err . . . give him the benefit of the doubt.'

'On what? That this woman isn't after him for his money? Or that she hasn't done this before and he'll end up heartbroken and stranded, with no home to go back to?' Guy's words are harsh and even Mum's eyebrows shoot up into her fringe.

'That's a little unkind, Guy. I know we're all concerned about Richard, but he's nobody's fool,' Mum reminds him, sharply.

'I also feel everything is happening too fast,' I agree. 'But whether he's selling up because of Angel, or this is his chance to take early retirement – the decision has been made.'

'Am I the only one who is concerned about Angela's motives? If there's nothing to hide, then wouldn't Richard have suggested she at least meet us all before their big day? What if he suggested it and she persuaded him otherwise?'

I stare at Guy, my gaze rather unforgiving. 'At the age of twenty-nine, of course it's unlikely I'd run off and tell everyone after the fact. But if I were in my early sixties, then I'd probably say: "Let's do it". In Richard's case, what has he got to lose? It's heart-warming to hear him sounding so happy and we can't stand in judgement of a woman we've never met.'

'His entire world will fall apart if he ends up regretting his decision, Marci. People who listen to their heart over their head either end up ecstatically happy, or in the pits of despair. I don't want that for Richard, in the same way that I don't want that for you.' Mum can't help but vocalise her thoughts about the man she sees as a brother.

It took two goes at serious romance before I realised that I was trying to make something work that was destined to fail. They both let me down and it wasn't because either of them broke my heart, but they made me feel unworthy of love. And that's what hurts.

Richard was always there on the other end of the phone to dispense sympathy and wait patiently as I sobbed my way through handfuls of tissues. Guy would simply give me a hug and then roll his eyes as if he'd seen it coming from day one.

Maybe I should take a leaf out of Richard's play book and start living my life one day at a time. I love my job, I have a lovely house – albeit with a sizeable mortgage on it – and I'm free as a bird. A huge smile breaks out on my face.

'I'm going,' I state, adamantly.

'Where?' Mum asks, puzzled.

'To Positano. Someone has to sort out Richard's things and that someone is *me*!'

June

3.

A Working Holiday

There's a tap on my office door and as it edges open, Guy appears.

'Marci, I appreciate that you're busy tying up loose ends, but you have a visitor. He's waiting in reception.'

'Thanks. I've got one more item to add to this list and then I can break off. Do you know who it is?'

Guy shrugs his shoulders nonchalantly. 'No idea. I'm just the messenger. One of your special clients, no doubt.'

It's a running joke between us that while he has a mixed clientele, mine is predominantly male and two-thirds are over the age of sixty. At less than half their ages, they find in me a willing student. I've learnt as much listening to the stories they tell about the history of the pieces they've collected and, in some cases, bought and sold, as I have from almost a decade in the business. And that's why they keep coming back to me. Patience, as they say, is a virtue and I enjoy that personal interaction.

I save the handover document I'm working on and stand up from my desk. Straightening my crisp cotton blouse and running my hands over the creases from sitting at the PC for the last couple of hours, I grab my jacket.

In this business you never know whether a customer is

bringing in an old family heirloom that's been lying in the attic for decades or is in search of a specific, must-have item. Sometimes I feel I'm like a private investigator in the world of antiques and my little black book contains the telephone numbers of some notable – and, in some cases, unusual – contacts.

As I hurry down one flight of stairs to the reception area on the second floor, I glance over the handrail at the sea of faces peering up at me.

'Surprise!' they all yell out in tandem, and Guy is grinning from ear to ear.

'You spoilt the moment,' he shouts up at me. 'You were supposed to use the lift!'

There are at least thirty people crowded into the space, as well as a table with an array of canapés and trays of champagne flutes. As I hit that last step, Mum comes hurrying forward.

'Oh, we're all going to miss you, Marci.' Goodness, if Mum is getting emotional then I'm in big trouble and I don't have a tissue with me.

'Don't,' I appeal to her, as she wraps her arms around me. 'Just think of it as another one of my buying trips. It's simply an extended one.' Admittedly, the thought of being away for two whole months is both exciting and a little daunting for me.

In all honesty, while I have a sneaking suspicion it's going to be a challenge, it's not like planning for one of my busy work trips. And I'm excited to meet the people Richard refers to as his *Italian family*. But as I stand here and begin doing the rounds, it occurs to me how lucky I am.

'Marci.' Mrs Krystyna Kaminski, one of my most frequent visitors, taps my shoulder and as I turn, today she's a vision in pastel blue. She's wearing a hat worthy of an appearance at Ascot, and everything is, as usual, colour co-ordinated. 'You are going – leaving us and what am I to do? The house still needs so much and now Jakub will wonder why nothing is happening.'

'Come, let me get you a glass of champagne. Please don't fret. I have briefed Briony, and she will continue the search for you. And I have some good news – I was about to call you. I have found the most exquisite French wall hanging.'

Briony is our shop floor manager and is also my closest friend. We met at uni and always have each other's back. I'm thrilled she agreed to step up and sit in my chair.

Mrs Kaminski's face lights up. 'Is it rare?' she asks, in her sing-songy voice.

'Yes, indeed. Right now, it's hanging in a monastery in the Languedoc area in southern France. We're still negotiating a price, but I think you'll be pleased with the outcome.'

Her hands fly up to her face with delight. 'It means so much to me, my dear. I am so grateful.'

The price tag is irrelevant to the Kaminskis and it's a pleasure to help them in their quest.

'And you will be back? You promise me, yes?'

'Of course. Now, here you go – let's toast.' I grab two glasses of champagne and hand one to her. 'And when I return, who knows – I may have found some special Italian pieces to delight you.'

'Did I hear the word "Italian"?' Anthony appears at my elbow, and I introduce him to Mrs Kaminski.

'A pleasure to meet you, dear lady,' he croons, shaking her hand and I watch as Mrs Kaminski's cheeks begin to glow under his scrutiny. Pastel blue certainly looks good on her, and it reflects her vibrant personality.

'You are also a client of Marci's?' she enquires when he finally releases her hand. 'Then we are competitors!'

The look on Anthony's face is priceless and I quickly jump in.

'That's where I'm extremely fortunate. You both have completely different and discerning tastes.'

Anthony's eyes light up. He appreciates someone who can banter, and with Mrs Kaminski he's met his match.

I excuse myself, seeing that they're more than happy to natter away. People who collect, even if they sell on, love to reel out the stories of their best buys. It's the thrill of the chase and that's why people often lose their heads and pay way too much for something at auction. Guy is brilliant at edging bidders up, even when they have already exceeded their maximum budget. It happens all the time.

As I stop to sip some champagne, it's clear that Guy has pushed the boat out. This is wine merchant quality, not the usual twenty pounds-a-bottle stuff. He must be feeling a tad guilty about the task I have ahead of me. Everyone is envious, acting as if it's a holiday, but both he and I know that it won't be.

A hand nudges my arm and I turn around to see Briony, looking at me sheepishly. 'Sorry I couldn't give you the heads-up as both Guy and Evelyn swore me to secrecy,' she admits. No one can find the heart to say *no* to my mum; even though she's a silent partner in the business these days, for a few years she was the driving force of the company.

'You're forgiven, especially as I can jet off to Italy knowing my clients are in safe hands!'

Briony catches her lower lip between her teeth and what I see is a moment of hesitation. 'What's wrong?'

'You really think I'm up to sitting at your desk?'

I reach out to give her a comforting hug, and when I stand back Briony's eyes look teary. 'Of course, you are! You passed your training with flying colours, as I knew you would. And I'm a phone call or an email away. Ring me as often as you like. I'll probably be in touch with you daily anyway, sending photos of Richard's collection to begin the valuations. You and I are a team, nothing can change that. But I think you're going to surprise yourself.'

The look of relief I see reflected on her face warms my heart. I understand the nervous apprehension, because that was exactly how I felt when Guy decided I was ready to undertake buying trips abroad. I didn't feel ready, but I was, and Guy could see that, just like I know Briony is.

'Have you had anything to eat?' Guy calls out, striding towards me with a huge smile on his face. I lift up my glass to avoid spilling champagne all over him, as he wraps his arms around me, hugging tightly.

'Not yet. My head is all over the place. I didn't expect to feel so conflicted today. I mean, it's only eight weeks, isn't it?'

Guy stands back, tilting his head to gaze at me. 'It was the same for me last year when Selena and I went on our honeymoon. I couldn't even imagine not coming into work for two whole months. I thought I'd get withdrawal symptoms. But once we were on our trip it was like stepping into another world. You'll soon adjust.' I can see the guilt from last year lingering in his eyes. 'And if you decide it's too much to take on, I can fly out for a few days. Mum will step in for me – you know that. Although I hate to think of the chaos that might ensue with her in charge!'

I shake my head, laughing. Mum hasn't been in charge of the business for years. 'I'll be fine once I get on that plane tomorrow. It's not like I'm a stranger to Italy, is it? Not after all my buying sprees there.'

'Yes, and it gave you and Richard the perfect excuse to meet up for a jolly and discover some interesting little places. And you're all set to go?' Guy prompts, sensing the change in my mood. 'I bet Richard has been frantically making arrangements ahead of your arrival. In hindsight I feel I overreacted to his news. Getting married is a risk no matter what the circumstances, isn't it?'

Is it? I wouldn't know.

'I guess it is, but I knew from the start that Selena was the right one for you. Otherwise, I would have been jumping up out of my seat when the vicar asked whether anyone knew of any just impediment,' I declare, and he chuckles.

'I don't think the fact that one's sister doesn't approve counts as a good enough reason. But the truth is that I wouldn't have asked her to marry me if you didn't approve. You've always had my back. And, if it helps, I knew that Everett Berkeley didn't deserve someone as wonderful as you – you're better off without him.'

Well, that's a surprise and his honesty is touching. I assumed the reason Guy didn't like Everett was simply down to a clash of personalities. At the time I was in love with the idea of being in love and Everett was very charming and attentive for a while. His parents were delighted when we started seeing each other, not least because my mum and Georgia, Everett's mum, socialised in the same circles. Everyone assumed it was the real thing – sadly, that included me. After a whirlwind romance and talk about getting engaged, Everett suddenly got cold feet. It was less than a week later that he was spotted with a new woman on his arm. In hindsight, I realise that the only person Everett cares about is himself, but the rejection dented my pride, and I felt humiliated. I vowed I wouldn't let anyone mess with me like that again.

'I'm going to miss you,' I sigh, and he nods his head in agreement.

'But just think of that beautiful Italian sunshine. And I'll be expecting a postcard – I can't wait to find out more about Richard's Italian family!'

The remarkably attractive guy holding up a piece of cardboard with my name scrawled on it – which looks suspiciously like it was hastily cut from a cereal box – has arms strong enough for him to take over the trolley with my suitcases on it and push it with one hand.

'Thank you so much. They're a little heavy,' I warn him. Even having spent a small fortune buying an entire wardrobe of new, lightweight summer clothing, the two large suitcases are still weighty, and I had to pay a hefty surcharge.

He flashes me an engaging smile and he's a vision of dark curly hair, white teeth, and bronzed skin. 'I'm Nico. And this is nothing. A lot of our guests turn up with twice as much and they're only here for a couple of weeks.'

That's obviously an Italian name but his English is perfect and spoken without even a hint of an Italian accent.

'Well, I'm so grateful to you for picking me up. I'm not sure I would have been up to the drive.'

'Oh, it's no trouble,' he calls over his shoulder, as I struggle to keep up with him. He weaves in and out of the steady stream of passengers filtering out towards the exit of Naples International Airport.

As we step through the automatic doors, the blast of heat almost takes my breath away and I'm reminded why Italy is one of my favourite places to visit.

'I told him I could rent a car at the airport, but Richard said I should settle in before I do that. Parking is a nightmare during the peak season, I gather.'

'It is. And driving in Italy can be a bit daunting for first-timers.'

'Oh,' I laugh, 'I visit Italy every year. I'm used to driving over here, but this is my first time in Positano. I don't usually travel quite this far south.'

'Ah, of course – Richard referred to his trips with you as his busman's holiday. We're going to miss him, but everyone is very excited to meet you.'

Everyone?

'We're having a party in your honour, this evening.'

We?

Oh, Richard, you gave me a long list of instructions but why didn't you warn me? And a party? They might be your family, but I don't really know these people.

'That's . . . very kind,' I reply, graciously, dismissing my thoughts.

'If it's your first time travelling this route, then I'll point out some of the highlights on the way. It's about an hour and a half drive from here.'

Nico is both friendly and charming – but I've already mapped out the journey and I'm well aware of how long it will take to get to our destination. I do hope he stops treating me like a tourist, because that's not what I am.

'Um . . . great, thanks.' Oh well, I guess I won't be sitting in the back seat and working through Richard's latest email, then.

Come on, Marci, I tell myself firmly, *the guy is only trying to make you feel welcome. It's time to switch off and relax – there's work to be done, but all work and no play makes for a dull life. And you'll soon whip things into shape, so relax and go with the flow.*

4.

Surprise!

Even with the air-conditioning going at full blast, my early start soon begins to tell on me. Once we pick up a little speed and the vibrant scenery starts flashing past the window, my eyelids droop. The next thing I'm aware of is being woken up rather abruptly by the sound of Nico talking to someone.

'We've just pulled into the car park.'

A woman's voice fills the car, and she sounds excited. 'I've been constantly checking the clock. I'll let everyone know!'

'Twenty minutes and we'll be with you.'

As he switches off the engine, he turns to look at me, apologetically.

'Sorry about that. But if I don't forewarn them, I'd be in big trouble.'

Rubbing my eyes, I gaze around but all I can see is a dusty car park in front of a rocky cliff. Even ducking down in my seat to get a better glimpse, the limestone seems to rise up endlessly.

'Where are we?' I ask, feeling slightly disorientated.

'On the top road. It's a bit of a walk I'm afraid, but we'll use the ramp where we can, although even that will mean negotiating a few flights of steps in between.'

Gathering my things together, I tie the arms of the

lightweight jacket around my waist. A mere six hours ago I was bemoaning the fact that it wouldn't keep out the early morning chill. Now, in the midday heat, it's just another thing to carry.

'Will you be okay to wheel one of the cases? Once we cross the road it's all downhill. Alternatively, I could make two trips.'

'I'm fine, really. I was up at two this morning to catch a coach to the airport so I'm just a little weary,' I explain lamely, hoping I didn't do that head lolling around thing while sleeping.

'I'm glad my driving was smooth enough to allow you to catch up then,' he replies, sounding genuine enough.

As Nico lifts the luggage out of the back of the vehicle, I glance around. On the far side of the half-full car park, a solid two-storey, pretty – although rather tired-looking – stone building is partly set back into the rock face itself. It's unusual, for sure.

'Here you go.' Nico extracts the handle for me, and if the cases weren't quite so large, I'm pretty sure he'd insist on wheeling them both.

The ground is a little bumpy as we walk towards the open gate next to a rather busy road. I glance up at the large sign: *La Grotta del Tesoro*. The shop is obviously shut, but I wonder why there are so many cars parked here. Perhaps the locals pay to use it. From the photos I've seen of Positano, the narrow alleyways that wind around properties which seem to cling perilously to the steep cliffs are only accessible on foot.

'Are you ready to sprint?' Nico asks, as we stand on the

edge of the road. I nod and when he calls out *now*, I'm hot on his heels. The wheels make a rumbling sound as we trundle the cases across the smooth surface of the road. It's so hot that I can feel the searing heat through the thin soles of my flat shoes.

'It's easier from here,' he says, as he helps me manoeuvre my case down a small flight of stone steps to access a long and winding ramp.

But it's the scenery all around me that's now commanding my attention. 'This is quite something,' I say, sounding a little breathless.

'I sometimes forget to stop and look. It's home for me and has been for as long as I can remember.'

We walk side by side, our pace slowing. There are people walking in both directions as it's narrow in places. Some of the passers-by greet Nico in Italian and that warm, low timbre to his voice is mesmerising. I could listen to him talking all day, even though I would understand very little of what he was saying.

'Are you available to book if I decide not to hire a car?' I enquire.

He starts laughing. 'Sadly, I'm a waiter, not a taxi driver. But I'll be around and I'm here to help with whatever you need during your stay.'

'Sorry – I had no idea you were doing Richard a favour. Now I feel bad for falling asleep. You must think me very rude!'

'Not at all. We owe Richard a lot and he's family. So that means you are, too. If we stop here for a moment, I'll point out the hotel to you.'

I've seen a lot of spectacular views on my travels, but this is captivating. My eyes sweep over terrace upon terrace of pantiled roofs, some partially obscured by the glossy leaves of lemon trees, tall Italian cypress and bushy shrubs, through which climbers blossom profusely. The enclave of hills that disappear down into the crystal-clear, azure-coloured sea, remind me of a tiered cake stand. The villas and clusters of houses in their ice-cream colours, are like cupcakes on display – pale pink and muted terracotta dominate, but there are blues, yellows and whites, too.

It's a vertical community which wraps itself around the cleft between two mountainous limestone formations. With its meandering slopes, linked by alleyways and flights of worn, stone steps, the vista is lavishly populated with greenery and bursts of colour which obscure many of the buildings. Leaning further over to trace the course of the ramp, it's like a ribbon, wrapping back on itself several times before it disappears out of view.

'If you tilt your head a little to the right, do you see a courtyard with a swimming pool and a rectangular stone building? There's a blue flag alongside the entrance – you might just be able to catch a glimpse of it if you move a little further along.'

'Oh, yes! I can see it now. How fabulous!'

'We managed to free up a corner room for you. It's small, but part of the wraparound balcony looks directly out over the sea.'

That's another thing Richard didn't tell me. I assumed he'd booked me into one of the local bed and breakfast places, not a hotel above a restaurant. A rush of excitement begins to shake off my tiredness.

'It's peak season, so I'm grateful simply to have a bed,' I admit.

'Luca feels bad we couldn't offer you one of the larger rooms. Anyway, let's get you out of this heat.' He turns his wrist to look at his watch. 'My shift starts in forty-five minutes and I need to change first, so the timing is perfect.'

Actually, from where I'm standing everything looks rather perfect. What I'm at a loss to explain, is why Richard never invited me here on any of my trips. I could easily have taken a detour and come to him, rather than him joining me for a little break. Well, maybe *break* isn't quite the right term for it. Armed with a lengthy list of appointments with prospective sellers often miles apart, at times it was a little stressful to say the least. Especially on the odd occasion when the sat nav decided to take an unexpected detour. But if this were my home, I'd never want to leave, so Angel must have truly captured his heart to entice him to turn his back on such a wonderful place.

Celia Romano fiddles with the key as I stand a few paces behind her, staring up at the sign above the door. *La Grotta del Tesoro*, which I'm fairly certain – with my limited Italian – translates into 'the treasure cave'.

'Our customers can park here for free,' Celia informs me. This smart-looking Englishwoman smiles back at me good-naturedly. 'Richard had some passing trade, but most of his business was conducted online and by appointment only. And, naturally, he travelled all over Italy. But you're well aware of that. Here we go, finally!' The lock slides to one side and the door opens, letting us inside.

I follow Celia in and it's surprisingly cool.

'I'll just pull up the blinds,' she says, leaving me to gaze around in the semi gloom which is broken only by the sunlight filtering in between the slatted blinds at the windows. It really does feel like a cave, and it's packed to the rafters.

'It goes way back,' Celia chatters away as I realise this is going to be a much bigger job than I'd anticipated. 'But what's wonderful, is that on the other side of the door to the rear it extends back a long way into the rock. It was a naturally formed cave and it helps to keep an even temperature.'

'Aren't caves damp?' I enquire, labouring under the impression that water finds its way through the tiniest of cracks in the rock.

'It was, but as soon as Richard settled in, he had it tanked. Luca told me that many years ago it was originally owned by a local farmer, and it was a *frutta e verdura* – a fruit and vegetable market.' Celia easily slips into Italian with the accent of a local. 'It was empty for a long time and quite rundown when Luca bought it. He intended to demolish the building, as all he wanted was the land as parking for his customers. But time goes on and, many years later and with a little TLC to freshen it up – here we are. I didn't realise Richard had such a large collection. It's been a long time since I was last here.' Despite her moment of nostalgia, there's a hint of sadness to her demeanour.

'I'm not surprised Richard made sure everything was

watertight; he always was very particular about how he stored his antiques but this . . .' I trail off, thinking this is more like hoarding.

'It can't be easy for him to let it all go,' she replies, as I look around.

'No. But his thoughts are elsewhere and I'm glad to be able to help. Richard has been there for me in times of need,' I reply, trying hard not to sound emotional. Celia is right, everything holds a memory for Richard, and I wish he was here to share his tales. It's a daunting task and something tells me the cave beyond is also going to be packed solid.

When you work in the antiques business you get used to the dust, the aging patina, the smell of musty wood and a few woodworm holes here and there. Every collector generally has a specialism, or an area that they focus on, but Richard's taste has always been eclectic. I liken him to a magpie – incredibly intelligent, inquisitive, and interested in any object that takes his eye. Contrary to popular belief, magpies aren't attracted to shiny things, rather they're attracted to anything they find even remotely curious. And that's what I'm seeing here. A pair of enormous cast-iron gates lean up against the back wall, but getting to them is nigh on impossible. In front of them is a sizeable dining table, but what it's made of I can't tell as every inch of its surface is obscured by a whole array of disparate items, beneath which appears to be a lacy cloth. Pieces of beautiful blue glassware grab my attention and my eyes wander over to a stack of wicker fruit baskets. Next to them are some tall jugs with lids, probably used for storing olive oil.

'You have your work cut out here, Marci.'

There's a general air of poignancy about her as she turns away from me and I begin to rummage through a few open boxes.

'Do you want me to wait for a while and then we can walk back to the hotel together?'

'Thank you, Celia, but no – I'll be fine. It's your busiest season and you have customers to attend to. Thank you for letting me in though and I enjoyed our little chat. I'll have a wander around to get a feel for what's here. Then I'll pop back, grab a shower and change ready for this evening's festivities.'

Celia hands me the bunch of keys. 'Well, I can see that Richard's treasures are in good hands. And if there's anything you need, you only have to ask. Luca and I have asked Nico to generally look after you while you're staying with us.'

She retraces her steps back to the door.

'Celia,' I call out and she turns around to face me. 'Thank you for the warm welcome. And for understanding that I felt a little overwhelmed earlier on.'

'Italians are warm and friendly, but they can also be noisy and exuberant. The restaurant was also busy, and I thought it best to whisk you up to your room so you could sit on the balcony and enjoy a quiet lunch. Tonight, however, it will be loud. There will be singing and dancing – so be warned!' Her smile lights up her face. 'To Richard you were like a daughter and that makes you special to us.'

As Celia disappears out through the door, I'm left wondering what exactly I've let myself in for. And then

I spot an old mirror, the heavily carved frame a thing of great beauty. I move things out of the way so that I can get a closer look, finally revealing it in all its glory. The silvering is corroded and at least a third of it is covered with what now looks like a giant spider's web of lines. Mrs Kaminski's hands will fly up to her mouth in delight when she sees a photo of this – well, that's one item potentially sold and it's a rare beauty. What's next?

After an afternoon of non-stop photographing, I've spent the last hour on my laptop uploading everything to the cloud and sorting them into categories. My phone pings several times and when I check, it's a text from Mum. I gave her a quick call after I landed and she's eager for an update.

> Well? The suspense is killing me! x

> Everything is great, Mum. I've been at Richard's place all afternoon. There's a party tonight and I need to shower and change, but I'll call you when I can! 😊

Honestly, one thing my mother needs is a little patience. It isn't just about checking up on me, but she wants any gossip I can glean about Richard's situation. Which still stands at zero. Instead, I call Briony.

'It's me. Don't tell Mum I've been in touch, but I thought I'd warn you that I've uploaded some photographs for you and Guy to look at.'

'Hey girl, I was on it as soon as I got the notification.

I'm just drooling over a mirror – it's stunning!' I can hear the enthusiasm in Briony's voice.

'I know, Mrs Kaminski will snap it up in a split second,' I laugh.

'It looks promising, then?'

I reach out with my left foot to push open the narrow patio doors leading out onto the balcony of my room. As I settle back against the chair, it's strange to be talking work with that view effortlessly attracting my attention.

'It's a much bigger job than I expected, for sure and I need to have a serious conversation with Guy before my next chat with Richard. I'm assuming Richard keeps a record of his purchases, the prices he paid and any provenance he's managed to glean. But at this stage I thought a few photos would help when I talk to Guy, and Mum will probably need to be a party to that conversation. We're talking serious money here.'

'Guy was expecting a few rather nice pieces, but this could come as a bit of a surprise then.'

My eyes keep straying as I watch a speedboat slicing through the water, leaving a turbulent white trail behind it. 'In my opinion, there isn't anything here we couldn't sell quickly in the UK. However, just packing this lot up would fill the time I have here. What worries me is that Richard has put out some feelers to his contacts and while no one has come back to him yet, if they suddenly start getting in touch it could slow things down.'

'Are you saying we might not get our hands on all of this trove?' Briony sounds disappointed.

'Ha! Funny you should put it like that, as Richard's

shop is called La Grotta del Tesoro – The Treasure Cave. When I originally spoke to him I suggested we price the contents as a job lot, but that was before I saw what was here. I'll need to have a frank conversation with him before we go any further. All he said was that everything had to go before the keys are handed back.'

'I still can't believe he's walking away from it all for this mystery woman. Who would have thought, eh? Are you calling from the B&B?'

I chuckle. 'I am. I'll send you a couple of photos of the room and the view from the balcony, in a bit. I feel dusty and hot, so I'm about to jump into a cold shower.'

'It's overcast here, so I'm envious! Anyway, it's good to hear your voice and this could be the first summer when you get a proper tan for a change – no tram lines if you have a private balcony, eh?'

'Me – lying about in the sun? I doubt it. Anyway, I'd better text Richard to let him know I've arrived safely. I think Italy is about five hours behind Thailand, but hopefully he'll pick it up before he retires for the night.'

'I can't wait to see more photos from La Grotta and those wonderful views.'

'Don't worry, I'm working on it. Has, uh . . . Jason been in touch by any chance?'

Briony lets out an irritated groan. 'We've exchanged a few texts, but I explained that I'm too busy to meet up with him right now.'

Jason is a client of mine and he and Briony recently got talking on one of his visits to the office.

'Don't give me that. He's a great guy and you like

him – what harm will it do to go for a quick drink together?'

'All right – no more excuses. Now stop worrying about my love life as you have much more important things to sort out. Take care, Marci and have some fun!'

Seconds later my fingers are tapping away on the screen.

I'm here and I've been to La Grotta. It's everything I thought it would be and more – MUCH more! I do need to speak to you before I make a start, though. Please call me as soon as you can!

Now, do I wear the cream ankle-length halter-neck dress decorated with tiny little blue flowers, or the vibrant lime-green knee-length one with cap sleeves? To check out what the other guests are wearing I saunter out onto the balcony. It runs the full length of the top floor of the building but is divided off. Rows of tall potted plants give a reasonable amount of privacy to each of the ten sea-facing rooms, and over by the pool two women are wearing long dresses, so the cream it is!

Below me, the double terrace of tables is almost full by the sound of it. I can only catch little glimpses as vines and climbers cover most of the old wooden beams, creating shade and a wonderful display of greenery and colour. Being on the top floor, the buzz of chatter and laughter is diffused.

Chatting with Celia on the walk up to La Grotta, she told me that breakfast is between 7 and 9 a.m., lunch is served from 12.30 until 3.30 p.m., and dinner from 7.30

until 11 p.m. She did warn me that when the restaurant is busy, they remain open until their last customer is ready to leave. Many are friends and family who dine here and tonight everyone has been invited.

When I asked her what time I should go downstairs, she shrugged her shoulders. 'Whenever you are ready. It's always chaotic and many of Luca's family work here. Our parties tend to include our customers, too. Life is very relaxed in Positano, as you will discover, and you are no stranger to Italy.'

I didn't like to point out that my trips are very different. Travelling for business and tacking on a couple of days to be a tourist, I'm used to being the single lady sitting at a table for two. When I arrived at the restaurant today, everyone whose path I crossed insisted on kissing me on both cheeks as if I were a long-lost relative.

Now all I need to do is to pin up my hair, pull out a few wispy strands, and don a pair of earrings. It's way too hot to wear make-up, so a quick brush of mascara and a slick of lip balm, and I can slip into that dress.

5.

A Sea of Smiling Faces

The moment I descend the guest stairs down to the rear of the first floor, the entry level to the restaurant, Celia is there at a tall lectern, tidying a stack of menus. She looks up, giving me a broad smile and then the introductions begin in earnest. If I thought that the reception I received when I arrived at lunchtime was full-on, this evening eclipses that and then some.

The restaurant is packed now, and Celia quickly hands me over to Renzo, whom she informs me is one of her nephews, who helps during peak season. Renzo starts by giving me a tour of the kitchen, where the biggest surprise is the banter between Luca and Nico. I watch the two men chatter away in Italian as plates are loaded onto a large tray. Nico lifts it high into the air, waltzing past us and turning full circle to smile at me, before putting out an arm to open the swing door and pass effortlessly through it.

'That's an art,' I remark to Renzo, as he disappears from view.

'Nico 'as been doing it for a long time. Nico is a good son and Luca is a good teacher.'

Nico is Luca's son? Oh, my goodness – then Celia is his mother, and I didn't even realise that. It makes my comment about him being a taxi driver even more embarrassing – and he told me he was a waiter!

The activity is frenetic and the noise level coming at us from all angles is an assault on the ears. Pans scraping against metal burners on the top of the huge cookers, several wall-mounted fans pumping out cold air in addition to a huge air-conditioning unit – and above all of that, voices fighting to be heard. Luca keeps up a constant dialogue in Italian, directing his team and moving from one to another, his eyes everywhere as waiters come and go.

'It is always loud in 'ere,' Renzo says, one of his hands flying up into the air as if denouncing them for being too playful. 'There is also an outdoor barbecue area and Luca – he wanted Nico to take charge of it. Is a lost cause,' he informs me, his accent adding a wonderful softness to the words.

'It is?' I enquire as he leads me back out of the kitchen and through into the sparsely populated interior. Naturally, most people want to sit outside and with another terrace of tables below, the waiting staff must get a good workout during each shift.

The main colours in here are white and blue, which is a perfect contrast to the vibrant hues of the abundant trees, shrubs and climbers nestled close to the main building. It's wonderful to see the daytime feel of a laid-back café, change for the dinner service. The white linen tablecloths and blue napkins, polished glassware and cutlery, and flickering candles, have turned this into an upscale dining experience.

'Naturally,' Renzo laughs, raising an eyebrow. 'Nico is

no cook. He burns the pizza every time, but Luca never gives up on his son!'

My heart squishes up in my chest. What a lovely throwaway comment for someone to make.

'Did you meet Angel?'

Renzo indicates for me to go ahead of him as we cross the upper terrace, weaving between the tables, and he points in the direction of the main garden off to the side.

'Of course!' he declares, as if that's a silly question. 'Richard is one of us. She 'as a good heart, but it is sad. We miss 'im, the awful jokes . . . but we 'ope, one day, they come back!'

There is quite a gathering ahead of us in what is a beautiful oasis of a garden. The height of the greenery makes this area quite private. The swimming pool shimmers and looks so inviting, as people sit at some of the metal tables, over which rather elegant white umbrellas cast a decent amount of shade. Some of the people milling around are obviously waiters from the restaurant, dressed in their pristine white shirts and blouses, and black trousers. Not all of them are serving, as there's an outdoor buffet going on here. Others are more casually dressed.

'*Famiglia e amici, e gli ospiti – tutti sono i benvenuti*,' Renzo states, checking to see whether I understand.

'I know a little Italian, but I understand more than I can actually speak, as I usually have an interpreter if I'm on a business trip. I'm guessing family, friends and guests are all welcome?'

He nods, impressed. 'Exactly. The private area of the garden is accessed via the steep stone steps over there, or you can reach it via the door in the corridor next to the kitchen. First, let me introduce you to our terrace chef – Giulia Amorosi.

'Giulia – this is Marci.'

Giulia's face is expressionless as her eyes sweep over me. The way everyone else has greeted me, I assumed she'd come out from behind the rectangular polished stone counter which fronts the enormous outdoor barbecue. However, she merely nods her head at me. Her not-so-friendly welcome makes me falter for a moment, unsure how to approach her.

Renzo gives me a sideways glance, placing his hand on my arm and leaning in to whisper in my ear. 'Giulia, she is difficult at times – moody, you might say, when she is busy? *Mi dispiace*. It is time you met Luca's two brothers – my father, Tomasso and 'is wife Xiamara, and my uncle, Vittorio, and 'is wife Francesca. Richard talks about you all the time, so we feel we know you already.'

Talk about being thrown in at the deep end! *Richard, all you have ever really shared about your life in Positano is that you are surrounded by people who are gracious enough to make you feel at home. However, Italians like to ask questions and they got you talking about your English family . . . the problem is that I have no idea at all what you've told them about me and that's a little unfair.*

Aside from a brief spell when I was at university and trying to fit in with the mad crowd around me, I've never been a party animal. I love a good meal, a couple of drinks and a dance, but tonight I've had the best fun ever.

Thinking that it's time I disappeared upstairs to

encourage the few remaining customers to wend their way back to their accommodation, I'm surprised when Nico waylays me.

'You're not going back to your room, are you?'

The barbecue coals are cold, and the restaurant is no longer serving.

'My voice is hoarse from all the singing and trying to talk over the background noise,' I declare. He gives me a rueful smile.

'I was rather hoping we could take a wander along the beach. If you're too tired, I understand. It takes me a while to wind down after a late one and tonight was special, wasn't it?'

'Absolutely amazing, and I can't remember the last time I had so much fun. I doubt I'll remember half of the names of the people I met when I wake up in the morning, though.'

'Well,' Nico states with a twinkle in his eye, 'I don't think that matters as they'll all remember you.'

Really? I thought I kept things low-key, and I look at him, arching an eyebrow.

'They're calling you the English antiques expert. *Esperta di antiquariato inglesa*. Richard has quite a reputation around here, as most of his clients are wealthy. Now that he's put his business in the hands of his goddaughter, all eyes are on you.'

Put his business in my hands?

'A walk on the beach would be lovely, Nico.' Who knows what I might discover if he's in the mood to talk as we walk?

'Great. Give me a couple of minutes to change and I'll meet you over by the steps on the other side of the gate.' He points in the direction of the entrance to the restaurant, and I give him a fleeting smile.

My intention is to discreetly make my way outside unseen, when I hear my name being called.

'Marci! Marci!' I turn to see Luca striding towards me. He's still wearing his white double-breasted chef's jacket, black-and-white houndstooth check trousers, but his tall white pleated hat is missing.

'It was busy tonight and Celia and I 'ave not stopped. It was good though, yes? And you enjoy yourself, eh?'

I smile at him warmly as he leans in to kiss first my right cheek and then air kiss the left one.

'It's been a wonderful evening, Luca, and I can't thank you and Celia enough for making me feel at home. And for finding me a room at such short notice,' I add, as that can't have been easy.

'Is no problem. Nico will sleep anywhere. My son is good.'

I'm in Nico's room? Why am I not at all surprised by that? Nothing, it seems, is too much trouble and I feel like an honoured guest. Why that should be, I'm still trying to figure out.

'It will have been a sad goodbye the day Richard left,' I reflect, thinking aloud.

'Sad for us, but for Richard . . . Angel is a special woman and will bring 'im much happiness. Like my Celia. What is life without love, eh?'

'It's good to know you've met Angel, Luca. Back in the

UK we were all rather surprised to hear Richard's news.'

'I understand that. She is a quiet woman – the sort of person who sees everything and says little. Angel's approach to life is very holistic and I'd describe 'er as being very in tune with nature and animals.'

Now I'm intrigued. Richard is the life and soul of every gathering – always fun to be around and spending a lot more time indoors than he does out. Perhaps he's had an epiphany. 'And Richard was instantly attracted to her?'

'Yes, 'e was. A party 'ad booked a lunchtime birthday celebration out on the pool terrace. It ran on into the afternoon and the staff who didn't 'ave to leave when the restaurant closed stayed behind to join in. Giulia and I were kept busy that day. Richard and Angel ended up chatting for quite a while. We thought no more about it. Then, a few days later, 'e invited 'er 'ere to dinner.'

'That must have been quite a surprise for everyone,' I exclaim, and Luca looks at me knowingly.

'Richard . . .'e is sociable, but it was a first for 'im to 'ave a date.' Luca's eyes are sparkling as he recalls that day. 'Angela was on a coach tour and when they left, she stayed behind.'

Oh, my goodness – I had no idea it really was instant karma. 'That's so romantic!'

'In my life I 'ave witnessed a lot of things, but to see my dear friend discover the love of 'is life was a privilege, Marci. They were truly meant to be together.'

'Oh, Luca – thank you so much for sharing that with me – I feel I can relax a little now, knowing that you were at ease around Angel.'

'Is my pleasure. It is good to 'ave you 'ere, Marci. Sleep well.'

'*Buona sera*, Luca,' I reply, smiling to myself.

I head out of the tall double gates and turn left to loiter, while I wait for Nico to join me. Luca has a gentleness to his nature, and his charming accent is endearing.

'Sorry,' Nico's voice calls out as he strides towards me. Having by now wandered down to the first turn in the steps, he's eager to catch up with me. 'My mother waylaid me. She was worried when she couldn't find you. I reassured her that you were in good hands.' He grins at me, shrugging his shoulders.

'Mums, eh? And why didn't you tell me?'

'I was messing with you. They do say that Italian mothers are strong-willed and loving. My mum might be English, but she was born to live in Italy.' He chuckles away to himself as we descend the second run of well-worn stone steps.

'Is it far?' I ask.

'Twenty minutes, probably. I've never counted the number of steps, but I'm told there are at least five hundred of them. It's well worth it, although the climb back up afterwards will test your calf muscles. You'll soon get used to it and it's good exercise,' he quips, making it sound as if he's throwing me a challenge.

'Don't worry,' I say a little defensively. 'I work in a repurposed four-storey warehouse with a basement, and each floor has two flights of stairs, so I'm used to it. There's only one lift and it's always in use.'

Nico smiles, indicating for me to go ahead and we begin the descent. It's enchanting, and even though the air is still warm as I draw in a deep breath, the fragrances in the air abound. A long run of jasmine cascades down over the high wall to our left and as we make our way further down, climbing roses intermingle with bougainvillea vines in a constant stream of colour.

Ahead of us, the steps are littered with lemons that have fallen from overhanging branches to our right, where the old stone wall is much lower. It's only a couple of feet shorter than the tops of the trees on the other side. I stop for a moment to glance over and see that they stand on a terrace belonging to a stunning pale pink villa some distance below us. With the grounds spread out in tiers that are heavily populated with trees, all I can catch is tantalising little glimpses. I see row upon row of tall canes, probably runner beans, peas or even courgettes. In between are large areas hidden by the canopy of leaves from a swathe of olive trees, but I manage to catch sight of a swimming pool and the flicker of garden lights surrounding it. The murmur of voices from below drifts on the air as we continue down.

The steps are wide and deep enough for me to take a good stride but when they take a sharp turn to the right, they suddenly become much steeper and narrower. I'm so glad I didn't wear flip-flops, as this requires a little more concentration to keep up a good pace. Even so, my breathing is getting heavier. Every time I think that we're almost there, there's another sharp turn and yet another flight of steps. It seems never-ending and I can't help but worry how I'll cope on the way back up.

When, eventually, we turn that final corner the scene before us is enchanting.

'And this is Positano's Spiaggia Grande,' Nico announces proudly.

To our right is a long line of restaurants abutting a wide promenade with several steps leading down onto the beach. As we stroll along, side by side, I catch glimpses of people still being served, others lingering over coffee, or liqueurs.

In front of us there is a pier, and several boats are anchored up. What a wonderful mode of transport to take you to dinner, I reflect. And the setting is perfect, like something out of a film.

'Come,' Nico encourages, 'let's wander along the shoreline. You'll want to keep your shoes on as it's a mixture of pebbles and gritty sand.'

The heat as the soles of my shoes gain contact with the beach is a surprise. When the sun is high in the sky, I can imagine it would be almost too hot to bear, as even now the warmth from tiny bits of gravel that creep into my shoes makes it slightly uncomfortable.

'That's a welcoming breeze,' I declare, as I increase my pace to catch up with Nico. 'Do you often venture down here this late?'

'In peak season, yes. It's too busy during the day. Do I gather you enjoyed yourself this evening?'

Poor Nico didn't stop throughout the entire evening. Most of the other waiters seemed to spend at least a little time mingling and grabbing something from the buffet next to the swimming pool. While Celia is obviously the one who is officially in charge, Nico's eyes are everywhere, ensuring things run smoothly by stepping in to help take the pressure off his mum. From the little I've seen, he seamlessly switches from taking orders, to plating up when Luca and his team in the kitchen are struggling to keep up. Then in the next moment he's clearing tables, to ready them for another round of diners.

'Have you always worked for the family business?' I ask, as he slows to allow me to catch up.

'Of course. It's expected of me. And I'm glad to do it. My mother had a tough time back in the UK as a single parent. One holiday changed everything for us.'

Oh, so Nico is Luca's stepson – I did wonder, as I couldn't see any likeness at all.

'How old were you?' I ask, hoping he doesn't feel I'm being nosy.

'I was two at the time. My father wasn't in the picture and Mum had to pay someone to look after me while she was at work. She said it was fate, as money was tight, but it's a long story I won't bore you with now.'

'Didn't she have family who could have helped out?'

He snorts. 'My grandparents' aspirations for her didn't include being saddled with a child at a young age, apparently. They've never been a part of our lives. It made her work twice as hard to prove she could cope without their financial assistance. And she succeeded in doing just that. She's one determined woman and Luca saw that the first time they met, according to Mum.'

'What a lovely ending to a sad story.'

'It is, actually, because Luca is unable to have children. Ironically, when his father died it was his eldest brother, Vittorio, who should have taken over the restaurant. The accommodation above and behind it was private back then.'

Our pace slows as we stop to look back up at the mountainous cliff face. The lights hanging on the terraces are like glittering necklaces. It doesn't even look real and yet it is, and they are mirrored. Two cliffs face each other and if I squint, it looks a little like two Christmas trees with lights wrapped around them.

'Oh my!' I sound as awestruck as I'm feeling.

'Magnificent, isn't it? And it's not until you stand here gazing up that you realise how incredible it is.' There's a catch in Nico's voice that takes me by surprise. It's obvious how much this place means to him. 'The oldest part is in the upper section of Positano. The mostly faded red or pink houses are decorated with Baroque stuccoes.'

'It's quaint – but on a huge scale. Everything appears to cling almost tenuously onto the cliffs.'

'John Steinbeck once wrote that Positano "is a dream place that isn't quite real when you are there and becomes beckoningly real after you have gone".'

'I read that somewhere and now I know exactly what he meant.'

'What, the tenacity of the people whose homes and gardens are perched precariously on a huge rock face, or the fact you'll miss it when you're back in the wet and windy UK?'

I laugh, good-naturedly. 'It's more than that – it's easy to fall in love with a place like this and imagine what it would be like to live in one of those pretty villas. With the lush gardens all lit up at night, each one stands out like a jewel against the rugged background. It's bewitching.'

Nico frowns. 'It's funny hearing you talk about it like that because it's all I know. You're comparing it to England, a place I can't even remember. Everything I know about the UK comes from the internet.'

'You've never had any communication at all with your grandparents?' I'm surprised they wouldn't want to keep in touch.

'I vaguely remember a few awkward phone calls when I was around the age of five or six. At the time I guess Mum was feeling a little guilty about the rift and she reached out to them, hoping they would grab the chance to get to know their grandson. All I remember is that I didn't know what to say and it was difficult making conversation. At the end of every call, Mum would disappear for a while and when she returned it was obvious she'd been crying. It didn't exactly endear them to me.'

'That must have been hard. But you never flew back to meet them in person?'

'Mum was essential to the running of this place, but I know for a fact she invited them to come and stay a few times as I was growing up. They never took up the offer and Mum hasn't spoken to them in a long time.'

'Is that a good or a bad thing?'

He takes a moment to ponder. 'Bitterness is a terrible thing, Marci, and I came to understand that Mum could forgive them for being angry with her, but not with me. Besides, this is the only home I know. Luca is the only father I've ever known, and he makes my mother happy. I don't think of myself as British, if I'm honest, neither does my family and yet strangers don't think of me as Italian. Does it bother me? No, is the simple answer; it never has.'

He scuffs the toe of his shoe against the swathe of sandy

grit, overturning a pebble. If I lived here, this is where I'd come at this time of night to relax. The little hubbub of noise as the late diners begin to head for home is merely a fleeting distraction.

'Let's wander over to the ferry landing stage at the end of the beach,' he suggests.

We head back up to the promenade and he waits while I slip off my shoes to dust the sand off my feet and tip out any remaining bits of grit before easing them back on.

'I never work on Mondays, so if you're free any time, a friend of mine has a boat I can borrow. Everyone should see Positano from the water – it's spectacular. We could take a little trip along the coastline and back.'

'It's kind of you to offer, Nico. That would be amazing. Until I speak to Richard to clarify a few things, I'm just taking photos ready to catalogue his collection, so I can't resist an offer like that!'

His mouth twitches and his eyes gleam. 'Great. Just tell me when and I'll arrange it.'

'And you didn't mention that you'd given up your room for me!' I add.

He gives me a mischievous look. 'It's nothing, really. We have a spare room above the extension with two bunk beds and a single in it, for staff who work exceptionally late and are too tired to drive home. It's not as if I'm sleeping on the floor.'

As we gaze out across the water, the light breeze blows a few strands of hair across my face, and I put my hand up to sweep them away. I watch the ripples going back and forth across the surface of the water, breaking up the moonlight as it dances on the surface. With the reflection of the darkening sky making the volume of water look dense, the movement sends out glints, like little shards of glass. I can't help but look sideways up at Nico, noting the look of pure contentment on his face. This is the closest thing to a perfect moment I can imagine and it makes the hairs on my arms stand up.

'The ferries and water taxis pick up from here or the pier,' Nico informs me. 'Some of the boats anchored up belong to diners visiting the local restaurants. That's the boat I was referring to a moment ago, the pale blue one – the *Serpente di Mare*. It belongs to friends of mine, Jack and Olivia Thornton. Jack works away a lot but is obviously back for a flying visit. He leaves a spare set of keys with me as I take her out for a run to make sure everything is ticking over nicely. They must be here somewhere enjoying a romantic dinner for two.'

How wonderful. I can't imagine anything more magical on a night like this, than to be sitting opposite the one you love in a cosy little restaurant and looking out over the beach. It's something I can only dream about.

'People like to see and be seen,' I remark, thinking out loud. 'I'm familiar with the *andiamo a fare qualche vasca*. One of my contacts who lives about a two-hour drive from here, always insists we have a meal and then go for a stroll, afterwards – see and be seen.' It's certainly not something I do in the UK. I usually drive somewhere to go for a walk but here everyone enjoys wandering around their neighbourhood, content to stop and chat to whoever happens to be passing by.

'It's the way it is here. If we wander back, we might bump into my friends. Olivia's mother, Patricia Boselli, is one of Mum's closest friends. Patricia was the person who taught Mum how to perfect her written Italian.'

'I'm assuming Patricia's husband is Italian, given the surname.'

'Yes, Aldo is a lovely man who worked in the UK for more than twenty years before returning to Italy with his family. Since he retired he's become a very keen gardener, which is handy for Olivia and Jack, given the size of their garden.'

'So how did Olivia and Jack cross paths?'

'It's a long story but to cut it short, Jack was over here on a secondment after the company Aldo worked for had its IT system hacked. At the end of his stay, Jack tacked on some holiday and Aldo and Patricia invited him to stay with them in Positano for a few days.'

'My goodness – when fate steps in there's no avoiding it, is there?'

Nico finds that comment amusing. 'I never looked at it like that, but you're right because it was a bit of a fluke. Jack could have just flown straight home, but he didn't. They kept in touch and he invited Olivia to fly over to the UK. They had a wonderful stay up in Scotland, one Christmas, and that sealed the deal. As soon as Olivia arrived back we all knew Jack wasn't going to be far behind her. Although it did take a while for him to tie up the loose ends and by the time he arrived here ready to set up his new life, Aldo was a man of leisure.'

'What a lovely story.'

'Jack's job requires him to spend long spells away from home. It mirrors Aldo's working life, so Patricia knows how hard it is to be a woman home alone. Olivia's parents help to keep everything ticking over at the villa, while she works. When Jack is at home Olivia insists it's down time for him, but it's a strain on her – I know that.'

'Do you have many other English friends?' I ask, naturally curious.

'No, not really. There are a few Brits who regularly eat at the restaurant, who I've come to know quite well over time through passing on the names of tradesmen or helping them to fill in various forms. And when Jack's around I often take a day off and we go for a trip in the boat. Working with family means we're all accommodating. The summer season is important to us, and everyone is happy to work long hours and make money while the sun shines, but we take care of each other. You probably understand more than most people, as Richard told me that you work with your brother and your mother.'

'I do. What else did he say about me?'

'Oh, Richard often talked about his life in the UK, especially after one of his trips back to see you all. But I'm curious about what exactly your role is – it sounds like an interesting job.'

We're almost at the bottom of the first steep incline of steps now and I hitch up my dress and knot it so that my hands are free. It does look a little daunting from this angle.

'Don't worry, I'm behind you. Just take care until they widen out,' Nico reassures me. There is lighting, but there are also shadows and it's been a long day.

I take it slowly, focusing on what I'm doing, and begin counting. There are fifty-three almost vertical steps until we round the corner, where it gets a little easier and we can walk side by side again.

'Right, that's the worst bit over for me. What were you saying – ah, yes – working with family. My mum is less hands-on these days. It's Guy who runs Anvil & Anchor Antiques and I'm his deputy and operations manager. But we're lucky enough to have a good team we regard as our work family. We firmly believe in rewarding effort and loyalty, it's a two-way thing. Besides, in our industry it becomes a passion – every single one of us collects something. None of our staff would do any other job. Work is a pleasure when you love what you do, isn't it?'

Nico turns his head to look at me. His eyes sparkle in the gentle glow from the hanging lights strung among a long line of lemon trees to our right.

'And it was easy for you to drop everything and leave, just like that?'

I hesitate at his words – does he think that was wrong of me?

'Our shop floor manager has a chance to step up and sit in my seat for a while. She's more than ready for the challenge and I'm easily contactable. This could be a big job for the company, as Richard has a lot of items that we could sell on. I also don't have a significant other at home to pacify, so it was a case of tying up a few loose ends, then packing my bags and heading off.'

'Oh, I see,' Nico acknowledges, but there's a strange edge to his voice. 'It must be nice to have total freedom.'

'You don't feel you have that?' I could kick myself for replying without thinking. It's none of my business.

'For now,' he mutters.

It's time to change the subject. 'How many more steps do you think are ahead of us?'

'Lightweight. We've done less than a hundred,' he smirks, and I start giggling.

'I thought it was at least twice that! My calf muscles are already beginning to complain.'

'Let's slow our pace, the night is still young.'

It's well after 1 a.m., I should think, and I've been up for twenty-two hours with only a couple of short naps on the plane and in the car. But Positano is tantalising, and this is an experience I'll remember forever. Who needs sleep?

6.

Aladdin's Cave

In my dream, I was – perhaps not entirely surprisingly – climbing steps and they seemed to go on forever. When I reached the top, I felt as if I were in heaven, as I was standing on a rather small plateau on top of a mountain and surrounded by wispy clouds. Ironically, I was strangely calm and wasn't at all fazed to find myself there. Instead, I felt an overwhelming sense of freedom. I was as light as a bird – and then I glanced down and realised that's exactly what I was! My feathers were pristine white with no markings on them at all and then, with absolutely no effort, I clearly remember the sensation as I spread my wings. Suddenly I was flying, caught on a breeze that carried me as if I were weightless. I swooped and soared out over the emerald-coloured sea and when I woke up a few minutes ago, seemingly mid-flight, my heart was beating so fast in my chest I wondered whether I was having some sort of panic attack.

Taking a few deep breaths to calm myself, I realise that I probably didn't drink enough water yesterday and make a mental note to keep better hydrated today. Especially with the long walk up to La Grotta del Tesoro and back.

The first thing I do is to check my phone and I'm

disappointed that there's still nothing at all from Richard. If he doesn't respond today, then I'll try calling him, but without knowing exactly where he is – or whether he's even within range of a signal – it's a long shot.

After showering and dressing, I gather my things together, determined to slip out before the staff begin their working day. There are two bottles of water in the small fridge in the room and I take both, leaving a tip on the small console table as I would if I were a tourist.

'*Buon giorno*, Marci, *come sta*?' someone half-whispers, as I fiddle with the key to get it to engage with the lock on the door to my room.

'*Buon giorno*,' I instinctively reply. Two young women are loading a trolley with neat stacks of towels and bedding from an enormous walk-in cupboard situated to my right. '*Molto bene, grazie*!'

I recognise one of them from the party last night, but I didn't catch her name. I think she's one of Nico's cousins, but I'm not sure. They both give me a little wave and return to what they're doing. I'm surprised by their early start, as it's at least forty-five minutes until breakfast service begins.

Downstairs, the entry-level terrace of tables have already been laid up ready for the guests and I can hear the drone of voices in the kitchen. As I walk past, making as little noise as possible, the double doors suddenly swing open and Nico appears.

'Ah, Marci – good morning! You're up early. I'm about to lay out the buffet table. What can I get you for breakfast?'

'*Buon giorno*, Nico,' I retort, a little awkwardly. I was trying my best to creep out unnoticed. 'I'm good to go, thanks. I took the two bottles of water from the mini-fridge – I hope that's all right. I need to go shopping to buy a few essentials,' I explain.

'That's not necessary, Marci. You are free to help yourself. Let me get you something – a bag of fruit maybe? You're heading up to Richard's place?'

I nod, nonchalantly. 'There is so much to do and I'm eager to make a start.'

Nico hurries over to a long table covered in a pale blue linen tablecloth and places the stack of plates he's carrying in the centre. There are several bowls of fruit, a couple of covered cake stands with croissants, and several trays of empty glasses.

'Please don't let me stop you,' I add. 'I'll grab two of those apricots for later, then. I'm not big on breakfast.'

'Me neither. I don't normally start work until elevenish, but we're one server down today. My cousin Viola, Vittorio's daughter, has broken a tooth.' He pulls a face.

Poor girl! 'Ooh, that's no fun. I think I passed another of your cousins on the landing. Long, dark hair coiled up on top of her head?'

He nods. 'That's Bianca. Her father is Tomasso. You'll soon get to know them all. Are you sure that's all you want?'

The two apricots fill my hand, and their scent makes my mouth begin to water. 'This is perfect, thank you. *Arrivederci*!'

That makes him smile. '*Vi auguro una splendida giornata*.' Nico's Italian is velvety smooth and hearing it roll off his tongue so easily, how anyone could think he isn't a native astounds me.

'Oh, I will!' Who wouldn't have a wonderful day in this beautiful setting?

'Richard is on his honeymoon, Marci, you can't go harassing the man. I'm sure we can work something out, but you need to start cataloguing everything. Keep the photos coming and leave it to me to work up an estimate of what it's all worth.' Clearly, Guy thinks I should just get on with it, but having texted Richard twice now and left a message for him to contact me urgently, I'm a little put out.

'There are piles of loose paperwork upstairs, as well as box files full of financial stuff. If you could see the size of the task, you'd understand my concern. It looks as if he just left without giving any thought whatsoever to what he was leaving behind!'

I take a deep breath and stretch out my legs; I'm sitting on the concrete step at the front of the shop, and the door behind me is wide open to air it out. It's not damp, but it's incredibly dusty and whenever I pick an item up to arrange it ready for photographing, the tiny particles tickle my nose, making me sneeze.

'I'm not sure it's do-able in the timescale, Guy, and it sucks up time having to constantly move things around to gain access.'

The flowerpot next to me is full of dark red geraniums, which I watered first thing. I watch as a bee is diligently working its way from one glorious flower head to the next. It isn't at all bothered by the noise from the road, which comes in waves. The most irksome sound is that of the scooters. Like a swarm of demented bees as the engines go full throttle to fight the drag of the long incline, maybe the bees themselves resonate with the sound. But when I glance up at the perfectly cloudless sky overhead, I feel guilty moaning.

'You sound hot and bothered,' Guy comments.

'I am.' I've already drunk both bottles of water and wish now that I'd saved one of the apricots, instead of scoffing them both as soon as I arrived. In hindsight, a late night wasn't the best plan to kick off day one and I am feeling a tad jaded.

'Thinking about our cash flow, selling Richard's collection on commission would also save you the task of photographing everything,' Guy points out.

We have a lot of floor space at Anvil & Anchor Antiques, and many of our visitors aren't seasoned collectors. They see something they like, and they buy it, but their budget isn't huge. Then there are the items that smaller dealers, and those in the business – interior designers included – are always on the lookout for, and there are a lot of decorator pieces here that will sell very quickly.

'A massive influx of stock like this would be a dream for us, Guy – it really would.'

There's a slight pause before he replies. 'I'll cost out the options for getting everything shipped back to the UK. Why don't you suggest we give Richard an advance on account?'

'I think it's the only practical solution, to be honest. I'll find out how much cash he needs upfront and we can take it from there.'

'Don't worry, Marci. Richard is hardly likely to go off travelling if he's short on funds. He's careful with his money.'

'I know and I'd be surprised if that isn't the case,' I agree. Looking at the task ahead of me, this would be by far the quickest and easiest solution. 'Anyway,' I continue, feeling a lot more positive, 'how is Briony doing?'

There's a little chuckle on the other end of the line. 'Trying to fill some big shoes!'

He misses me already and it's been, what . . . thirty-six hours? It feels like forever in one way as I draw up my legs, which are now feeling uncomfortable in the searing heat.

'I'll let you know when I've spoken to Richard. And in the meantime, I'll continue to download photos of the higher-end items so you can get a better feel for what's here. Give everyone my best!'

As I stand to go back inside a car pulls into the car park and I watch as it draws up alongside the building. All four doors open and two adults, a teenage boy and a younger girl walk towards me, chattering away to each other excitedly.

The man speaks to me in a torrent of Italian, his hands pointing to the shop as if he's checking whether it's open.

'*Non è aperto*.'

Simply telling him that the shop isn't open, merely makes him look at his wristwatch, puzzled. It's a good half an hour until noon and he frowns. Lots of shops close between noon and three in Italy, as that's when people flock to the restaurants, or head home to eat lunch and take a nap.

His wife joins in, and he turns around to face her, his hands flying up into the air. For all I know they could be arguing, or she could have noted the dusty windows and realised I didn't mean simply closed for lunch. The teenage boy is loitering, looking bored but the little girl is nowhere to be seen. She must have crept around behind me, unnoticed, while I was talking.

'*Ciao*, Marci,' Nico's voice calls out as he approaches, a cool bag swinging from one hand.

Surprised by his appearance, the couple immediately stop talking and turn around. Nico walks up to them, smiling. What follows is a long conversation and as far as I can tell they take the news that the shop is no longer trading with good grace. Then the man seems to be asking directions and Nico is very obliging. The woman calls out for her daughter and glances at me, embarrassed, when she appears in the doorway. I give the mother a warm smile in return as she turns to lecture the child, pointing in the direction of the car.

As we watch them drive off, Nico gives a wave. 'I assume you don't have time to let people wander around. They're on a road trip, so not serious buyers. Any news from Richard?'

'Nothing yet. Your arrival is timely. I don't think the woman was very happy to be turned away and they started to argue.'

Nico laughs. 'Italian conversations can often sound like an argument when they're not. They were fine when I explained, if a little disappointed. There aren't many places to stop where there's parking and sometimes people just want to stretch their legs. But I told them that a few kilometres further on there's a lay-by on the right-hand side of the road with panoramic views. There's also a large fruit stall and the two women who run it sell freshly made lemonade. It's a nice place to stop for a little break. Anyway, I'll have a word with Luca about the sign at the entrance – maybe we should add a banner making it clear that the shop is now closed.'

'Thanks, but only if it's not a hassle,' I state, firmly.

'It's no trouble. I know it's a bit early,' he says, indicating to the cool bag, 'but I brought you some lunch before the restaurant gets busy, courtesy of Luca.'

'That's so thoughtful of you all, Nico. Do you need to head straight back, or can I tempt you to sit down in the shade of the rear courtyard for a moment?'

He isn't in his work clothes, but even in knee-length shorts and a T-shirt, it's a hot climb up to the road.

'Oh, I think they can manage without me for a while longer. That would be great, thanks.'

I realise we're standing here just staring at each other as my eyes flicker over him. With that short, dark, curly hair, those hazel eyes, and naturally tanned skin, he looks and sounds like a local. Watching him talking to that Italian couple, I envy the skill of being able to slip effortlessly between two very different languages.

'Right, follow me.' Forcing myself to focus, I wish I could offer him something to drink. It's time I went shopping, but the thought of carrying some supplies up here is daunting. And unless I need to travel further afield, I can't see the point in renting a car to just let it sit in the car park.

'Hmm . . . you've certainly succeeded in having a bit of a tidy-up in here,' Nico remarks, impressed by my attempts to impose some semblance of order.

'I'm using the chest of drawers as my photographic area. Moving it back against that plain wall means I can take some good shots.'

'I love your temporary lighting solution,' he grins at me. 'You've done this sort of thing before, I see.'

Having lined up a semi-circle of five side lights, I trained them at the general direction in which I'm working. 'It's not perfect, but it's good enough. My photos aren't going online or being used for an auction catalogue – they're simply for Guy to put together some guide prices.'

Nico follows me along the newly created aisle leading up to the door separating the front of the shop from the section hewn into the rock – that's the *real* cave, I think to myself. We walk past the cloakroom to our left and take a right turn into a small corridor, off which is the door into the kitchen.

Outside, a large courtyard patio is separated from the wild, overgrown orchard by a low wall. To our left the rocky cliff isn't completely vertical, but it's a domineering backdrop and the other two sides of the garden are enclosed by a tall, beautiful old stone wall. A small area of the patio is shaded by the building and a pergola extending out from it. Covered with several intertwining climbers, the powerful scent of jasmine is delightful. It's certainly a relaxing place to sit and chill.

'My mother packed the cool bag herself,' Nico informs me, as he places it down on the weathered metal table. I indicate for him to take a seat. They aren't the most comfortable chairs, but they lend a rustic charm with their amazing patina.

'Oh, that's so kind of her. But in future I will sort myself out, so you won't have to worry about me when I'm here.'

I sit down and unzip the bag. 'So much food! Have you had lunch?'

Nico shakes his head. 'I don't usually eat this early.'

'But we can't waste anything. Oh, there are two bottles of *birra al limone* and a couple of bottles of water. You deserve a beer for carrying this up here!'

The truth is that it's rather nice to have someone to chatter to.

'My mother probably thought you needed a little company. She's not happy that you're here all alone working, but I have an idea to resolve that. And she suggests you keep the front door locked if you're out in the garden. There's been a couple of incidents quite recently. One where a woman had her phone snatched out of her hand by someone on a scooter, when she was distracted by a guy in a van asking for directions.'

I glance at him, raising an eyebrow. 'Please thank Celia for her concern and tell her I'll be very careful.'

As I pull out two ceramic dishes and ease off the lids, the aroma of bittersweet rocket and caramelised onions makes my mouth water.

'It's homemade pasta, like short spaghetti, with a spicy *melanzane* sauce . . . stewed aubergine . . . with calamari, prawns and rocket,' Nico kindly explains as I pass one of the bowls to him.

'Here – take a fork.'

'Someone obviously thought you should eat, too,' I

laugh, and he nods, his mouth already full. Seconds later he holds out his hand.

'Pass me the beers and I'll open them,' he says, putting his dish down on the table and pulling a bunch of keys from his pocket. Does every man walk around with a bottle opener at the ready? I muse.

'This is wonderful. A rare treat for me, as I usually eat at the end of my working day – just don't let Mum know that her little plan worked,' Nico says as he hands me a beer. He holds up his bottle and we chink.

'*Cin-cin*!' I declare in my best Italian accent.

Nico's eyes crinkle up. '*Cin-cin*, Marci!'

'Can I ask you a personal question?' He nods, looking amused. 'I'm assuming your name wasn't always Nico . . .' I venture.

He puts down his drink and begins eating again, talking in between mouthfuls. 'No. I was born Nicholas Griffiths, which is Mum's maiden name. I was three years old when we finally settled in Positano and Mum married Luca shortly afterwards. When I started school, the only name I knew was Nico Romano. It wasn't a big deal.'

The calamari and prawns are amazing, but I'm also enjoying the company and hearing more about Nico's past. 'That's a good thing as it turned out, isn't it?'

Nico nods his head as he finishes eating, then takes a swig of beer before sitting back on the hard metal chair.

'Yes, and it made it easy for me. No one really talked about the time before my mother and I came to live here, but I was curious as the years went on. Just before my tenth birthday, I asked her about my biological father and she told me that genes are one thing, love is another. Luca, she told me, treated me as his son from the very beginning. Out of respect for her, we never talked about it again until years later. I asked her if she ever thought about the man who chose not to be a part of our lives and she simply said that she was happy with things the way they are. Afterwards, I realised that talking about it was painful for her and it didn't really matter to me anyway.'

'It's funny how things work out, isn't it? I mean . . . how people get together, like it's destined to be. Even when they're born in different countries, fate finds a way to make their paths cross.'

Nico's lips twitch. 'I only have one regret,' he replies, but his eyes are smiling. 'Luca deserves a son who is a chef and, sadly, that's not one of my strengths. Now appreciation of good food, that's a different matter entirely!'

Despite the humour, something in his words makes me hold my breath for the briefest of moments. For him it is a sadness. 'I think you do him proud, Nico. He sees the way you keep an eye on everything and everyone. Your mother is a very strong and capable woman, but it's obvious to me that you are her silent tower of strength. Luca is well aware of that.'

He tips his head, his smile fading. 'It's the least I can do. Luca made this life happen for us and I wouldn't want to be anywhere else. I should get back.'

'Well, thank you for coming to my rescue as I was beginning to flag and that really hit the spot. Here, take one of these bottles of water to drink on the way back.'

As I hand it to him, our fingers touch briefly and it's an

awkward moment. I pretend not to notice as I put the lids back on the dishes and wrap the forks up in one of the paper napkins. 'I'll wash these in the kitchen and bring them back in the cool bag later, if you like.'

'No. It's not a problem – I'll sort it out when I get back. You have work to do. Maybe we can catch up later tonight, and I'll tell you my idea to stop Mum and Luca worrying about you being here alone.'

The image of a guard dog flashes into my head, and I look at him, narrowing my eyes.

'Some help?'

'You'll have to wait. That's the price you pay for encouraging me to talk about myself.'

As I follow him back through to the shop, we continue the banter.

'I'm sorry, I didn't mean to pry.'

'Oh,' he replies, 'you can only pry when there's something interesting to discover. My life is exactly what you see and I'm not complaining.'

I escort Nico out, lingering to watch as he walks down to the gate. He stops, turning to give me a brief wave and a smile, before disappearing out of sight. Curiously, there's no sign of a significant other in his life and yet family life is all important to him. I bet Celia would dearly love to see her son settling down before too long. I'm guessing that he's a couple of years older than me. Being single as I approach thirty, with all my friends bar one having already tied the knot, everyone assumes my career comes first. It does, but sadly in my case it's not by choice, but the direction in which my life seems to be taking me.

7.
A Sense of Relief

'Marci, my darling, I'm so, so sorry. Angel and I met up with a British couple who settled in Thailand almost ten years ago. We all headed off to this incredible retreat at Haad Tien Bay. They advertise it as a place where the jungle meets the sea and it was an amazing experience. So amazing that we didn't take our phones with us.'

Oh, Richard! Looking at the world through the rose-tinted glasses of new love is one thing, but this is crazy.

'I'm glad you're safe and you've had a great time, but it would be useful if . . . um . . . I mean, there are times when I'm going to need your input.'

A low and rather guilty-sounding 'Hmm . . .' reverberates down the line. 'Slapped wrist acknowledged. No more disappearing off the grid for me, I promise. And I'm all yours right now – so ask away.'

'Having talked to Guy, how urgently do you need some cash?' I might as well get straight to the point.

'Cash? Oh, I'm fine. There's no rush, Marci. I just don't want you exhausting yourself on my account and ending up returning home in need of a holiday!'

'If that's the case then, I've spoken to Guy, and he suggests we ship this lot back to the UK for the team to catalogue properly. We'll auction off as much as possible and the general, low-value items we can sell on the shop floor. As it's all sold on a commission-only basis, if you do end up needing something upfront, I'm sure we can advance you a lump sum percentage based on the lots that will go to auction. Obviously, you'll incur the cost of shipping it over to the UK in a container and the packing materials, but I think you'll end up getting a better return. And I'm confident that I can get that done in the timescale you've given me.'

'You are a star, my dear. It's good of you and Guy to put yourselves out to come up with a great solution, but an advance is not necessary. I just need the peace of mind of knowing that it's all in hand. And if it's going back to the UK, that would save Luca storing my personal effects. Would you mind renting a storage unit near Gloucester for me? I'll pay for six months at a time – let me know the cost and I'll transfer the funds directly to your account.'

'You won't be coming back to Positano?' I gasp.

'I'm sure Angel and I will be back at some point, but where we'll end up settling – only time will tell. Knowing that you can get your hands on my paperwork and documents means a lot to me, Marci. There's no one else who understands me like you do, and I trust your judgement implicitly.'

'I'll do my best, Richard. By the way, you have a mounting pile of post at the shop. Can I forward it on to you?'

'I'm not sure how much longer we're going to be here before we move on—' There's a muffled sound of voices in the background and someone is obviously trying to attract Richard's attention. 'Sorry, Marci. Our transport has just arrived. I'll call you in a day or two, if that's okay? Perhaps we can go through those letters then and I'll decide if there's anything that needs actioning. And find my ledger – it'll give Guy all the provenance he needs for the real treasures. There's a key in a pot on the shelf above my desk. It opens the big cupboard in the master bedroom. We'll speak soon. Take care, Marci!'

Before I can utter another word, the line goes dead and I slump back in the chair, staring out at the wonderful vista from the balcony of my room. Richard has succeeded in turning my life, as well as his own, upside down! But the relief at hearing his voice has quickly been replaced by a sense of unease. I'm not happy poking around in his private files. Surely Mum would be better taking care of that side of things than me? Although, she'd never swan off leaving David to fend for himself and if I'm struggling to cope, then Mum would probably be tearing her hair out by now!

That evening, back at the hotel, there's a loud rap on the door to my room and I hurry over to see who it is.

'Oh, hi, Celia. Come in.'

She steps inside, looking at me with a slight frown on her face.

'You've had a long day and you haven't had dinner. I came to see whether you'd like a tray in your room.' She gazes across at the desk and my laptop, alongside which several notebooks lie open.

Glancing at my watch I'm surprised to see it's gone nine already.

'Time seems to have flown this evening. And I've literally just got off the phone with Guy. Look at me – I haven't even changed yet.' In all honesty I'm not sure I can be bothered now.

'The restaurant is full and noisy, but it seems a shame to eat up here. Why don't you put your work away and I will ask Luca to make you a pizza? I'll set up a table for you under the pergola. It'll be quiet there and you can relax undisturbed.'

'That's extremely thoughtful of you, Celia, and much appreciated. As was lunch.' We exchange smiles and there's amusement in her eyes.

'Richard would never forgive me if I don't look after you. I know Angel will be taking good care of him, but I hope he realises what a task he's asked you to take on.' Her frown is back, and I can see she's not happy about it.

'We've agreed an action plan and I'm feeling much happier now. It will take a little arranging, but I know what I'm doing.'

Her expression immediately lightens. 'That's good to hear. He has a great fondness for you, Marci.'

For Celia to acknowledge Richard's feelings for me is a complete surprise, but it warms my heart nonetheless.

'Richard had a sadness in his life,' she continues, 'and he told me that you helped him get over it. Sometimes it's the things we do to brighten someone's day that make all the difference. He said you were a constant joy to be around, a happy soul full of positivity and sparkle.'

Me, sparkle?

'I think it was more the other way around. He was there for me after my dad died and I went through an angry phase for a while.'

'Maybe you helped each other through difficult times.' She turns to go, but I stop her.

'Celia, did anything unusual happen just before Richard met Angel?'

Her eyes meet mine, a look of surprise flashing over her face. 'An old childhood friend of his back in the UK died, quite suddenly.'

'Oh – I had no idea!'

'Richard wasn't his normal, lively self and I pressed him about what was wrong. He told me that he'd received an email that one of his old friends had died of a heart attack. It hit him hard, and I'm not surprised he wasn't able to talk to you about it.'

'It must be tough not being able to say goodbye to someone,' I remark.

'I think it was a bit of a wake-up call, Marci, and he said it was a sharp reminder of how precious life really is. A couple of months later, Angel arrived for a two-week stay and the attraction was instant. I'm happy for them both. I know you haven't met her yet, but they were made for each other. So, relax – splash some cold water on your face and head down to the quiet spot!'

I might not have all the answers to the long list of questions buzzing around inside my head, but despite feeling shattered I'm also content. Sitting beneath a wooden structure at the far end of the terrace, I'm surrounded by a huge vegetable and fruit plot, with pathways running off in all directions.

I stare up at the greenery above me. I should imagine that it's pretty unusual to have courgettes hanging down, rather than tendrils covered with blossom. And as I gaze along the entire length there's a wonderful old vine with a mass of bunches of tiny green grapes. At the far end, a vibrant pink bougainvillea drips blossoms everywhere. I'm glad I'm sitting at this end, as even from here I can hear the incessant buzz of the bees busily harvesting the nectar.

I'm so engrossed in looking around, that it's a surprise when I hear a voice next to me.

'*Buona sera*, Marci.'

I look up to see Giulia, carrying a large wooden platter at shoulder height, on her upturned hand. Like the other sous chefs, she's wearing a black double-breasted chef's jacket, plain black trousers and a black-and-white pin-striped bandana covering her hair.

'*Buona sera*, Giulia. *Grazie*!'

'You are alone and Luca he has made you one of his large specials,' she replies, shrugging her shoulders.

I didn't think I was hungry until I catch a waft of that heavenly smokiness from the wood-fired oven; my mouth is watering.

'That looks and smells wonderful.'

'Simple is best!' Giulia declares. '*Pomodoro*, a leetle bazil, and some *Mozzarella di latte di bufala*.'

She places the platter down on the table. 'I thought you 'ad a drink already. I will ask someone to bring that together with a salad.'

'That's very kind, thank you.'

She takes a moment to straighten the small blue tablecloth and I lift the cutlery to make it easier for her.

'You return 'ome in August?' she enquires, casually.

'I'm due to fly back on the thirty-first of July. Hopefully I will get some time to relax and enjoy the beautiful scenery once the packing is under way.'

'Naturally. I enjoy to wander around Richard's cave of treasures in the past. It is full of interesting things. But so sad to see it closed and Luca misses his good friend.'

All the staff here can speak at least a little English and I've overheard French and German being spoken, too. However, Giulia is more fluent than I thought, because she was a little frosty at first and not very talkative. Renzo did warn me that she can be moody at times, so it's nice to see her feeling more relaxed around me tonight.

'I know. Hopefully, Richard and Angel will come to visit you all very soon.'

On her way back along the path, Giulia passes a waiter I haven't met so far and they stop to exchange a few words. The sound of her laughter as the guy reaches out with his free hand to place it briefly on her arm, reaches my ears. He turns to walk in my direction but I notice that he stops, briefly, to glance back at her. Giulia is still watching him and gives a little wave, as if she was expecting him to do that and it's a curious moment.

As he comes closer I can't help but notice the spring in his step.

'Goodness – all of this is for me?' I remark as he lowers the tray, placing a large salad next to the pizza, together with a glass of water and a bottle of wine in a cooler.

'You no starve with Luca in zee kitchen. I am Dario, Viola's brother. Sadly, I missed your welcome party. I pour for you?'

He points to the wine bottle, but I put up my hand to indicate that I'll help myself. '*Grazie*, Dario. How is Viola?'

He rubs his hand along his left jaw, screwing up his face. 'Sore, but back tomorrow. Enjoy!'

Viola, if I remember correctly, is Vittorio's daughter – that's Luca's eldest brother. I'm assuming that neither of his brothers are in the catering business, given that they both have offspring who work here.

Although nowhere is off limits to the guests, unless someone wanders into the narrow corridor running alongside the kitchen, the only access point to this part of the gardens is up that steep flight of stone steps the other side of the barbecue. It's about as private as you can get in such a relaxed and busy place.

I can hear the strains of music filtering up from down below, but it's a pleasing background sound as I manoeuvre a slice of pizza onto my plate. The salad is so fresh, with herbs, peppery rocket, black olives, capers, and small slices of something white that I don't recognise. Picking one up, I take a bite and it's lemony, which is a surprise. The dressing is simple – virgin olive oil and balsamic vinegar, by the look of it.

Pizza is one of my favourites back home because it's easy to order in when I haven't had time to go food shopping. But this is something else. The smokiness from the wood-fired pizza oven contrasts perfectly with the sweetness of the tomatoes. A little charring here and there, together with the creaminess of the buffalo mozzarella, is divine. This is without a doubt the best pizza I have ever eaten – the previous winner of that accolade was a small restaurant in Rimini. No wonder Giulia is happy to work here – she's learning from the best.

Considering I didn't think I was that hungry, I manage to eat just over a third of the pizza and make a dent in the salad. As I sit back, my stomach feeling pleasantly full, I spot Luca striding along the covered pathway between the runner beans and the tomatoes. He waves to me as he approaches.

'I no disturb you. Just make sure you like?'

'Please, sit down and that was absolutely delicious, Luca. Look how much I've eaten!' I grin at him. 'Can you sit and enjoy a glass of wine with me?'

'I stay for a moment only. Celia tells me you 'ave heard from Richard? They are good?'

'Yes. He sounds very happy indeed. They're still in Thailand but may well move on very soon.'

'Ah! I wish them well. I miss our late-night talks over a glass of limoncello. I told him not to empty La Grotta, but he said that it should be a home, not a place to store dusty things from the past. Richard is right.'

'What a great idea, Luca. The parking could so easily be divided off and the front made private. Richard has now decided that everything will be shipped back to the UK, so I'll be able to start packing very soon.'

Luca presses his lips together, accepting that it's the end of an era. 'Then is time for me to make plans for my future. My old friend Richard says Celia and I work too 'ard but work is good. It is my life, but I do it for Celia, eh?'

I didn't realise the full impact of Richard's departure. Will Celia and Luca renovate La Grotta and enjoy some sort of semi-retirement?

'Sit and enjoy your wine, but I will ask Nico to come and join you. It is quieter time now and it 'as been a long day for 'im, too.'

I don't like to say that I was just about to head back to my room. I guess I'm in for yet another late night.

8.
Reading Between the Lines

It isn't long before Nico appears, an empty wine glass in his hand.

'Let me clear the plates first,' he insists. 'I need to grab something to eat if that's okay with you.'

'Of course.'

While Nico is gone I pour him some wine and top up my own glass. However, when he returns, he's carrying a plate in both hands.

'Dessert?' He slides a small platter in front of me.

'I didn't know what you liked, so there's a choice. You might want to try my pasta dish, too,' he says, as he places some cutlery wrapped in a napkin down on the table. '*Spaghetti alle vongole*. You won't taste better anywhere – just try it.'

Clams aren't my favourite seafood, but these are small and surprisingly sweet when mixed in with the flavoursome sauce and the perfectly cooked spaghetti. I love that they don't overcook it, as pasta loses a lot of its taste when it's soft.

'Simple, and yet a delight to eat. The pizza was fabulous, too. I thought Rimini did the thinnest bases and I love it when there's a crispness to it, but Luca's base is light and flaky.'

'Giulia also makes a good pizza,' Nico informs me.

I watch as he expertly twists the pasta around his fork and pops it into his mouth. 'Luca has trained her well, but he always says that a chef is born, not made. Once the techniques have been learnt it's all about the combination of flavours and the quality of the ingredients.'

I look at him quizzically. 'That sounds to me like it came from personal experience.'

A mirthful look comes over Nico's face. 'Sadly, he eventually gave up on me, but it was a long time after I'd given up on myself. Luca doesn't like to accept defeat.'

'Were you disappointed?' I ask.

'A little, but I wasn't surprised. Apparently, my biological father worked in an office, so it's hardly in my genes. When the time comes, Giulia will fill Luca's shoes and I'll run the business side of things. Hopefully, that time is still a way off, yet.'

Oh dear. After chatting to Luca just now, maybe that's wishful thinking on Nico's part.

'It must be satisfying running a family business, knowing you can rely upon each other as the next generation steps up. When did Luca open the restaurant?'

'Oh, it's been here since the fifties. He inherited it when his father died.'

'But he's the middle son, isn't he?'

'Yes. Vittorio was already working for his father-in-law's business alongside his wife, Francesca. Tomasso, the youngest of the three, runs his own business.'

'Who did Luca take after, to inspire him to become a chef?'

Nico tilts his head, indicating for me to try one of the desserts.

'I think you'll find the lemon tiramisu refreshing. Giulia is what you might refer to in the UK as the queen of puddings,' he interjects. 'Luca took after his mother and grandmother. In fact, his mother worked here in the kitchen until she died following a fall. She was in her mid-eighties, and it was sad because she was young at heart. When Luca took it over the building was badly in need of updating. One of the terraces was in disrepair and a supporting garden wall needed to be fortified.'

'That sounds expensive.'

Nico nods, while he finishes eating. When he's done, he sits back, wiping his mouth on the napkin. 'It's a large property and the restaurant wasn't making enough money to cover the overheads. There was talk of everyone putting up capital so that all three of the brothers had a share in the business, with Luca running it. In all honesty, it wasn't a good investment at the time as the rooms above weren't being let out. In the end it was agreed that Luca would buy them out. He sunk in every penny he had to get the structural work done and the restaurant area spruced up. Sadly, his first wife passed away in a tragic car accident. At the time, things almost came to a halt, apparently, as he fell apart.'

'He was left entirely on his own?'

'Yes. They were unable to have children and with his brothers involved in their own businesses, things started to go downhill.'

What a sad story. 'But he managed to pull it all back because it's thriving now.'

'He did. When Mum brought me here on holiday I fell in love with the beach and the boats, while Mum fell in love with Luca. When this became our new home, together they gradually reclaimed the gardens, which were wildly overgrown. And Mum was responsible for the setting up of the kitchen garden.'

'Goodness. That must have been hard work for Celia with a young child to look after, too.'

Nico looks off into the distance for a moment before replying. 'I must admit that I've never really given it any thought. My earliest memories are all happy ones, of running around in a wonderful environment, full of sunshine and people eating and having fun.'

'Why did they decide to offer accommodation? Isn't that an additional pressure?'

'That was Richard's idea.'

I do a double take. 'Richard?'

'Well, the result of one of Luca and Richard's late-night discussions. I assumed you knew that they were partners. All that was needed was a little extra capital. Within eighteen months of Richard moving here it went from a restaurant making an okay profit, to two thriving businesses.'

My head is reeling. What possible reason would Richard have not to mention any of this to me? Here I am talking about clearing out La Grotta, as if Richard is merely a tenant, and not an integral part of the business. Poor Luca must think me insensitive.

'You haven't touched the *torta di ricotta e pere*. It's traditional here on the Amalfi coast. Ricotta cheese with freshly baked, brandy-soaked pear cake and hazelnut-flavoured pastry,' Nico chides me.

'I'm full, really. Don't let it go to waste.'

He pulls the platter closer to him, eager to tuck in, but I'm reeling. Now that I've met everyone, I don't relish the thought of being in the middle of something that could affect them all. Richard's decisions going forward could have a serious impact on this family. I can only hope an exit strategy isn't a part of the plan.

Suddenly life doesn't seem quite as sweet as it did just a few short hours ago and my conscience is beginning to feel uneasy.

'Morning, Mum, I know I said I probably wouldn't call again for a few days, but I thought I'd better let you know that Richard has been in touch.'

'Oh, he phoned me, too, Marci. Shortly after he rang you, that's why I didn't bother letting you know. He's so grateful for what you're doing.'

So grateful, that he's only telling me half the story, I reflect, as Mum continues.

'It was only a quick call, but long enough to reassure me that he hasn't had a change of heart . . . I mean, it's full steam ahead.' She sounds confident about that.

'I'm reassured to hear you say that, Mum. I like to think that if Richard were in some sort of trouble, he'd be straight with us.' Last night my mind went off on a rather bizarre tangent. *Richard wouldn't get involved in any dodgy deals*, I told myself firmly. But when I awoke this morning that ugly worm of a doubt was still lingering.

When someone who is settled, suddenly ups and leaves, it is puzzling. Angel and Richard could easily have returned from honeymoon to sort everything out together, and then decide what they wanted to do next. In my opinion that would be the sensible option, but who knows what the plan is. I hope at some point the two of them will share it with the rest of us.

'That's taking your concern a little far, Marci. Besides, you know what a stickler Richard is for rules – everything he does is by the book. And yes, I've been a little apprehensive too, as it's a big step for him to take, but I've known him long enough to read between the lines. He's in a genuinely good place.'

'And he's in good health?' I check, that niggling fear still sitting at the back of my mind.

'As far as I'm aware, he's fine. Unless you're about to tell me something I don't know. You aren't – are you?'

Now I'm unsettling Mum and that wasn't my intention. Quickly I backtrack, determined not to worry her.

'No. I'm just nervous as he's a little blasé about everything, as if none of it matters. When I hand back the keys to La Grotta, if he decides to return to Positano with Angel he will be starting from scratch again.'

Mum sighs. 'I warned him this wouldn't sit well with you.'

'What wouldn't?'

This time she draws in a deep breath. 'This didn't happen overnight, Marci. Richard confided in me before he pressed the *go* button. He said that going with his heart was the right thing to do because Angel was his future, and they'd build a new life together. He knew that you'd be concerned over whether he was being cavalier, and Guy would be shocked – which made me laugh, as he knows you both so well. I offered to sort things out for him, but he said David wouldn't approve. He thought you were the right person to handle this on his behalf and he pointed out that the break would do you good. In all honesty, I was in total agreement with him on that point.'

'So Guy wasn't in on it, either?'

'No, of course not. Richard made the offer to both of you and it was genuine. If Guy had stepped up, then you'd be here at home keeping everything ticking over – wouldn't you?'

But both Richard and Mum know that Guy wouldn't have been able to do that for two reasons. Firstly, because I'm not an auctioneer and secondly, because he and Selena are coming up to their first wedding anniversary.

'Richard thought an adventure might shake me up a little?'

There's an awkward pause. 'Marci, Richard means well, and I went along with it because if I were your age and single, I'd have jumped at the opportunity to fly off to Positano.'

'Yes, but if you could see the size of the problem that he left behind you'd think differently. Besides, at my age you already had Guy, and I was on the way,' I remind her.

'You know what I mean. I said *if* – we're two different people, Marci. All I wanted was to settle down, have a family and do whatever I could to help your dad build the business.'

And Mum did just that – they were a team. In between

school runs, dental appointments, keeping us all fed and the house ticking over, Mum tackled everything and anything that needed doing. Dad's head was always elsewhere, being up to his eyes in paperwork and keeping a close watch on the cashflow. As I approach thirty, my life couldn't be more different.

'What's really worrying you, Marci?'

'Richard's total lack of planning at this end and the problems it's causing. It's so unlike him, he's thrown me.'

'He told me that when he made his will, a few years ago, he organised his finances so that he could take early retirement when he was ready. Now that time has finally arrived, he can relax and enjoy himself and he's more than happy with the way things are going, Marci. And both Guy and I agree with Richard that a change of scenery will do you good. The last year you've been so focused on work that you've had little time for yourself.'

'Thanks, Mum. It's just that—'

'—Richard stepped in to fill Dad's shoes when David couldn't, and you're hurt that he didn't let you in on his plans. I know. Richard takes his role as godfather to you and Guy very seriously and I appreciate that fact. Sadly, David isn't a family man, but love isn't something you can sidestep. It just happens, I'm afraid. There's nothing wrong with letting Richard worry about you as if you are his daughter. It's a role he took on willingly and without hesitation – that's rather special and what I love about Richard.'

'What if his little bubble of happiness bursts, Mum?

What would he do then? There was a time when I thought Everett was the one I was destined to spend the rest of my life with – and look at what a disaster that turned out to be.'

It didn't help that Guy's wedding more or less coincided with the news of my break-up with Everett. While it pains me to even mention my ex's name, I want to explain to Mum why I'm so concerned for Richard.

She utters a sigh. 'Oh Marci – just when you're beginning to let go of the hurt, this has, unwittingly, raked it all up for you. Nothing in life is guaranteed and Richard is very aware of that, but without hope life would be pretty miserable, wouldn't it? Just know that you are repaying Richard's kindness and love by being there for him at a time when he's ecstatically happy. He also wants you to have a little fun. Flirt, laugh . . . perhaps even have a summer fling!'

I start laughing. 'Me? Have a fling? It's been so long that I can't remember how to flirt. Thanks for listening, Mum. It's just a little weird coming here and everyone I talk to acts as if they know me, or at least something about me.'

'I rather think that was the point Richard was trying to make, Marci. You laugh and joke with people, but how many do you let cross that line you draw? Open up a little, step outside your comfort zone and what happens in Positano stays in Positano after you leave.'

Maybe Richard and Mum are right. I mean, there are good-looking Italian men all around me and some of them are bound to be single. There's certainly one who immediately springs to mind and that thought is enough to make me break out into a shameless smile.

9.

The Hard Work is About to Begin

'Right, it's all set up!' Guy sounds mightily pleased with himself. 'The packing materials will be delivered first thing tomorrow morning. I'll email you the company's details in case you need more, but they've based it on our guestimate that we'll be able to fill a twenty-foot container. Worst case scenario is that we've underestimated it and you'll run out of space. If that's the case, then we could get Richard's personal stuff sent later.'

I can finally breathe a sigh of relief. 'You have no idea how good it is to hear that, Guy. I've been here five days already and the time has flown by. When will the team arrive to load everything up?'

'The earliest date I could get was the twenty-eighth of July and that was a cancellation. You'll be flying back three days later. That gives you a little over six weeks to fill those boxes. I've ordered some wooden crates for the over-sized and heavy items, like the gates and the high-value pieces we've already identified. The guys who load up the lorry will be responsible for packing up the crates. You're still going to need help, though, as you have a lot to get done. It's the small items that take up the time, especially the glassware.'

'Nico says he knows someone who might be able to help. Monday is his day off and we're having lunch with a friend of his.'

'Well, with the money we're saving Richard by not getting the professionals in to do everything, whatever it costs to get another pair of hands onboard will still mean it's a good deal. I feel bad not offering to fly over and get stuck in myself, but things are busy this end. Mum was here on Thursday and Friday, helping out. The temperatures have suddenly shot up and this weekend has been manic. We probably had twice as much footfall today as we did last Sunday.'

'That's great and it's good of Mum to make herself available. I bet David isn't too happy, though.' I can imagine Guy grinning at that comment.

'Selena said the exact same thing. But it's family first for Mum, always. David accepts that, even though he can't really understand it. We both know his attitude is that people either sink or swim. He's built a successful business on his own and in his eyes no one is indispensable. There's always someone out there looking for a job and he uses that tactic to keep his employees sharp. It's made him a lot of money.' I sigh, knowing he's right, but it doesn't make it any less frustrating.

'Hmm . . . that's why I can't stand to be around him. David thinks I'm a lightweight, doesn't he?'

The line goes ominously quiet for a second or two. 'Um . . . no. I think that's a little unfair of you, Marci. He doesn't know you, that's all. You never gave David a chance, did you? It was Richard you turned to every time.'

'That's true. But in fairness, he's not the type of man to sit down and listen to anyone's growing pains, is he?'

Guy laughs. 'Maybe you scared him off. Even I had trouble being around you at times. It was either loud music blasting out, groups of giggly girls having sleepovers, or doors being slammed and tearful outbursts.'

Teen years aren't easy to get through.

'Thanks for that!' I exclaim, laughing. 'It was easier for you, being that bit older. He's never asked me to go horse riding with him.'

'Did you ever show an interest?' Guy points out and he's right. I wouldn't have wanted to go anyway.

'As long as he makes Mum happy, that's all I care about. As for Richard – well, they're really missing him here, Guy. He's such a character, isn't he?'

'Yep. He sure is. But we've got his back and if this is what he wants, then we'll get it sorted between us. It's going to be a lot of work when you get back, but Briony's confidence is really starting to grow. I think when you return, we need to give her more responsibility. Maybe recruit a new floor manager to replace her, so that she can take on some of your workload. What do you think?'

I know where Guy is going with this. He wants to train me up as an auctioneer, so it doesn't fall to him every time. Mum knows that I don't feel comfortable being up on a podium and the pace is fast. You can't miss one bid in the room and now it's also online too, the back and forth is frenetic.

'She deserves a promotion,' I agree, but I fear I'm going to disappoint Guy. 'You know where my interests lie, and we need to have a frank talk about that. Anyway, I must go. They're busy in the restaurant and I've offered to help.'

'Oh, my goodness, you really are settling in – aren't you!'

'Without experiencing it first-hand, it's hard to explain what it's like here, Guy. But everyone jumps in without hesitation and from the moment I arrived, I wasn't a stranger. Well, not to them.'

'You always were Richard's favourite. You shed enough tears on his shoulder over the years.' Guy doesn't often show his emotions, but I can tell from his tone that he's talking from the heart.

'I did, didn't I?'

'Actually, Marci, I was glad you had someone you could run to.'

He speaks the truth, but forgets that he too, steps up for me whenever I need help. He's beavering away in the background so that I can – at last – get things started at this end.

'Thanks, Guy. I appreciate you're swamped and taking time out to make the arrangements is more than I expected. I've finally begun going through some of Richard's paperwork and I've found his ledger. Would you believe that it's handwritten? I'll send it recorded delivery as it lists the date he purchased each item, any provenance that exists, as well as the sum he paid for it. As I pack stuff up, I'll record it on a spreadsheet and then we can marry the two on my return.'

'Sounds like a plan, Marci. You saved the day – you do know that? We both owe Richard a lot. He kept Mum going when grief was threatening to suck the life out of her. And don't be too hard on David. Mum needs to be needed. He fills that role and when she's fussing over him, she isn't here wistfully wishing she could turn back the clock. Anyway, good luck tomorrow – hope you find yourself another pair of willing hands!'

Celia gives me the nod of approval – dressed in a white cotton short-sleeved blouse and a pair of black trousers Viola kindly found for me, I blend in perfectly.

'You look the business,' Celia remarks kindly, but I'm nervous.

'Relax. Nico will direct you and anything you can do to help is much appreciated.'

Nico comes hurrying towards me, beckoning with his finger and I give Celia a parting smile as I race to catch up with him.

'You look good,' he calls over his shoulder, sensing I'm hot on his heels. 'We're going to clear tables and get them set up.'

I watch as he shows me a few tips on the correct way to stack plates without risking things falling off on the trip back to the kitchen. There's a sequence and it doesn't take long to get into a pattern. Clear the plates first, then the glasses and empty wine bottles using the brown trays with a lip. Make sure there's nothing left, like a receipt, before folding up the tablecloth. Place it straight into the washing machine en route to the linen cupboard to get a replacement.

The lunchtime tablecloths are blue, with white paper napkins and the cutlery isn't laid out, as it is for dinner in the evening. Instead, there are paper pockets bearing the restaurant logo into which a knife, fork and dessert spoon are inserted.

'Steak and fish knives are kept in the large drawer next to the coffee station,' he informs me. He continues working while he's giving me my instructions, as there's no time to stop and chatter. I simply follow his example and when I catch his eye, I see that he's smiling at me.

'What?'

'You're a quick learner.'

Someone calls out Nico's name and we both turn around to see three guys striding through the open doors. They greet each other enthusiastically, laughing, joking and chattering away in Italian.

'Sorry, Marci, I didn't mean to turn my back on you. Meet my friends – Enzo, Cristian and Marco.'

Not sure quite how to react, I simply hold up my hand and give a little wave. What follows is a torrent of words I can't even begin to keep up with and Nico gives them a dismissive look.

'They're ribbing me for not telling them how beautiful you are and that it isn't just work that's keeping me occupied.'

I give a little laugh, a blush slowly creeping up my face, feeling slightly embarrassed as they continue to check me out. Nico waves out to Dario to get them seated, but I can see it isn't merely because of the banter.

'Marci, can I leave you to it? Luca's ringing the bell and food is waiting, but everyone is busy.'

'I'll be fine. Go!'

It's rather nice to be doing something useful, and great

to see how jovial Nico's friends are – they all look like they know how to have a good time, that's for sure.

It's non-stop and although the restaurant only serves until 3 p.m., by the time the last of the lunchtime diners leave, it's nearly a quarter to four.

'Pizza on the terrace, everyone?' Celia calls out as Nico carries the sign out to place across the entrance to the restaurant. It displays this evening's menu and gives the details of the app for anyone wanting to book a table. I hang back, but he doesn't realise I'm waiting for him and on the way through he can't resist stopping to slide in a chair a little further and straighten the candles in the centre of the tables. When he realises that I'm watching he gives me a huge grin.

'Small things annoy me,' he says, throwing up his hands in typical Italian style. 'I like neat and tidy. And straight.'

'How did I do? I notice that you didn't stop at any of the tables that I've just laid up ready for tonight.'

'Which means you did a good job.'

Now I know he's just being kind. 'I didn't drop anything, but I'm slow compared to everyone else,' I admit.

'Which is why there weren't any breakages. You did great and it makes a difference. The quicker we clear tables, the more meals we can serve. People don't like waiting, even if they haven't booked, and it's hard to turn anyone away. They're more likely to come back again if we make them feel their custom matters. It's good business sense.'

As we join the others in the side garden off the terrace, it's the first time Nico has talked about the restaurant business in general. He's very deferential to Celia, but he knows what he's doing. We walk past the swimming pool and the beautifully clear blue-tinged water as we approach the outdoor buffet bar. Giulia is busily cutting up pizzas fresh from the oven.

Celia is standing at one end passing out plates and she greets us warmly.

'What kept you two? I hope Nico congratulated you, Marci. But you aren't one of us until you smash a plate.'

Everyone stops what they're doing to turn and watch, starting a slow handclap. I raise my eyebrows as Celia passes me a plate and points to the patio area. Glancing at Nico, he nods his head and the clapping speeds up.

Walking over, I stand hesitantly looking down at the floor. This feels so wrong and yet everyone is egging me on. I raise the plate level with my chin, and let it fall. I'm relieved when it doesn't smash into smithereens, but into five or six pieces, and there's a massive round of applause. Dario appears at my elbow with a dustpan and brush. I reach out to take it from him, but he indicates for me to re-join the group.

'Well done, Marci,' Luca calls out. 'There is always a job for you 'ere if you want it!' he declares loudly, and I start laughing.

'I think you could do better,' I smile, as everyone tucks into the food.

It's lovely to mingle and I end up standing on the far side of the swimming pool, looking down onto the Spiaggia Grande and the colourful rows of umbrellas. All I can think about is my first night here and the long walk back up a seemingly endless number of steps.

'Is beautiful, no?' Viola interrupts my thoughts and I turn to look at her.

'It's spectacular. How's your tooth?'

She grimaces. 'Sore, but I have tablets. Now you are officially one of us,' she grins. 'It is so busy and it make everyone happy today.'

I can see that. 'I think I should have worn flat shoes, though,' I admit, and she stares down at my feet.

'Ah, yes. Always flat! Richard, too, would help. He was a good wine waiter.'

'I can imagine. He's a wine lover, for sure, and a bit of an expert,' I reply before taking a huge bite of pizza. 'Mmm . . . this is different. What are the toppings?'

'Smoked *provala*, *Piennolo* cherry tomatoes and bazil.' I love the way sometimes the Ss sound like Zs. 'There is a little sweet salami, too. Giulia, she experiments.'

'The flavours are incredible.'

'She loves what she does. She is also a *chef pasticcere* – eh . . . *I dolci*?'

'Desserts – a pastry chef, yes. I tasted the lemon tiramisu the other day. It was amazing.'

'One day she will take over from Uncle Luca,' Viola says, lowering her voice as she gazes around to check that no one can overhear us. 'She has promised me a job in the kitchen.'

I'm a little surprised as it seems that Viola is taking me into her confidence. It hadn't occurred to me that there was a hierarchy, or that some jobs might be more sought after than others.

'Do all four of Luca's nephews and nieces work here?'

'No. My cousin, Renzo he come occasionally to help, but he works for my Uncle Tomasso. They build swimming pools – they built this one for Uncle Luca.'

'Oh, I didn't realise. Your father, Vittorio, also has his own business?'

'Yes. *Agente immobiliare*. Uh . . . sell villas?'

'But you prefer to work here?'

'Yes. It is my mother's family business but now my father, he is in charge. It is not for me or my brother, Dario. They do not get on, they argue much.' She shrugs her shoulders.

'I'm sorry to hear that. But he's happy working at the restaurant?'

'Very happy, as am I. They fall out because he broke up with his fiancée. My father does not approve.'

Oh dear. Perhaps the less said, the better.

'That's sad, but one day maybe they will make up.'

Viola rolls her eyes. 'My mother hopes Dario will change his mind. I don't think so. He won't admit it, but I think he might have feelings for another person. Do you have someone special in your life, Marci?'

I wasn't expecting that question. 'Me? No. I'm too busy,' I try to laugh it off.

'Richard said you are married to your job?'

'Did he, now? Well, I love what I do, that's true. But love, well – that's down to fate.'

We both start laughing.

'I have not met *the one* yet, either!' she whispers. 'Someday soon, I hope.'

'What are you two laughing about?'

Nico comes to join us.

'*Il matrimonio*,' Viola retorts and Nico raises his eyebrows.

'My least favourite subject,' he moans, and Viola giggles. It must be some sort of private joke, but Nico makes no attempt to explain. Instead, he changes the subject.

'Luca is asking whether you know how to cook, Marci.' Nico's face changes in an instant as he grins back at me.

Before I can answer, Viola jumps in. 'Nico, he is teasing me, Marci. He knows how I long to swap my serving uniform and join the team in the kitchen!'

I can see it's true, as Viola gives Nico a withering look. But she's not angry with him, it's all in fun and she offers to take our empty plates back to the kitchen.

Once she's out of earshot, we stand together just staring out at the gently rippling waves, watching a dozen speed boats zipping along.

'It doesn't feel like a Sunday,' I mutter, my eyes dazzled by the sparkling sea.

'You haven't forgotten our plans for tomorrow, have you?'

'No, of course not. In fact, I now have a deadline as Guy has arranged for the packing materials to be delivered tomorrow morning. The pressure is on.'

'Perfect timing, then. I'll pick you up some time around eleven? It doesn't matter if you need me to hang around for a bit as I can always get lunch delayed.'

'Great. Should I bring anything? It's the first time I've been invited to eat in someone's home over here.'

'Flowers are a nice gesture, but we'll pick them up on the way, so don't worry.'

'Is there anything I can do to help in the restaurant tonight?'

Nico shakes his head. 'Renzo will be here. He likes the company. Besides, you've done enough for one day. You should relax and put your feet up – or go exploring.'

Maybe I will.

The beating heart of Positano is the town, which is a stone's throw away from the beach, albeit I lose count of the number of steps. Made up of narrow, bougainvillea-covered alleyways lined with boutiques, the main street is Viale Pasitea. It's pedestrianised – which is just as well given how tightly packed everything is.

Nearby is the beautiful little church of Santa Maria Assunta and it's the first place I head towards. The cupola is especially commanding when viewed from the beach, as it's covered in the most glorious yellow, white and green majolica tiles. It's a popular landmark and one you simply can't miss. But to see it up close as evening descends is a special moment for me. As I stop to take in the sights, sounds and smells all around me, I feel a little fizz of excitement in the pit of my stomach. I wouldn't have missed this for the world! And I have my godfather to thank for that.

It's fun wandering around at leisure, people-watching and finding myself constantly drawn to some of the interesting little stalls along the way. The main street leads to Piazza dei Mulini, which Celia informed me was probably a twenty-minute walk, but tonight I'm in search of a few things to tide me over when I'm at La Grotta.

The shops I pass display a wide range of items from brightly coloured cloth bags and beachwear decorated with beads of turquoise and coral, to ceramics and the finest linens. There are even craftsmen ready to make sandals for you while you wait. It's tempting to stop, but I'm a woman on a mission and it's already getting dark.

What's strange is that I don't feel like a tourist, and I suppose I'm not in the truest sense of the word. I feel very at home, and it dawns on me that it's because I'm not a stranger abroad – I'm surrounded by people who are looking out for me, even though I hardly know them and that's comforting.

Would it be nice to be wandering along hand-in-hand with the man of my dreams? Yes, of course it would, but this is still an experience I will never, ever forget. And I'm grateful.

10.

A Good Wife Makes a Good Husband

The next morning it takes me a couple of hours to clear enough floorspace at the front of the shop for the delivery of packing materials. However, I seriously underestimated the amount of room it would take up. While I've packed up thousands of individual lots to send out to customers, when I go abroad on a buying trip Guy is the one who organises the professionals to come in after me. By the time the goods arrive I've usually been back in the UK for a while and I'm more interested in the unpacking bit.

I ask the two delivery men to leave some of the massive – albeit deceptively light – boxes and rolls of padded wrapping outside on the small deck in front of the shop. As I'm trying to manoeuvre one of them through the door without scraping my fingers on the doorframe, a scooter pulls into the car park and begins tooting. Great, another potential customer who isn't going to be pleased to find out that we're shut. But when I look up, it's Nico's smiling face I see, as he slips off his helmet.

'*Buon giorno*, Marci. It seems I arrived just in time!'

He strides forward, indicates for me to stand back and is tall enough to reach his arm over the top of the box to tilt it slightly and then uses his foot to slide it effortlessly inside.

'Ha! I thought it was going to be heavy. What's in here?'

'Just loose packing to put around the more delicate items.'

'And you'll need all this?' He stares around in amazement.

'If we want everything to arrive intact, yes. On removal day they're bringing some wooden crates to protect the more expensive pieces and things like the hefty pair of wrought-iron gates over there.'

He looks at the pitted and weathered decorative metal monsters leaning against the wall and shakes his head. 'Those will fetch enough to warrant the cost of transportation?'

'And give a healthy profit on top. This is history we're looking at, Nico. There will be a story to go with those and Richard has kept a record of it – where they came from and maybe who made them.'

'Richard has all that?'

'He does. That's a major selling point and attracts a premium. Guy will be trawling through his records once I get those off to the UK very shortly. And then I just have the rest of the paperwork to sort out.'

A look of astonishment flashes over Nico's face and I can see it's dawning on him that Richard's collection has some importance attached to it.

'I might not be the best person to help with the packing, unless it's stuff that can't easily slip out of my hands, but sorting paperwork I can handle. My mum is very particular with the accounting side of the business and I'm her number one assistant.'

'That's useful to know, thanks. I might take you up on that offer.'

It's not long before we get everything inside and when we're finished, I take Nico through to the garden.

'Grab a seat, I won't be a moment.'

When I return with two cold bottles of water and two glasses on a tray, Nico looks up, surprised.

'You have supplies?'

'I do. I took your advice and had a wander last night before dinner. I found a little shop and bought a few things. Not much, because I wasn't sure how heavy it would be carrying it all the way up here. But this morning I cleaned out the fridge and switched it on.'

'Home from home,' he laughs.

It's pleasant sitting here quenching our thirst, because it's hot again and despite the traffic on the road to the front, it's a little oasis of greenery and colour. It's just a shame that most of it is so overgrown.

'Oh, how I'd love to attack this garden and reveal its true beauty,' I sigh, thinking aloud.

'The whole place needs a lot of money spent on it. Oh, before I forget, Luca has arranged for someone to fix a closed sign across La Grotta's logo at the gate.'

'That's very kind. I suppose it'll disappear entirely if Luca decides to sell the property. This could be turned into an amazing home for someone.'

Nico shrugs his shoulders. 'At the moment it's the landmark we use on the website to direct our customers to the parking area. If the plot was split into two, selling off the building is an option, but Italians tend to hold on to what they own. I don't know if Luca has enough money to get the necessary work done, but anything is possible.'

Is it my imagination, or does Nico avoid any talk about the future, even his own? His reaction when Viola said we were talking about marriage seemed to press a button and he immediately changed the subject.

'We should think about leaving,' he says, standing and loading up the tray like a true gentleman. 'I have a helmet for you.'

'We're going by scooter?'

He laughs. 'It's too hot to walk the whole way, but it's a pleasant ride before we park up and tackle the steps.'

I don't like to inform him that I've never been on the back of anything with two wheels before. To my eye, scooters look so flimsy.

'I'll . . . um . . . just go and tie my hair back and grab my bag.'

Thank goodness I'm wearing leggings and a long-sleeved cotton shirt, as this was the last thing I was expecting. I lock the back door and make my way out into the sunshine. Nico is sitting on the pale blue Vespa, his feet firmly planted on the floor as the engine kicks into life. He turns to look at me as I hesitate for a moment; I feel awkward when he passes me a helmet over his shoulder.

Ramming it on, I slip the strap of my bag over my shoulder so that it's behind me. Pretending it's the most natural thing in the world to cosy up tight to Nico's back, I'm desperately trying to work out how I'm going to hang on. I'm only glad he can't see how flustered I am.

'Are you all set?'

'Y . . . yes,' I say, my voice wavering.

'It's not your first time – is it?' he queries.

'I'm more a four-wheel type of person.'

'You might want to put your arms around my waist, then. Just relax. You're in expert hands.'

As he pulls away, I screw up my eyes, my fingertips desperately working their way around the edge of the seat in search of a lip to grasp. However, as soon as he turns to the right, I fling my arms around his waist and cling onto him for dear life! This is so not fun. Not fun at all.

It seems like an eternity before he eventually slows down, and I ease open my eyes to see we're pulling into a layby. He points to a florist's shop on the opposite side of the road.

Once the scooter is stationary, I hop straight off, unclipping the strap beneath my chin. 'I'll get these,' I say, my legs a tad shaky as I hurry away from him.

Am I shaking because of my nerves, or because of the way my heart was thudding in my chest as I sat with my arms clutched around Nico?

Get a grip, Marci, I tell myself firmly as I push open the door and a young woman appears from the back room. After a short conversation in both Italian and English, I ask her for a small bouquet suitable to give my host. It doesn't take her long to put together some pale pink roses, white Marguerite daisies and a couple of stems with a small profusion of tiny white flowerheads. She tells me that it's mock orange blossom and I thank her. Carrying the bouquet over to the scooter, the smell wafts up and tickles my nose.

Gritting my teeth while smiling at Nico, this time I'm more prepared and I slip onto the seat behind him as if it's something I do all the time. However, now I only have one free hand, the other holding on tightly to the small bouquet. The only option is to literally glue myself to his back to ensure I don't embarrass myself and fall off.

It's a great relief when just a few minutes later he pulls to a halt in a section of private off-street parking.

'That wasn't so bad, was it?' he enquires, waiting as I try to elegantly alight, while encumbered with flowers in one hand and the strap on my bag beginning to slip down my left arm.

'It was fine,' I reply, trying to sound cool and composed. But I can see from the way his mouth twitches that he isn't fooled.

Nico tucks the two helmets underneath the scooter, and we set off.

'More steps?' I ask and he nods.

'Naturally! Do you have your bearings? When we were on the beach on your first night here, we looked up at the two cliffs with a cleft between them. We've now crossed over to the other side.'

I am listening as Nico chatters away, but whereas before I felt comfortable around him, now I'm feeling awkward. Thankfully, he's oblivious to that fact. It's been a long time since I threw my arms around a man, albeit this was not the usual scenario. But feeling the warmth and firmness of Nico's body while experiencing an adrenaline rush triggered by fear, has left me shaken and a little confused.

We traipse along a ramp, then down several winding

sets of well-proportioned steps, drawing to a halt at a narrow gate.

'We're here,' Nico informs me as he swings it open.

In front of us a long, straight path leads to a large pergola covered in climbing roses and jasmine. Beyond is an amazing garden filled with colour. I stare at the bouquet in my hand, reminding myself that it's the thought that counts.

'Nico!' a woman's voice calls out as we increase our pace.

We walk up the three steps leading onto a wide patio area in front of a gloriously pretty villa, with pale pink stucco and a faded terracotta roof.

As they greet each other, kissing alternate cheeks, the woman smiles at me over Nico's shoulder. 'And this must be Richard's goddaughter, Marci. Welcome!'

Goodness, is there anyone in Positano who isn't in the know about me?

'This is Olivia Thornton, Marci, she's married to Jack, my boating buddy.'

Ah, I remember Nico telling me that Olivia's mother, Patricia, is Celia's best friend.

'It's lovely to meet you, Olivia, and what a stunning home you have!' I hold out the flowers and Olivia takes them from me smiling, before leaning in to kiss first my right cheek and then the left.

'These are so beautiful, thank you – that's so kind. Daisies are my favourite! But, oh, that mock orange blossom. I keep saying to Jack that it's the one shrub we don't have, and yet even back in the UK, I remember it well from my childhood. Anyway, come inside and I'll get you both a cold drink.'

Glancing around, I notice the terraced gardens are very lush, vibrant with greenery – orange, lemon and olive trees abound. But there's also a vegetable plot with its carefully tended, neat little rows and someone has been weeding, because there's a huge pile of debris at one end. As I follow Olivia and Nico, I notice that beyond the end of the path leading up to the villa, there are several interesting outbuildings clustered together. They look a little sad and the exteriors are most definitely in need of a re-paint – but it's all very charming.

Nico's phone suddenly kicks into life and he disappears as I follow Olivia through to the kitchen.

'We've been dying to meet you, Marci. Jack is away and won't be back again for another two weeks, maybe a month if things don't go smoothly. I'm in between jobs and I gather you're in need of a little assistance?'

I watch as Olivia grabs some scissors and within less than a couple of minutes has clipped all the stems of the flowers in the bouquet and effortlessly assembled them in a white jug. 'There, don't they look and smell gorgeous?'

She stands back and turns to me, smiling. But when she begins speaking it's not about the flowers.

'You're quite a surprise, Marci, if you don't mind my honesty. I was expecting someone . . . older.'

Before I can reply, Nico appears, looking apologetic.

'I have to head back, I'm afraid. One of the refrigerators has broken down and Mum is tied up trying to accommodate the food, so it doesn't spoil. I'm sorry to cut and run like this. It will probably take an hour or two if I have to get someone out to look at it, but give me a call and I'll come back to collect Marci when you've eaten.'

'Oh, Nico!' Olivia pouts, looking sad. 'Our first lunch in ages and you get an emergency. Seriously, that place would fall apart if you weren't there! Go – sort them out and don't worry, I'll drive Marci back.'

Nico turns to me, trying not to smile. 'I know how much you enjoyed the ride here, Marci, but I'll catch up with you later. Have fun, ladies.'

I bat my eyelashes at him, and he starts laughing as he turns to walk away, leaving Olivia wondering what the joke is all about. It's a pity Nico can't stay, but the thought of four wheels instead of two is a relief.

Olivia is one of those people you instantly feel comfortable being around. She talks almost non-stop, in between frying off some giant king prawns, which fill the air with the piquant smell of the chilli sauce they've been marinading in. She assembles two plates of spaghetti, then scoops the succulent seafood on top, drizzling the juices over the top and finishing off with a sprinkling of coriander.

'Would you mind grabbing that basket of bread, Marci, as it won't fit on the tray? I think we're ready to eat. We'll take this down to the lower level. Oh, and can you grab that small packet of dog treats on the side – thank you!'

As we walk Olivia gives me a running commentary on the work they've had done since they bought the place almost four years ago.

'This lower level we kept unobstructed because the

views are simply divine. Jack thinks that we should put the swimming pool here, but I'd prefer it next to the villa.'

'You have ambitious plans still, then?'

'We do! Given that I'm self-employed, my income stream fluctuates so we use that to fund the work. We can only do that because of Jack's job, but unfortunately it's quite stressful for him at times and requires him to work away a lot.'

We step down onto the long terrace with its pretty flagstones, surrounded by the most fragrant lemon thyme as you walk over it. The views are panoramic, with only a half-wall that has dark pink bougainvillea draped over virtually the entire length as a barrier.

'Goodness, this is incredible, Olivia. It takes my breath away.'

She laughs. 'Just don't peer over the wall – it never feels precarious from this angle but it's a steep drop. Luna – come and meet Marci.'

From the shade of a little doghouse, hidden by the low sweeping branches of a ruby-red acer, the cutest little dog appears to greet us.

'Luna is an Italian Bolognese. Say hello, Luna.'

'She's so small and sooo adorable!' Well, she is the colour of cooked pasta, I smile to myself. 'I've never heard of that breed before, though.'

'The Bolognese is a small toy breed in the Bichon family. They have a coat that is fluffy and slightly curled and they don't shed. They love attention and make a wonderful companion dog, but they're very active,' Olivia explains as I watch Luna jumping around excitedly.

Placing the breadbasket on the table, I watch – fascinated – as Luna stands on two legs and begins rolling her paws in the air.

'Good girl,' Olivia croons. 'Would you mind giving her a few of those treats, Marci? She'll head back into the shade afterwards, as it's her nap time.'

As I stoop to open the packet, Luna sits watching me, tilting her head from side to side as she waits patiently.

'There you go! What a gorgeous coat you have, Luna.'

'It's a labour of love keeping her tangle-free, but she's such a cutie and perfect company for me when Jack is away. Nico said you're looking for someone to help you pack up Richard's wonderful collection?'

Giving Luna one last smooth, I straighten, and Olivia beckons me over to the table. It nestles inside a re-purposed shed, which has just three sides and a roof. In the back left-hand corner is a wine cooler full of ice set on a tall stand, with several bottles of water and a bottle of white wine.

'As I'll be driving you back, I'll stick to water. Would you like a glass of wine?'

'No, water is fine for me, too, thank you. This is wonderful, Olivia and so very kind of you. And to answer your question, yes, I'm desperately in need of some help at La Grotta.'

She passes me a packet of wipes and I take one, flashing it over my hands and dabbing at my cheeks. 'That's so refreshing, thank you.'

'You are most welcome. I'm a translator by trade, mostly women's fiction from English into Italian. I also write articles giving advice to people who are relocating to Italy.'

'Oh, Nico didn't mention that you translated *books*.'

'My next project has just been delayed by a month and a little break has turned into a bit of a black hole. I get bored easily, especially when Jack isn't here,' she explains as she twirls some spaghetti around her fork.

'Well, if you like I could pay you by the hour. I'm there every day from about 8 a.m. Thankfully, the shop doesn't get too hot, as the sun is only on the front and I keep the blinds down most of the time. Direct sunshine is the enemy of antiques.'

'Is there a lot to do?'

I'm just savouring the first mouthful of prawn and it literally melts in my mouth. I wonder if that's because everything here is so fresh, or Olivia simply knows the best way of cooking them.

'Mounds of it. Some pieces are more delicate than others, but it's common sense really. Glass, for instance, needs to be double-wrapped in tissue paper and carefully placed in boxes. Then we pack it out with something called paper void fill. It's one hundred per cent recyclable and comes on rolls. You simply crumple it up and stuff it around the item to secure it during transit.'

Olivia is just about to pop her fork into her mouth, but she stops for a moment to give me a beaming smile. 'That doesn't sound too difficult. I'd love to get involved.'

'You have no idea how grateful I am, Olivia. And the company will be most appreciated.'

'It sounds like this is going to be a summer you'll never

forget,' she remarks, her eyes searching my face. 'You haven't upset anyone back at home by escaping to Positano for a few weeks in the sun, have you?'

Breaking off some bread to dip into the sauce, I pop a small piece into my mouth as I take in the view. 'It's not an easy job, so the answer to that is no. In fact, my brother is feeling a little guilty as the offer was extended to both of us.'

'And you were the one to take up the challenge. Is there a special someone at home counting down the days until you return?' Her eyes twinkle as she poses the question.

'That's a firm *no*, too. It's just me until the man of my dreams waltzes into my life.'

'Oh, I see. But you wanted to come, anyway . . . I can tell.'

'Richard and I have always been close, and I'm pleased to do this for him. I think it would have been a bit of a painful process for him. Besides, he's having the time of his life!'

Olivia and I exchange a knowing look.

'This is a summer adventure for both you and Richard, then,' she says, watching for my reaction.

'I suppose it is.'

'It's also Nico's last summer of freedom,' she remarks, casually.

'It is?'

'Giulia has served her time and she's fed up with playing the waiting game, but until Nico commits to her, Luca won't consider taking a step back and handing over his chef's toque.'

This throws me and I'm not quite sure how to respond. Feeling a little uncomfortable, I go for the safest option.

'Toque?'

'That pleated hat worn by the head chef. Sometimes they wear a pointy one, too – don't ask me the difference. I think it's personal preference.'

'It must be difficult for her,' I reply, cagily.

Olivia purses her lips. 'It will please both families and Luca has been training Giulia ever since she gained her qualifications.'

'That sounds rather . . . business-like.'

Olivia sits back in her chair, biting her lip as she considers her reply.

'It's hard to explain. There is an old Italian saying: *La buona moglie fa il buon marito* . . .'

I understand enough Italian to figure that out for myself. 'A good wife makes a good husband – and I'm sure that's true in most cases. But marriage is a huge commitment.'

'Nico needs someone like Giulia,' she explains. 'If he's going to take over the running of the business it will complete the team. Giulia could leave and get a job anywhere, but what she wants is to be a part of the legacy, not merely an employee. But she isn't family – yet. Everyone is watching and waiting.'

I find myself toying with the last few strands of pasta on my plate.

'Family first, I understand that, but getting married should be for love, not . . .' I cast around for the right word, not wishing to cause offence. 'A sense of duty.'

'It's complicated, Marci. Giulia's father is a business associate of Vittorio Romano's. In southern Italy, life is more traditional and it's a slower pace than the more commercial centres like Rome, Milan and Venice. Family isn't motivated by *duty*, as much as . . . let's call it *goodwill*. Luca could not have taken over the business if Vittorio, the eldest son, had not decided to allow him the opportunity to do so.'

Now I'm confused.

'But I was under the impression that neither Vittorio or Tomasso were involved in the restaurant as they both have different interests, and Luca bought them out.'

'That's true,' she confirms. 'But while there is no obligation, Luca owes his eldest brother a debt of gratitude. Reputation and honour are everything here in Italy. *La bella figura* – the good image – affects one's entire family. What you do, what you say, and how you look – it's a matter of pride and reflects on one's parents. Luca knows full well that Vittorio is expecting Nico to ask Giulia to marry him – that's the reason she came to work here. Two problems will be solved in one fell swoop.'

'And that's why Luca will push for Nico to make a decision, because he and Celia are ready to step away and Luca hopes everything will slot into place rather neatly.'

Olivia nods her head, studying me for a moment. 'Perhaps you're better off steering clear of it while you're here. But it makes me sad. Nico hasn't found his true soul mate yet – he came close, a few years ago, but Tiziana preferred the buzz of city life.'

'Nico was in love?'

Olivia pauses for a moment, as if she's not sure. 'I like to think if that were the case, then somehow they would have made it work. But she's a model and while her parents live in Positano, she couldn't wait to escape.' Her tone is sombre. 'The clock is ticking and now you're here.'

I can feel myself frowning; there are so many questions whirling around inside my head that I don't quite know where to start.

'What has that got to do with anything?'

'I saw the way Nico was looking at you. He didn't want to leave, whereas usually he's gone like a rocket if there's a problem.'

'I think he has more than enough to cope with at the moment, don't you?'

All I receive in return is a silly grin. 'You can't help who you find attractive. I fell in love with Jack the first time our eyes met, and it was all so easy. But here you are, for a short time the two of you have been thrown together and you get to experience something truly wonderful.'

I glance at her, questioningly.

'A couple of months in Positano is a bonus, right?' However, there's a look of amusement reflected on her face.

As I help to stack the plates and carry them back up to the kitchen, my head is whirling. I'd rather spend my life alone than forgo finding true love. But what if Nico has already given up? Lots of people settle rather than spending the rest of their lives alone, don't they?

11.

A Whirlwind of Activity

Beep beep! Beep beep!

The sound of an insistent car horn pulls me reluctantly away from the rather delicate task of packing up a 1950s Italian clock and two matching candelabras. Finally relenting to the noise, I stop what I'm doing to go outside and explain for the umpteenth time that the shop is permanently closed. But as I step out into the sunshine, raising my hand to shade my eyes, it's Olivia I see stepping out of the small pale blue Fiat 500.

'Your newest recruit has arrived, and I have a few things that need to go into the fridge!'

I hurry towards her, and we greet one another as if we're old friends, Italian style.

When Olivia opens the hatchback, there is an assortment of small plastic boxes that fill the limited space. 'Unfortunately, I must leave by 4 p.m. at the latest. My mother is happy to look after Luna, but she is cooking for friends this evening and I promised I would head back early.'

'Oh, that's fine. I'm just delighted to see you. Here, let me take those.'

As I grab a small stack of boxes from Olivia's hands, she balances the rest with one arm as she locks the car.

'This looks like a feast,' I laugh, and she smiles at me as we walk over to the shop.

'I know La Grotta probably has more vases than our local florist's shop, but I thought you'd appreciate a good lunch instead of some flowers.'

But as we enter the gloomy interior, Olivia immediately sneezes as she begins to gaze around.

'Maybe flowers might have been better. It smells a little . . . dusty in here.'

'The whole place needs airing and I do leave the front door open at times, but it's easy to forget if I end up sitting out on the rear patio for a break. Now I have some company, let's head to the kitchen and put these things away, then I'll open the back door, too. Getting a breeze through will soon freshen things up.'

I'm relieved to see that Olivia has come prepared to work, as I forgot to warn her that everything is a little grimy. She's wearing a well-worn pair of knee-length navy shorts and a sleeveless navy top. She still manages to make it look much more fashionable than I do with my calf-length black leggings and a burgundy short-sleeved cotton shirt.

Olivia raises her eyebrows. 'Hopefully, that breeze going through will soon blow away the cobwebs,' she chuckles.

Fortunately, there are plenty of small, heavy items to use as doorstops and then – although it wasn't a part of the plan – we decide to do the first proper clean-through. It's rather satisfying to get to this stage, at last. Olivia sweeps the floor as I follow on behind with a wet mop. What a difference it makes as we start working – the floor cleaner adds a fresh scent of eucalyptus to the air and even the dust, as we move a few items around, is nowhere near as bad.

'Right, give me a quick lesson on how to pack up valuable items so they'll survive a long journey.' Olivia pulls a face, as if she's a little nervous. 'I can't wait to get stuck in – I've never done anything like this before.'

The large dining table, which is now the packing bench, is fully organised and relatively dust-free.

'This is a three-piece collection. I've already double-wrapped the clock and now it's a case of wrapping the matching pair of branch candelabras.'

'I'm not a bronzed cherubs, gilt work and marble base type of girl, but I can imagine this would look amazing sitting on a grand mantelpiece in a historic *palazzo*.'

'It's very collectible, although not as old as you might imagine. All the packaging we use is either recyclable and/or biodegradable. When this load arrives in the UK, everything, with the exception of the paper tape, will be reused. I'm on the fence about offsetting the carbon footprint if it's used as a cop-out. Shipping worldwide is difficult, of course, but we use what is called a green freight service.'

'Goodness, it's not something I've really considered. You sound like a woman on a mission.'

'I guess I am – sustainability is one of my special projects.'

'Go you! Right, show me how you would wrap these awkward candelabras and then just keep an eye on me until you're happy I know what I'm doing.'

In less than an hour, Olivia is confident enough to pack and talk, as we share our respective life stories. We commiserate over teenage angst, laugh over broken hearts that, in hindsight, felt more like fate rescuing us. And then talk about the things we love in our lives. For Olivia, it's Jack, Luna and her garden. For me it's my job. The stark difference in our conversation makes me think that maybe Richard was right after all – perhaps I do need a summer of love!

'How is life in sunny Positano?' Briony asks, her voice sounding a tad wistful. 'It's raining here, and Guy quit early for the day to go shopping for an anniversary present for Selena. Am I interrupting you?'

'No. It's gone four in the afternoon, and I've just arrived back at my room. I'm helping out in the restaurant tonight.'

'The restaurant?' She sounds surprised.

'Oh, anyone even remotely connected to the family steps in during the busy season. This will be the second time they've let me loose. It's mainly clearing tables and laying them up, but I'm also going to try my hand at serving coffees and desserts tonight – Nico thinks that's enough to begin with.'

'That name has such a romantic ring to it . . .' Briony lowers her voice, imagining goodness knows what.

'He helped find me an assistant, so I owe him big time. And this is a real experience for me. I'm seeing a side of Italian life I've never encountered before as someone on a business trip, or as a tourist. Anyway, Guy leaving early – that's a first!'

'He keeps ringing me for gift inspiration as he browses, but so far, Guy has rejected every suggestion I've made.

That's why I'm calling – he asked if I could sound you out for ideas.'

'Guy couldn't call me himself?'

'Um . . . he's not in the best of moods today.'

'That'll teach him to leave his present buying to the last minute! I suppose he thought he could simply pop into a shop and find the perfect gift without any forethought.'

Briony's tinkling little laugh says what she won't – that she's in total agreement. 'He has been rather tied up,' she replies, sympathetically.

Now I feel guilty because I'm not there, and what does Guy know about gift shopping? Absolutely nothing. I usually come up with the ideas for him and, in return, he comes to my rescue when I'm left scratching my head over something. Like the time my fuse box kept tripping out and the earliest I could get hold of an electrician was three days later. Seriously! It turned out to be a dodgy ceiling light, but Guy is good with practical things like that. At least it meant I could get back online. 'I know just the thing.'

'Ooh, what is it?'

'A handbag, one Selena admired when we popped out for coffee together a few days before I left. You know that little boutique dress shop . . . the one on the edge of town?'

'Yes, I know it. Elegance, isn't it?'

'Guy will probably raise his eyebrows at the price tag, as we didn't look that closely. It's not something Selena would treat herself to, but I know she'd love it! Tell him it's cream with a black trim and it's a shoulder bag – they'll know the one. They also had it in black with a cream trim – that would be the second choice.'

'Everything begins to fall apart when you aren't here,' Briony says, sounding a little maudlin.

'Really? I sincerely doubt that. But what's up?'

'The truth is . . .' Briony hesitates for a moment, and I find myself holding my breath. 'I feel like I'm telling tales, but Guy and your mum had a big row about an hour before he stormed off. He decided he needed to cool down. Except he's not cool, he's angry.'

Goodness, it must be bad for Briony to mention it.

'Do you know what the argument was about?'

'Your mum has been . . . how can I put this . . . um . . . tinkering with things behind his back.'

'Like what?'

'The layout in the gallery, for one.'

Uh-oh. 'She's still helping out?'

'Yes. She keeps finding an excuse to pop in even when we're fully staffed. And Guy isn't happy.'

'Thanks for the heads-up, Briony. I'll have a word with her.'

'She means well, Marci, but everyone is on edge.'

I can imagine. The staff won't know whose bidding to follow. Guy is the boss, but they all have a great affection for Mum. There's a reason why she handed the running of the business over to Guy and she can't step back in now and start meddling. That's not helpful, it's unsettling.

'And how are you doing?'

'Trying to be diplomatic when things get a little tense. Aside from that it's going well and I'm enjoying the extra responsibility. I accompanied Guy on a trip to Ravensdale

Manor yesterday. We picked up some wonderful items for the next auction. One of the paintings should attract a lot of interest. They're raising funds to pay for some extensive renovation work to the main house.'

I chuckle. 'I didn't mean *at work*!'

'Oh, right. Well . . . Jason messaged and we're having lunch together on Sunday.'

My smile immediately turns into a huge grin. 'Now that's promising.' Their casual drink together must have gone well.

'Don't go reading anything into it. I'm not entirely sure that Jason is my type. He's a bit too serious for me.' Briony is immediately on the defensive.

'Too serious? That's a first. We've had *too young*, *too blasé*, *too disorganised* . . . so this is a vast improvement.'

Now she's laughing. 'He's a real gentleman but a little awkward at times. I hate dating a friend of a friend, though. You know what it's like. The friend insists on asking you how it's going.'

'I'm not sure he'd class me as a *friend*, Briony. Jason just happens to be someone I've known professionally for a while, that's all. There's no pressure at all from me,' I declare, but I am delighted they are having a second date. It wasn't easy getting them to cross paths without it looking obvious, but I managed to pull it off. Jason owns a small jewellery shop in Stroud, and I often give him the heads-up if we have any items going under the hammer that I think might be of interest to him.

'Yes, well, we'll see how it goes – just don't get your hopes up. Anyway, I'd better give Guy a call and put him out of his misery. And I suppose that helping out in the restaurant is a bonus – coming into contact with lots of handsome, single Italian men is a great way to brighten your day.'

'Men of all ages,' I laugh. 'I have no idea what Richard has told them about me, but I've been welcomed with open arms, it's as though they've known me forever. That has been a little overwhelming, if I'm honest, as you know me – I like my own space. But I'm learning to relax and go with the flow.'

'It sounds like quite an experience. You'll be back here before you know it, so make some fun memories. And soak up a little sunshine while you can. Everyone here is moaning about the weather and it's a nightmare keeping the floors dry with all the dripping umbrellas.'

I'm actually missing the rain, although I wouldn't admit that. It is wonderful to wake up each morning to a glorious blue sky, though.

'You did well tonight, Marci. It means a lot to the family that you're prepared to give anything a go. I hope you don't mind getting roped in to help out.' Nico gives me a whimsical little smile.

'It's my pleasure. Everyone has been so kind and welcoming. And Olivia is a real bonus – I can't thank you enough for putting us in touch.'

'You needed help and Olivia is at a loose end for the next few weeks. I'm glad it helped solve a problem.'

'It certainly has. I'm avoiding Richard's office for now but I can't put if off for much longer,' I admit. 'He's a great keeper of records, but that's why there are boxes and boxes of paperwork. He sent me a long email this morning explaining his complicated filing system. His folders and boxes all have reference numbers on them, but he wants some of them combined when I begin packing them up for transit.'

'It sounds intense. Why don't you save that for my day off and I'll give you a hand? It's the least I can do as you certainly saved me a few headaches tonight.'

We're sitting on the small terrace next to the swimming pool, enjoying the calm of a twilight view out over the sea and having just rewarded ourselves with a slice of lemon tart with a scoop of vanilla ice cream. My empty plate has one or two tiny crumbs on it and I only left those because they're too small to scoop up on the spoon.

'Here you are!' Celia calls out, as she walks towards us carrying a tray. 'I thought you might like an espresso and the cocktails are from Dario.'

Celia and Nico exchange a cautious look.

'Ah, that's perfect and please thank Dario for me,' I reply.

'Maybe reserve the thanks until you've tried it,' Nico jumps in. 'Dario is still learning, and he can be a little heavy-handed with the alcohol.'

As Celia places the small cups and glasses in front of us, she raises her eyebrows at me. 'It might be best to take a small sip first,' she advises, apologetically.

'I will, but please tell Dario that it looks absolutely gorgeous. Ten out of ten for presentation.'

'That I can do!' She beams at me before heading back inside.

Knowing what I know after talking to Olivia, I'm curious about Nico and his future. Is he in a hurry to take over the business? He doesn't appear to be fazed by anything but seems happy to take whatever comes his way in his stride.

'You were deep in thought there for a moment,' he remarks.

'Just a couple of thoughts running through my head. While I'm away my mum has decided she's going to be extra supportive at work and from what I gather, it's driving Guy mad.'

'She's interfering?'

I shake my head, because it's not as simple as that. Picking up the small espresso cup, I take a satisfying sip. The smell is as good as the taste – robust, not too bitter and the perfect thing to follow on from the tartness of the lemons and the creaminess of the ice cream.

'When she handed over the running of the business to Guy, gosh, it must be almost ten years ago now, it was on the understanding that she took a back seat. I guess she's bored and the fact that I'm not there gives her an excuse to make herself useful. For Mum it's nostalgic – it takes her back to when my dad was alive, but the business is very different now.'

'Ah, I see.' Nico shakes his head. 'There's useful and there's *useful*, isn't there?'

'Precisely. I'm not saying that Guy didn't make a few mistakes early on, but Mum's second husband, David, certainly won't be happy for her to get involved on a regular basis. If only she could stop herself from making *improvements*, Guy could get through this period while I'm away a little easier.'

'I learnt that lesson very early on,' Nico smiles to himself.

This is my chance. 'There are things you intend to change once you're in charge?'

As he settles back in his chair, coffee cup in hand, his eyes flash over my face.

'What has Olivia been telling you?'

I try not to look a little guilty for being inquisitive. 'Not much, only that one day you will take over the business. I wondered whether you'll have similar problems to Guy. Can parents ever really walk away from their life's work and just relax? David would probably have suggested Mum sell up if Guy hadn't been able to eventually take the reins. I was just heading off to university, but Guy was Dad's assistant buyer, and a trainee auctioneer. He still had a few things to learn, though.'

We finish our coffees and Nico passes me the long-stemmed cocktail glass. The rim sparkles with a tiny edge of frosting, probably sugar crystals, and it has a small red stirrer, a short black straw, and a slice of lemon hooked over the top.

'I'm guessing it's limoncello?' The smell of it alone is slightly intoxicating.

Nico picks up his own glass, holding it under his nose before giving it a vigorous stir.

'Yes, but I wonder what else he's put in it. I suggest you mix it up really well to avoid ending up with a shot at the bottom that might end up taking your breath away. It won't be the first time and we can discreetly tip the contents away if it's too bad. That's why we don't allow Dario behind the bar very often. He's running out of family members willing to try his concoctions.'

'Well, here goes – *cin-cin*, Nico!'

After a quick stir I tentatively use the straw, making a concerted effort not to suck up too much liquid on my first attempt.

'Ooh, there's a slight fizz to it. Nico, this isn't bad. I'm not really a cocktail person but this is very drinkable. There's that little kick, which I think might be a splash of vodka, and the limoncello is delicious, but I think the fizz might be soda water.'

I watch as Nico bravely follows suit. 'You're right! We might have a winner here. Thank goodness. I hate giving feedback and seeing the disappointed look on his face when I admit it's too strong, or – on a couple of occasions – way off the mark.'

'Why doesn't he try them himself, first?'

'Dario prefers not to drink alcohol. He will occasionally have a beer, but that's it. Uncle Vittorio was a heavy drinker when Dario was young, and I think he saw enough to understand that some people struggle to know when to stop. He said it turned his father into a stranger at times and drove his parents' marriage to the brink.'

'It's sad to see someone spiral out of control. I witnessed something similar when I was at uni, and a good friend had to leave partway through the second year. But it could so easily have been drugs, overeating, or running up unnecessary debt,' I observe, thinking out loud.

'It's tough when it happens to someone you know and

there isn't anything you can do to help, because they don't understand why you're so concerned for them. From what you've seen, how does the family ethos over here compare to the UK?'

That makes me pause for a moment and I take another, longer sip of my drink before placing it back down on the table.

'Well, working for a family concern myself, I'd say similar in some ways. I certainly couldn't imagine still living at home, though. But then I don't really get on that well with David, anyway. We don't have anything in common except for Mum.'

'Would you ever leave your job and go to work for someone else?'

'Probably not. But I don't think it's out of a sense of duty, but—' Before I can finish my sentence, Nico jumps in.

'You think I'm waiting in the wings, biding my time until I do the dutiful thing?' I can tell from his tone that it's a light-hearted question and he's merely interested to hear my thoughts.

'It wasn't supposed to sound like a criticism. You'll run this place without a hiccup – that's obvious. But you mentioned that it must be nice to have total freedom as if you feel that's not the case for you. That comment stuck with me.'

'Ah – what's the term? Loose lips? It was a throwaway remark, no more.'

If he doesn't want to talk about it, that's his prerogative. I turn my attention to the ever-darkening skyline, thinking how wonderfully relaxing it is with that light breeze after a very humid day.

'Sorry.' Nico sighs and it's a heart-rending sound. 'That touched a bit of a raw nerve. Luca and my mum can't firm up their plans until I'm settled.'

'Settled?'

'Married.'

I've just taken a long, slow sip and as the slight kick from the vodka hits the back of my throat, I swallow hard to avoid coughing.

'That's a lot of pressure to put yourself under.'

Nico toys with his drink, swirling the stirrer aimlessly around before setting it back down on the table.

'It's just the way it is. Giulia and I have this sort of pact that unless either of us suddenly discovers the love of their life, we'd make a great team running this place together. She's ambitious and so am I; however, Giulia isn't family but she wants a stake in it. Luca won't step back until I have a wife, and she's well aware of that fact.'

'But Giulia's a chef and a good one. What does it matter whether you're married or not?'

Nico sighs. 'Luca has spent his entire working life building something to pass on to his son, and, hopefully, his grandchildren. As my mum has been his never-failing tower of support, together they achieved a lot more than he would have done on his own. Family might squabble and have their disagreements but, when it matters, they forgive and forget because family always comes first and business second. If Giulia and I marry, then the restaurant's reputation for the highest quality food and impeccable service is guaranteed going forward.'

'That's a huge commitment for you both and a decision

that shouldn't be rushed,' I empathise, picking up on an undercurrent of uncertainty.

'You're right, Marci. Olivia keeps on at me, saying that I'm running out of time. Time to do what, though? Suddenly discover the love of my life? And what if that special someone has no interest in the hotel and restaurant industry – that would probably end up pushing us apart anyway, because this is my dream too. Maybe I have to accept that it's not always possible to have it all.'

I can only assume he's thinking about Tiziana, after what Olivia told me.

'But you get on well . . . you and Giulia?' I check and he immediately nods his head.

'Yes, we always have done. Maybe friendship and mutual admiration can grow into love – who knows? Giulia has worked hard to prove herself and Luca didn't go easy on her. There isn't a test she hasn't passed with flying colours and she's ready to wear that chef's hat. Besides, Luca has always treated me like his son, never his stepson. It means a lot to me to keep his and Mum's dream alive. And yet something is holding me back and I don't know what, or why.'

The silence between us grows as we both stare out at the moon and the stars above us. The velvety sky looks so perfect that it's hard to believe it's real. An artist could have painted it as a backdrop, and we could be actors speaking our lines.

'Olivia was probably right when she said it was your last summer of freedom then, because things are coming to a head. But you and Giulia don't appear to be regarded as a couple.'

Nico's eyes meet mine and the honesty I see reflected back at me is raw emotion.

'That's because we're not – yet, anyway. Olivia thinks I'm about to make a big mistake. But she doesn't understand – she just thinks she does. Giulia is also doing this for her family and if it doesn't go ahead, then I'm letting down two people who put their trust in me.'

'And your mum?'

His expression softens. 'She simply wants me to be happy. Luca does, too, of course – but he thinks I'm just taking my time and it's already a done deal.'

It's a sobering end to a long, hard day. Mine was filled with a lot of laughter, new experiences, and a heart-wrenching reminder that few get to do just as they please. But what if it were possible to take a little time out? Would that be foolhardy, or brave?

12.
Simple Pleasures

'It's sad, Marci. Nico should sit down with Luca, Celia and Giulia to talk it through. What if Giulia and Nico end up locked into a loveless marriage? How will that impact on the ambience of their family-run restaurant?' Olivia states indignantly, as she wrestles with the packing tape.

It was a mistake answering her questions as she quizzed me about my conversation with Nico last night. Olivia is living the fairy tale and she wants that for Nico, too.

'What's important to both Giulia and Nico is family and work. As a team running the restaurant and the hotel, Nico thinks it's possible that their friendship could grow into something more,' I confide.

She tuts under her breath and I'm glad that the item she's packing up is solid silver and not glass. She tears off some tape with her teeth and presses down on it as if daring it not to stick.

'Yes, well – I'm not convinced about that because from what I've seen, love doesn't work like that. Nico needs something to open his eyes, something to make him stop for a moment and consider what he really wants out of life. Even Celia's beginning to have her doubts.'

That makes me pause for a second as I stop what I'm doing. 'She is?'

Olivia places the heavy package inside the box in front of her and picks up a duster to begin polishing the small oval tray that accompanies the silver jug.

'Up until about six months ago, Celia would take every opportunity to pull Giulia's name into a conversation. To the point at which it became uncomfortable and Nico told me the only way he could handle it was to switch off. Oh, Celia is very supportive of Giulia, but she has definitely taken a step back now and is leaving them to it. I think her worst fear is that Nico won't go with his heart, but his head – and to Celia that would be a tragedy.'

'What about Luca?' I ask, interested to hear her opinion.

'As far as he's concerned it's a done deal – he knows Giulia is ready and waiting. Vittorio sowed the seed a long time ago, the Amorosi family are great friends of his, and from Luca's point of view it's the perfect solution. Luca recognises Giulia's growing frustrations, but from what I'm picking up, Celia is worried that Nico is dragging his feet because he's having second thoughts. Obviously she doesn't want to upset Luca, so she's keeping it to herself for now. But she will speak out if necessary, I'm sure.'

'Maybe Nico and Giulia have been so focused on their respective roles that it's only now they're at a stage where they need to relax a little and talk openly to each other,' I add.

'There's a lot resting on their decision, given how many relatives depend on the restaurant and the hotel for a living.'

I was thinking the exact same thing and it's time to change the subject. 'When you've finished filling that box, shall we start emptying the old chest? If we stack everything on the table, I can begin sorting through to see if there's anything of interest in there. I'm assuming most of it is inexpensive decorative items and it's not worth the cost of packing and shipping them.'

'Will you sell those locally?'

'Yes. Richard sent me details of a contact who is happy to buy general bric-a-brac as a job lot.'

'That's welcome news. It would take forever to wrap everything up individually. Oh, before I forget – I'm really sorry to spring this on you, but I might not be able to make it here next Monday.'

'It's not a problem. I'm simply grateful for whatever time you can give me.'

She smiles back at me appreciatively. 'An old friend has invited me to her thirtieth birthday celebration on Sunday night. It's a four-hour drive and she suggested I stay over and drive back after breakfast on Monday. It's not definite, as my parents are away too, and they usually sleep over to look after Luna. I'm hoping that one of my neighbours will come to my rescue but it's tricky, as they both have dogs of their own. Luna is fine when she's on her own, but she's jumpy around other animals.'

'Oh, poor thing. Could I look after her for you?'

Olivia's eyes instantly light up. 'You'd be prepared to stay at my place? I'm not sure how Luna would handle all the people milling around at the restaurant.'

'It'll be a change of scenery for me.' It's a beautiful house and Luna is a cutie, so why not? Besides, Olivia is a real treasure and she'll turn her hand to anything, so it will be nice to repay her hard work with something more than just cash. 'Draw me a map of Luna's favourite walks and I'm sure the two of us will be just fine.'

'Ah, Marci – you have no idea how grateful I am for your offer. I'll make sure the fridge is full. You have so made my day. That's the problem when one's other half keeps flying off on work projects – he's never around when I need him! If he didn't happen to be the love of my life, I'd trade him in for someone who comes home every night to his lonely wife, and adoring pet.' She shrugs her shoulders and starts laughing.

'It must be hard at times, but wonderful to know you've found *the one*. With every passing year I'm finding the art of dating more tiring. It's such a lot of effort getting to know someone new, only to discover after a couple of dates that my interest quickly wanes.'

I stoop to grab a couple of items from the wooden chest, and Olivia follows my lead. Everything is wrapped in old newspaper and as we discard the dusty coverings, I can see that some of the items are rather pretty.

'These blue-glass tea-light holders are gorgeous,' I remark, changing the subject. I lift one of them up to the light. 'They're obviously handmade, as there are a couple of flaws – air bubbles trapped within the glass – but they're a good weight.'

'Would you consider dating an Italian guy?' Olivia poses the question as she holds up a small ceramic chicken for inspection, making me laugh. 'Hmm . . . not quite as good a find as yours. Anyway, what do you think? I could introduce you to someone.'

'It's not exactly an heirloom, but someone will buy it. And thanks for the offer, but I can't see the point. It's not like I'm staying, is it?'

'I know, but what harm would it do to mingle a little?' She looks at me, raising her eyebrows. 'Even better when you both know that holiday romances are usually short and sweet – which means there are no strings attached.'

This is rather like being at home, where all my happily married acquaintances keep suggesting a double date. There's always a single male *friend* in mind. I understand this would be different, but it's hard enough meeting someone new, without the language barrier.

'It's not my thing, I'm afraid. Especially given that my Italian is so basic. Oh . . . what's that you have there?'

I watch as Olivia lifts a rather large parcel up onto the table and as she peels back the outer cloth wrapping, an old book is revealed. The leather is well-worn, and we stare down at it with interest.

'It's a family bible,' she says, grabbing a duster to gently wipe the cover and we can just about make out a cross emblazoned on the front.

'You see,' she states, with a grin. 'Neither of us were expecting this! They do say that there's a surprise around every corner if you have the patience to wait for it. And I'm not giving up on the thought of a romantic summer for you just yet!'

Oh dear. Friends always mean well, but I'm going through a jaded phase when it comes to the dating game. I can usually tell within the first ten minutes where it will end up. Then it's the embarrassment of faking it to get through the entire evening, only to then do the exchange of numbers thing because it's expected, while keeping my fingers crossed that I don't get a follow-up call.

'I'm happy to settle for a quiet life, Olivia, and I like hanging around the restaurant in the evenings in case they need an extra pair of hands. Really, this is the perfect way for me to unwind while I'm here.'

Olivia is no longer listening to me, as she's absorbed in leafing through the dusty pages in front of her.

'It's in Latin,' she exclaims. 'This is probably quite valuable.' Olivia sounds in awe, as she points to the most exquisite example of biblical art.

'Let's see if there are any other little gems waiting to be discovered.' At least it brought our rather uncomfortable conversation to a halt. Besides, antiques are a far more interesting topic and what we're discovering is that Richard's collection might be worth an awful lot more than either Guy or I first thought.

'We didn't get a chance to talk – are you off to bed?' Nico's voice rises up from behind me, as I reach out to grasp the metal handrail on the staircase. I turn, giving him a smile.

'You've been busy, and I was late coming down to eat,' I reply.

'I can't tempt you with one last coffee, given that it's such a beautiful night? I hate drinking alone. I was hoping for an update on how your new assistant is doing. I'm in Olivia's bad books, so she isn't talking to me and, unfortunately, Jack isn't around to take my side.'

It would be rude of me to refuse when I know that Nico

finds it difficult to unwind after a long and busy shift. For some reason he enjoys our little chats and I don't have the heart to refuse his request.

'Why not?' I turn around and follow Nico to the bar. There are still a couple of waiters out on the terrace clearing tables and I hesitate for a moment, wondering if I should offer to grab a tray and lend a hand.

'Don't even think about it, Marci – they can manage.'

'I know, but I like to make myself useful.' I slide onto one of the bar stools as I watch Nico making two double espressos. He disappears into the kitchen and I gaze around.

The restaurant is blissfully quiet at this time of night and Luca and Celia are nowhere to be seen. I notice a small collection of framed photos in an alcove – something I've walked past many times but never really registered. I decide to take a closer look and it's obvious some of them go way back. I should imagine that the older couple in one of the photographs is Luca's parents, as they proudly stand next to the entrance to the property. Some of the other group photos have a party look to them, so they're probably milestones, or special family occasions.

'That one on the top right was the party to welcome Richard into the family when he became Luca's business partner,' Nico explains, walking towards me carrying a tray. 'Are you ready?'

'What have you got there?' I muse, as he turns, and I follow on behind him.

'Trust me, it's never too late in the day for a frozen treat.'

Glancing at the clock on the wall, I notice it's a

quarter-after midnight and a little late for ice cream. Well, this will be a first for me!

I assume we're heading for the patio alongside the pool, but Nico keeps going, climbing the flight of narrow stone steps in the far corner beyond the barbecue. He leads us over to the covered area in the vegetable garden. This is fast becoming our go-to place, even though it's a little out of the way.

'We're less likely to disturb anyone here,' he explains as he sets the tray down.

'I'll sort the candle,' I offer, picking up the rechargeable arc lighter. We have a new replacement tonight – a porcelain pot decorated with lemons and vibrant green leaves. The yellow wax gives off an instant whiff of something floral and grassy, as the flame touches the wick.

'The citronella should help to keep the midges at bay. Right, one double espresso and one classic *Zuppa Inglese*: biscotti and sherry mixed into a custard-flavoured gelato. Trust me, on a humid night like tonight it will hit the spot.'

We settle down and I use one of the small spoons to add a little brown cane sugar to my coffee. As I take a sip, the robust, dark roast instantly gives me a boost. It isn't just the taste as it coats my mouth, but the aroma as I breathe in seems to stimulate all my senses.

'Coffee is an addiction, isn't it?' Nico states as he watches me, his eyes smiling. 'Now try the gelato. You'll be surprised, I promise.'

In truth, I'd rather just settle for the coffee, but it's too hard to resist. The long-handled ice-cream spoons are probably three times the size of the dainty coffee spoons, so I take a modest scoop. As the creaminess mingles with the lingering aftertaste of the coffee, the cold makes my tongue tingle a little and then the sherry adds a zing.

'Well?' Nico demands. 'I'm right, aren't I?'

He is right. It's a surprisingly perfect way to end the day. 'Maybe . . . but I won't know for sure until I repeat the process a few times,' I reply, teasingly. I'm feeling happy and as the days go by it's as if my problems and worries are falling away. I know they'll all be waiting for me on my return, but do I care? No, not sitting here enjoying a surreal moment like this, I don't.

'Wait until you discover the biscotti chips. Giulia adds grated lemon zest to them, which she insists on preparing herself. She says if there is any pith left on the peel, it gives it a bitter taste and she's right.'

I sit back, watching Nico as he sips his coffee and then attacks his dish of *Zuppa Inglese*.

'Do you do this often?' I enquire and he looks across at me, raising an eyebrow.

'The staff all eat together before the diners arrive, but I prefer to have a late-night feast and as people rarely wander up here, I'm usually on my own. You're the first person I've ever invited to join me.' I'm not sure whether he's teasing me, or telling the truth, but I reward him with a big smile anyway.

'Then I'm honoured. The ambience might not be quite the same back in the UK, of course, but I'll definitely give it a try, late one night.'

'Some good company helps.' Nico lowers his eyes from mine and pops a loaded spoon into his mouth.

Seconds later he takes another sip of coffee, letting out a satisfied sigh.

'This isn't really conducive to sleep, though, is it? I mean, caffeine, sugar and icy cold.'

'Sleep is for those who have nothing better to do,' he replies, sounding amused as he quickly polishes off the last of his dessert and settles back into his chair.

'Or those who can't switch off their thoughts,' I point out. I can see from his reaction as he pulls a face that I've hit the proverbial nail on the head. 'Would it help to share?'

'Luca informed me today that the building work on La Grotta will begin in September. He showed me the plans he has had drawn up and it came as a bit of a shock.'

I finish off the remainder of my ice cream and follow up with the last dregs of coffee, a satisfied smile on my face. 'Why?'

'You know when you said it would make a great home? Well, that's exactly what he has planned for it. The car park will be walled off and the building extended.'

'It makes perfect sense to me. The views from the front are amazing and the boundary has some wonderful trees, shrubs and climbers. The property is far enough back from the road for it not to be a problem and the walled garden to the rear is a little oasis.'

'And it appears it's going to be *my* new home.'

Nico's look is one of acceptance and I'm not sure what to say, but he doesn't wait for a response.

'I know why he's doing it, of course. It's a signal.'

Now I'm a little perplexed. Even in the gloom of the flickering candlelight, his expression looks dour.

'A signal?' I prompt.

'Well, a gesture, let's say. He thinks it's time I had a place of my own away from work and that will encourage me to think about my long-term future. It's my mum's wish that I accept his offer.'

'But you're not happy about it?' My enquiry is hesitant, because Luca's gesture is generous and thoughtful.

Nico avoids my gaze and instead looks back at the hotel, which is mostly in darkness. Outside, the solar lights around the garden bathe everything in a soft glow.

'I have money, Marci, and if I wanted a place of my own then I'd sort something out. This is all I need for now, but Luca is growing impatient for me to settle down and take the reins.'

Does Nico see this not as a gift, but as a reward for doing the dutiful thing as Luca's son?

'Oh. I see.'

We lapse into silence and suddenly the tiny sounds around us that I don't usually notice seem much louder. The annoying buzzing of the mosquitos, which are drawn to the flame of the candle when it's supposed to repel them. Then there is the raspy sound of the grasshoppers, which – for all I know as I haven't seen one up close – could be cicadas. As my thoughts have my eyes darting everywhere, looking for every little movement in the tightly packed vines overhead, it's a few minutes until I realise Nico is frowning.

'Time is running out,' he mutters, before turning his head to look at me. 'And Olivia is right. Maybe I have until the new year, at best.'

'But if you won't be living on site, does that mean Luca and your mum will remain here?'

Nico nods, his mood lifting. 'I should give you the tour in daylight. They live in an apartment off to the side of the main building. It's completely separate and even has its own gated garden.'

'It sounds lovely. As is this – simply sitting here and chatting at the end of the day. It's so relaxing.'

'My days of late-night treats in the garden are numbered,' Nico says with a robust laugh and I raise a finger to my lips.

'Shh . . .' I berate him. 'We might be wired, and wide awake, but it looks like everyone else is asleep.'

'So, Marci, do you have someone at home you can talk to late at night when you can't sleep?' It's a fair enough question but he's not smiling.

'Not anymore, no. It's only my brother, Guy, who sleeps like a log but on the odd occasion when I've had to call him he always pretends he was awake to make me feel better.'

'Everyone is looking for that special someone, aren't they?'

'Yes, Nico – but it needs to be a like-minded soul who is on the same wavelength.'

The look we exchange is one of empathy. If I had someone special in my life, then I like to think I'd never feel alone. But Nico is implying that Giulia wouldn't appreciate gazing up at that phenomenally starry sky while most people are safely tucked up in bed. That's such a shame because she doesn't know what she's missing – this is truly magical.

I guess we're both in limbo and can understand what it's like to know that life as we know it will change at some point. For me, there isn't even a glimmer of a timeline – assuming the right man does eventually decide to put in an appearance, of course.

As our eyes become more accustomed to the velvety mantle overhead, more and more stars reveal themselves. The universe is so vast and there is so much that we don't know, maybe fate does have a plan mapped out for each of us and life isn't simply the result of our sometimes hastily made decisions. I hate to admit it, but my choice of university hinged on the flip of a coin because one involved uprooting myself and moving away, while the other was a bus journey away from my parents' house. I can't help wondering if it had been heads, rather than tails, what I'd be doing now. I chuckle to myself, thinking this is absurd.

'Why are you laughing?' Nico stares at me, puzzled.

I have no idea why I suddenly feel so happy. Or am I buzzing because I'm overloading on sugary things I wouldn't normally consider eating at this time of night?

'Oh, I think the caffeine is wearing off and tiredness is kicking in.'

He gives me a guilty look. 'Sorry for keeping you up, but thank you for humouring me tonight, Marci. It's been a bit of an unsettling day and I think I might have overreacted a little. It's nice to have someone I can be totally honest with.'

'Change isn't easy when you're staring it in the face, but sometimes when you look back, all you see are the positives.'

As I turn to glance at Nico and his eyes search mine, a warmth begins to spread up from my chest and I'm glad of the shadows so he can't see my cheeks as they start to glow.

I need to be careful here. Being empathetic is one thing, getting dragged into someone else's problems is another.

'I hope so,' he says, his words hardly audible. 'Let's see what today brings.'

Dragging my eyes away from his face, I stand and begin loading up the tray. Ever the gentleman, Nico insists on carrying it back to the kitchen and I follow him in silence. This is a little piece of heaven and I'm so glad I didn't refuse Nico's request to join him in the garden. It's one of those memories that I will treasure when I get home.

13.

Making Good Progress

'Good morning, my lovely Marci, assuming I have worked out the time difference correctly.' Richard's cheery voice is good to hear, even though it's only just after 6 a.m.

'At last! You never respond to my texts,' I complain, chiding him.

'Sincere apologies, but time flies when you're having fun!' he exclaims, before giving a huge belly-laugh. 'Angel accused me of abandoning you and I'm afraid she has a point. I have rather landed you in it, my darling, so I'm checking in. Feel free to let off steam if you want.'

'Oh, Richard. Well, as hard a task as this is, I will admit that I am having fun. And Positano is like stepping into another world. I sat with Nico in the early hours of this morning drinking espresso and eating ice cream in the vegetable garden.'

That elicits a little chuckle from him. 'I knew that once you got into the spirit of things, you'd enjoy yourself. Dare I ask how the packing is going?'

'It's going very well indeed. A friend of Nico's named Olivia – you probably know her – is helping. We're paying her by the hour and it's a cost saving if we can get the lion's share done. The company we've hired will come in once we're ready to transport the boxes and they'll crate up the bigger items. You can relax – it's all in hand.'

'That's brilliant news! And the fact that you're getting on so well with everyone.' There's an inflection in Richard's tone and I can imagine the look on his face. He's feeling pleased with himself.

'The Romanos have been very good to me, and I have helped out a couple of times but only to clear tables, although I did get to serve coffee and aperitifs.'

'Ha! I knew it. You'll turn your hand to anything and I'm proud of you, Marci. You're beginning to loosen up a little.'

'Are you saying I'm uptight?' I throw back at him, accusingly.

'No. Reserved is the word I like to use, my darling. Life is about taking risks and to do that sometimes feels a little uncomfortable at first.'

'Says the biggest risk taker of them all, as it turns out!'

'Well, come to think of it, that is true in my case. After all, I turned my back on the UK and settled in Positano. And once again, when a new opportunity presented itself, I grabbed it. There is always an element of risk involved, naturally, but you don't shy away for fear of making a few mistakes. You would have had a boring summer in the UK and now you're experiencing Italian life up close.'

I shake my head at the way Richard's mind works. 'Ah, the point being that I should be grateful to you for my unscheduled trip to Italy. If it helps ease your conscience for throwing me in at the deep end, then I wouldn't have missed this for the world. But from what I'm hearing, Mum is causing problems for Guy.'

A loud 'harrumph' travels down the line. 'Is she, now? Leave that to me – you have enough on your plate and it's my fault, so I'll have a word with her.'

Oh no . . . it'll be obvious I've said something to him. 'Maybe it's best to leave them to sort it out between themselves,' I suggest.

'What your mother needs is something to occupy her mind. She has too much time on her hands. I know exactly how to distract her.'

'You do?'

'Angel and I haven't firmed up our plans for the future yet, but Angel has been away from the UK for a long time and she misses it. That's a little project your mother would enjoy getting stuck into – having a place we can go back to would be a start. I'll get Angel to give her a call and explain exactly what we're looking for.'

That's a surprise. 'Don't forget that Guy is more than happy to make you an advance payment ahead of the auction. It might come in handy for a down payment,' I remind him gently.

'Oh, that's not necessary. I'm not about to run out of money but I do appreciate you thinking of me, Marci. If you spend your life in the antiques business and don't end up with a few pounds in the bank, then you can't really call yourself an antiques expert, can you? Oh, and when you start rooting around in the office upstairs, there are a stack of paintings that aren't for sale. It's my *personal collection*,' he whispers, lowering his voice. 'You know how I like to pick up a brush, even though I have no skill whatsoever.'

'Don't worry, I'll make sure to ask Guy to put them to one side and they'll go into storage, together with the boxes from your office. I hope to make a start up there really soon.'

'Good. I can tell Angel that you're happy, then, and everything is falling into place?'

'Into place?'

Richard pauses for a second. 'Um . . . your plan, my dear and a jolly good one it is, too. I promise to be in touch in a few days' time, but if you get any problems text me.'

Text him when he rarely responds? 'I will, Richard. And it's good to hear you sounding so upbeat. Give my regards to Angel, won't you?'

'I will and I'm transferring some money into your account as a little thank you. I'm delighted Nico has been looking out for you, given how busy he is, and it might be a nice gesture if you used some of the money to hire one of those expensive boats for the day. His dream is to own a luxury speedboat. It's something he'd really enjoy, and it would be an amazing experience for you to see the Amalfi coast in all its glory.'

'Ah, Richard. You didn't need to do that but thank you. As soon as an opportune moment presents itself I will arrange a fabulous day out for Nico and try to tie it in so that Jack and Olivia can join us.' Nico did promise me a boat trip, but something tells me that he'd find this experience much more thrilling.

'It's only money, dear Marci, and you deserve it. And buy yourself a nice piece of jewellery, or something. A memento that will always remind you of your time in Positano. Right, enjoy your day – I'm off to take my wife for a walk with some new friends. Take care, lovely, and leave your mum to me!'

As the line disconnects, I wish I hadn't mentioned the situation back home, but it's done now. I did intend to phone Guy this morning, but now I think I'll just send him an email about the extra wooden crates for Richard's personal canvases and leave it at that.

I'm really looking forward to today, again. Working with Olivia, we get to talk about all sorts of things. When we stop for lunch, we sit out in the courtyard, and she always brings something delicious to eat. Mostly it's simple food, but the ingredients are freshly picked, and I admire her skills in the kitchen.

Oh, and I must ask her advice on where I can hire a boat, as Richard suggested – something that will give Nico a thrill to captain for the day. It would be nice to surprise him, so that means enlisting his help on some pretext, or other. I'll have to give that some thought, as it isn't going to be easy to pull off.

'I cannot express enough thanks to you, Marci, for your 'elp this evening.' Luca's expression is one of pure gratitude. 'It is not often that Giulia is unwell, as we rely so much upon 'er.'

Celia nods her head in agreement as we stand in the kitchen talking. The rest of the team are finishing the clean-up, and everything is beginning to sparkle.

'The one thing I can make,' I reply, gaily, 'is biscuits. It's about the only thing I can cook.' It's just as well, because not only are they used in one of Giulia's gelato dishes, but they accompany two of the other desserts on the menu. I was very conscious of the fact that I couldn't make a single mistake, but it reminded me of the shortbread biscuits that Mum and I often baked when I was growing up. It was our favourite mother-and-daughter tradition.

I really am beginning to feel as if my contribution is appreciated, given the limitation of my skills.

'Many hands make light work of a task, as my grandmother would have said,' Celia replies. 'The problem with both Luca and Giulia is that they make it all look so easy and we know it isn't. We are lucky that when everyone pulls together, we seem to make the impossible happen. Tonight, was a big test for us all—' she raises her voice '—*tutti, venite*!' Throwing up her hands, she encourages everyone to gather around us.

'*Ben fatto e grazie a tutti*. Thank you, everyone!' As she begins to clap, Luca joins in and soon we're all clapping each other. I've never felt this sense of inclusion before and I simply can't stop smiling at how at home I feel among them all. And yet, rolling up my sleeves and listening to Luca's instructions, my sole purpose tonight was not to let them down. Nico is standing at the back grinning and when the group disperses, he walks over to me.

'You remembered not to leave on any of the pith. Giulia will be impressed. She suffers from migraines and it's a sure sign that she's been working too hard. I'm sure she'll be back at work tomorrow, but it's not pleasant for her.'

Nico is obviously saddened to think of Giulia suffering

and his concern is touching. If everyone backed off and left them alone, maybe they would naturally gravitate towards each other. They have a lot in common, but when do they get any time at all to spend together and just discover who they are as people? I wonder.

'As long as I didn't disappoint anyone, I'm happy.'

'Guess we need to try them out for ourselves a bit later, then?'

'Sadly, I can't tonight. Guy asked me to ring him as soon as I'm back in my room. He wants to go through the updated list of the items that Olivia and I have already packed.'

Nico quickly shrugs off his disappointment. 'I understand. But you stepped up for us tonight, Marci, and we're all grateful to you. If there's any way in which I can repay your kindness by helping out up at La Grotta, I'm free every Monday as you know.'

This could be my chance to spring that surprise upon Nico. I haven't had time to sort anything out yet, but I could start the ball rolling. 'That would be great, Nico. I'm about to start going through Richard's office to pack up his paperwork and his personal collection. I might call on you in the next week or two, if you really don't mind giving up your day off.'

His eyes sparkle as he looks at me. 'I'm all yours. Every Monday until the job is done.'

As he walks away I'm a little stunned. I wasn't expecting such enthusiasm – I mean, it's not exactly a riveting job, is it? But it gives me time to sort out his surprise and I'm sure Olivia will be only too delighted to help me make the arrangements. I just hope she doesn't read anything into it, other than the fact that it's a nice gesture from Richard.

'Is everything all right, Celia?'

She's on the terrace looking out to sea, a cloth in her hand after wiping down the tables, but Celia is miles away.

'Oh, Marci – yes, I'm fine, thank you. Did you and Olivia have a good day?'

'We did,' I beam at her. 'La Grotta del Tesoro might look a tad cluttered, but Richard has filled it with some wonderful pieces.'

'Some of his clients travelled a long way to visit him,' Celia informs me.

I know Richard has a vast network of dealers around the world, but he keeps everything very close to his chest. His shop could have been based anywhere and it wouldn't have made a difference, because these days a lot of business is conducted online.

'That's good to hear, Marci. I wish him and Angel well. He deserves to be happy and to let go of past hurts.'

Past hurts? 'Oh, his first love. He told me once that you never forget your first love, so be wary to whom you give your heart. I thought it all sounded rather melodramatic, but I was only fourteen years old at the time.'

She looks at me, shaking her head, but there's a faraway look in her eyes. 'It's taken Richard a long time to find the woman of his dreams,' she confides in me. 'Suddenly it has given him a new lease of life. But – oh, how we miss his gentle humour and his gravelly laugh. Luca is at a loss without his companionship.'

Now, a part of me wonders how unsettling this is for Celia and Luca, being on the verge of handing the restaurant and hotel over to Nico. With their business partner travelling the world, is that a complication for them going forward?

'I can understand that. And I can't wait to get to know Angel. She sounds lovely, and I'm sure she is, as Richard isn't usually impetuous. Everything he does is meticulously planned and suddenly nothing else seems to matter to him.'

Celia looks at me, her gaze intent. 'That's a good thing, Marci. Richard is kind-hearted, a giver. When he settled here, he said little at first, but it wasn't long until he sat down with Luca and told him straight that he was fighting an uphill battle. Richard was right, of course. The restaurant alone wasn't making enough money to keep us going and everything was looking tired.'

'It was a tough time for you both, by the sound of it, Celia.'

'It was, Marci, and the worry was unbearable at times. Luca is a proud man, but Richard managed to talk him into accepting a partner and six months later we had a relaunch. For our wider family it came at just the right time. Their children were getting to an age where they were about to make some big decisions – if they can't find employment locally, they move to the city and everything changes overnight. Oh, they come back for weekends and holidays, but we have all witnessed what happens. It's not the same – they begin to grow away from you. That's why I'm so grateful that Nico loves what he does. I couldn't bear the thought of not seeing him every day.'

There's an air of sadness about her and I hesitate to say anything.

'Are you in a hurry?' she asks, placing the wet cloth back into the small bucket on the chair next to her. 'I have something I'd like to show you.'

'I'm done for the day, so please do!'

'Come,' she says, leaving everything exactly where it is and heading off in the direction of the kitchen. But instead of going through the double swing doors, she steers me to the left-hand side of the sweeping staircase and along a narrow corridor. There's a door at the end of it with an inset panel of stained glass in blues, greens and yellows. It's like a rainbow of colours. She withdraws a key from her pocket to unlock it and we descend a spiral metal staircase.

'Oh my!' I gasp, as we step down into a large open area. 'This is wonderful, Celia. Nico mentioned that you had your own entrance and private garden, but this is such a surprise!'

While the hotel bedrooms reflect a contemporary Italian style, I hadn't expected Luca and Celia's accommodation to be so modern. This is a delightful, large open-plan living, dining and kitchen area. One whole side of the room is comprised of four sets of bifold glass doors, with small panels in between them. Each separating panel is decorated with a cascade of leaves in a vibrant green which seems to bring the garden into the room.

'This is beautiful, Celia. I love those panels.'

'It was Richard's idea,' she confirms, proudly. 'It was so dark in here and when we did the renovation work, he talked Luca into trying something a little different. Have you seen the plans for La Grotta? Richard and Luca spent hours with the architect going over every little detail.'

'It's been a long time in the planning then?' I ask, quite casually.

'Oh no, quite the reverse. But as soon as Richard broke the news that he was leaving, Luca knew exactly what he wanted to do with La Grotta. It's partly the reason why Richard wasn't able to get his things all packed up before he left. Poring over the plans together reminded Luca and Richard of the early days, pulling together their ideas for updating the hotel and restaurant. I left them to it, but it gave Angel and me some time to get to know each other a little better.'

'If it turns out half as good as this, then I'm sure it will be amazing,' I reply, doubting it even crossed Richard's mind that it would lead to putting Nico under pressure.

'I hope so, Marci. Sometimes I feel . . . I feel . . . oh, I don't know!' she exclaims, sounding a little frustrated. 'We had no support net, you see.'

It's obvious Celia is in a reflective mood and is desperate to talk to someone. However, while I'm happy to listen, I think the less I say, the better.

'My family was shocked when I announced I was pregnant,' she continues and I'm a little taken aback by her honesty. 'They saw my refusal to name the father as an indication that I didn't know because I'd slept with a lot of men – which wasn't the case at all. But it taught me something – all that mattered to them was what other people would think. I knew then that somehow I'd build a better life for my son and myself.'

'That's sad, Celia. You must have been devastated by their reaction.'

'I was heartbroken at the time, but it made me much more aware of other people's acts of kindness. What surprised me, Marci, was how total strangers often reach out to help when they see a young mother struggling. It restored my faith in human nature. Luca was one such person. We met at the beach, and he had no idea I was a single mum. He insisted on carrying the pushchair back up to the apartment where I was staying, so that I could hold Nico in my arms to negotiate the steps. The next afternoon we bumped into each other at the beach again and he invited us out to lunch. I didn't know he was a chef, or that he owned the restaurant, because he wasn't trying to impress me. I had trust issues at that time, and he seemed to sense that. Our last day together was emotional, but he told me firmly that it wasn't goodbye. And, on my return to the UK, he rang me every single day and we'd just talk . . . about anything and everything.'

'How wonderful!' If that's not true romance, then what is?

'Luca's kindness was born out of love and, eventually, he flew over to propose to me. The moment he held me close to him once more, I knew that it was meant to be – he succeeded in capturing my heart and true love doesn't lie. When Nicholas and I returned to Positano a few months later, Luca welcomed us with open arms. When my son became Nico Romano it was the best gift that Luca could give me to prove his love, and my boy finally had the family he deserved. Just to know that he would never be alone and someone who loved him would take care of him even if I weren't here, was a blessing. But now I wonder if my son is sacrificing . . .' Her words tail off and she gazes out over the beautiful garden. It's so full of colour and even though it doesn't have a view, it's even prettier than the walled garden at La Grotta.

I watch as Celia swipes her hand across her eyes but, from where I'm standing, I can't see her face full-on. 'I've seen how you've grown close to Nico over the last few weeks, so I'm sure you're aware of the situation here and I can talk to you honestly about it. I was so grateful for a fresh start, Marci, and I instilled that in Nico. He feels indebted to his Italian family because Luca embraced him as his son, and he's always been treated as if he were born here. But he wasn't. Like it or not, he might sound like a local when anyone hears him talking, but is his hesitancy about the future triggered by the fact that he's obligated? I've tried talking to him, but he simply says the things he thinks I want to hear. What if his life here ends up making him miserable?'

Goodness, I know that's not a question aimed at me, but something Celia needed to voice in front of someone. And better a stranger who will soon be gone, than a family member who might repeat it.

'It's a dilemma, Marci, and it will break Luca's heart if Nico decides to walk away.'

'Nico is happy here, Celia, so why would he do that?'

While he might be ready to take on the responsibility of running this place, that doesn't mean he's ready to propose to Giulia. Silence is the only option, as it's not for me to point that out.

'I sense the hesitation in him, Marci. I don't want him to feel trapped. Maybe if he took a year off, travelled a little and visited the UK even, it might help him to put his life into perspective. This is all he knows.'

Wow – that's more or less exactly what Nico said to me one day when we were talking. Is Celia right and this isn't to do with his feelings for Giulia at all, but Nico wanting to know what else life has to offer before he commits to anyone? That would be devastating for everyone here, because there is no one else qualified enough to step into Nico's shoes.

'Or it could be a good sign, Celia. When big changes are on the horizon it doesn't benefit anyone to jump in before they are good and ready.'

She turns to look at me and her eyes are glassy with the tears she's trying to hold back.

'I hope you're right, Marci. Thank you for listening to me. What I wanted to show you were some photos of Nico as a toddler. Photos that no one else has ever seen. Come, take a seat at the table and I'll fetch them.'

Celia is gone for a few minutes and I gaze around, rather surprised by the artwork on display. There are some super large canvases, and the style is modern, vibrant and dashing – not at all what I expected to see and it's delightful.

When she returns there's a smile on her face.

'Look,' Celia says, laying a photo album down in front of me and lifting back the cover.

'Aww . . . how lovely!'

On the first page are photographs taken on a beach

and Nico is very small. He's piling up some pebbles as he sits on a padded blue cushion. Celia is next to him and throughout the series of snaps she's either laughing, trying to stop her hair from blowing across her face, or talking to someone off camera. I assume that someone is Luca.

'How old was Nico here?' I begin to turn the pages and am shocked to see the restaurant and glimpses of the extensive gardens in a wild state. There was no swimming pool or terrace, and what is now the barbecue area was dense shrubbery.

'We celebrated his second birthday a month or two after this was taken. It was such a wonderful holiday, as you can imagine. It was a fluke really – a colleague I worked with broke up with her boyfriend and was offering a cheap deal on a two-week stay in a one-bed apartment here in Positano. It was owned by a friend and came at a time when I had a little money put by. My Italian was pretty good, having studied it at school for a few years, so I went for it. It was mad, of course, managing a baby, a pushchair and the steps, but we coped and for Nico it was his first real holiday.

'I never believed in love at first sight until I met Luca, but that's exactly what happened.'

I'd love to ask about Nico's biological father – I'm curious to know more about how this family came to be, and what the man who left them was like – but it would be wrong of me to ask such a pointed question. 'It's a wonderful story, Celia. And what a life you have made here together. Many would envy you, not just the location and the sunshine, but the closeness you all enjoy. It reminds me of my childhood when my dad was alive.'

'It's different now?' Her tone is warm and inviting; she's not prying, or making polite conversation. Celia genuinely wants to know more but is giving me the space to say what I want.

'I was at university when my mum remarried. David has a relationship of sorts with my brother Guy, but David and I aren't close. The best I can say is that we tolerate each other.'

'I'm sorry to hear that, Marci, that's rather sad.'

'It's fine. David makes Mum happy, which is all that matters.'

'That's why you're so close to Richard, I presume?'

'Yes. He's always been there for me, especially during some tough times.'

Celia gives me a little smile. 'He's good at listening but also good at talking when you can't find the words you need. Richard told me that you're a very private person and I think that's why Nico feels comfortable being around you.'

'Like minds, I suppose. But Richard's right, coming here has shown me that I was opting out of things when I should have been out enjoying myself. Being home alone is nice at times, but it's not good to become isolated.'

A frown appears on her forehead. 'I said to Luca that Nico needs his own space away from here. It's too confining to live, and work, constantly surrounded by the hustle and bustle of so many people. Do you think I'm right, Marci?'

Oh, this is awkward, but Celia is waiting for an answer, her hand pressed against her chest as if her heart is wildly beating.

'I think it might be a good idea to explain that to him, Celia. My family aren't exactly role models for good communication, but when we do get a chance to sit down together it helps to talk through our worries. At least it ensures there aren't any misunderstandings.' Goodness, that wasn't easy to steer myself through without putting my foot in it, but I hope Celia takes it in the spirit in which it was meant.

'That's helpful, Marci, thank you. If you turn to the last page, there's a photo of Nico and Giulia on one of our picnics here in the garden. They were probably around five or six at the time.'

I don't know why, but I got the impression that Giulia's appearance in Nico's life wasn't until she started working here as a trainee chef. If they were around each other since early childhood, maybe that's a part of the problem. How can he see her in a different light if she's always been there?

'They look so happy. What a wonderful place to grow up,' I remark wistfully.

'I hope Nico feels the same way, Marci. I just want my son to be happy. Come, let me show you the garden. Luca built me the most wonderful little waterfall in the far corner. It's my favourite place to sit and put my feet up for an hour.'

Celia's anxiety levels seem to have lessened and I hope I haven't misled her in any way because that wasn't my intention. But Olivia is right in what she said, and they do all need to sit down together and talk openly and freely about the future.

It's strange how being a part of a tightknit family, and

working together, can cause a whole raft of different problems. It's important to be able to give each other breathing space and recognise that everyone sees each issue from their own perspective. That's not something I've ever given any real thought to before now but I'm fast waking up to that fact.

14.

By the Light of a Full Moon

Luna is curled up on my lap, but every time I try to move she howls, and I don't know why. After a long walk this afternoon, along a trail Olivia told me Luna loves because it begins in a wooded area and then leads down to the water's edge, she's been listless.

It's growing dark outside, and I really should turn on the side lights but we've been sitting here quietly for what feels like hours now. It's not that Olivia's house is spooky, but it's rather big and everything is new to me. With Luna's sad little whimpers even when she's still, I'm beginning to feel uneasy.

Leaning over to smooth her ears, I whisper to her, 'I know you're missing Olivia, Luna, but I'm here. You're not alone and there's nothing to fear.' But the truth is that it's also an attempt to boost my flagging morale. What if she's sick? I wonder.

Gently scooping her up into my arms, I lay her on the sofa and her low whimpers turn into a high-pitched whining. I slip off the thin cotton shirt over my strapless top and nestle it around her. It does the trick, and she settles back down, laying her head on her front paws, but she won't curl up and she's lying awkwardly. I quickly walk around turning on lights to comfort us both and it's reassuring.

When my phone kicks into life I rush over to grab it from my bag, hoping it won't start Luna off again, but she immediately begins to howl.

'Marci?'

'Hi, Nico. Can you wait just one second?' I pull the phone away from my ear as I head back to the sofa and put it down briefly while I lift Luna back onto my lap. 'Sorry, Luna is really disturbed, and I don't know if she's just missing Olivia, or there's something wrong with her.'

'You sound worried. Do you want me to pop over?'

It's not even 9 p.m. and he won't have finished his shift, but I am beginning to get quite concerned. It's a huge responsibility looking after someone's beloved fur baby and the only other option is to call Olivia.

'I feel bad asking, but I'm at the point where I need to do something about it. I don't really want to panic Olivia as she's at least a four-hour drive away, but I might need to take Luna somewhere to get her checked out. I wouldn't know where to start looking for a vet at this time of night.'

His reply is immediate. 'It's not a problem, Marci. I'm on my way.'

It's silly, but the minute the line disconnects my eyes fill with tears as I gently cuddle Luna. Her body language tells me something is wrong; she's usually so full of energy, and on the walk I could hardly keep up with her. But less than an hour after we arrived back, there was a change in her. I've racked my brains, wondering whether she ate anything she shouldn't, but she didn't wander far from me and all she did was snuffle around.

Fear sends a sudden chill to my stomach, and I feel a little light-headed.

'Please don't get sick, Luna,' I whisper, smoothing her head gently. 'Olivia would never forgive me if anything happened to you!'

A tear plops down onto her head and she makes a little moan. Her eyes are closed, but she's only resting.

It seems forever before there's a tap on the patio doors, and I indicate for Nico to come in as they aren't locked. I'm so delighted to see him that I could burst into tears, but I take a deep breath to calm myself and give him a welcoming smile.

'Thank you for coming straight over, Nico. I'm convinced now that there's something wrong with her, but I don't know what.'

The look of concern on his face tells me that he's in agreement with me, as Nico kneels down next to us.

'Hey, Luna. What's up?'

Nico runs his hand very slowly down over her head and then along her back.

'Can she walk?' he asks, his face grave.

'She was jumping around as normal earlier this afternoon and managed what must have been at least a two-mile trek, but shortly after we arrived back, she seemed to flop. I assumed she was tired, but all she wanted to do was sit on my lap. We've been here for hours now. I tried to get her to drink some water, but she wouldn't get off the sofa. When I moved her to bring the bowl over, she started howling and it took ages to settle her down again.'

'Has she been eating?'

'No. Not since we returned. She had her usual pouch of food before we went out and I swear I didn't see her eat anything at all on our walk. I watched her like a hawk because a part of the route was really steep, and I was worried that she'd go too close to the edge.'

My words are tumbling out; now that I have company I can't hide how frantic I'm becoming as my worry builds.

'You might be right. This could warrant a trip to the vet.' I watch as Nico very gently checks each of Luna's legs. I'm surprised she's allowing him to do it and she doesn't make a sound. As he checks her final paw she yelps, and it makes Nico visibly jump. 'Oh, poor Luna – I'm so sorry puppy. I didn't mean to hurt you, I promise.'

Aww . . . he's gutted, but clearly there is something wrong and he's found it.

'Marci, can you try to distract her, and I'll be as quick as I can, but I need to take a closer look.'

Sliding my arm under Luna's neck, she turns her head to look at me and as I smooth her ears, I begin talking to her in a hushed voice to keep her calm. Her gaze doesn't waver from my face, and she instinctively seems to know that Nico is trying to help.

'Try to keep her still. It's some sort of thorn and it needs to come out. I'll count to three and hopefully it will be quick.'

I lean over her, my other hand supporting the back of her head.

'One, two, three!'

A heart-rending howl fills the air, but Nico sits back

on his heels looking relieved and holding up an inch-long thorn.

'Poor Luna,' he croons as he leans in to smooth her back. 'No wonder you weren't happy.'

'She wasn't limping – I would have noticed it,' I confirm, feeling guilty now.

'It didn't go in vertically, but horizontally. As the afternoon went on her paw has become sore and swollen, but there wouldn't have been much to see at first. I'm going to make a call and get some advice. It's nothing to jump in the car and take her somewhere if need be. I'll put the kettle on at the same time, you look like you need a strong cup of coffee.'

As he heads into the kitchen area, the tears I shed are out of sheer relief as I continue to cuddle poor Luna.

'Our late-night feasts seem to be turning into a bit of a habit,' Nico grins at me as we sit on the terrace, staring up at the full moon.

Having eaten nothing at all since shortly after noon, I didn't think I had an appetite until I began eating.

'I thought you didn't cook?' I remark.

'Olivia loves simple food, and she knows what ingredients work. Fresh salad leaves from the garden, a few herbs, some feta cheese that I'm pretty sure was made by her neighbour. They swap veggies for cheese and cured meats.'

'And the pasta?'

'Just a few fresh tomatoes, a little garlic and onion, and some homemade linguini. I doubt there's a single Italian man who couldn't make something out of the ingredients in Olivia's fridge.'

I smile at him. 'But you're not really Italian.'

Nico raises his eyebrows. 'You're right. I guess I'm not, but it's how I see myself.'

Should I mention the chat I had with Celia a couple of days ago? On balance, I figure it's better to take Olivia's advice and stay out of it.

'Thank you for coming to our rescue tonight, Nico. I love dogs, but I've never had one of my own. Cats, yes, but not dogs.'

Inside, Luna is snuggled up on her fluffy doggy bed, which we placed on the sofa. Between us we cleaned and bandaged her paw, although she's still feeling very sorry for herself. But Luna is on the mend and it's a big relief. She even managed to eat a handful of treats and as I lifted her up in my arms, Nico held up her water bowl so she could have a long drink. The vet told Nico he'd see Luna in the morning if it's still inflamed and to ring him if we're worried, no matter what time of the day or night. Well, it's just after 11 p.m. and the fact that Nico stepped in and sorted it all out so quickly makes him a hero.

'I knew immediately from your tone of voice that you needed help and Richard told me in no uncertain terms that I was to look after you.'

Hmm. Look after me? 'Why?'

'He said – and I quote – "Marci is special, Nico." He went on to say that this was going to be a summer in which your eyes would be opened to the endless possibilities of life.'

'Did he now!' *Richard, seriously what WERE you thinking?*

Nico lifts the wine glass to his lips and takes a sip, letting out a sigh of satisfaction. 'Jack knows his wines and I'm sure he won't mind us cracking open a bottle. It appears to me that we're two people standing on the brink of big changes to come. You know what Richard is like – he wants the best for everyone. The question is – what are you running away from this summer, Marci?'

A forkful of pasta is on its way to my mouth and that stops me in my tracks. I glance at Nico, narrowing my eyes. 'A drizzly British summer – that's all.' I continue eating, surprised by such a direct question.

'It's more than that. Richard is worried about you. I know him well enough to read between the lines.'

And so do I!

'Richard thinks it's time I had a little fun in the sun, but that's easy to say and not so easy to do, is it? It's certainly not the reason I came to Positano.'

Nico shakes his head, laughing as he places his glass back down on the table. We both instinctively glance towards the house to check on Luna, who is sleeping peacefully and hasn't moved for the last twenty minutes.

As we turn back to look at one another, it's an awkward moment. 'What if he's right?' he replies. 'Try living in the moment while you're here, Marci, and enjoy yourself – what harm can it do?'

'Is this simply advice you're giving *me*, Nico, or is this really about *you*? You're free to do whatever you want until you make a decision about your future and you don't need anyone to tell you that.'

'Until I know what I want, how do I communicate that without upsetting the people I love the most?'

The truth, at last!

'You sit them down and explain how you feel. Is this just about Giulia, or is it about the business, too?'

He looks surprised, laughing off my comment. 'You think I'm having second thoughts about being in charge of Ristorante Sul Mare and the hotel?'

Wiping my mouth with the paper napkin, I shake my head. 'I think you've been waiting all your life for this opportunity.'

'But . . .' Nico tails off, waiting for my response.

'But I think you're paying lip service to the plan, rather than getting onboard with it.'

His response is one of confusion, 'What does that mean?'

'You grew up with Giulia, something you omitted to mention. How much time have you spent together aside from when you're at work, or involved in family parties?'

I can tell Nico is uneasy with my take on the situation.

He laughs, but it's dismissive. 'We often sit and chat over coffee before a shift, but we're busy people.'

'That sounds like an excuse to me. Are you avoiding each other, or are you simply pushing her away because you can't give her an answer yet?'

Nico is growing increasingly uncomfortable as I point out the obvious.

'It sounds so easy when you put it like that. Sadly, not everyone is lucky enough to find their perfect match. But you're right, I guess that's not exactly a sound reason to marry someone you know you aren't in love with, and simply hope for the best, is it?'

'I rest my case; it seems to me that you regard each other as a means to an end. If you tell Giulia how you feel – that you're not sure about the future and whether you can commit to marrying her – maybe she'll open up to you in return. It's a good starting point, Nico.'

He falls silent and we sit, looking up at the luminescent moon in all its glory.

'Funny things happen when there's a full moon,' Nico states, as if it's a fact.

'Really?'

'Yes. It's Italian folklore – men and dogs become wolf-like during a full moon.'

'Are you talking about werewolves?' I jest.

'In Italian the term is: *lupo mannaro*.'

'I don't think Luna has been feeling anything other than her sore paw this evening, bless her. And you're definitely not going through any sort of transformation.'

'Perhaps that's the problem.'

I'm done eating, and I feel so much better. Gone is the light-headedness and seeing Luna now curled up in a ball, I can finally relax.

'I don't understand. Why don't you explain it to me?'

Cradling the wine glass in my hands, I sit back and watch Nico, who is deep in thought.

'How does anyone know what they really want? Mum asks me if I'm happy and I say *yes* because it's true. Every day has a purpose and I meet a lot of interesting people.

I'm a part of something much bigger than just me and that means a lot.'

And yet I can tell there's something niggling away in the back of his head, something more than just his worries about the future.

'Life is perfect, then,' I reflect, thinking that on a night like this those words could certainly ring true.

He gives a deprecating little laugh. 'No, it isn't but that's where I'm at right now and I can't see how I could have done anything differently to change the outcome.'

Nico sounds disheartened, and it's obvious he's talking about a person from his past who touched his heart.

'It's gutting when you find someone with whom you feel that initial, euphoric buzz, only to end up having your hopes dashed because, for whatever reason, you're not the perfect fit.' I realise that I'm thinking out loud as I look across at Nico. The glance we exchange tells me that he understands exactly what I mean.

'And it's easy to torture yourself over whether you made the right decision, but you can't change the past,' he remarks, as if he has regrets. 'It's funny – Richard and I would often sit together late at night and talk about life in general. He said that the day he realised he was faking it, was the day he faced up to the truth.'

My stomach does an involuntary somersault. 'Whatever did he mean by that?' But the other question whirling around inside my head is why that struck a chord with Nico.

'He'd had a fair bit to drink that night, but it was to do with his first love – the woman who broke his heart.

Richard said he woke up one morning realising that simply being around her wasn't enough.'

Did Tiziana break Nico's heart when she left, I wonder, but he can't bring himself to admit that? I don't know what to say, so I sit quietly waiting for him to continue.

'The only way to shake him out of the comfortable but sad little life that he'd settled for, was to start again. That's why he came here.'

'We all thought it was some sort of mid-life crisis,' I admit, candidly.

'I can see why. Richard is a great philosopher on occasion and at other times surprisingly unpredictable. I can imagine the full moon having an effect on him.'

I giggle, the wine relaxing me a little too much, perhaps. 'Before I accepted a place at university, Richard took me to one side and said he thought I should take the opportunity to gain a little life experience and travel – can you imagine my mum's reaction to that? He said I should see the world and then come back ready for the next part of my life.'

'Richard has a tendency to do that, doesn't he? Wax lyrical at a time when what you need is practical advice.'

'He sees life as a complicated timeline with lots of different options. But the reality is much simpler. Even when we don't realise that we're making choices, we are – whether it's just the people we're attracted to, or by utilising our natural-born skills. Sometimes I feel Richard thinks I'm capable of more and he's trying to wake me up. But I'm good at what I do, and I'm surrounded by people I love and respect. Maybe that's precisely the point he's trying to make.'

'Reverse psychology?' Nico is finding this amusing now, but I'm serious.

'More like a test. I was overdue a holiday, but as I'm required to take a lot of short business trips away to various European countries every year, a break for me is being at home. I like to potter in the garden, decorate the house and I love spring cleaning. It sounds boring, doesn't it? But for me it's energising. Richard perceives that as locking myself away.'

'So, the real reason he didn't just call in one of his business associates and sell off his collection is because he wanted you to step outside your comfort zone for a while. Isn't that rather manipulative?' Nico sounds genuinely surprised, but I'm feeling mellow about it.

As I breathe in the warm, fragrant air of another balmy night, I let out a grateful sigh. 'Yes, and he even admitted that to me – after I got here, of course.'

'And you forgive him?' Nico raises an eyebrow, questioningly.

'Richard is the best godfather anyone could ever wish for. He only wants the best for me. He's never let me down; he picked me up when I fell – not literally, of course, but emotionally. Richard says that mediocrity is the fate of those who don't listen to their inner self. Those who switch off aren't even aware that they are settling for less than they deserve.'

Nico is deep in thought. 'That's pretty thought-provoking.'

'Yes, it is. Did you know that Richard has two degrees? One in fine art, and he is a painter himself, and the other in psychology?'

'No, I didn't. I mean, we've had some amazing conversations but that explains a lot.'

I stretch my arms, conscious that I have no idea what time it is, but I'm exhausted.

'You should go. I didn't mean for you to stay so long, and you have all those steps to negotiate. At least the moonlight is a blessing, it would be rather tricky if it weren't so bright tonight.'

'I'm not going anywhere,' Nico states, adamantly. 'I'll sleep next to Luna on the sofa. You look absolutely shattered and my day was certainly less stressful than yours. If all goes well tonight, I'll pop home first thing in the morning to change. If you call me when Olivia gets back, I can drive you up to La Grotta. We can work all afternoon and into the evening if you like.'

'Isn't there anything more exciting you'd like to do on your day off?' I reply, feeling guilty for commandeering his time.

'Not until Jack returns and we can all take a trip in the boat.' Nico's smile is wistful.

If all goes well tomorrow, then I'm going to enlist Olivia's help to arrange an amazing day cruising the Amalfi coast and put Richard's little plan into action. Jack's boat is fine but hiring a luxury speedboat for the day will put an even bigger smile on Nico's face!

'I'd love to accept your offer, Nico. Richard is getting a little anxious about his office. He wants me to sift through his paperwork and sort it out into boxes ready to go into storage in the UK. And he has even more little treasures hidden away up there, so he tells me. Those will need taking downstairs for Olivia and me to pack.'

'Great – maybe I'll learn something about antiques at the same time. Now, let's clear this lot away and get some well-deserved sleep.'

As we ferry things back and forth, it's the perfect end to what has been, in part, a bit of a traumatic day and I'm grateful to Nico for coming to my rescue.

Locking the patio doors, all that's left is to say goodnight as I walk up to Nico.

'Thanks for . . . well, being there for me and Luna. I'm more grateful than you can possibly imagine.'

I lean over to smooth Luna's head and she opens one eye, but doesn't move – she's exhausted.

'I enjoy our chats, Marci.' Nico steps forward as I straighten up, and suddenly I'm looking directly into his eyes. 'I guess I miss Richard more than I thought. But it's also been illuminating finding out more about him. I think of him as one of those wise old professors who at first glance appear to be quite staid but turn out to be full of surprises.'

My heart begins to thud in my chest as I cast around for something amusing to say. 'Like running off to Thailand to get married?'

The look we exchange is strangely intimate – together we've sussed Richard out and found him endearing, inspiring, and at the same time just a little bit crazy. I'm waiting for Nico to step back but he doesn't move and for one second there's a sense of hesitation between us. *He has to kiss you first, Marci*, that little voice inside my head tells me firmly. And then Luna lets out a little whimper and the moment is lost.

'Well . . . um . . . I'd better see if Luna's thirsty before we settle down for the night. Sleep well, Marci.'

From the look on Nico's face he's equally as disappointed as I am. Given that we're in Olivia and Jack's house, maybe it would be disrespectful, I reflect, as I head towards the guest bedroom. But that doesn't stop me wondering what it would be like to feel Nico's lips on mine . . .

15.
Diving into the Unknown

'Oh, Marci – I am so sorry this happened. It isn't the first time Luna has injured a paw but it's such a rare occurrence that I didn't think to leave the vet's number handy.'

Olivia is holding Luna in her arms, a wildly wagging tail flailing around like a little whip.

'Well, she's certainly pleased to see you and I hope she doesn't hold it against me.'

Luna turns her head and begins to lick Olivia's neck, which makes her start laughing. 'Oh, she wouldn't be this perky if she was feeling really sorry for herself. She is a bit of a diva at times.'

'It was a huge thorn, though – but Nico sent the vet a photo and he said the swelling was due to fluid. Once it was out, he said unless there's an obvious sign of infection just keep her inside until it's back to normal. He said to ring if you have a problem.'

'Calm down, Luna,' Olivia croons as she struggles to keep hold of her. 'I don't think there's much wrong with you now, is there? You should be very grateful to Marci and Nico for being so attentive.'

'Talk of the devil . . . and here I am!'

Nico steps through the sliding door, surprising us all and Luna yelps to get down to greet him.

'It's good to see the patient looking so lively,' he says, kneeling to give her ears a rub as she collapses in a heap next to him. But his attention is firmly focused on the bandage around her paw. 'We raided your bathroom cabinet, but by the looks of it now that she's feeling more perky it won't stay on long.'

'That's a good sign,' Olivia confirms, looking first at Nico and then at me. 'You two have been amazing, really you have. I'm so grateful to you for taking such great care of her.'

'Nico slept on the sofa with Luna all night,' I explain. 'I slept comfortably in bed and didn't wake up until nine this morning so really it was Nico who played nurse all night. How was the dinner party?'

Olivia's eyes gleam. 'The food was wonderful, but after a couple of hours of dancing around like mad women, singing at the tops of our voices, we all woke up feeling a little jaded this morning,' she declares. 'Right. I assume Nico is here to give you a lift back?'

'Oh, we're going straight to La Grotta,' he jumps in. 'I only went back to change and run through a few things with Renzo as it's going to be super busy today. Are you all packed up, Marci?'

Olivia is watching us with interest. 'And did you manage to at least enjoy a quiet meal together last night?' she enquires, looking directly at Nico.

'I raided the fridge and thanks to you, it wasn't a total disaster.'

A look flashes between Nico and Olivia, as she raises her eyebrows. 'You might not be a chef, Nico, but every Italian man knows how to throw a few things together.' They both start laughing and I assume that it's some sort of ongoing joke between them.

'I'm sorry, Marci. I'm married to a man who doesn't even barbecue – can you imagine? Even assembling a salad would have him yelling out to ask what he should pour over it. At least Nico isn't afraid to have a go. Unfortunately, Jack doesn't show the slightest interest. Or, in his case, maybe I mean *fortunately* . . . he's clueless!'

The next couple of hours are spent dragging a few boxes through from the back room. Nico manages to manoeuvre some of the larger items around to allow us to gain access. Together we unpack them and get rid of the dusty old paper and cardboard. Olivia now has enough items waiting to be packed to keep her busy for a couple of days at least. Then we head upstairs to the study.

'Where do we start?' Nico grimaces as he looks around. There are piles everywhere, and boxes that look like they're about to fall apart. Most are stuffed to overflowing with paperwork and even what looks like it might be a sofa bed is covered with neatly laid out stacks, as if someone meant to file them away.

'Richard asked if I could separate out his personal stuff and he'll go through those boxes first. This is his life we're looking at – not just a record of every item he's ever purchased but photographs and letters going way back.'

Why didn't Richard whittle this down before he made the move to Positano? And now he's doing the exact same thing. He doesn't want anything thrown away, but he expects me to make some sense of it so that he can then sort it out once and for all.

'Let's clear an area in here and then bring up three of the new packing boxes. One for financial stuff, one for personal things and one for business-related documentation.'

'Okay.' Nico heads downstairs and I begin moving the dilapidated boxes out onto the landing. When he returns, he gives me a hand and it's hot, sweaty work.

'I hope this stuff is worth going through,' Nico comments.

It is a lot of effort, but once it's done there's enough floor space for us both to spread out.

'Richard said he has a special stash up here and some personal artwork. We ought to check that out before we begin.'

There's a cupboard set back into the wall over in the corner and this is the first time it's been accessible. I open it rather gingerly, and peer inside. It's bigger than I thought.

'The shelves have been taken out to accommodate a shipping crate. It's nailed down, so that's one thing less to worry about, I'm glad to see.'

'Are they his prized possessions?' Nico asks.

'They're not stock. You're probably aware that Richard likes to dabble with a paintbrush. He's pretty good, if my memory serves me well. He showed me a couple once, many years ago but given that I haven't yet stumbled across an easel or any art equipment, I suspect most of these are from his younger days.'

'Of course. It's a shared passion that Luca and Richard spent hours talking about and Mum would usually leave them to it. Are there any more cupboards up here?' Nico asks.

'One in his bedroom, but it's a double cupboard. We might as well check that out next. I'm half expecting something to run across the floor when we start pulling things about,' I confess, as we squeeze along the landing. We're just moving piles around, or that's what it feels like right now.

'It's dusty, that's all. There's no damp and all I'd expect to see is maybe a few spiders here and there, as nothing has been disturbed for a while.'

'Do the spiders in Italy bite?'

Nico begins to laugh. 'As long as it doesn't have spots, then you have nothing at all to worry about.'

'And that's supposed to be comforting?' I ask, as we enter Richard's bedroom.

Nico strides over to the ceiling-to-floor double doors which are set into the wall that backs onto the landing. He tries the handles. 'It's locked.'

'Oh, right . . . hmm . . . Richard mentioned something about a key in a pot on the shelf above his desk.' Sure enough, when I go back into the study to check, there it is.

'Result! Hopefully it's the right one.' I throw the key over to Nico and he catches it in mid-air, turning on his heels to insert it into the lock.

He gives the cast-iron knob a hefty turn. 'The key seems to have unlocked it, but the door won't budge.' This time he turns and yanks, and the left-hand door flies open, sending him sprawling. 'Guess it was just stuck,' he grins, as I offer him a hand to get back onto his feet.

'Are you okay?'

'I'm fine. Fortunately I bounce well. It feels a little intrusive poking around in someone's cupboards,' Nico comments as he steps back.

I know exactly what he means as I'm feeling much the same way. Everything is very neat in here, the bed fully made up and a colourful handmade throw adding a little vibrancy to the dark wood furniture. There are a few bits and pieces on the top of a tall chest of drawers and a bedside table, but it's rather spartan. The huge double cupboard seems to dominate the room.

When I look inside the open door it's empty. There's a hanging rail and a few shelves at the bottom, but they're not even dusty. 'This must be where Richard kept his clothes. There's a dividing panel, though.' I try the right-hand door, to no avail. Nico steps forward to investigate.

'Ah, there's a hidden bolt at the top – here you go.'

When it swings open, there are a dozen shelves and each one is stacked with little boxes. Most of them are in almost pristine condition, although it's clear some of them are quite old.

'This wasn't at all what I was expecting to find,' I admit, as Nico and I glance at each other. I reach out and pick up a navy blue oblong box and carefully ease off the lid.

'Jewellery!' I exclaim, surprised.

'That's pretty,' Nico comments as we stare down at it.

'It's a vintage triple-strand pearl necklace with a gold

lapis lazuli clasp. It's Italian – see the mark on the back? RM means it was made in Rome and the number next to it identifies the maker.'

Placing the top back on, I slide it onto the shelf and ask Nico to hand down one of the wooden boxes that are beyond my reach.

'Heck – it's really heavy,' he says, carrying it over to place it on top of the chest of drawers. 'It could be full of gold coins.'

I shake my head at him dismissively, but as I ease up the lid it's stacked full of little bars, each in its own plastic case. Picking one up I lay it flat on my hand and it's weighty. Nico and I stare at it.

'This is the maker – ITALpreziosi, Italy,' I confirm. It's stamped 5 oz. fine silver 999.0. 'This is the serial number. How many are in here do you think?'

'Thirty, maybe? I'd say the whole lot weighs at least four kilos.'

And it isn't the only wooden box on the top shelf. 'This should be in a bank vault somewhere, not a cupboard with an old iron key and one shunt bolt to secure it. What was Richard thinking?'

'I agree, Marci. I suggest you give Richard a call. You can't just pack this up and leave it lying around until the lorry arrives, can you? What if a box went missing?'

It's just after four in the afternoon here, so it's probably late evening in Thailand. I'm dusty, thirsty and hungry and I look at Nico, appealingly.

'I know – it's time we stopped for a break, anyway. I'll head off and grab us something to eat and drink. You make that call. I'll be back as quickly as I can. And lock the door behind me,' he says firmly, but I don't need telling.

'Sorry, that took a little longer than expected. Giulia insisted on making a black olive and basil pizza, then Luca disappeared to make a salad. Mum added a bottle of prosecco and then went off to find some tea towels to wrap up two glasses. When they began fussing over a dessert, I said we'd grab something later when we get back.'

I turn and Nico follows me inside, shutting the door behind him. 'It's been a long time since breakfast and I'm sure you're just as hungry as I am. Shall we eat outside?'

'We can't, I'm afraid, unless it's at the front. A man is coming to collect the wooden boxes.'

Nico looks surprised. 'Oh, you managed to get hold of Richard, then. At least he's on the ball. I'm glad he's not leaving it to you to sort out.'

'I told him straight that it isn't something you leave lying around in a cupboard that's easy to break into. He simply said, "It was remiss of me, Marci. I'll make a call and get it sorted." Then he called me back about ten minutes later to let me know what was happening. It's the fastest response I've had from him so far!'

'And you just hand the boxes over?' Nico queries, obviously feeling as nervous about that as I am.

'Yes. It's odd, though – he wasn't at all fazed to think he'd left his personal stash of silver behind, and he didn't say anything about the person he contacted. I mean, that was one quick phone call. Richard said the man will give me a receipt, which is a little reassuring. He was actually quite apologetic at that point, and he said he'd *forgotten* they were there.'

'Forgotten?' Nico shrugs his shoulders. 'I don't know many people sitting on a small fortune like that who would be likely to forget, but that's Richard all right. Okay, let's sit out the front. There's enough furniture knocking around here to make ourselves comfortable,' Nico says, scanning around. 'Let's use those two chairs over there and um . . . we need a small coffee table – I thought I saw one somewhere.'

I laugh. 'There are several, but I moved them into the back room. I'll find something suitable.'

It doesn't take long for us to settle ourselves down. It's not quite as pleasant as the courtyard, but there's enough greenery around. And we're at least twenty metres away from the main road. There's also a tall hedge in front of the solid stone wall that runs along the boundary of the property, and it helps to diffuse the sound of passing traffic.

'Gosh, I'm loving these ad hoc picnics. I feel spoilt. That's quite a salad and it was so kind of Giulia. It's a little early for her to have the wood-fired oven going, isn't it?'

'She was still doing prep work, but there's nothing like a good pair of bellows to get a fire roaring. I didn't like to refuse her offer, so I felt it was only fair that I get the fire going while she made the dough.'

'I thought Giulia doesn't like anyone messing with the oven?'

'She doesn't, usually. But uh, I asked how her parents were as I was piling in the wood, and she didn't stop me, otherwise I'd still be there now. So, you see, I can make polite conversation with Giulia that doesn't have any connection at all with work.'

I'm busy scooping some of the wonderful *insalata* onto my plate and he's unaware of the fact I did a quick roll of my eyes. That hardly counts as conversation.

'What are these?' I ask, picking out some inch-long pieces that look very similar to leeks.

'Palm hearts. It's an *insalata di rucola* – rocket salad with basil, grated zucchini, and cherry tomatoes. A little salt, garlic, black pepper and shavings of Parmigiano-reggiano with a drizzle of olive oil.'

'I rarely have a salad with pizza at home, but then our pizzas are usually quite doughy,' I explain.

'I've cut you a big slice, hold up your plate.'

'Oh, I'll eat it with my fingers.' Balancing the plate on my lap, I pick it up and fold it lengthways to make sure nothing slides off. One bite and I groan as my stomach gratefully acknowledges that food is on the way. 'The olives are so sweet and there's a little roasted garlic, too.'

'Watching you eat is fascinating,' Nico says, staring at me, his own food untouched.

'What do you mean?'

'You savour every mouthful. Some people pick at their food and that's annoying. Others eat without any real appreciation of the individual ingredients, or the seasonings and sauces. Often, you taste everything separately before you combine everything on your fork. With pizza you simply stuff it into your mouth.'

That makes me laugh, and I hold a hand up to my face as I continue eating. 'Do I? I wasn't aware. Are you going to have something, or just continue to sit there watching me?'

Nico gives me a look of pure amusement and then picks up a slice of pizza and takes an enormous bite, just as a car turns into the car park.

'This must be Richard's contact.'

Nico looks up. 'Oh, it's Hans Wagner and his son, Freddie. It's going to be fine. Shall I carry the boxes down for you?'

The fact that Nico knows the men reassures me a little, but I am nervous about handing over something so valuable in exchange for a signature on a piece of paper.

'Thanks, they are rather heavy. He certainly drives a very smart car. I hope Hans speaks some English.'

'Mainly Italian, with a German accent, of course. Don't worry. I've got this. Why don't you give Richard a call and let him know they've arrived? Luca introduced Richard to Hans many years ago. He's a savvy businessman – trustworthy and well-respected. Just relax and enjoy that pizza.'

I watch as two men get out of the car and the older man waves to us. I'm surprised when Nico suddenly places his hand on my shoulder, giving it a reassuring squeeze before he strides away from me.

While they're inside I try Richard. It's probably midnight in Thailand and I hold my breath, hoping he's still awake and will pick up.

'Marci, my darling. It's a bit noisy here, give me a moment.'

There's loud music in the background and I listen as it recedes into the distance.

'Sorry. That's better. We're surrounded by a group of thirty-something backpackers here tonight and they're letting their hair down. It's great fun. Problems?'

'No. Hans Wagner and his son are here and Nico is about to hand over the boxes to him. He's brought some paperwork in an envelope by the look of it, but is there anything we need to do – will it require a signature, or should I check it?'

Richard's baritone voice rumbles with a little chuckle. 'The money has already been transferred to my account, Marci. Hans was the person who procured the bars for me in the first place, so you can relax.'

'Great. I just um . . . thought it was best to double-check,' I reply, trying hard not to sound a little on edge.

'There's nothing dodgy going on, my dear, if that's what's worrying you. Physical silver is a good long-term investment and, yes, it should have been in a bank, but I have a special reason for keeping it separate. No one knew it was there and I'm cross with myself that it slipped my mind. The remainder of the items in the bedroom cupboard are mostly jewellery, with a handful of collectible coins, all of which will require an expert valuation prior to auction. Now stop worrying and enjoy the rest of your evening. Give my best to Nico – he's a handy guy to have around. Ciao, Marci, we'll speak again soon!'

I sit back, sipping my glass of prosecco thinking this is crazy as I watch the men carrying the boxes over to the car. Hans turns and gives me a polite wave before they drive off.

'Why are you frowning?' Nico asks, looking at me rather

nervously as he hands me an A4 envelope. 'Did you speak to Richard?'

'Yes, and he said he'd already received the funds. I guess we can relax, but I wish I'd checked out that cupboard sooner, rather than later. What if someone had broken in and stolen them?'

Nico sits down, eager to get back to eating. He picks up the pizza box to offer me another slice and I can't resist.

'Perhaps now is not the time to mention this, but you know that fruit stall I told you about? Well, their cash box was snatched yesterday. One guy acted as a distraction while the other swooped in, and it was over in seconds. So, an antique shop could be a bit of a sitting target and a haul of silver would be like winning the lottery to this duo of thieves. Richard is a trusting sort of man and I doubt he's even given it any thought but just in case, you really should keep that front door locked at all times.'

'I will.' I can see he's trying not to panic me, but he is concerned and it's time to change the subject. 'How did Richard and Luca meet?' It's a question that's been on the tip of my tongue for a while.

'Like a lot of customers, he came to eat at Ristorante Sul Mare one evening, enjoyed the food and kept coming back. I often helped out for the odd hour here and there, back then. No one knew who he was, but he appeared regularly. He never made a fuss, always left a tip and he became a familiar face. Then, one day, we had one of our family celebrations and he joined in with the late-night dancing. Luca and Richard struck up a friendship over time. I think it was when Luca was trying to hide his financial problems and even Mum didn't know how bad things were. Richard is rather like you, someone who is easy to talk to – maybe a little too easy!' He raises an eyebrow, accusingly.

'I talk to you as honestly as you talk to me.'

'Hmm . . . but once something has been said, it can't be unsaid. Anyway, where was I?' Nico pauses to stuff the last of his pizza slice into his mouth while I try not to think too hard about what he meant by that. He takes a moment to think before he responds. 'When Luca sat everyone down and said Richard was going to invest in the business, we all knew him quite well by then. It wasn't really a big deal, more of a reason to celebrate, actually.'

'I'm assuming that a part of the deal included the use of La Grotta?'

'Yes. Richard had been slowly amassing his collection, apparently, but everything was in storage. He loved being up there. He didn't get much passing trade, but buyers would turn up, usually by appointment.'

I put my empty plate down on the coffee table in front of us. 'I know that he was constantly in touch with Guy, and we sold quite a few things at auction for him.'

'I guess none of us knew how successful he was,' Nico says, impressed. 'Clearly, it's given him a good living. Perhaps the hoard of silver, together with his investment in Il Posto di Luca and Ristorante Sul Mare, is his retirement fund.'

I was thinking the exact same thing. Richard isn't worried about money because his financial interests are spread out. Meeting Angel has upset his plan a little, as he wasn't as prepared as he should have been. No one overlooks what is probably well in excess of fifty thousand pounds' worth of silver bullion. Unless you're in love, that is, and your attention is elsewhere. Well, at least the boxes are now in safe hands and it's one problem less for me to concern myself with.

'I think you're right,' I reply, topping up our glasses. 'Richard knows what he's doing, I'm sure.'

'I have a feeling Richard and Angel may well end up back here at some point, Nico. I understand why this place resonated with him. But I think his days of collecting antiques are over – he's been doing it for a long time, and he's made his money. It's time to enjoy the fruits of his labour, as they say. But I know Richard, and while travelling is exciting, a part of him needs a permanent base. Being selfish, I'm glad that's likely to be in the UK, but I think he'll have a bolt hole here, because Positano was his home for so long.'

'Life isn't quite the same without his vibrant personality to brighten our evenings. My Uncle Vittorio would love to find Richard and Angel a new home – being in the business. There isn't a property on the market that he isn't aware of, so I do hope you're right – for all our sakes.' Nico raises his glass. 'To future happiness,' he says, as we clink glasses.

The car park is beginning to fill up with customers for the restaurant, and while we're tucked away on the far side of La Grotta, it's a little distracting.

'Shall we clear up and go back inside?' Nico suggests.

'I think it's time. If you want to head back, then don't feel you have to stay. I'm not tired and I'm going to start going through some of that paperwork.'

'I'm not a quitter,' Nico exclaims. 'Besides, we have the rest of this bottle of prosecco to finish off and you might need a steady arm to negotiate those steps.'

I throw back my head and laugh. 'I doubt it, two small glasses is my absolute limit. But, seriously, it's a long time since I felt this fit. All those steps are like a workout. I'm eating more than I ever have and yet I know I've lost some weight, it's crazy!'

Nico's eyes flash over me and I feel self-conscious. 'Positano suits you, Marci. When you first arrived you were so pale, I thought you were unwell and now you're glowing.'

'Oh . . . that's a positive, then,' I reply awkwardly.

'Why is it that most British women can't seem to handle a well-meaning compliment?' he asks, clearly puzzled.

I shrug my shoulders. 'Perhaps it's because we're not used to receiving them?'

Nico bursts out laughing. 'Guess I'm a true Italian at heart in every way. What man doesn't want to compliment a beautiful young woman? That makes no sense at all to me!'

And what woman doesn't long to hear it, I reflect as a warm glow envelops me . . . I only hope it's not obvious to Nico.

16.

Throwing Caution to the Wind

It's the wine, I tell myself. And the fact that Nico and I are working in such close proximity. Sitting cross-legged on the floor as we sift through a mountain of paper, it's boring enough for the mind to begin wandering. It hasn't really registered with me before how fresh Nico smells, despite the dust that lingers in the air and the odour of staleness from the boxes we're diving into. Nico reminds me of the scent of citrus, but when he jumps up to carry over yet another box to place in front of me, the warmth of his body in action seems to accentuate it.

'That's an interesting cologne,' I eventually ask, my curiosity getting the better of me.

'It's a body spray I buy from a friend of Olivia's. She has a little shop in the heart of Positano – Bellezza Naturale. The ingredients are organically sourced and chemical-free. I'm sure Olivia will end up taking you there at some point. Sorry if it's a bit overpowering.'

I didn't mean to make him feel awkward. 'No, it's nice . . . fresh.'

'Thank goodness! It's rather warm in here – do you mind if I open the window a little wider?'

'Not at all – it's a little stiff and that's as far as I could get it to extend.' As Nico turns away, I discreetly sniff myself. Not too bad considering and, thankfully, the spritz of perfume I sprayed over my top still lingers. The light, floral tones aren't overpowering, but still pleasantly fragrant.

My eyes stray over to Nico as he reaches over the top of a stack of boxes and pushes against the glass. His muscles strain against his pale blue T-shirt and from the contours it's obvious that there isn't an ounce of fat on him. I suppose he's on the go most of the time.

'Do you have any hobbies, other than boating, whenever Jack is around?'

'There's a gym in the basement of the hotel,' Nico informs me as he settles down again. 'I really must give you that tour.'

'Your mum showed me her and Luca's accommodation. It's wonderful – so modern and bright.'

'She did? You're honoured, then.'

He doesn't seem put out and I continue leafing through. Most of what I'm sorting out here are receipts for various purchases over the last two years.

'Uh . . . I think you should take a look at this,' Nico interrupts.

'What have you found?'

'Most of this stack seems to be mainly auction brochures. They go back a long time, but I found this pile in among them. I'd better flick through each one to be on the safe side.'

He passes me a handful of envelopes of various shapes and sizes, some of which look like birthday cards. It's obviously personal correspondence. 'Maybe we'll set up a separate box for handwritten letters and photos. I'll go and get one. Do you fancy a cold drink? There's lemonade in the fridge.'

'Perfect. Where do you want me to put the auction stuff? There are an awful lot of these.'

'How about over there in the corner? Some are more collectible than others, but Richard might not want to part with them anyway. Thanks for being thorough, Nico, as I know it's a tedious job, but I'd hate something of sentimental value to Richard to be missed.'

'It's not a problem.'

'I'll see if I can find some shallower A4 boxes.'

When I return, Nico has already made two huge stacks in the corner and there's a pile of other items he's found in between the old catalogues. With some flat-packed boxes under one arm and a glass in each hand, he jumps straight up to help.

'Here are a few to be going on with, but I know there are more somewhere. There's no point using the deeper ones as I doubt I'd be able to carry a full one downstairs,' I inform him, as he eases the cardboard from under my arm. He leans them up against the wall.

'Here you go . . .' Nico reaches out to take a glass from me.

'I'm more than happy to do the carrying. I enjoy being useful.' A cheeky smile lights up his eyes and suddenly I'm standing here with a silly grin plastered over my face. 'I'll . . . uh . . . just make up these boxes and label them,' he continues.

Is it just the stuffiness in here that is making me hot,

or did we have a moment there? I silently berate myself for being ridiculous and letting my imagination run riot.

'Let me clear away the general rubbish to give you some room. You enjoy creating order out of chaos, don't you?' Nico ventures, watching my face with interest.

We're at the stage where we've only just scratched the surface in here, but the original boxes have seen better days and wouldn't survive the journey, even if they didn't need sorting through.

'This level of disorganisation would drive me nuts. I suspect it was the same for Richard, as this isn't his style.' It's puzzling and I can't help but wonder why he suddenly got himself into this mess. It's like his routine went out the window and judging by the size of the backlog we're talking months and months. Long before Angel captured his attention.

'He was constantly on the go and he travelled the length and breadth of Italy. It probably just got too much for him.'

Is that the reason? Or did Richard have something else on his mind to distract him? What exactly, I have no idea, but I do my best to shake it off as I don't want Nico to think anything is wrong. However, I can't help but think there must be more to Richard's sudden change than just love.

Nico makes two trips with his arms full and by the time he's done we're both ready to take a little break. He sits down next to the desk, leaning against the wall and stretching out his legs, glass in hand.

I lower myself down in front of the window, leaning back and letting out a gentle sigh. 'My back is beginning to ache. Have you had enough for one day?' I check, conscious that it's not much fun for Nico on top of everything else he has going on. At least the lemonade is refreshing.

He shakes his head. 'I'm good for another hour or two before we head back for dessert and coffee.' That playful grin of his gets me every time. Immediately responding with a smile of my own, I'm beginning to feel all hot and bothered again. 'Besides, the way it looks now is worse than it did when we started, and even I'm not happy to leave it in this state.'

'You're a man after my own heart,' I laugh and then realise that sounds a little odd. 'I mean . . .' What do I mean?

'I think we're very alike in many ways, Marci. Are you only just noticing that?'

Nico's gaze is intense, with a mischievous glint to his eyes that I can't miss.

'Um . . . I suppose the answer to that is no.'

'It's beginning to bother me,' he replies. 'How about you?'

I gulp, hoping the noise wasn't as loud as it sounded to me and I take a hefty swig from my glass, conscious that Nico is still watching me closely.

'A little. But I have to be clear, Nico, I don't flirt, and I don't believe in holiday flings.' Ooh . . . that sounds like I'm putting him in his place and that's not how I meant it. I'm simply trying to be honest with him.

'Neither do I.' The seconds pass and it's awkward avoiding eye contact. 'Look, I'd hate it to turn into a problem between us, Marci, but, uh . . . I really do enjoy spending time with you – just being in your company.'

'Even sorting through dusty old paperwork?' I jest.

'Look, that came out all wrong. It would be a lie if I didn't admit that the highlight of my day is when we sit beneath the pergola having supper together. Olivia says I should enjoy myself and that holiday romances can be fun. It's not really my style, though, and how does anyone know how they are going to feel when it's over? I'm not sure I'm the sort of person who can switch their feelings on and off, quite so easily.'

Nico stares down into his glass, smiling to himself. 'That's Olivia, her heart rules her head. I'd rather hoped you'd see that it isn't my thing, either. I can't help how I feel, and it wouldn't be fair on you if I didn't admit that I find you attractive, Marci. Even if it's means you choose to steer clear of me.'

'Oh, Nico! I wish I could just breeze through life, but—'

'—but if we both have the same understanding, would it hurt to enjoy the time that we're around each other?'

My mouth is suddenly so dry I'm having difficulty swallowing, and my heart is literally pounding inside my chest. 'Just one, brief summer and then we step back onto our separate pathways? It sounds way too easy and that's a big red flag for me based on what I've seen of life.'

'I understand that, Marci. This is the last thing I expected to happen and maybe it's because you're not like any other woman I've met before. Anyway, your presence is giving me the little boost I need and I'm grateful, so we'll say no more about it. You have a willing pair of hands and I'll make sure my focus doesn't waver. Now, let's make a dent in this, it's the least I can do to make amends.'

I look across at Nico, glad of the distance between us

right now, but the smiles we exchange so naturally are genuine. Mine is with a heavy heart because I feel the exact same way, and it's a scary thought.

'Ah, there you are!' Dario stops wiping down the bar counter as we enter. 'Uncle Luca made me promise I would hang around until you both returned. There's a snack for you in the fridge and two portions of Giulia's cappuccino tiramisu.'

'Is everyone else gone?' Nico asks.

'Yes. It was quieter than usual tonight.'

'Of course! They'll all be at home glued to their TVs. There was an important football match on this evening,' Nico explains. 'Supporters will either be partying it up now or drowning their sorrows.'

'I keep telling Luca we should get a big TV screen – football brings in the customers,' Dario states, adamantly. 'Anyway, I'm done here. All of the external restaurant doors are locked, and Viola is covering reception.'

'Thank you, Dario, and that's a great idea of yours. Maybe we could consider fixing something up in the garden, a little away from the main dining area to keep all of our customers happy.'

'Or on the lower dining terrace.' Dario's response is instant, and I can see he's given this some thought. I wonder how many other family members are patiently waiting for the day that Nico is in charge?

'Probably best not to mention that to Luca right now, as his head is full of his plans for La Grotta. But that's worth considering. Right, Marci – you must be tired, but you can't go to bed on an empty stomach.' He breaks out into Italian and the only words I understand are good night, but Dario looks happy. Was Nico reassuring him that there will be changes, and he simply needs to be patient a while longer? Dario holds his hand up in the air and they bump palms. It's the first time I've seen anyone do that since I've been here.

'*Buona sera*, Dario,' I say, as I turn to follow Nico through to the kitchen.

'Sleep well, Marci!' he calls after me.

The first thing Nico does is to head for the small basin to wash his hands and I follow suit.

'Can I help?' I ask.

'If you can grab a couple of dessert spoons and some napkins – oh, and a bottle of white wine from the chiller cabinet – I'll sort the rest.'

I love it in here. It's all so perfectly organised and while during service it often appears to be chaotic with staff criss-crossing and waiters ferrying dishes, at the end of each day it's left sparkling and orderly.

When I return to the long preparation counter with a bottle of wine pressed tightly under one arm, and my hands full, I'm surprised to see that Nico has turned on the oven.

'Isn't it a little late to be cooking?' I remark, expecting to see a cold platter and not an assembly of small covered dishes.

'This is Luca's version of a platter. It won't take long.'

Considering Nico doesn't think of himself as worthy in the kitchen, he seems to know exactly what he's doing. He heats up a pan of a delicious-smelling tomato-based sauce before tipping in a small dish of tiny meatballs, as we wait for a tray of some rather interesting-looking canapés to warm through. I fetch two wine glasses and go in search of some plates.

'We're going to need two trays,' he instructs me and off I go again.

'It won't be assembled with the same level of perfection Luca brings to the plate, but here goes.'

I watch with interest as Nico pulls everything together and we each carry a tray outside, carefully negotiating the path between the long run of vegetables. Most of the lights in the garden are still on as it's only just after 11 p.m. and not all the guests will have arrived back yet.

'This is beginning to feel very decadent, you know. I appreciate how Luca and Giulia cater for us, but tonight you surprised me. You know what you're doing, Nico, so don't try to tell me that you don't.'

'There isn't a job in the kitchen I haven't done over the years, it's true. But if I'd excelled at any of them Luca would have me on his team. Let's place the trays down and pull two of the bistro tables together, Marci.'

It takes a little re-jigging and my stomach is rumbling, but when we're finally seated it's good to take the weight off my feet.

'Are you suffering?' Nico asks, frowning.

'Only my calf muscles are complaining. Too many steps,' I reply, truthfully and he smiles, sympathetically.

'You've adjusted quickly. You only need to take two breaks on the uphill climb and that's something.' Now he's teasing me.

'So, what have we here?' I ask, sitting forward to look more closely at the platter in front of us. Each canapé is bite-sized and the aroma wafting up makes me impatient to begin eating.

'Meatballs reheated in a rich garlic and tomato sauce, with a pearl of mozzarella and a fresh basil leaf. Then here we have *crostini di polenta*. A square of warm polenta with a sliver of smoked cheese, a slice of speck, and a sage leaf.' Both of which are secured with a small wooden pick. 'And finally,' he continues, 'salami and green olives on sourdough bread with herb butter. Tuck in!'

Grabbing a paper napkin I reach out for one of the skewered meatballs but it's in my mouth before any of the thick coating of sauce can drop off. 'Oh, yum!' I groan, holding a hand to my mouth as I chew. 'That is so amazing.'

The sound of laughter down by the swimming pool filters up through the trees and Nico looks at me in surprise. 'We have some late-night swimmers. It's good to hear.'

'You don't seem to get many young families staying here, it's mainly couples.'

'You're right, and I think that's a shame. There's plenty of room to have a playground and a small pool. It wouldn't be too much work to create a child-friendly area.'

'Where?'

'The boundary is the other side of this huge orchard behind us. You can't really get a sense of the size of the area because the trees need thinning out.'

So Nico does have plans, well – a vision and that's a good sign.

'Thank you for your honesty earlier on, Nico and I'm

sorry if it appeared that I was shutting you down. It's just that instant attraction rarely lasts, it always dims disappointingly quickly I've found, and wouldn't that leave a sense of awkwardness between us?'

'You think that attraction is a dangerous thing to indulge? Even when people declare they have fallen in love at first sight, I've seen enough friends in that position to know that it's hit and miss. So, to me it's tantalising because it's fun while it lasts.' He laughs softly to himself as his hand hovers over the platter. He changes his mind, picking up the wine bottle and pouring a little into each glass, then handing one to me. 'Maybe we should be counting our blessings. There's a lot to be said for freedom.'

'To freedom, then, unless fate has another plan – but one that actually works,' I acknowledge as our eyes settle on each other. 'It must be nice to find someone you want to be with forever and know that they feel the same way.' I really must stop and think before I speak. That sounded a little defeatist.

'There's someone you can't quite get out of your head?' Nico asks, a gentleness to his tone that sets me on edge.

'No. I let myself believe something that wasn't true and as I didn't learn my lesson the first time around, let's just say that the second time stung a little.' Unwilling to dwell over that fact, I pick up a slice of the polenta with what looks like cured ham. 'What did you call this?'

'It's speck – s-p-e-c-k – a type of cured, lightly smoked ham made in South Tyrol, a province in the northeast. Unlike prosciutto, it's browner in colour and much denser.'

Nico begins eating again and our mood lightens.

'It isn't as sweet as prosciutto – there's a savoury, smoky taste and something else, a different flavour, but I have no idea what it is.'

'It's laced with spices – juniper and bay leaf, but it's the juniper that you're probably picking up on.'

'There's a first time for everything,' I muse, not sure if it's to my liking. 'It's slightly earthy.'

Nico's eyes gleam. 'You're obviously not a gin drinker. But you're right. I liken it to rosemary. Anyway, what were we talking about . . . ah, yes. You were about to tell me about the man who broke your heart.'

I stop mid-chew and swallow quickly before I choke. 'No, I wasn't, and he didn't!'

'Ah, it's worse than I imagined, then.'

Is Nico teasing me? But his face looks serious and now if I change the subject, he'll assume he's right.

'His name is Everett. He is a charmer and knows how to make a woman feel special. Unfortunately for me, I believed every word he said because why wouldn't I? Everyone was eagerly awaiting the announcement of our engagement and I got swept away in the excitement. The next thing I knew, Everett was telling me that it was over and he couldn't really explain why.'

'Some people don't care about anyone but themselves,' Nico remarks, angrily.

'I'm over the embarrassment now, well, almost.'

'That's a painful experience to put behind you, Marci,' Nico replies, his voice full of sympathy.

I pause for a moment, because I know now that it was as much my fault, as Everett's. 'I closed my eyes to the truth – so I got hurt but I won't let that happen again. Have you ever been in love, Nico?'

I can see from his reaction that he's startled by my question.

'Once. Well, I thought I was at the time, but when it all falls apart it usually means something wasn't right, doesn't it?'

'Are you still struggling to let go?'

Nico leans his head back, closing his eyes for a few moments before re-opening them. 'I don't subscribe to the romantic idea that everyone has a soul mate waiting for them. If that were true, what would be the odds of stumbling across that person, given how many people there are on this planet?'

I thought *I* was a little jaded, but that statement stops me in my tracks.

'What a sad way to look at it. I know your mum obviously had a hard time, but she found Luca, didn't she?'

Nico takes a swig from his wine glass, cradling it in his hands as he turns his head to stare up at the sky.

'And Olivia found Jack,' I add.

'I'm beginning to wonder whether I'm one of those people who doesn't need someone to make them feel complete. Tiziana – my ex – thought it was her job to rescue me from my tedious existence here and entice me off to her swish apartment in Rome.' He starts laughing as he turns to look at me.

'That sounds rather exciting,' I reply, trying not to sound intrigued. She obviously had money, then, and real feelings for Nico.

'Maybe, but I love it here, which therefore makes me boring. Until a stranger comes along,' he adds, pointedly, 'who reminds me what it feels like to be alive. And then I get excited about taking up my next challenge.'

'Boring is not a word that springs to mind when I'm with you,' I tell him, firmly.

'You're fun to be around, Marci. You make me stop and consider things I don't usually ponder over, which is a good thing.'

Without thinking, I find myself leaning into him, and suddenly my lips are on his and Nico's response is instant. As each moment passes the blood seems to rush to my head. He's right – because being around him is also a reminder of how exciting it is to feel that raw attraction to someone.

It seems that our late-night suppers are about to get a lot more interesting.

17.
A Deep Dive

I'm lying here nervously waiting for Nico to wake up. The dawn chorus is signalling the start of a new day and he shouldn't be here, but I don't have the heart to awaken him. Not least because I'm not sure last night was such a good idea. It was wonderful, but impetuous.

Fighting the temptation to reach out and run my fingers down his bare arm, instead I study his face. A strong chin with a dimple, a long narrow nose and dark eyelashes against that glowing tan – Nico is beautiful to look at, even when you can't see his eyes. And with a little stubble and his curly hair a bit messy on top, he still looks gorgeous.

Me – well, half an hour ago I slipped out of bed and ran a brush through my hair before pulling on a short white cotton slip decorated with pale pink roses. Staring at myself in the mirror for a moment, my face and arms have a little colour now, but the rest of me that has remained covered looks woefully pale.

'What . . . oh. I guess we both fell asleep.' Nico rolls onto his side to face me. 'Were you watching me sleep?'

'I was. You need to go, really you do – or my reputation will be shot to pieces.'

Nico looks at me, his eyes widening. 'This wasn't

supposed to happen, was it?' he asks, meekly. 'It's all my fault – I should have kept my thoughts to myself.'

'If my power of recall is correct, I was the one who made the first move. Anyway, it doesn't matter. What does matter is that you get dressed and leave my room before anyone else is up and around.'

He closes his eyes briefly, a hint of amusement causing his lips to twitch, but he says nothing until he opens one eye, gazing up at me.

'You'd better look away. I seem to have lost my clothes.' He's jesting because there is no way he could possibly be embarrassed after the passionate few hours we just spent together.

I stare at him, amused, before placing my hands over my eyes. Given the circumstances, this is a little awkward though, I will admit.

'Just make sure you don't leave anything behind.'

There's a jolt as he leaps out of bed, and I hear a flurry of activity as he retrieves items from the floor on his way to the bathroom. Peeking between my fingertips, I stifle a laugh when I catch the rear view of a naked man making a hasty retreat.

'I'll be quick, I promise. No one will know I was ever here,' he calls over his shoulder, softly. 'If the birds are up, then I haven't got long.'

He reappears a couple of minutes later and stands there, unsure of what to say or do. It's not like this is something either of us expected to happen last night.

'We'll catch up later,' I say, encouragingly and he grins back at me – his teeth the brightest thing in the room.

'You're still talking to me – I'll take that as a good sign. And Marci . . .'

'Yes?'

'Everyone deserves to stray outside the lines occasionally. When you return to the UK, I'll always be just a phone call away – and I mean *always*.'

'Morning, Briony. How is life treating you?'

'Well, after a fabulous long weekend away, the sunshine has decided to grace us again today, so I'm one happy bunny. And Guy is in a good mood because your mum is tied up trying to find a suitable home for Richard and his new bride.'

'Oh, he did mention it briefly, but I didn't realise he was going to press ahead so soon.'

'Your mum is in her element and she seems to be getting on well with Angel. Guy is thrilled, of course, because it means Evelyn doesn't have time to keep popping in.'

I offer up a silent prayer. Richard is a genius.

'I'm calling to let you know that I'm about to upload a folder with photos of over fifty different coins. Can you organise for them to be forwarded on to one of our expert contacts? And also alert Guy, as I'm just about to head out and I won't be back until late. If he wants me to parcel them up and send them on ahead so they can go into the end of July auction, let me know as soon as possible.'

'Will do. You sound like you're motoring along. I bet it's made a huge difference having some help.'

I'm glad she can't see the satisfied little smile on my face right now – it's a little too smug this morning.

'Oh, yes – it's made *all* the difference,' I enthuse. And Olivia's help is also appreciated. The moment Olivia steps through the door to the shop her jaw drops.

'What happened in here? Where did all of these boxes come from?'

'Richard's office, I'm afraid. And there are more to come.'

Nico and I were too tired last night to rearrange what we'd dumped down here to give us some floor space upstairs. But walking into it this morning I was a little dismayed. It's like being back to square one.

'How's Luna's paw today?'

'Oh, she's back to normal – sticking her nose in everything, as usual. Mum is in charge and Luna will follow her around as my parents are going to do some weeding for me. I'll put the kettle on, then we can get stuck in tidying this little lot up.'

'They're heavy,' I inform her, and she shrugs her shoulders.

'After what I ate at the dinner party on Sunday night, I could do with the exercise. Oh, and Jack is coming home for a long weekend!'

Her face is radiant as she shares her news. 'I know how busy you are, but the only day Nico is available is on Monday. It would be marvellous if the four of us could get together. I know it means losing a whole day here, but I'm more than happy to work the following Saturday so we can make up for it. What do you think?'

A lightbulb switches on inside my head. 'That won't be necessary – there's still plenty of time to get everything sorted. I love the idea of a day to relax and hang out.' This is just the opportunity I've been waiting for. 'Ooh, let me make that drink and then we'll talk as we work. I'd like to enlist your help to pull together a little surprise that Richard has asked me to organise, which I think Jack, too, will really appreciate.'

I do love it when a plan comes together. Olivia is bound to know where to go to hire a speedboat, something a bit special, and I can't wait to meet Jack. I just hope that Olivia doesn't suspect that anything is going on between Nico and me. It's best kept between the two of us, I think. In hindsight, it is a little foolhardy given that I'm surrounded by Nico's extended family and the woman he'll probably end up marrying. Goodness, I scold myself, what was I thinking? But it's too late now. As long as no one finds out, what harm can it do? I seriously doubt anyone will give me a second thought after I fly home at the end of July.

After lunch I head upstairs with the intention of finishing off the box I started sorting out, but didn't have time to complete. It was one of the few that seemed to be a bit of a dumping ground. It's slow going. I discovered a lot of unopened envelopes from well over a year ago and after a little hesitation, I decide to open them up and file them properly. There are bank statements in some, others contain general business correspondence. It seems that up to that point, Richard was managing to keep things pretty much together. The row of well-ordered and labelled box files on shelves above the desk are even sorted into relevant years.

I'm assuming there will be space within them to file some of these things away for him.

As I empty out the last handful of yellowing paperwork at the bottom of the box, I notice a hole in one corner and it reminds me to be careful plunging my hand into anything that might have been standing around undisturbed for so long. The cardboard is old and has little rigidity left in it and it collapses with ease once it's empty. One less, I grin to myself as I throw it over my shoulder on the ever-growing rubbish pile.

When I look down, I notice there are what appear to be more photos in between a small stack of faded envelopes. All are handwritten and addressed to Richard here in Positano, but as I flip through looking at the postmarks, I'm surprised to see that some have his old UK address on them. The photos go back even further, and a lump suddenly rises up in my throat as I spot a photo of Richard and Dad, a pint of beer in their hands as they lean against a car. Taking a closer look, I wonder if it's the infamous Ford Capri – the second car that Dad owned, and he was always going on about it. He said it was one of the classics and if only he'd hung onto it, he would have had it restored. Sadly, he didn't have any photos of it and yet here I am, looking at two long-haired young men on a lads' day out, posing with what could be Dad's most prized possession. 'The one that got away,' he once confided in me, 'but it was good enough to snag your mum.'

I remember giggling at the thought of Dad trying to impress Mum. He looks like he should have been in a pop band with his collar-length hair and that sleeveless shirt. Mum would love to see this, and I wonder if it would be wrong of me to take a photo of it with my phone and send it to her. Maybe after all these years some memories are best left as just that.

As I tidy the pile, several envelopes slip out. They're old birthday cards, by the look of it, but as I scoop them up one has an old UK stamp on it which hasn't been franked. I'm intrigued when I take a closer look and see that it's addressed to Mum. It isn't sealed and I flick it open. It's one of those cards you buy that is suitable for any occasion. The print on the front is an artist's impression of a bowl of pale pink roses. The sort where the brush strokes are visible and yet the overall effect is pleasing to the eye. On the back it says:

Grant Galleries, Chelsea. Pink Profusion by Edward Jay.

When I finally get up the courage to open it, what was a blank card with no verse is covered in Richard's tell-tale flamboyant handwriting and I feel the blood drain from my face as I begin reading.

My dearest Evelyn

When I left for Positano, I couldn't find the courage to voice the words I'd practised over and over again in my head. And for good reason, but one I know that you will understand as we both know that some things are best left unsaid.

I'm hoping that starting a new life in Positano will set me free but I want to thank you from the bottom of my heart for your unwavering friendship over the years. From the moment I first saw you, hiding the truth wasn't easy, but my stubborn sense of pride is all I have to offer as an excuse.

I feel blessed and privileged to be godfather to both Guy and Marci. It's more than I deserve, but I will always be there for them, no matter what.

So, please understand that I wasn't running away, I was running towards a new life. And I know that admission will bring you a sense of true peace.

With love, always,

R.

Sitting back on my heels I'm reeling, and I instinctively reach for my phone.

'Mum, it's only me – can you talk?'

'I'm on my way to look at what could be the perfect little cottage for Angel and Richard, but I can talk as I walk. I'm only five minutes away from it, though. Everything is okay with you, is it?'

'Yes. I'm fine but, um . . . maybe we can have a chat after your appointment? I've found something in among Richard's things and I think Guy should be in on the conversation, too.'

'That sounds intriguing. I hope it isn't a potential problem.'

'No, just something that probably needs to be discussed to get it out the way. I'll schedule a video call for later this afternoon and send both you and Guy a link.'

'Great idea, Marci. You can give us an update on your progress, as well. I know Guy is quite excited about the coins and I'm sure you're discovering more little gems with each passing day.'

'I am and a few other things I wasn't expecting. I hope the viewing goes well and we'll speak later.'

Placing the card back inside the envelope, I quickly put the other papers into the personal box and head downstairs with it clutched tightly in my hand.

'How's it going up there?' Olivia asks, looking up as I enter and casually pop the card into my handbag.

'Good, there's just so much to go through that I decided a change would be as good as a rest. I thought I'd start nosing around in the back room – inside the real cave!'

'Ooh . . . can I join you?' Olivia reaches her arms up in the air to stretch her back and I realise we've been at it for several hours.

'Let's go exploring,' I reply and her eyes light up.

The part of the building that goes way back into what I assume was a natural formation in the rock, is pleasantly cool. Only the rear wall is natural stone, the ceiling and side walls have been lined. What little of the floor tiles we can see, are natural limestone. This would make an amazing dining room.

'There's heating in here too,' Olivia points out. 'And an air-conditioning unit.'

'That's why it's dry, then. Oh – is that a wine cage over there in the corner?'

We shift a few of the lighter things out of the way and aim for the far left-hand corner. New ground.

'There's a massive crate tucked behind this huge cupboard,' Olivia calls out. She has totally disappeared, but I can hear her and the sound of wood scraping on wood. 'I think there are paintings inside!'

I ease myself around a wonderful example of a classic Louis XVI lacquered armoire which will fetch a very good price indeed. Olivia has managed to squeeze herself into a two-foot-wide space between the back of the cupboard and a crate.

'The top isn't nailed down but there's not enough room to lever one of them out. What a shame – this looks really promising.'

'Oh well, maybe that's a Monday task for when Nico is here,' I acknowledge. 'I'm going to check out the wine store.'

It's wonderfully cool at the rear and I see there's a vent high up in the side wall. It must be visible from the courtyard, but I can't say I've ever noticed it.

'I hope there aren't any creepy crawlies lurking in the shadows,' I call out over my shoulder, as I undo the latch on the filigree metal doors and swing one of them open. When you see wine bottles covered in a layer of dust it's a very good sign indeed. 'It's tempting to take a closer look, but I think I'll ask Richard if these are likely to be really valuable before I risk taking one out. It might not be wise to disturb the sediment – it's not unheard of for bottles to suddenly pop their corks if the wine has turned. They might not even be for sale.'

Olivia appears next to me, craning her neck to get a better view.

'This place is a little goldmine, isn't it? I had no idea what was here, did you?'

'No. I doubt anyone who hasn't been inside and taken a good around would believe it.'

'It just goes to show that you can't always judge a book by its cover.' I can't help but smile at her words. She's certainly got a point.

18.

A Revelation

After reading aloud the words in Richard's card, Mum flashes me an awkward look. I glance at Guy's image on the screen in front of me and turn the card for them both to see. He looks stunned and Mum looks shell-shocked.

'Every family has their secrets, Mum, but we're all adults here. You need to tell us what this is about.'

Mum sucks in a deep breath, collapsing back against the cushions on the sofa. Her body language reflects her unease, but she says nothing.

I glance at Guy, and he looks back at me, guiltily. 'You knew about this?' I challenge him accusingly.

Seeing their images side by side on the screen, they have both averted their gaze.

'Richard was in love with you from the very start and you knew that? Did Dad know?'

It's beginning to look like the sofa is swallowing Mum up as she sinks even further back into it. I'd laugh if I wasn't so distraught.

'It's a long story,' Mum mutters, looking flustered.

'I bet,' I retort, mortified. 'Why ask him to be our godfather, in that case?'

'So that he wouldn't feel alone?' Mum frames it as a

question and I can see a sadness reflected in her eyes that makes my stomach begin to churn.

'Marci, calm down and cut Mum a little slack.' Guy glares at me and I take a deep breath, trying to still my nerves. 'Go on, Mum, when you're ready. No one is here to judge.'

She tilts her head for a moment to gaze up at the ceiling, as if her thoughts are taking her back in time.

'My best friend suggested we try a new restaurant that had just opened in the heart of Stroud. Naturally, when we arrived, they were fully booked, but the handsome young waiter was very helpful. There were two seats spare on a table of four. As it turned out, your dad and Richard were delighted to have some company and we had a lovely evening. But when we arranged to meet up for a drink together a few nights later, I realised that Richard wasn't really interested in my friend, Beth. But the moment he saw the way your dad and I were together he left the two of us to get to know each other a little better. Richard never said anything at the time, of course, but his initial look of disappointment was obvious to me. They were best mates all through school, and I certainly wasn't going to edge Richard out of your dad's life, as he's such a lovely man.'

That's the last thing I was expecting to hear.

'Richard was best man at the wedding, and then our godfather. Didn't Dad feel that was a bit . . . weird?'

Mum looks directly at me this time. 'No, of course not. It might have ruined their friendship if your dad had realised. Richard never said a word out of place in all that time. Yes, I had my suspicions, but I respected him for his silence.'

The pieces begin to slot together in my head. When Dad died, Richard was already in Positano and that's why Mum didn't reach out to him. It would have been too awkward.

'You should have said something,' I state, firmly.

'Why? Richard regards you both as his family, as you do with him. That man doesn't have a bad bone in his body! He's never been waiting in the wings to swoop in for me, this is all in the past and he loves us all in a very different way.'

The passion in Mum's voice as she speaks is enough to stop me in my tracks. 'And you knew about this all along, Guy?'

'No, Marci. But one day I caught Richard looking at Mum and put two and two together. I didn't feel it was any of my business.'

And judging by his tone now, he doesn't feel that it's any of my business, either, but seeing it in black and white shocked me to my core.

'I knew from the start that Richard and I weren't right for each other, Marci. There was absolutely no doubt about it,' Mum says, softly. 'We'd have driven each other mad. Now your father – well, it was obvious that he was the one for me as soon as our eyes met across that table. When you know, you know – trust me.' I do trust her, and I live in hope that one day it will happen to me too. But this is different.

'Don't you think that Dad deserved to be told how Richard felt – I mean, it doesn't feel right that he was kept in the dark, Mum,' I remark, tentatively.

She lowers her chin to her chest. 'In hindsight I can

appreciate why you think that it was wrong of me, but while I've never been in love with Richard, he has always been a big part of our family. And he was my listening ear at times when I was worried about your dad overdoing it, and at the peak of our financial worries. Your dad and I went through some rocky times with the business after Richard moved to Positano. But there are things I could say to Richard, that I couldn't to anyone else and I rang him often. He kept me on an even keel so that I could support your dad. It was never anything more than that, Marci – believe me.'

Her words are heartfelt, and Guy's right, it's not my place to judge. But I suddenly feel a little disloyal to Dad, for some reason.

'Well,' Guy jumps in, his voice firm, 'I can't see what good it would have done anyway, if you want my opinion. Richard never was a threat, Marci. You know that. He's a gentleman first and foremost. Dad was like a brother to him, and Richard was a good influence on us, wasn't he? I have no quibbles now it's finally out in the open and you need to let this go.'

They both stare back at me from the screen. How will I push all thoughts of this out of my head next time I speak to Richard? I wonder.

'It was just a surprise seeing your name on the envelope, Mum, that's all. I wish I hadn't looked, now. I'll slide it back in among the growing pile of Richard's personal things.' Let's just hope I don't find any more unexpected revelations. Of all the people I know, Richard is the last person I'd think about when it comes to having secrets – buried treasure, yes, but buried secrets, no. 'Thanks for your honesty, Mum. And I'm sorry for blurting it out, but—'

'—Richard helped you get over your loss when Dad died and now you feel that might have been a betrayal, but it wasn't, Marci. There was nothing to betray, in fact it's what Dad would have expected his best friend to do – to comfort his grieving daughter.'

On that tearful note I make an excuse to end the call, saying we'll catch up again soon. I'm upset, I can't deny that, and I can't face going downstairs to eat, so I ring reception. Viola answers and I ask if I can have whatever is tonight's special on a tray in my room as I have a lot of work to do.

Thankfully, fifteen minutes later it's Dario who turns up at my door – if it had been Nico, I would have ended up crying on his shoulder. Is Mum right and if Dad had known how Richard felt, would he have understood?

A while later, Nico texts me, checking that I'm all right and asks if I'd like some company. I can tell he's hopeful, but I need a little time to myself.

A new day dawns and after sleeping on it, I realise I overreacted a little yesterday. If there was anything going on between Richard and Mum, then she wouldn't have married David, I assure myself. Instead, Richard would have returned to the UK to comfort her, but he didn't and that tells me all I need to know. It's my fault for reading something that wasn't meant for my eyes. That's a lesson to remember for the future.

However, I'm in no mood to talk to anyone right now

and I sneak out quietly and head up to La Grotta. I text Nico to say sorry for being a bore last night but I had a bit of a headache – which is true – and that I'm starting early, but will catch up with him this evening. I don't want him to think that this has anything to do with us sleeping together because the timing is unfortunate.

As I unlock the front door to La Grotta and step inside, I don't know what I'm looking for – but I can sense that there's something I've yet to discover. I can't help wondering why Richard wanted me here and not Guy. Didn't he know there were things that might pass before me that would be a little unsettling, to say the least? Guy, I'm sure, would simply have employed a couple of people to pack everything up, and spent his time getting the valuations pinned down. Perhaps that confirms Richard has nothing to hide. Did he think I'd twigged that Mum was the mystery woman who broke his heart and he wanted to prove he had nothing to hide?

'Right – let's see what today throws up,' I mumble to myself.

It's really stuffy in here this morning, so I prop open the door for a few minutes. As I make my way to the rear of the shop, an unsettling thought pops into my head – am I simply trying to distract myself from getting too close to Nico? Even when I'm head down working, I find myself suddenly thinking about him and I can clearly see his face smiling back at me playfully. *It's called having fun, Marci*, that inner voice confirms. I guess it's been a while for me and I'm nervous. What if I'm not one of those people who can simply jump into a casual relationship, without having a glimmer of hope that it could lead somewhere?

Desperate to halt this train of thought, I head straight to the crate conveniently hidden away out of sight behind the impressive armoire.

The lid is still ajar, and I lift it off, careful not to hit the expensive piece of furniture which is irreplaceable. It's a specialist crate made to transport half a dozen paintings, each sitting within a groove with guide rails at both the top and the bottom. Unfortunately, it makes it difficult to grasp one of the canvases, especially given the tight space I'm in. Just as I'm about to give up, my fingers manage to find a lip and I gingerly ease one of them out. Resting it on the top of the crate and leaning it carefully up against the wall, my first impression is that it's very well executed, although I can't see a signature. There's no room to turn it around to check the back, unfortunately. The colours are muted blues with an orange ball of light reflected on water, as the sun begins to rise above the horizon. The sky above is brushed almost wildly with a pale orange glow. I slip out my phone and take a quick photo, wondering if this is an undiscovered artist. Guy will be having his breakfast about now and I'm curious to get his initial reaction. This looks special to me. I have some knowledge about modern art, as one of my clients is always on the lookout for interesting pieces by unknown artists, but Guy is an expert in this field. I point out that it's unsigned, as I know that will spark his interest.

Suddenly there's a loud bang as the front door slams shut, making me jump. When I go to check, it's obvious that a breeze has sprung up, but something isn't right.

I'm sure I propped it open with the first thing that came to hand . . . what was it? I even open the door to check that whatever it was isn't lying on the porch, but there's nothing in plain sight.

Stepping back inside I turn the key and scan around. Nothing has been disturbed and I rack my brains to think what on earth it was that I picked up. Perhaps I was so preoccupied, I meant to find something and got distracted.

'You're losing the plot, Marci,' I say out loud, as I return to put the canvas back into the crate.

As interesting as it is to poke around the antiques, the reason I'm here so early this morning is to head up to the office. The next time that Richard calls me I will ask him outright if there's anything he'd prefer me not to see, but until then if I stumble across anything else . . . well, that's hardly my fault.

There's a gentle tap on the front door and my heart begins to beat a little faster. It takes me a couple of minutes to extricate myself and head back into the sales area. Hurrying forward it's a huge relief when I see Nico peering at me through the glass.

'Another skipped breakfast,' he grins, as he steps inside. 'What's wrong? You look like you've seen a ghost!'

'Do I? It's just the wind – I had the door open for a bit and it slammed shut, which put me on edge.'

'It is a little windy out there this morning. I'm not here to stop you but I have a couple of hours off and thought you'd appreciate some company before Olivia arrives.' He slips off his backpack and pulls out a container.

'I have brioche, *fette biscottate* and some fruit.'

'Wonderful, then I'll make the coffee.' I smile at him gratefully and he leans in to softly kiss my lips. We linger for a few seconds, and a little buzz courses through me like an electrical charge.

'Let's sit in the courtyard,' I mutter a little breathlessly, as I reluctantly pull away.

Isn't it funny how once that invisible line between two people has been crossed you instantly become aware of each other's presence in a completely new way? I notice the hairs on Nico's arms are a pale golden colour against the bronze of his skin. And the way he arches his back when it begins to stiffen, as he works through yet another stack of auction catalogues. Every now and again, he sifts out something totally unrelated and places it into one of the boxes in front of us, most of which are now full and need sealing up.

As I'm wading through yet another stack of receipts and separating them into different years, a question pops into my head. Nico said Richard told him about his first love and I wonder if he said anything else on the subject.

'Richard must have been a little lonely when he first arrived here,' I observe, watching out of the corner of my eye for Nico's reaction.

'Probably, although he's the sort of man who can easily strike up a conversation with anyone. His Italian was good, so that made it easier for him but when you consider that he started his business from scratch, he was constantly working.'

'It's a pity it took him so long to find Angel, but he never mentioned any significant friendships along the way. It's kind of sad, really.' I'm fishing and I know I shouldn't, but I can't help myself. I know Richard talked about me and Guy to just about everyone in his Italian family, but did he ever talk about Mum? I wonder.

'I suppose that if you compare everyone you meet to your first love, your expectations might be unrealistic. It's hard for me to understand why he couldn't just get over it and move on.'

Nico doesn't know anything, then, and I'm glad about that.

'And yet he seems to have instantly fallen in love with Angel,' I point out.

Nico hands me a few sheets of folded paper and some more loose photographs. 'You might want to check these before they go into the personal box. As for Angel, I think their paths crossed at the right moment. La Grotta wasn't always in disarray, but I think Richard's interest has been waning for a while.'

'That's something that hadn't occurred to me. I really hope their bubble doesn't burst, though. Love can be a rollercoaster ride.' It would devastate Richard if all of this was for nothing.

'No doubt they're happy to live each day as it comes and that's a wonderful position to be in after a lifetime of hard work.' Nico pauses for a moment. 'I missed you last night.' His voice is low as he glances across at me cagily.

'Sorry, I was exhausted. I think the heat got to me, too. It's much cooler today.'

'I think we might even get a little rain later on,' Nico replies, raising his eyebrows.

'Rain? Really?' I remark, playfully, as I glance down at his hands and what look like some old bank statements.

'More bits and pieces.' He hands me the little pile held together with a large silver paperclip, this time. 'I see you ventured into the rear of the cave. Is it as bad as you thought?'

'It's packed solid and there are some monster pieces of furniture that will require specialist packing by the removal men when they're here. There's a wonderful old wine cage in there – have you seen it?'

'No. Is it very grand?'

'I love it, although it's French and not that old – early twentieth century, maybe. But it has a rustic charm to it.' There's a loud rap on the door. 'It's probably Olivia.' I jump up. 'Don't feel you have to stay, Nico. You have a long day ahead of you but I'm grateful for what you've done, yet again.'

I leave Nico to get his things together and, for some silly reason, I quickly pop in to check Richard's bedroom and then the bathroom. I'm still feeling a little on edge after the door incident, but everything is fine – of course it is! I silently berate myself as I hurry downstairs, conscious that I'm keeping Olivia waiting.

A few minutes later Nico joins us. Olivia heads straight over to him and they kiss and embrace.

'I'm on countdown,' she grins at him. 'My man is coming home, and I can't wait. But what are you doing here this early?'

'Breakfast delivery and then I got roped in again. Oh,

and where's that wine cage, Marci? I'd love to have a quick look at it, before I go.'

They both follow me through to the back room and we walk in single file, weaving in and out. The moment Nico spots it, I can see he's impressed.

'That's every restaurant owner's dream. I bet it will fetch quite a bit and the wine, too. Some lucky connoisseur will snap that up at auction. It puts our stainless-steel racking in the cool room to shame. Anyway, I'd better leave you to it. *Buona giornata*, ladies.'

And with that he's gone – no kiss goodbye for me, obviously, but this was a nice little bonus to start my day and I'm not complaining.

'You two look so good together,' Olivia says, wistfully. 'It's such a shame you're only here for a short while.'

Before she has a chance to go any further, I grab the nearest thing that will fit in two hands and hold it out to her. 'How do you fancy having a go at wrapping this?'

It's a vintage Capodimonte vase with a moulded rose on the front. Olivia takes it from me as if I'm handing her the crown jewels. 'I'll have a go, but I want you to double-check it afterwards.'

'Just make sure the rose is well protected and I know you'll do a great job of it.'

It's probably nowhere near as valuable as Olivia thinks it is, but at least she now has something to occupy her mind, aside from Nico and me. Anyway, I'm eager to get back upstairs because the small clip of papers that Nico handed over looked interesting. But when I return to the office, I can't seem to put my hand on it. There are so many piles everywhere that it's time to tape up the full boxes and make up some more. Those papers will turn up at some point.

The phone in my pocket begins to buzz, and I grab it, delighted to see that it's Guy.

'Good morning. I wasn't expecting a call.'

'Hmm . . . you send me a photo of what is obviously an unsigned copy of one of Monet's paintings and you didn't think I'd be curious about it?'

I open my mouth to speak, but nothing comes out and I quickly assemble my thoughts. 'The style was what caught my attention, but without looking it up on the internet I can't say I can recall it from memory. Are you sure it's an exact copy? Richard's skill as a painter isn't that good, surely?'

'Of course I'm sure and it's a pretty good copy, too. It's Le Havre, the port. Monet's main residence was close by. At least there's no signature – if there were, we'd be in trouble,' he scoffs.

'But even if it's not one of Richard's, he would have known it was just a copy and can't be sold.'

'Is there anything written on the back of the canvas?'

'I can't tell as it's buried and there's no room for me to safely get it out so I can turn it around.'

'I'm probably right. You've uploaded photos of three different paintings, but they're all signed and by lesser known, albeit popular artists. I'm sure when I get to see them up close, they will turn out to be originals.'

'It is curious, though. There are several others in the same crate, as if he was getting them ready to ship. Unfortunately,

I can't access the others until a couple of really solid items of furniture are moved out of the way first. It's all too heavy for Olivia and me to manage and I'll need to organise some assistance.'

'If you're going to speak to Richard, then I strongly suggest that you don't mention Mum, or what we discussed. It's in the past, Marci, and there's no point raking it up. I believe what Mum said,' Guy states, firmly. 'Judging by the look on your face at the time, I know you – a part of you will want to hear it direct from Richard, but you must let it go. If anything had happened between the two of them, don't you think it would have come out way before now?'

It's beyond annoying when Guy can still prod my conscience like this. Being the elder, he was my protector at school and there were times when I was very grateful, but there have been times when he ratted on me to Mum and Dad. I remember yelling at him once that it was my right to make mistakes without him constantly pulling me up for it. We were walking home from school together and his words have always stuck with me.

'And it's my job to keep an eye on you. Your trouble, Marci, is that half of the time your head is in the clouds, and the other half is spent analysing every little detail. You can't have it both ways, you need to be more like me – in the middle. And if you think I'm going to let that shifty-looking kid follow you home, then think again.'

At the time, I was only eight years old, and Guy was thirteen going on thirty, or so it felt to me. Later in life I blamed him for making me look at every guy who talked to me with suspicion. Until the day when Mum happened to mention the fact that Dad had once told Guy that it was his job to look after his little sister. It was then that I felt sorry for Guy, because there must have been times when keeping an eye out for me was a pain, to say the least.

'You're right and I know it. Thanks, Guy. It benefits no one and changes nothing, does it?'

He gives a disparaging grunt. 'If Richard thought for one moment that it would affect how we felt about him, he would have told us himself well before now.'

There's no point arguing when I'm in total agreement. Besides, I know that Mum was truly heartbroken when Dad died. The only thing that I can't get over is that she then went on to marry David. I mean, he's nothing at all like Dad. And that never made any sense to me. How can Mum love two men who are so completely different? And Richard – well, his heart is in the right place and the connection that Guy and I have with him is special. But when I think of David, for me there's . . . nothing, no connection at all. And that isn't solely down to me.

19.

Sometimes Things Just . . . Happen

'I told you we'd get a shower before the day was out,' Nico leans forward to light the candle as the gentle rain falls almost imperceptibly around us. The irony is, it's strangely comforting and reminiscent of home.

'I can almost hear the garden letting out a sigh of relief as it soaks up the raindrops,' I declare, and Nico gives me a strangely wistful smile. 'What?'

'We do worry about the lack of rain during prolonged dry spells, but I've never heard anyone celebrate the fact that nature, too, feels a sense of relief.'

'One of the many differences between us, then,' I observe.

'And what else have you discovered since you've been here?' Nico enquires, his eyes full of laughter as he uncovers the platter Luca left for our late-night supper.

'That Italian people take the world at a more leisurely pace. They seem to be able to relax more readily – whether that's sitting down to enjoy a coffee, chill with friends, or simply enjoy their surroundings. Admittedly, it's much easier to do that when the weather is so delightful.'

'We call it: *il dolce far niente*,' he informs me.

'Which means?'

'Literally speaking, it's sweet to do nothing. When we

eat, it's all about the food and the wine. A meal is a relaxing thing, and we don't like to be hurried.'

I had noticed and I love that Nico says *we* when he talks about Italian people.

'How do you usually unwind when you aren't spending your spare time looking out for a stranger as a favour to a good friend?'

He bursts out laughing. 'You make it sound like it's a duty. It's not. I enjoy your company and I think I've more than made that obvious. And as you seem happy to be here, I'd say it was mutual.'

There's a thin line between banter and flirting, and we're teetering on the edge. 'When in Rome, do as the Romans do . . . or in this case, Positano!'

Nico rolls his eyes at my attempt not to flatter his ego. 'You've dragged me away from zipping around on my Vespa, catching up with friends over a glass of wine or an espresso. Although I do go swimming most afternoons. Sadly, with Jack away it has ruled out our regular boating activities.'

I hadn't given any thought to what Nico does when the restaurant closes around 3 p.m. until it opens again around seven in the evening. I'm not usually here as I'm either up at La Grotta, in my room having a nap, or catching up on phone calls and emails. But on Monday, Nico is in for a surprise, because with Olivia's help, I've managed to hire a luxury boat that she assures me will make his eyes light up. Richard will be over the moon when I send him a picture of it, as I think it's exactly what he had in mind. Normally, the hire includes a captain, but as the company know Nico personally, it was simply a case of paying a little extra for insurance so he could take the wheel.

'Italians have a way of doing things that seem stylishly casual,' I reflect. 'And they do everything with such easy grace. Yes, the roads are crazily busy, and they all seem to drive very fast, but it isn't as intense as it feels in the UK. We have lots of scooters, mopeds and bikes, but it's different. Certainly, it's a lot less glamorous in the rain and the cold, that's for sure. What do we have tonight?'

I lean forward as Nico uncovers the platter. It's the first evening we've had to cover everything up to carry the food outside, but there was no hesitation on either part. Under cover of the pergola, with its mass of vines and greenery, it's totally dry and the smell of the rain on the dry earth and the plants is truly wonderful. It's refreshing.

'This dish is tuna tartare with avocado and a citron sauce. Here we have grilled octopus dipped in olive oil with a little cayenne and paprika, and some wonderful anchovies. And, finally, a mixed salad with Emmenthal cheese and pan-fried pancetta. There are some slices of ciabatta to accompany the octopus.'

Nico pours us both a glass of wine and afterwards he stops to show me the label. 'This is one of my favourite local wines: Costa d'Amalfi Tramonti Bianco. Tenuta San Francesco grow their wines on the steep terraced hills in Tramonti, in the heart of the Amalfi Coast. Try it – I bought this specially for us to enjoy tonight.'

Nico passes me a glass and I pretend to know what I'm doing. I swirl it around as I hold it up in the air to inspect it. 'I love the pale-yellow colour.' Then I lift the glass to my nose and breathe in appreciatively. 'Ooh . . . it's both fruity and flowery!' I remark boldly, before taking a sip.

Nico looks delighted. 'Do you get the hint of white peaches and there's that satisfying aftertaste of aromatic herbs – sage and thyme.'

'You're right, but I don't think I could have identified that if you hadn't pointed it out.'

'Most people say it has a slightly mineral taste, for the same reason. I like it because it's both smooth and refreshing. It goes perfectly with fish of any sort. Anyway, you must be starving.'

I am, although Olivia always brings a hearty lunch. But it's just after 11 p.m. and I'd better eat something quickly, as this wine is going to slip down all too easily. In my present company, I think it's wise to keep a clear head.

Leaning on my elbow, so I can gaze down at Nico as he fights to keep his eyes open, I realise the decision I made earlier on that this should not happen again was half-hearted.

'Why are you frowning?' he murmurs in his dreamy state.

'Because it's 3 a.m. and you shouldn't be here. Can you imagine how awful it would be if someone spotted you creeping back to your room?'

Nico stretches out his arms in front of him, his muscles flexing as he groans a little. 'What business is it of anyone's, Marci?'

I shake my head at him, closing my eyes for the briefest of moments – not because I'm sleepy, but because I feel uncomfortable.

'You know exactly what I mean, but it's easier not to think about it, isn't it?'

Nico rolls onto his side as we continue to make eye contact. 'Is this about Giulia, or about my mum and Luca?'

I sigh, heavily. 'It's about having respect for your whole family, Nico. I'm not happy sneaking around like this. Would they make me feel as welcome and a part of life here, if they knew what was going on between us?'

Nico's expression changes and now he's wide awake. 'I'm expected to take care of you while you're here and there's no reason for anyone to be suspicious. It's not as if we're walking around holding hands and kissing, is it?'

'That might be true but having been welcomed into the fold, my conscience is troubling me. Fun is one thing, sex and fun is another, and that's just the way I am. We can't sleep together at the hotel, Nico, and now you really must get dressed and leave – quietly.'

The problem is that my resolve weakens all too easily when I'm around him, but the risk is simply too great. A look of disappointment flashes over Nico's face but he can see I'm serious as he reluctantly slides out from under the sheet.

'What if I don't stay so long next time?' he asks, as he dresses.

I stare at his bare back, watching the way his torso moves and wanting so much to reach out and feel the warmth of his skin beneath my fingers again. 'That's not the answer,' I reply firmly, as I make myself look away.

'What about when we're alone together at La Grotta?' He half-turns to look at me.

This isn't just about someone spotting him leaving my room, but if we continue like this it's going to be even tougher when it's time to say goodbye and where do we draw the line? Will the odd night here and there turn into every night?

The look in his eyes makes my stomach flutter. When I leave at the end of July, will I regret the moments we didn't spend together locked in each other's arms? Or will I be glad I slowed things down a little when I did, because I saved myself from a potential sense of . . . loss. Knowing this can only be a transient thing between us is easily said, but what if there is a bigger price to pay?

'Nico, I'm a guest here and the last thing I want to do is to upset anyone. Can you see how that places me in a very difficult position?'

He sighs, then turns around to find his shoes. 'I understand and I will respect your wishes. I promise.'

I slip out of bed and into my knee-length silk robe. Nico is standing in front of the doors leading out onto the balcony and I walk over to glance out.

'This isn't easy for me, Nico – you can see that. But I'd end up hating myself if I leave behind a trail of unhappiness because we get discovered.'

His answer is to lean forward and brush his lips gently against mine, before reaching down to clasp my hand.

'This is magical to me, being here in Positano,' I murmur. 'But it's not real life as I know it and it's also not a holiday. It has become something in between and I'm not sure I can cope with that if we don't put on the brakes a little.'

'I'll obey the rules if you promise in return that this won't affect things between us for what time we have left. I can still spend time with you at La Grotta?'

'Of course,' I reply, brightly.

'And you're still up for Monday with Olivia and Jack?'

'Yes, I'm looking forward to meeting him at long last.'

For a few seconds we stand together looking out at a starless sky, the clouds masking everything and making the sea look dark and soulless tonight. Only the twinkling lights from the terraces of homes nestled on the steep limestone cliffs to our right are a distraction. We instinctively turn to face each other, and it is with regret that we part. Nico says nothing but places a finger on his lips and smiles, gently. His eyes search mine and I wish I could pretend that he isn't leaving me standing here, my body aching to be with him but knowing this must be the last time we sleep together under this roof.

'Marci, my dear – how are you?' Richard's voice booms down the line and I sit back on my heels, grateful to take a break.

Sweeping the hair back from my face, I stand and walk over to the window. Today it's open wide and the breeze is welcoming. It is a little fresher after last night's rain and as I look down onto the courtyard garden, everything seems to be a little more radiant this morning – except me. And I'm feeling jaded.

'I'm good, Richard. I'm standing in your office as we speak.'

'Oh dear, then I'm probably not your favourite godfather,' he chuckles.

'You're my only godfather, Richard, so you know I'll forgive you. But I'm glad you called. I found another crate of paintings downstairs in the back room. Are they . . . uh . . . for sale?'

The pause is ominous. 'Oh. Hmm . . . I forgot about them.' I note once again how forgetful Richard has become, between the paintings and the silver. That sense of unease begins to stir in the pit of my stomach again. 'No, they're not for sale, either. I meant to get that sorted before I left. If you can nail up the crate and ask Guy to store them with my personal collection, that would be marvellous.'

Do I mention what Guy said?

'He'll be disappointed, as he was hoping to have a few more pieces to put into a separate fine arts sale he has planned in November.' I don't feel comfortable, now, admitting that I looked inside.

'I'm sorry but, no, they definitely aren't for sale. There isn't anything of value, but they're pieces I might put up on display once Angel and I get settled.'

I'd better warn Guy not to say anything, then.

'Does that mean Mum has found you and Angel a place in the UK?' I enquire, surprised at his response.

'A little place in Gloucestershire, yes, and Angel is very excited about it. But we're off to Australia very soon and I'm not sure how long we'll be there.'

Australia? 'Gosh, that's unexpected.'

'Angel has family there and we'll be doing some sightseeing as well.'

'Wonderful. Um . . . I have a big stack of post here for you and now that I'm beginning to pack up the paperwork in your office, I thought it was best to check that there isn't anything that's likely to be particularly sensitive?'

'Why, what have you found?' Oh, that's Richard's serious voice.

'Nothing, but you said it would need some sorting and I wanted to check what exactly you wanted me to sort?'

'It's a ghastly mess I've left you with, Marci, I know that. It's worse because I did start pulling things out before I became distracted. You'll find a small wooden trunk with a padlock on it. It's a French apothecary's medicine chest. It contains most of my private documents. If you come across any photos I pulled out and didn't put back, and other personal bits and pieces, I'd be very grateful if you could pop them back inside. The key is taped to the underside of the top drawer of the desk. If you could keep that safe for me, I'd rather not have to end up prising open the lock at some point in the future if it goes astray.'

That's reassuring. If Richard had anything to hide about Mum, then I'm sure he would have ensured the card and the photos were put straight back into the box. Perhaps he looked through them as a way of letting go, before he began his new life with Angel.

'What about your post?'

'Hmm . . . I don't want to risk having things forwarded on in case it goes astray. Does anything look urgent, or is it all boring stuff?'

'Let me grab the pile, hang on a moment.'

It's quite a sizeable stack now.

'There are quite a few with the same postmark – Harrison & Company Financials.'

'Oh, they're pension fund statements and can be filed away. There's a box on the desktop for those. I get a monthly bank statement for two different accounts and those can be filed, too. What else do you have?'

'About a dozen – some with Italian postmarks, but not all. It looks like they're from various antiques dealers and a few that could be circulars.'

'Throw them in the bin. My days of hoarding are over. Anything else?'

'A couple of what looks like cards from the UK, probably congratulating you and your new bride.'

'I made a point of telling everyone we were off on our travels, and we'd have a party when we fly back to the UK, but it's kind of them.'

Hmm . . . I note that there's no mention of a party in Italy.

'Oh,' I exclaim, glancing at the next envelope in the pile. 'There's one here addressed to you, but marked for the attention of Luca!'

'Ah, that's business-related – if you would be so good as to hand it to him in person, and not Celia, that would be much appreciated, Marci. He's expecting it and it's just some outstanding paperwork that needed tidying up.'

I'm a little surprised, to say the least. 'Of course. It would be difficult for them if you wanted to end your partnership,' I venture, thinking that's a fair enough comment to make.

'Ah, yes, my involvement in the business . . .' There's an awkward pause before he continues. 'There's nothing to worry about on that score, my dear – I can assure you.

I'm sure my days spent basking in the Italian sunshine are not over and visits will be even more enjoyable with Angel by my side. However, Angel's heart is set on a place in the UK, which I'm extremely happy about naturally. Once things are sorted in the UK, it won't be long before we visit Positano again. After all, it's where we met and fell in love, which means it's a special place for us both. I think Angel feels the draw too, so who knows what might happen in the not-too-distant future? But I want to know that my wife isn't just going along with what I want because of my business interests. Luca doesn't need my input anyway, although I can take credit for the carefully selected, yet affordable wine list.' Richard chuckles to himself and I can't help smiling. Ah – what an old romantic he is and that's encouraging news, because I think he might be right.

'Of course, Richard. But it's something that needed saying now that I'm aware of it. Positano is a very special place indeed and you're missed more than you know.'

'It has a charm, doesn't it, Marci, as do the people. You can tell them that my wife and I will be back before too long. Anyway, enough about me – I promised you a summer you wouldn't forget, and I hope it delivers. And have you managed to arrange that boat trip, yet?'

'On Monday. It will come as a total surprise to Nico, but we're spending the day with Olivia and Jack onboard a very chic-looking *gozzo* boat. And we'll be toasting your generosity!'

'Marvellous – and an excellent choice! It will be made by a local company – Fratelli Aprea. They still build their crafts according to *sorrentino* artisan traditions, but today's models are luxurious. I wish I could be there to see Nico and Jack's faces on the day. And, while I remember, do make sure you get plenty of fresh air. I don't want you spending all your time inside La Grotta, even if there is a tantalising new discovery to keep you occupied everywhere you look. If you don't fly home with a tan that everyone will envy, it will be an opportunity missed. A big hug, Marci – how would I manage without you in my life?'

As the line disconnects, I can't help feeling a little confused. Flipping over the envelope marked *Alla cortese attenzione del Signor Luca Romano*, I compare it to one from the pile Richard said were bank statements to be filed. A little shiver begins to creep down my spine – the return address on the back is the same. I appreciate that the hotel and restaurant employ a lot of people, but business looks brisk. And if Luca has reached out to Richard for a cash injection . . . well, Celia runs everything except the kitchen and she's the one balancing the books. Now that is a little odd.

I don't suppose Richard and Luca have another business on the side? One that Celia and Nico aren't aware of, to bring in some extra cash? Who knows . . . ? At this point nothing would surprise me.

20.
La Bella Vita

Jack steps forward and it's clear that he's homing in to greet me as if we're old friends. He's every bit as handsome and charming as I expected. With sandy-coloured hair, he's a little shorter than Nico. The full beard is a surprise, but it suits him.

'I feel as if I already know you,' he smiles at me. 'And you've kept Olivia busy, which is good, because it means she's not constantly texting me.'

Olivia's face is a picture of happiness as she looks lovingly across at her husband. 'I do not. Well, only when I'm missing you.'

'I was expecting someone a little older from what Olivia has been saying, Marci,' Jack responds, giving me a playful wink. He turns to give Nico a man hug and then a fist pump.

Olivia gasps. 'I said Marci is an experienced antiques *expert*, not an antique,' she groans. 'I'm sorry, Marci – he often switches off when I'm talking to him. Besides, he should have known better as Richard always referred to you as his English rose.'

'I try my best, but Olivia talks non-stop,' Jack says, shrugging his shoulders. 'I'm sure you're well aware of that by now, Marci, but I bet the two of you have had some fun.'

'We have and I couldn't manage without her,' I reply. 'We're hoping both you and Nico will enjoy the little surprise we've arranged for today, eh, Olivia?'

Jack bursts out laughing as Olivia waggles her finger in the air, mischievously.

'Are you two ladies going to share the details of this little plan of yours?' Nico enquires, as he glances across at Jack a tad nervously. Maybe they think we're going sightseeing or shopping, and I doubt that either of those options would be high up on their preferred list of ways to spend a day off work.

'Oh, it's not really down to me. I was just the middleman,' Olivia states, looking for me to explain what's going on.

'It's Richard's treat, really – he's footing the bill for today.' I'm conscious that Nico has moved closer to me, but there's an awkwardness between us now. Ever since our frank exchange in the early hours of Thursday morning, we've both struggled to find the right balance. We've had our usual suppers together each evening in the garden, but afterwards we walk down to the beach to while away some time. I'm sure we've both been thinking about what else we might have been doing, but Nico has been true to his word.

'If everyone has their beach gear packed, we'd better set off.' I glance at my watch, conscious of the time.

'It's not a coastal walk then, if we're taking swimming costumes and beach shoes are in order?' Nico turns to look at me, his eyebrows knitting together.

'No. Trust me, you're going to love this surprise.'

'And we don't need to take anything with us – drinks in a cool box, for example?' Jack enquires, but Olivia shakes her head.

'Everything has been taken care of, guys, so you can relax. And Mum's here to look after Luna, so we don't need to rush back.'

'Can we at least book a table at Ristorante Sul Mare then, so that we can spend the evening catching up with everyone?' Jack looks across at Nico, an artful expression on his face as he tries to suss out our plan.

'No, that won't be necessary,' Olivia interjects, giving Jack a pointed stare.

Hopefully, they think we're going to have a bit of a party on the beach and that other people will be wandering along to join us throughout the day.

'Okay – let's go, then,' I chivvy them, as we're going to be late at the meeting point if we don't leave immediately.

Luna whimpers, sensing that we're about to leave and Olivia's mum appears to bid us goodbye. 'She'll be fine. I'll take her for a walk, shortly. You enjoy yourselves and don't rush back on my account. If it's very late, then Papa will join me and we'll stay over.'

Olivia places her arms around her mum, giving her a grateful hug. Jack begins fussing over Luna, and as Olivia and I walk past them I notice that he's talking to her in Italian and she's loving it. Living and working in Italy, and with an Italian father-in-law, Jack slips seamlessly between Italian and English.

Animals must wonder what's happening when one of their owners is away for long periods of time, I reflect. It must be confusing for her and she probably misses Jack almost as much as Olivia does.

'If you guys can each carry one of the beach bags, that would be very gentlemanly,' Olivia calls over her shoulder. We grab our backpacks and I follow her along the path at the side of the house and out through the gate.

It's a much shorter walk down to the beach from Olivia and Jack's villa than I thought. The property isn't as high up as Il Posto di Luca, situated on the adjacent limestone cliff.

'It's a steeper route towards the end,' Olivia warns me, 'but it's the walk back that is the real workout.'

'Hey, wait for me!' Jack calls out, but Olivia is more intent on checking her watch. We don't want to be late, and I give her a nod to step up the pace.

The landing stage is at the end of the magnificent beach and there is usually a collection of smart boats anchored up close by. The water taxis tend to use the pier, I've noticed. I can only hope the boat we've hired doesn't disappoint. The photos in the email made it look amazing.

'It's going to be busy,' Nico points out. 'We could always take the path to Spiaggia di Fornillo, instead – the beach there is a lot quieter.'

He's probably right, if we were merely sunbathing, as tourists tend to head straight for Spiaggia Grande. With line after line of sunbeds and umbrellas for hire, it gets packed. I suppose if you're just lying in the sun, either your eyes are closed, you're reading, or people watching – so what does it matter how many people are around you, as long as you are comfortable and can enjoy that amazing view? Everything you need is a short walk away anyway, with a variety of eateries and places to grab a cold drink to accommodate all budgets and preferences.

'Just keep walking, guys.' Olivia casts me a sly glance and I try hard not to laugh. From the stuffed beach bags, it does rather look like we're going to spend the day sunbathing.

Olivia is right, there are several long runs of incredibly steep steps and by the time we get down to the beach it's a welcome sight.

Nico and Jack go on ahead of us, instinctively drawn to check out the boats first and several people wave to them as they walk past. Trudging along behind, we slow our pace a little, as if this isn't the direction in which we need to be heading.

Taking a moment to gaze around, I still feel like pinching myself as the setting is so unique. It's like stepping into someone else's life, certainly not mine. And yet I'm a part of it and not just a tourist. I am lucky to have this experience and it's time to switch off and simply enjoy myself.

Thankfully, there's hardly any breeze at all today, which is just as well given that both Olivia and I are wearing floppy hats. When I told her I didn't have anything suitable to keep the sun off my head, she disappeared and came back with a choice of three. Wearing a flowery strapless dress with an elasticated top that flows gently out over my hips down to mid-calf level, I feel summery and cool. And colourful, in pale blues and greens.

'Here, you'll need one of these hat pins – just to cope with the sudden gusts when we get on the boat. Are you all right?' Olivia asks, sensing my reverie.

'I'm just tired,' I reply, taking one from her as we amble along, side by side.

'Well, hopefully we'll have a few relaxing hours onboard and you'll get your first breathtaking view of the Amalfi coastline!'

The guys are already at the landing stage, and it looks like they've just sussed out what's happening. Nico and Jack are laughing, as a very dashing young man in shorts and wearing a T-shirt sporting a company logo, hands something to Nico. Nico immediately turns to look at us as we get closer, holding up an envelope and his face is sporting the biggest grin ever.

'You did this?' he calls out as we step off the gritty sand and onto the landing stage.

'It was Richard's idea. A way of paying you back for helping me at La Grotta.'

Nico takes a step forward, opening his arms as if he's going to hug me and then he stops short, slightly embarrassed.

'I'll text him to give my grateful thanks. He knows what a thrill it is to get behind the wheel of *La Fortuna* – it's a dream come true for me. And thank you, Pietro, I'm truly honoured that you're allowing me to take her wheel.'

Nico waves the envelope in front of him, which I assume contains the insurance document.

'Only you, Nico – or Jack, of course! And I get to spend some time on the beach for a change,' Pietro replies.

I guess that he's in great demand throughout the busy summer period and he certainly looks like he intends to make the most of his day on the beach. Olivia explained that it's unusual for the company to hire out *La Fortuna* without one of their captains, but Pietro and his father, who own the company, are long-time friends. They know this very expensive boat is in safe hands.

'Your lunch is onboard, as requested, ladies.' Pietro turns to me and Olivia, giving us a charming smile.

Nico is trying to catch my attention. I leave Pietro and Olivia to chat, as I walk towards him. Jack, I notice, is already checking out the boat.

'Richard didn't need to do this, you know,' Nico half-whispers as he leans in to me. 'It's a pleasure to . . . I mean, uh, I'm enjoying having something different to do.'

He scuffs his foot along the surface of the ground, the toe of his beach shoe making a swirl in the fine layer of gritty sand.

'Richard insisted and you deserve it.'

'It's a lot better than Jack's little boat, which would have been a bit of a squash for the four of us. I've been longing to take you on a cruise along the coast, there just hasn't been an opportunity, has there? Anyway, let me help you climb aboard.'

Nico can't see my eyes, as they're shaded by sunglasses, but I look up at him and study his face for a second before he turns away. It's clear he's overjoyed and what he wants to do is to whisk me up in his arms. It's both ecstasy and agony at the same time.

'Give me your hand.' Jack reaches out to me from the deck of *La Fortuna*, and I can see that he, too, is delighted with the surprise. This isn't going to be simply a nice little sail along the coast, but a taste of the luxurious lifestyle you see in glossy magazines.

Nico hangs back to assist Olivia, as she gives Pietro a parting wave. Jack busies himself carrying our bags over to the small wooden doors that lead below deck.

'What fun!' Olivia sounds as excited as I am, as she joins me. The boat bobs a little and I lose my balance. When I let out an involuntary shriek, she reaches out to catch my arm.

'You haven't found your sea legs yet, come on, let's sit down.'

'Ready when you are, Captain,' Jack confirms, as he casts off.

Pietro is watching; he gives a little salute, and Olivia and I wave to him. This sleek ultra-white boat, sporting a six-inch flash of dark blue painted a few inches below the stout handrails, is without a doubt one of the smartest among those anchored up. To the rear is a large moulded fibreglass hard top giving blissful shade to the seating area and the cockpit. Upholstered in an off-white leather, it feels decadent. I watch as a line of lifebuoys hanging from the handrails either side begin to sway.

'Hold onto your hats, ladies,' Nico calls over his shoulder as Jack makes his way over to stand next to him.

'Talk about boys' toys! Look at the pair of them – Jack will be wanting to upgrade our little *Serpente di Mare*, now. Well, in his dreams!'

As we each sit with a hand firmly securing our headgear, we exchange wide-eyed glances.

'This is such a glamorous boat, Olivia. I'll take some photos to send to Richard – he'll be over the moon! Thank you for sorting it out. I'm grateful to Nico for giving up his spare time because I'm sure his friends are missing him a little.'

Olivia gives me a knowing smile. 'Oh, I don't think he minds,' she retorts.

Nico looks at home sitting in the captain's chair and Jack settles into the wide corner seat on the other side of the cabin doors.

It's another beautiful day and it's going to be a hot one. The fact that we can sit in the shade is a real bonus for me. I love getting a little sun on my skin, but I don't like the sticky feel after slathering on the sun lotion. So, this suits me perfectly.

As the shoreline gets further and further away, the boat begins to rock from side to side and my grip on the rail behind me tightens.

'It's a little choppy until we turn, and then we'll be going with the current and not against it,' Nico confirms.

I'm surprised by how many boats there are and the ferries certainly churn up the water, but all of them are like tiny dots on the massive expanse of mesmerisingly deep-blue water.

'It's a bit scary – I hope I turn out to be a good sailor,' I whisper to Olivia, trying not to grimace.

'You'll be fine,' she replies, confidently. 'We're in good hands. If Nico wasn't in the restaurant business I'm sure he'd spend his life on the water. I can just imagine him taking tourists out for the day, can't you?'

As I gaze at him, all I see is the nicely fitting navy blue T-shirt and the way his arms flex as his hands move the wheel to change direction. He's in his element and totally in control. Watching him literally takes my breath away for the briefest of moments. He looks so happy and relaxed, and my heart skips a beat before I force myself to look away. Something about Nico makes me want to throw caution to the wind and my deepest fear is that I'll end up getting hurt.

'Are we heading to those little islands?' I ask, determined to get myself back under control.

'No, the Li Galli islands are privately owned, but we can moor nearby and swim offshore. The clear water inlets between the three crags are wonderful. They were originally known as the Sirenuse. The legend is that they were the home of the mythical sirens who lured sailors onto the rocks.'

'That doesn't sound very appealing,' I mutter.

'Relax . . . it's time to be a tourist and this is a trip you'll remember forever – I know *I* will.'

A day in paradise with a cloudless sky, and the sea a blue I can't even begin to describe because it keeps changing – from turquoise in places, to areas of an impenetrable indigo. And as for the view looking back at the Amalfi coast, it's a vision I will never forget. The terrain might be difficult and the constant influx of tourists no doubt both a blessing and a trial to the locals, but it's magical. I feel alive. The sun, the sea . . . the glamorous boats . . . this is little old me, Marci. The person who always plays it safe and is happy with her lot. And yet, as I let my surroundings sink in – new friends, new and exciting experiences – suddenly I begin to feel homesick. How crazy is that?

Then I gaze across at Nico. Once again my heart involuntarily skips a beat. Maybe Richard and Olivia are right. When a moment presents itself to step outside your life and take things as they come, it's a gift. And now I'm in deep trouble. What if this is my moment and I don't have the courage to enjoy it to the max?

'You're away from prying eyes, Marci, and I do hope that the two of you feel you can just be yourselves today. It's obvious how close you've become, so there's no point in hiding it on our account.' Olivia gives my arm an affectionate squeeze and I'm both touched and – if I'm honest – a little relieved.

'You seem to have settled in quickly, Marci,' Jack asks as we make our way to the sun deck at the fore of the boat.

'I have, the Romano family has been most welcoming.'

Nico and Olivia are off snorkelling in one of the small inlets leaving the two of us onboard. Even from this vantage point, anchored a short distance away where the water is much deeper, as I look across it's so clear that I wish I were a more confident swimmer.

'And your task is going well?' he asks, as we lay out the large striped beach towels. It's too hot to lie directly on the leather-upholstered pads which sit inside a wide border of decking.

I grimace. 'Without Olivia I think I would have struggled. Not only does she treat every item as if it's a treasure, but we have a good laugh.'

His warm smile is engaging, as we make ourselves comfortable.

'My fascinating wife likes to talk about everything and anything, and I miss that when I'm away.'

'Well, it makes the task a lot more fun! The big problem we have is making enough space to drag even more items out of the cave at the back. It's more than the two of us can manage.'

'Pass me your phone and I'll pop in my number. If you need a couple of burly young men, just text or give me a call. That's an easy problem to solve, as I'm owed a lot of favours being in the IT business.'

He's serious and I ferret around for my phone, panicking a little until I find it wedged between two of the cushions. 'That's extremely kind of you, Jack. It would probably only take an hour or two to straighten things up and it would make it so much easier.'

'I'm surprised that Olivia hasn't mentioned it to me, but she should have done as it's nothing to make a call. Especially given how guilty I feel for being away at a time when she's between projects. Every day that we're not together is one day we'll never get back, isn't it?'

My goodness, for a second or two, my heart constricts as if someone is squeezing it. Jack is right and it touches a nerve because it also applies to me and Nico. Nico isn't as relaxed as he should be today because the truth is that neither of us want to slow things down, as we're both conscious that my time here is speeding by.

'If ever there was a saying to remind us to live in *the now*, that's it, Jack.'

He laughs. 'Oh, I'm full of wisdom but all talk and no action. Just ask my wife. One day I'll find the right job and we'll grab all the quality time we want.'

How sad. 'You're not happy in what you do?'

'Upgrading IT systems is a stressful business. Clients always expect it to be a smooth process, but that's seldom the case. There is a bedding-in period and I need to be on site to troubleshoot the problems. Olivia hates it when I'm away and, to be frank, I'm tired of it now. It's a necessary evil, though.'

Wow. I wasn't expecting such raw honesty from someone I hardly know.

'Is Olivia aware of that fact?'

Jack looks at me, narrowing his eyes.

'Richard was right – he said that you and I would get on. Something about being on the same wavelength. The answer to your question is probably not to the full extent that I'm feeling it now, but it pays the bills. Aren't we all simply chasing the dream that one day we get to do what we really want, instead of what we need to do to get by?'

Now I understand why it was love at first sight between Jack and Olivia. They are both trying to make the best of what is a difficult time because they share the same dream.

'That's truer than I care to admit,' I laugh, but it's tinged with a grim acceptance. 'It came as a bit of a shock to know that Richard seems to have talked to everyone about me. I'm a very private person.'

'My experience of Richard is that he doesn't just prattle on, like many people tend to do. If he tells you something, it's for a reason. He knows I'm feeling frustrated with life – this wasn't where I saw myself, you know, going through the motions. At least with Olivia and me, we aren't connected to a family business. I've seen what it's doing to Nico, and I guess from what Richard told me about his UK family, that might be true for you, too.'

How can I not come clean after that exposé?

'I guess it is. My brother runs the business, but he relies very heavily on me.'

'You're happy, though?'

I turn to face Jack, giving him a rueful smile. 'Most of the time. Family politics aren't easy to navigate when you feel that you're in the middle. Nico and I are on similar paths in some ways. My mum and my brother adore each other but are both stubborn people. I'm the one who steps in to calm them down.'

Jack nods his head, understanding my dilemma. 'You have other, personal commitments back in the UK?' He's choosing his words carefully.

'No. Only two failed relationships and no intention of launching myself into a third until I'm one hundred per cent convinced that I won't get hurt again.'

Goodness, did I really just blurt that out to a complete stranger?

'I see how you and Nico look at each other. He's trying to play it down, but I know him too well. I just wasn't sure where you stood. You do know that Olivia has high hopes for the two of you? She's a natural-born matchmaker, I'm afraid. But please don't tell her I said that, or I'll be in serious trouble.'

It's hard not to chuckle. 'I've tried to explain that it's not simple. I love my life in the UK and while this is all truly wonderful, it's not where I'm supposed to be. My brother, Guy, and my mum would be devastated if I turned my back on them. It was bad enough when Richard upped and left.' I can't share what I now understand to be the reason why. But at least it makes sense. 'And the Romano family are such a tightknit group – how could I upset their plans for the future when Nico is at the very heart of it? He's accepted his fate and so have I.'

'That's three of us who live in the real world and yet my ever-optimistic Olivia believes that dreams can come true.'

'Maybe it's people like Olivia who keep us all sane.'

'Richard was going to get one of his business acquaintances in to clear out La Grotta and then, out of nowhere, Olivia mentioned that his goddaughter was coming over to sort everything out. No doubt her mind went into overdrive. Maybe the two of them put their heads together – I wouldn't put it past them.'

'This conversation is just between us, right?' I query.

'That's a big yes – Olivia would be horrified to hear us discussing this and so would Richard. But the moment I saw Nico's face when you arrived this morning, I knew I had to say something. People who mean well can unwittingly stir up a hornets' nest. You're staying at Il Posto di Luca, in the bosom of the family. Celia dotes on Nico – as does Luca – and you've walked into a situation that is a little sensitive because of the timing.'

At last – someone who understands my caution.

'Now that I know them all, I don't want to upset anyone.'

'Olivia's romantic view of the world is sometimes a little impractical. She wants me to give up work and find something local, saying we can live on her income in the interim. The truth is that we can't because of times like this when a project gets delayed. So, I do what I can for the time being. One day my dream is to make her really happy, but until then it is what it is.'

My eyes are beginning to smart, and I try my best to hide it.

'Is it a little too hot for you, Marci?' Jack checks.

'Yes, it is rather. I'm not really used to lying in the sun.'

'Then let's figure out how to erect the awning over the sun deck. When Olivia and Nico get back it will be time for lunch, and rather pleasant to be able to sit here in the shade to eat. What do you think?' Jack sits up and I follow suit.

'Sounds perfect to me. And thank you, Jack, for your candour. Like it or not, few people are truly free to do whatever they want with no restrictions whatsoever.'

'Don't let it spoil your time here, Marci. None of us know what will happen in the future. But Nico will never leave Positano and, by the sounds of it, you'll never turn your back on the UK. I'm a great believer in fate. Maybe people's paths cross and then they're destined to move on. Olivia can't accept that. She feels very strongly that we each determine our own fate.'

'What's your ultimate dream then?'

'To set up my own IT business and spend every weekend out here on the water. It would eat away at Olivia if she knew just how hard it has become for me to get up each day and motivate myself. I poke fun at her for missing me, but what I'm clinging on to is the fact that the harder I work, the sooner we'll pay off our debts and be financially free. It's the dream and I'm going for it.'

As I reach out to touch Jack's arm, the empathy between

us is tangible. It makes me consider my own fate. In five years' time will I still be valuing dusty antiques to keep up the payments on my mortgage? And constantly stepping in between Mum and Guy as a referee to keep the peace? The last thing I expected to find today was a confidant in Jack. But he's a realist and I respect that – because I am, too.

When I return home, I'm not going to slip back into my old role. They've managed without me and Briony is doing a great job of proving herself. It's time I carved out a role that works for me. I'll always enjoy working with my own list of clients, but as a company we haven't even looked at online advertising and we've only dabbled with social media. I have so many ideas that I'm sure would help to grow the business. Just before I left, I finished writing a detailed report for Guy that would have a big impact on the business. Like Jack, where I am now is just a means to an end, and what better time to set the framework for the future than after a break away? Mum will regard it as a risk, but I now see clearly that I've outgrown my old role and I want to be the one implementing, and steering, the changes.

21.

The Plan – Seriously?

Even with the blue-and-white-striped awning erected over the sun deck, it's way too hot to set out the food in advance. However, bringing the cute matching scatter cushions up from below deck to make the area more comfortable for lounging is a great idea.

As Jack and I are in the tiny galley kitchen pulling out plates, glasses and cutlery, there's a flurry of noise and the boat begins to sway. The sound of laughter filters through to us.

'They're back onboard,' Jack confirms, poking his head out through the double doors and looking towards the rear of the boat. There's what he referred to as an aft platform extending out a couple of feet from the stern – it's perfect for diving off, or a place to sit and put on snorkelling or diving equipment.

'I'll start getting the food out of the ice chest,' I call out.

'They'll probably want to shower first, so if we unwrap everything and lay it out on the table in here, we can cover it over.'

Jack narrowly avoids banging his head as he takes two steps back and turns around. 'I hope there's some wine in this fridge!' He swings open the door. 'Ah – you thought of everything, Marci. It's loaded with small bottles of still water, too – we've almost emptied what's in the cool box up on deck, already. I'm assuming Luca organised the buffet?'

I nod at him, grinning.

Olivia appears, bending low to negotiate the three steps down into the hull of the boat, her wet hair scraped back from her face. It's obvious they enjoyed themselves.

'That was invigorating,' she declares. 'Seriously, Marci – I know you aren't a strong swimmer, but Nico could get the boat a little closer to the beach and it's fun to snorkel in the shallows. You'd love it!'

I screw up my face, not convinced.

'I'm starving.' Nico is a couple of paces behind her. He bends double to step down into the cabin space and it's starting to feel a little cramped in here. I slide onto one of the banquette seats to begin laying out the food.

'Ha!' Nico says, pointing a finger at the stainless-steel ice chest. 'Luca said it was for a luxury cruise and he wouldn't let me help. Now I know why!'

By the time everything is unwrapped and covered with freshly laundered white tea-towels, Jack has popped the cork on a bottle of wine. Olivia is dressed and waiting patiently while Jack pours.

'I see Luca has raided his special collection and not given us the house wine,' Nico exclaims, as he steps through from the door leading into the bedroom and the smart, albeit rather bijou, bathroom.

'Yes, I thought the same. A bottle of Monte Rossa Cabochon, no less – we are honoured. Have you tried this before, Marci?' Jack asks and I shake my head. 'It's a mix of Pinot Nero and Chardonnay grapes, and it has a refreshing fizz to it.'

'It's one of my favourites,' Olivia adds. 'It's not cheap – at least fifty euros a bottle.'

'That's very generous of Luca, as this is way more than the little lunch and drinks hamper that I ordered.'

I was lucky, as I caught Luca sitting all alone, enjoying a quiet drink on the terrace. He invited me to take a seat. I told him about the surprise we had planned for Nico and that we needed a buffet lunch. It was a little awkward, as Luca didn't want to take any money from me, but he eventually accepted two fifty-euro notes because I pressed them on him. It was then that I remembered the letter Richard had asked me to give him and I retrieved it from my bag. He thanked me and, without further comment, slipped it into the pocket of his chef's tunic. He didn't look at all surprised and I found that reassuring.

'Right, everyone grab a glass and we'll head outside to toast before we pop back to fill up our plates.'

In all honesty, it's quite a squeeze in here, although with the windows and the hatch doors open, there is a cooling breeze circulating. But once we're outside the air just makes you want to keep breathing it in, that fresh, salty tang and the exhilaration of a view that is breathtaking. The mountainous terraces of the land mass in front of us seem to literally drip with pastel colours, contrasted with bursts of lush greenery. I watch enthralled, as a ferry packed with tourists makes its way along the coast. Behind it, a small speedboat cuts through the water as if it's ploughing up a white field of foam, the bodywork glinting in the sun.

A few of the boats have sails, I notice, and they look so graceful against the backdrop.

Nico coughs to clear his throat. 'I think we should raise our glasses and toast Richard for his generosity, Luca for the extravagant bottle of Cabochon, and Marci and Olivia for pulling this off! What do you say, Jack?'

'Hear, hear!' Jack replies. 'And not only is it a pleasure to finally meet Marci, but being able to spend the day together as a foursome is a real tonic.'

Well, that was spoken from the heart and when Jack leans in to kiss Olivia, Nico reaches out to catch my hand in his. Standing together as we all clink glasses, it feels so natural to be here and I don't feel like a stranger in their midst.

Nico suggests that Olivia and I go back inside to grab some food while the guys take our drinks over to the sun deck.

'Did Jack bore you to tears talking about work?' Olivia questions me, as we descend the steps into the cabin. 'This job he's on has been a total nightmare and I did say to him that if I hear a whisper about it today, I'd immediately shut him down. He needs to switch off and relax while he can.'

I guess we did talk about work but not in the way that Olivia means.

'Oh, it was fine. We lazed around in the sun until it was too hot and then it took us a while to get the hang of the awning. To be honest, half an hour in the sun and I was glad to get in the shade.'

'You do look a little pink-cheeked,' she replies, passing me a plate. 'But your tan is definitely coming along nicely.

Mmm, I love a cold pasta salad, especially when it has roasted and charred red peppers in it.'

It does look appetising and colourful, but I go for the platter of cold meats first, because the wedges of green olive ciabatta are calling to me. There are thin slices of pizza with anchovies that look irresistible, and *piadina* – a flatbread pocket with lettuce, juicy, ripe tomatoes and brie. Another dish I'm looking forward to trying is the broad bean pods, inside of which are three individual cubes of cheese, each pinned with a cocktail stick to a broad bean, which has been drizzled with olive oil and possibly a touch of balsamic vinegar. It looks intriguing.

'I'm going to come back for more,' Olivia states. 'These plates are too dainty. Come on, the guys will be waiting impatiently. And don't worry, I told Nico to lighten up.'

Lighten up? Oh dear. As I follow Olivia, my right hand cautiously grabs the handrail as I inch along the narrow walkway to the sun deck. The guys have transformed it. Two of the large upholstered cushions which form the main body of the sun deck have been stacked up as a back rest. A collapsible table in the centre has been unfolded and there's enough room for at least six people to sit and eat. At each end of the highly glossed surface, there is a recess to take glasses and small bottles.

'Every little detail has been well thought out, hasn't it? Oh, what it must be like to have enough money to buy whatever you want and do whatever you like,' Olivia mutters, heaving a little sigh.

The guys are already out of earshot, and I lean into her.

'We can dream,' I agree, somewhat wistfully.

'What's the real problem between you and Nico, Marci?' I glance at Olivia as she fixes her gaze on me.

'I told Nico that he can't sleep in my room anymore.'

'I knew it! But in hindsight you feel it was a mistake?' Her eyes widen as she looks at me, questioningly.

'I'm staying in his family's hotel – it feels wrong. They treat me like a relative and we're . . . well, not anymore – at least, not under their roof. I can't handle it – but what else could I do? It just makes everything so awkward.'

The sound of some raucous laughter calls a halt to our conversation, and we begin eating. This food is way too delicious to waste and I'm delighted when Nico pops back to bring out a metal bucket filled with ice and small bottles of water.

'You are a star,' I say, as he places one in the recess alongside my plate.

'I have my uses', he replies, smiling down at me, and we hold each other's gaze for a moment longer than necessary. Olivia laughs.

'They've had a little tiff,' she explains to Jack, touching his arm. 'I think they're ready to make up.'

'We did not have a tiff,' Nico replies, firmly, lowering himself down next to me.

'It was my fault,' I mutter, mainly to stop him from going into detail.

'How can anyone have any privacy with so many Romanos around?' Jack declares and both Nico and I look at each other, awkwardly.

'That's easily remedied,' Olivia states nonchalantly, as she expertly delivers a loaded forkful of pasta into her mouth.

'How?' Nico asks and I can't even look up. I focus on twisting a slice of dried ham onto my fork and manoeuvring it onto a piece of ciabatta.

Olivia raises her index finger, waving it around until she's able to speak. 'There's a bedroom at La Grotta, isn't there?'

This is crazy. 'There is no way I could sleep in Richard's bed!' I interrupt, sounding scandalised. 'He's my godfather and that would be weird. Besides, La Grotta is dusty and there are cobwebs – no, that's not an option.'

That's ignoring the fact that everyone around this table has accepted that Nico and I are having casual sex. Telling Olivia in confidence is one thing, talking about it in general conversation is another.

'There's a sofa bed in the study,' Nico points out.

'Seriously, though,' Olivia joins in, 'all those antiques, some now packed up and ready to transport make it incredibly risky to leave the premises unattended at night. I'm sure Richard's insurance company wouldn't be happy about that.'

Nico casts me a sideways glance but doesn't linger when I refuse to turn and look directly at him. This is so embarrassing.

'Naturally, you'd need someone to stay with you overnight, Marci,' Jack continues.

Olivia isn't giving up, either. 'Luca and Celia would insist on that, I'm sure, if they knew you'd already had a couple of scary incidents. Especially as there are two bedrooms.'

'What do you mean?' Nico demands, staring at me.

'It's probably my vivid imagination playing tricks,' I reply, breezily.

'No, it isn't,' Olivia chimes in. 'We both know that at least one item has disappeared and it's high time we acknowledged that fact. A solid metal snake paperweight doesn't just disappear into thin air – someone took it.'

'Okay, maybe that once someone got lucky,' I concede, reluctantly.

'And what else have you neglected to mention?' Nico is not amused, but Olivia is wrong to make a big deal out of this.

'There have been a number of occasions when a vehicle has slowly driven around the car park before pulling back out. I always alert Marci, but by the time we rush outside it's too late to capture the number plate.'

'Is it always the same vehicle?' Nico quizzes Olivia.

'Two, actually. I've seen a small blue van and also a white Renault.'

'Oh, come on,' I declare, not wanting to add fuel to the non-existent fire. 'People see a large car park and use it as a place to turn around. Anyway, I only leave the door open if there are two of us inside and I'm very careful about that,' I admit. Well, that's certainly been the case more recently.

'In hindsight, putting up that closed sign at the gate wasn't the best idea – it's like a red flag to opportunist thieves. I seriously doubt that Luca and Celia will brush this off quite so easily when I tell them, though,' Nico replies, firmly. His tone highlights he's cross with me for not mentioning it and I watch as he stands, grabbing the empty plates and makes his way over to the cabin.

'Come on, guys, it's not *just* that, is it?' I address Olivia and Jack as soon as Nico is out of range.

'I don't see the problem – it's the perfect solution.' Olivia shrugs off my concerns as if they're nothing.

I'm conscious that they're both watching me intently as I lean over my plate, fiddling with salami and a chunk of crusty ciabatta.

'Oh, for goodness' sake! The place needs a thorough spring clean, for a start.'

'That's easily resolved,' Olivia replies, dismissively.

Nico is back and when I turn to look up at him, it's as if everything around us has faded into obscurity. There is only the two of us, staring at each other.

'How would you feel, Marci, if the place were ransacked overnight?' he throws at me, frowning.

This isn't just about having some alone time together, there's an element of real concern reflected in his voice. And it has nothing at all to do with Richard's precious antiques.

'If anyone is watching the shop they'll quickly suss out that there are periods of the day when you're there alone, and that the property is empty at night. If they think it's lived in and they see a couple coming and going at frequent intervals it'll put them off,' he continues.

'But what will your family think? I mean—'

Jack jumps in. 'It's a security issue and simply a case of ensuring your safety and protecting Richard's valuable stock. If there are lights on in the late evening, that confirms someone is living there again. Nico simply joins you every evening and leaves in time for his shift the next day.'

There's a distinctly uncomfortable pause.

'Right. I think I'm going to try the broad beans next.' Feeling flustered and uncomfortable, I jump up, leaving them to it.

It's one thing to sit around and convince ourselves that no one will bat an eyelid over this plan, but another to put it into practice. I'm sure that even Richard would be raising his eyebrows to the heavens if he were here.

After a leisurely lunch and an hour spent lazing around chatting, Jack is dying to get behind the wheel. He takes us for a pleasant run along the coast, with Nico egging him on to increase the speed. It's late afternoon when we anchor up a short distance away from Spiaggia di Fornillo. It's another dark sandy beach just west of Positano's Spiaggia Grande.

And now, here I am, about to discover it up close and personal.

'Trust me, together we can do this!' Nico's optimism is hard to resist. I'm sitting on the aft platform, wriggling my toes in the water as my legs dangle over the side. Nico is waiting for me, his hand extended.

'Go on,' Olivia encourages. She's kneeling on the bench seat at the rear of the boat to cheer me on.

If I don't do this, then I'm going to look and feel like a wimp, and I know it.

'Okay . . . here I come.'

Grabbing Nico's hand a little tighter than he was probably expecting, I notice that he winces as I lower myself down into the water.

'Wow! It's—' The initial shock as my warm skin reacts

to the chill momentarily takes my breath away. But as I let go of Nico's hand and begin moving my arms, my body quickly acclimatises.

'This is wonderful,' I exclaim, experiencing the crystal-clear waters of the Tyrrhenian Sea for the first time.

'See that small, rocky inlet over there? Are you happy to swim that far?'

'I can manage that.' It's not a lack of skill, it's just that I'm not one of those people who swim regularly. It's like driving a car, though, isn't it? You never really forget, you simply have that moment of hesitation, which soon passes.

Nico doesn't race but keeps up a slow and gentle pace alongside me. I'm glad I tied my hair up and I'm feeling pretty good in my bikini. It's pale green, with a profusion of flowers in dark purple and rich burgundy. My tan lines spoil the effect a little, but I hope today will help to even that up a little. I'm not expecting to go home bronzed all over as sunbathing isn't my thing, but hopefully the bits that show will have a healthy glow.

As we approach a group of jagged rocks to our left, Nico swims in front of me and I follow him. It's not dangerous, as it's getting shallower but as the water crashes against the tiny shore and then retreats, it requires additional effort to avoid being dragged back out with it.

Seconds later, I'm heaving myself up to sit on a small rock next to Nico, watching as he runs his hands through his hair to sweep it back from his forehead. His upper body is evenly tanned, but from the knees up, his thighs are paler and every time I see that it makes me grin. He catches me looking at him.

'I know – I need to laze around in the sun more. It's easy to work outside on the garden for an hour now and again shirtless, but I don't think our guests really want to see me in my swimming gear.'

'You might be wrong there,' I chuckle. 'Look at my arm – there's hardly a tan and yet I have two distinct lines.' It does look odd, but he simply smiles back at me.

'You look lovely just as you are, but then you always do.'

That's one thing I really love about Nico: he's never made me feel uncomfortable, whatever state of dress – or undress – he's seen me in. I don't mean *love*, of course . . . I mean . . . admire. I avert my gaze to take in our surroundings.

'The scenic walkway behind us leads from Spiaggia di Fornillo which is a little further along, past the watchtower over there.' Nico raises his arm and I turn my head. 'Beyond that is the landing stage at Positano.'

'It looks like a lovely walk, maybe we could do it some time?'

'That would be awesome.'

And just like that what felt like a barrier between us instantly fades away.

'I'm sorry about Jack and Olivia getting carried away – but if any of what Olivia was saying is true, then she's right, Marci. Give it some thought, because whether you like it or not, that place is beginning to attract attention. I know for a fact that Mum and Luca have already discussed this subject and had cross words over it. But it's entirely up to you – just promise me, please, that you'll keep that door locked at all times from now on.'

Before I have a chance to respond, Nico literally throws himself back into the water. He returns seconds later, splashing around to entice me in. A family of four ambling along the path in single file stop to take in the view. One of the children points to Nico, laughing, as I dodge the water droplets.

'Come on in,' Nico coaxes as he stops messing around and beckons to me with his finger. Taking a deep breath, I dive in.

Nico launches himself forward to catch me in his arms when I surface, and the full-on body contact is agonisingly delicious. He's such a temptation but none of this feels real. It's like being in a dream. One where anything can happen until you finally wake up.

As I gaze up at him, that connection between us makes my heart beat erratically.

'We should get back,' I murmur, softly. 'I think I'm ready for a second glass of wine.'

'And I want to grab the captain's chair again. We need to make the most of it – there's so much I want to show you, which includes some wonderful craggy grottoes, and we must take a cruise past the island of Capri. Even from the water, the main harbour is colourful, with its village setting and restaurants.'

Nico's enthusiasm is infectious – I'm becoming increasingly aware that if I don't tread warily, my heart could be in danger of getting broken and I promised myself I wouldn't let that happen again – ever.

It's 7 p.m. and we're due to meet up with Pietro in an hour.

It's been a truly wonderful day but we're all hungry now and Olivia has offered to cook for us.

When we finally approach the gate to the villa, set back off the narrow, stone-walled incline, it's a relief to know we'll soon be able to take the weight off our feet.

Jack and I have been talking, but it has slowed our pace and Nico and Olivia are nowhere to be seen. Jack stops for a moment, pointing to the view. 'It's worth it, isn't it?'

I can't disagree.

'Did you know we still use mules to bring up the fuel pellets for the boiler, ready for winter? Olivia feels uncomfortable about it, but they're well treated and it's an age-old form of transport. They're sure-footed and people with heavy sacks on their backs aren't. They're well looked after and appreciated here.'

'One thing is for sure, it's good exercise for all. I'm feeling lighter and fitter in just the few weeks I've been here.'

'Will you miss this when you return home, or will it be a relief to slip back into your normal routine?'

It's a question I try not to think about.

'I think I'm incredibly lucky to be here, experiencing all this, but I'm hoping to make some changes when I get home. Changes that are long overdue. It anyone had told me just six months ago that I'd be spending a couple of months here, I'd have shaken my head and thought they were mad. And yet, here I am.'

'There's a problem with constantly overthinking things, Marci,' Jack's voice is full of empathy.

He tilts his head to stare up at the sky and I follow his gaze.

'If you had to describe Positano in one word, what would it be?' he asks.

'I guess, I'd say *romantic*.'

'Then that's how you're experiencing it – that says a lot if you think about it. You could have used so many other words, but that's the one you chose.'

'Goodness, you're right!'

'Being apart from Olivia so often, I've had to teach myself how to cope by switching off a little when I'm not here and make sure I grab whatever moments of happiness I can when I am. It's what keeps me going. If I spent the time I do have with Olivia, fretting about the next parting of the ways, life would be very miserable indeed. Enjoy the remainder of your time here, Marci, and see it as life bestowing you with a little unexpected happiness – something to simply enjoy. I might be misquoting it slightly, but this line has always stuck in my head. "Yesterday is the past, tomorrow is the future, but today is a gift – that's why it's called the present."'

22.
Getting Set Up

'I really can't see the point in buying anything more than the minimum I need to get by, when I'll only be using it for a few weeks,' I point out to Olivia.

We're wandering around the main town in Positano in search of bed linen and this is the last thing I ever imagined myself doing.

'But a very *special* few weeks,' she reminds me. 'And now that La Grotta is sparkling, a little splash of colour will breathe life back into it.'

I'm fighting a losing battle and I knew that from the moment Olivia suggested we take the afternoon off to go shopping. We've already stopped by her friend's shop – Bellezza Naturale – where I purchased some wonderful scented hand soaps and shower gel.

'All things considered, I think everything has worked out brilliantly. Did you know that it's usually Viola and Bianca who sleep over in the staff bedroom? They haven't been able to do that when they're on the late shift since Nico's been using the room.'

'Of course! I didn't think about that.'

'As it turns out, everyone is happy.'

Yes, so it would appear, and tonight is the first night Nico and I will spend together at La Grotta. The transformation is unbelievable. We stripped the study bare, except for the sofa bed and underneath the throw, I was relieved to see that it was in pristine condition. I wondered whether it had ever been used for anything other than as a temporary filing space.

The royal blue heavy-weight linen was hardly faded and there were no visible signs of wear. With some crisp white cotton sheets and pillowcases, a thin colourful blanket to use as a bedspread, it should look cheery.

The windows gleam now, and Olivia brought along a pair of long voile curtains earlier, which frame them perfectly. The floorboards cleaned up a treat, too, and now I'd happily walk around barefoot.

Downstairs, what was once a cluttered sales floor, has a sitting area, but mainly to make anyone peering in through the blinds think that we've just moved in and are unpacking. The two single wicker chairs and the double sofa are more suitable for the garden, but they serve a purpose for the time being and look homey with their vibrant orange cushions.

The old signs for La Grotta have been taken down and packed up ready to go into the container. Luca was touched when I asked if I could have them. We both knew that they represented a very happy time in Richard's life, and he would treasure them forever.

The room at the back is now the main storage area, with the oversized and heavier items the experts will pack set to one side, and boxes neatly stacked ceiling to floor on the other. The remaining items waiting to be boxed up have been moved upstairs into Richard's bedroom, together with the packing materials and a small table. It's the new workroom, although there isn't a lot of space to move around, but it will do.

Outside, the windows sparkle and the dusty façade is pristine. Either side of the front door the newly replanted stone pots create a warm welcome and La Grotta looks lived in once more.

'Do you feel in the mood to splash out on a little rug to put next to the bed?' Olivia encourages, running her fingers over a vivid green, leaf-shaped mat.

I bat my eyelashes at her. 'It's gorgeous, but that's a firm no. Come on – I have everything I need right here.'

It's embarrassing. I feel like I'm turning Richard's old home into a love nest. I mean, two people can sleep in the same bed without jumping all over each other constantly, can't they?

'Why are you blushing?' Olivia asks, peering at me as she holds up some brightly patterned tea-towels for my inspection.

'I'm not and that's a no, too. I'm off to pay as I still have a lot to do.'

It's an excuse, of course, because there's plenty of time. But I told Nico that I'd cook supper and I'm nervous about that.

Olivia disappears as I place the pile of items on the counter. By the time the sales lady has filled several smart-looking carrier bags, Olivia reappears, swinging a bag of her own.

'You see – I can simply pop into a shop and pick up what I need without having to spend ages deliberating over each little item.'

I shrug my shoulders. 'There's a difference here. I can't get too comfortable,' I laugh.

'You want to make what time you have left together feel cosy and romantic, don't you?'

Saying a swift, '*Grazie*,' I steer Olivia firmly in the direction of the door. 'Enough! Anyway, I have some news.'

'Good news?' She instantly perks up.

'Not really. I had a text from my ex-boyfriend.'

'You did?'

Someone bumps into me, almost knocking everything out of my left hand.

'Here,' she says, 'let me take one of those carrier bags, or you'll do someone some serious damage. It's not too far to the car.'

'Thank goodness—' As I'm about to follow on behind her, I find myself doing a double take. Is that Dario and Giulia over there? Craning my neck to get a better view, as they've already disappeared, suddenly I spot them again as they sidestep the throng of people to linger at one of the stalls. I'm rooted to the spot when I notice that they're holding hands.

Olivia is oblivious to the fact that I've stopped, and I force myself to turn away and step up the pace. I guess there is a little anonymity to strolling along Viale Pasitea, given how packed it gets. But even so, it's very close to Positano's main beach and Dario and Giulia are taking a big risk.

It is quaint and rather romantic, though. I wonder if this is where they come to grab a little time together, hoping to blend in with the tourists? They can easily duck into a shop if they spot anyone they know coming towards them.

'Keep up, Marci,' Olivia shouts over her shoulder, 'I want to know more! Were you surprised?'

As I draw up alongside her, for one brief second I fear that she spotted them too, then I realise she's still talking about Everett.

'Absolutely, given that we broke up a little over a year ago,' I mutter, trying my best to push any other thoughts out of my head. 'Everett called into the Anvil & Anchor showroom, asking if I was around. I'm not sure who exactly he spoke to, but I doubt that it was Guy. They never got on very well.'

'What did the text say?'

'Nothing much. Just asking how I was and if I was enjoying Positano.'

'I thought for one moment there you were going to say he was flying over. He's obviously still thinking about you.'

It's not easy having to weave in and out of people going in both directions as we make our way towards the first run of steps on the way back to the car.

'I don't intend being a shoulder for him to cry on if his new lady friend has decided she's had enough,' I explain, trying my best to keep up. 'I gather he's had a number of girlfriends since we parted ways.'

'Ooh, he sounds like a commitment phobe to me!'

'You could be right. I might not know exactly what I want, but I do know what I *don't* want. And that's someone who is going to mess me about. The next time I let someone get that close to me everything must be perfect – well, not totally *perfect* but as near to perfect as possible.'

As I fall in alongside Olivia, what I'd like to say is as perfect as her and Jack's marriage, but I don't. She pretended she was fine after Jack left, but it's taken her almost a week to get over it and readjust. Olivia didn't admit that, but it was blatantly obvious. What she did say was that Luna isn't sleeping well. I bet they end up snuggling together for hours in one of the deep wicker chairs outside under the stars.

'Hey, Marci – how's it going today?' Guy sounds tired and it's unusual for him to call on a whim.

'Problems?'

'David had a word with me. Well, he rang to suggest we grab a pint after work, and I knew then that something was up.'

Oh dear, a feeling of unease seems to instantly settle around me. Just when I'm done putting the finishing touches to La Grotta and sitting back sipping freshly squeezed lemonade in the courtyard garden.

'Don't tell me . . . he's tired of Mum feeling that she has to step in and get hands-on because I'm not there?'

'Yes. I guess I sort of fired back at him, though, because for me it's like one step forward and two steps back.'

The line goes ominously quiet.

'What do you mean?'

'Let's be honest, Marci. Mum's involvement in the business is sentimental, and she doesn't like change. She comes here and spends her time . . . hmm . . . how can I say this without sounding mean? Reminiscing about old times with the staff, but how many of them were here when Dad was alive? Four, maybe five?'

Ooh, that is cutting. 'That's only natural. We all have good memories of those early years.'

'Yes, but she's worrying about our plans to expand the online side of the business and increase the number of specialist auctions we hold.'

My jaw drops. 'You're seriously considering the report I did for the new system?'

'I am. I think you're right. When you get back your first task ought to be to cost it out and we'll take it from there.'

'If things aren't easy between you and Mum, maybe it would be best to wait a while,' I advise, diplomatically.

'David thinks he can tempt her into walking away from her – well it's a joke to say hands-off role, because she's still very vocal – but reduce her shareholding.'

This is a bombshell I wasn't expecting. The problem is that we're all equal partners and it's increasingly becoming a case of Guy and me voting against Mum. The stumbling block is that Mum hasn't been a part of the daily running of the business for so long, she's out of touch.

'Don't tell me – he's going to create a little job for her.' Oh – that sounded rather disparaging, but that's David's style.

'If it's something she'll enjoy doing, why not?'

Now Guy is trying to sow the seed that it's for her own good, because he wants me to agree with him.

'Have you talked to Mum about it?'

'No. David asked me to wait until he'd set something up.'

I bet he did.

It's hard not to heave a sigh, because if I were there, I could help diffuse the situation. 'Just don't try to push Mum into anything she's not happy about for David's sake, Guy. That wouldn't be fair.'

Guy clears his throat, uneasily. 'The thing is, Marci, the business is going from strength to strength, but correct me if I'm wrong – we're looking at a significant investment if we go with your suggestions, am I right?'

'It would take us up to the next level and that comes at a cost, Guy.'

'I know, and David and I have been talking about just that. He agrees that what we need is some capital investment and someone with enough business acumen to help guide us as we grow. He has a good point.'

'And that would sit well with Mum?' This is beginning to sound like a scheme David has come up with and it happens to suit Guy's agenda.

'Listen, I'm just telling you what David said. Mum hasn't mentioned a thing, although she's not talking to me again and I haven't seen her for a few days. I did think she'd call to make up over the weekend and when that didn't happen, I realised it wasn't simply one of our usual mother-son disagreements.'

I knew there was a big problem looming on the horizon. Every time I try to ease Mum into a discussion about upgrading our IT system, her answer is always the same. 'It if isn't broken, then why fix it?' But I don't want her to feel she's being pushed out.

'Thanks for the warning, Guy. I know how difficult it is for you at times. You get all the pressure, but you do know that Mum means well?'

He sighs. 'I know. But I think David is right. Mum isn't happy because she's out of her depth. I think it's time for her to let go.'

Maybe Guy's right, but I'd want to hear that directly from her, not via David.

'I will tell you this now – if this is a way for David to buy into the business, it's a firm no from me.'

'Hey, hang on there! That's definitely not an option. Even I don't like him enough to take his money. However, I'm not in a position to buy Mum out, even partially, are you?'

I'm stunned. 'Of course not.'

'Well, we're agreed on that then. Let's wait and see what happens. I didn't mean to upset you but Mum isn't happy and we both know that. Anyway, dare I ask how the big clean-up is going?'

Hmm . . . is changing the subject a diversionary tactic?

'It's clean and tidy, and my clothes are now hanging in the wardrobe upstairs.'

'And you feel safe, whenever you're there alone?' Guy asks, pointedly.

I only mentioned it in passing and now I wish I hadn't.

'Yes. There are sturdy locks on the doors and people pop in to check on me all the time,' I reply, quickly dismissing his concern. No one at home is aware that Nico will be staying here, and I want to keep it that way. I can't tell Richard, either, but it's not likely to reach his ears. He's much too busy enjoying the honeymoon of a lifetime.

* * *

It's only by chance that as I go back inside to grab some more lemonade, I hear frantic knocking at the front door. With two side lights on in the sitting room, all I can see is a shape looming up against the patterned glass.

My heart begins to thud, as I glance at the clock on the dresser to my right and see that it's just after 10 p.m. Sunday is usually a late one as the restaurant is always busy.

Leaning up against the panel to peer through, I quickly unlock the door as soon as I realise that it's Nico standing there grinning at me rather sheepishly, a holdall in his hand.

'It's only me. I didn't mean to scare you.'

'Why are you so early?' I ask, as he follows me inside.

'That's down to Luca. He said he'd never forgive himself if anything happened to you, or Richard's precious antiques. He's been worried sick, apparently, and they'll be kicking me out each night the moment things start to quieten down.'

I'm trying to act normally, but this is anything but normal. And now a little worm of guilt begins to twist and turn in my stomach.

'Don't do that!' he instructs, dropping his holdall on the floor and coming towards me.

'Don't do what?'

Nico wraps his arms around me, and I stare up at him, trying to look calm and collected, when I'm anything but.

'Worry so much. Everyone agrees that this is a sensible move. Especially since that theft of the cash box from the fruit stall – the two women were quite shaken up by the episode. These opportunists don't mess around, Marci.'

Despite my concerns, my resolve begins to dissipate as I relax and sink effortlessly into Nico's arms.

'We should have thought of this before,' he murmurs huskily.

'Hmm . . . I think you'd better reserve that judgement until we've had dinner. It's not going to be fancy, that's for sure.'

'Come on, we'll do it together. Simple is best, as Luca always says.'

After a lot of chopping up of onions, tomatoes and garlic, Nico leaves me to begin frying them off in a little olive oil, while he settles in.

When he returns, he's carrying a box.

'I'll set the table up in the courtyard. Is there anything I can do in here first?'

'No, I have everything under control. As soon as the water is boiled the pasta will only take a couple of minutes.'

'It's not dried?'

I laugh off his comment, as he places the box under his arm and gathers a few things together. 'Shout when it's ready and I'll help carry the plates through.'

It's just warm, sliced ciabatta, a simple salad and fresh pasta with my version of a tomato sauce. After Nico expertly plates up the food, the air is filled with a delicious smell that gives me a smug sense of satisfaction. I add a few black olives and some shavings of fresh Parmigiano Reggiano and we're ready to go.

As we carry everything outside, I follow a pace or two behind Nico and then stop in amazement. There is a large scented candle burning in the middle of the table and a waft of citrussy lemon fills the air. White linen napkins from the restaurant lie next to each place setting. On the low wall dividing the patio area from the unruly garden, a long line of tea lights cast a flickering glow. I pause to take it in and Nico glances across at me on his return trip.

'Is it too much?' His look is earnest, almost apologetic.

'No, it's perfect,' I murmur. As he draws close, I lean in to kiss him softly on the lips. All day I wondered what this moment would feel like, whether I'd be disappointed, and it would fall flat. Instead, it's perfect and truly magical.

Lying in each other's arms, it's hard to believe how wonderfully cosy the old study feels having been transformed into a bedroom.

'The plant was a touching gesture,' I acknowledge. 'I thought it was a mistake when I answered the door this afternoon to see a delivery guy standing there holding out a potted orchid!'

'It's not just any old orchid, it's a rose orchid,' Nico murmurs, sleepily.

'Well, it's beautiful,' I reply, turning my head to the left to gaze at it, taking pride of place on the windowsill.

'You don't think it was a daft idea given that before long all of this will become a building site?'

'No – maybe we can plant it in a sheltered corner of the garden before I leave. I rather like the idea of doing that.'

As Nico begins to drift off, I lower my voice to a whisper. 'A little piece of us.'

He stirs, suddenly, opening his eyes but I don't think he heard what I said.

'The orchid wasn't the only delivery I had this morning,'

I continue, softly. 'Dario carried up a cool box on your mum's instruction.'

Nico yawns. 'From Mum?' His voice is barely audible.

'It was freshly made pasta and a ciabatta. You didn't think I made it all from scratch, did you?'

'Mmm . . . that's . . .' He pauses to yawn once again. 'A no!' Nico flexes his arm as it's wrapped around me, and I feel protected in a way that I never have before.

It's funny, but I finally get what living in the moment is all about. I'm not thinking about the past or wondering what tomorrow will bring. I'm lying here with my head on Nico's chest, listening to his heartbeat and feeling incredibly at peace. Everything suddenly feels right with my world and there's nowhere else I'd rather be right now. With the crisp, new bedding, the leaf-green rug that Olivia gave me as a present lying on the floor next to the bed, and no clutter – it's as if this is our space, mine and Nico's.

'I don't want to fall asleep, but I'm so tired.' Nico's voice is apologetic. I shush him and snuggle even closer. With the window slightly ajar, the light breeze coming through it is pleasantly cooling to the skin. This is the first time we've lain together in bed without the feeling that we're doing something wrong.

Visions of Giulia hammering on the door no longer haunt me after my chat with Dario this afternoon. It's not something I can share with Nico, though. Dario happily accepted the offer of a coffee on the patio before he went on his way. At first he was simply asking questions about how Richard and Angel were doing. Then he asked whether I thought they would ever return to settle here in Positano and I knew then why he'd offered to carry up the cool box for Celia.

I simply said what I believe to be true – that Richard's links with Positano would always draw him back here.

'Giulia will be relieved to hear that,' he'd confessed.

'She has concerns?'

An anxious look travelled over his face and there was a moment of hesitation as he stared back at me with a troubled expression. 'Eh, we were just talking, that's all.'

'But she's worried?' I pressed him.

And then I realised why Dario broke up with his fiancée – he's in love with Giulia and if they're talking about a future together, they both have a vested interest in what happens.

'Her position is not clear if she does not marry Nico,' he'd replied, sounding slightly apologetic.

'Oh – I see!'

'You will say nothing? I should not have asked, it is not my place but . . . it is difficult and a huge worry. Thank you for sharing your thoughts, Marci – I appreciate it.'

I assured him that he needn't worry, I fully understood it was an anxious time given the situation.

After he left, I felt rather sad for them both and, admittedly, a little frustrated at not being able to share what I've learnt with Nico. It doesn't change anything between the two of us, but it means I can enjoy this time we have together without guilt. Knowing that the time we have together is limited doesn't take away that joyful, exquisite buzz of excitement I feel when we're around each other. And it can be enough of a fix until, well . . . hopefully until we each fulfil our true destiny.

Nico and Giulia will eventually end up having that conversation at some point very soon, because it's inevitable. I wonder how Luca will react if Giulia marries Dario instead of Nico? She'll still be a Romano, just not his son's wife. Nico isn't ready to settle down with anyone right now and I'm sure that Luca will accept that something like that can't be forced – it has to happen naturally when the time is right.

As for me, the one thing I know for sure is that Everett Berkeley is not going to step back into my life.

23.
Trouble on the Horizon

'Happy Monday! You look radiant this morning!' Olivia enthuses, grinning at me from ear to ear, as she steps over the threshold. 'I guess last night was a success, then?'

'Stop it!' I groan, putting a finger to my lips. 'Nico is spending his day off attacking the jungle area outside and he could walk in on us at any moment. I'm not going to let you quiz me, either. But I do have a question for you.' I glance around nervously, but judging by the noise filtering in from outside, Nico is busy felling branches.

'Fire away.'

This is awkward as it would be wrong of me to share – even in confidence – anything at all about Richard's personal affairs. Especially when it's financial, but another little discovery this morning has set me off again.

'Is it possible that Richard knew Luca *before* he moved to Positano?'

I follow Olivia through to the kitchen as she unloads the contents of the cool bag she's carrying into the fridge. She pokes her head out of the back door, but Nico is nowhere in sight. However, the squealing sound of a chainsaw struggling to get through a tough piece of wood makes her pucker up her face.

'Poor Nico – you two should have taken yourselves off somewhere nice for the day. Anyway, I digress. Hmm . . . that's an odd question to ask – why on earth would you think they had history? Surely, if that were the case then Richard would have moved straight into La Grotta and set up his business from day one. I think it took him over a year to get everything sorted.'

'Yes, of course. I just wondered why he decided to go into partnership with Luca.'

'Oh, well, you had to be here to understand the size of the problems Luca inherited. The restaurant was a huge success – every single night it was packed, but one of the terraces was in a bit of a state and unusable. That's a third of the tables less than they have now. Plus, the building had issues – a large retaining wall in the garden was failing. And while reviews for the food were great, the décor was tired. Luca invested what money he had, but it wasn't anywhere near enough to make a real difference.'

'But Richard had never been in the restaurant business before. He loves to eat and he is a bit of a wine buff, but it's not as if he brings any expertise to the partnership.'

Olivia closes the fridge door and straightens, shrugging her shoulders.

'Isn't that what businessmen do? Spot an opportunity to invest in something they believe will flourish – which has been proven right in this case.'

'I suppose so, but it's easy to assume that just because a place is busy, it's making a healthy profit.'

'It must be doing well, as I hear Luca is excited about

getting the builders in to start work on the renovations here.'

What I'm after is a little information without having to give too much away, but now Olivia is staring at me and frowning.

'I just wondered whether Richard was still putting money into the business to keep it afloat, that's all.'

Her face relaxes and she gives a little laugh.

'Is this your way of avoiding the burning issue? How did it go last night with Nico?'

Obviously Olivia isn't aware of any problems, which is a comfort of sorts.

'No. Suffice to say that everything is, um, fine.' Suddenly I'm feeling distinctly hot and bothered, and I can see that Olivia is amused, thinking that I'm a little embarrassed.

'Oh, well – moving on rather quickly, I'm going to take it as good news because he's still here,' she continues, flashing me a knowing smile. 'Am I working up in Richard's bedroom again today?'

'Yes, that's the plan. Anyway, how is everything back at the villa?'

'Mum is with Luna and Papa is going to spend the day hacking back an area of the garden where I'm losing the battle. Aren't we lucky to have willing volunteers when we need a little help?' She bats her eyelashes at me suggestively, implying that my volunteer might have an ulterior motive. 'The climbers seem to have had a huge growing spurt this year and they're stifling one of the grapevines.'

'And how is Jack?'

'He said that another week, two at the most, and he

hopes to be able to wrap it up, barring any unexpected complications. Seriously, Marci, I'm not sure how much longer we can live like this.'

I turn to look at her and I can see how jaded she's feeling this morning.

'Have you told Jack how you feel?'

'No. It wouldn't be fair on him. He's under pressure and I can't add to his worries.'

'Sometimes it's the things we don't say that matter the most,' I reply, gently.

Olivia's eyes begin to well up. 'It's like a growing chasm between us, Marci, and it scares me. He has this goal in his head and he won't stop until he's achieved it.'

It would be wrong of me to meddle, or pass on anything told to me in confidence, but Olivia is clearly concerned about him.

'Why don't you begin the conversation and see how willing Jack is to open up? What harm can that do?'

'I suppose he could always shut me down if he doesn't want to talk about it. We don't need a place like the villa to make us happy, Marci. Not if we end up having to spend so much time apart. I'm living in a lovely setting and he's living in hotels.'

'Then you've answered your own question, Olivia. Be honest with Jack. You don't have to go at this full throttle, just explain how you feel when he isn't with you and see what reaction you get.'

As we start work, Olivia lapses into silence. After a while I decide to leave her to it, but when I return a couple of hours later to see how she's doing, she's rather subdued.

Olivia is so deep in thought, that even when my phone rings she doesn't look up from what she's doing, and I decide to take the call outside to leave her in peace.

'Hi, Mum, how are you?'

'Wondering what's going on and thinking that David and Guy are up to something! Sorry, Marci – David and I have just had words, which is unlike him, and I so wish you were here.'

'Calm down, Mum. I'm sure it's not as bad as you think it is. Tell me exactly what happened.'

'David said the business needs additional *resources* if it's going to survive. You know how he talks . . . he said that's what is holding you and Guy back. Is that true, Marci?'

She sounds distraught.

'Oh, Mum! That was a bit unfair.'

'Ah – but you're not disagreeing with him!'

This is not a conversation I want to get pulled into when I'm getting everything second-hand, but Mum deserves an honest answer. 'The world has changed a lot since Dad passed. Over the last decade things seem to have speeded up and if we don't keep abreast of what's happening, we'll end up lagging behind our competitors, Mum. The sheer volume of items we handle now means we need a state-of-the-art upgrade.'

The line goes quiet, and I strain my ears because I'm sure Mum has been crying but doesn't want me to know.

'In my humble opinion,' I continue, 'weighing up the risk of keeping the status quo, against making some pretty big changes . . . well, it's the difference between growth and stagnation.'

She sniffs, and I wish I were there to give her a reassuring hug.

'Then David is right, the time has come. My children are all grown up and they no longer need me!' As sad as it is to hear Mum so upset, her words make me smile. She has always been a bit of a drama queen.

'Aww, come on, Mum. That's not true and you know it, but the things you're worrying about aren't a sign that we're struggling, but a sign of our success. And yet both Guy and I look to you because that's what Dad wanted. This isn't about Guy, or me, ousting you, but you choosing to let go. Be honest with me – would it be a relief?'

Mum lets out a huge sigh. 'Oh, Marci, Richard is right – you are like a mini version of your dad. I suppose I'm floundering because I'm out of touch and everything I say, or do, seems to push Guy further away. I love my son, and I hate the constant arguments. I feel guilty at times as it's not your job to always be the voice of reason stepping in between us. It grates on David how upset I get and he says I shouldn't take things so personally. He pointed out that if I'm not a part of the solution, then I'm a part of the problem. There – I've said it, but please, please don't repeat this to Guy.'

'Don't you think it's time to focus on what *you* want for a change, Mum?'

Now she's choking back the tears and I wait while she pulls herself together. It's heart-wrenching sitting here listening to Mum sounding so distressed.

'You're the only one who can truly understand my

dilemma. I miss you so much, Marci. If I bow out now, would your dad think of me as a traitor?'

'Oh, Mum! Dad wouldn't want you stressing like this. Whether we succeed or fail, it's not down to what you do or don't do. Hopefully, the two of us will take the right decisions and make you proud.'

'It's that simple?'

'It is – and I know this is going to sound strange given that David and I don't see eye to eye, but maybe David sees it as a slight, the fact that you won't let him take care of you. It's time to decide for yourself what you want to do going forward, Mum, and talk to him about it. If I don't think he's putting your interests first, believe me, I'll be straight on the phone giving him a piece of my mind.'

'What I really want . . .' Mum stops to blow her nose and I wait with bated breath, 'is to get a little job, something I'd enjoy doing that would be fun. The local library is looking for volunteer storytellers. You know, for mother and toddler groups. As I don't have any grandkids of my own yet . . .' She pauses for dramatic effect, before continuing, 'I'd love to get involved.'

Well, talk about a shock – that's the last thing I was expecting to hear but finally, Mum is thinking about herself for once and it's a start.

'What a great idea, Mum. Whatever you decide will be fine with us all, just so long as you're happy. It's funny because this trip has made me think about my future, too.'

'You are coming back, aren't you?' The pitch of her voice creeps up a couple of notches.

'Of course I am. But Briony has proved her worth and I want to focus on other areas to push the business forward.'

I wait for a few seconds, allowing Mum to catch her breath.

'All Dad and I wanted was to create something that would set both you and Guy up for the future. Family is everything, Marci. You two are formidable together because you genuinely have each other's back.'

Mum's words touch my heart.

'It's tough being a parent. All that responsibility lying heavily on your shoulders and then how do.you know exactly when to stand back and let go? There are no guarantees in life about anything, but with Guy in charge he'll be just like Dad – exercising due diligence, but fearless and visionary. Those are the true qualities of an entrepreneur. Anvil & Anchor Antiques is in good hands, Mum.'

'Thank you, Marci, for being such a comfort. You are the voice of reason in our family. Do you remember when Dad and Guy used to butt heads?'

That makes me smile to myself. 'I do and I was the one dragging Guy out of the office while Dad cooled down. So, crisis over?'

'It is and I wasn't trying to put pressure on you. You know, about children or anything. All in good time. Bye for now, Marci, and take care of yourself.'

As I stand here feeling relieved that Mum finally has a plan, the sound of Nico wielding a hedge trimmer down at the far end of the garden ceases. A moment later he appears, his forehead beaded with sweat and damp patches on his T-shirt.

'I need a cold drink,' he says, swiping an arm across his face. 'Is it lunchtime yet?'

'It is. I'm sure Olivia will be more than ready for a break, too. Sit down, I'll grab you a towel and something refreshing, then see what's on the La Grotta menu today.'

He grins back at me, stepping closer and even though he's hot and sweaty, I can't resist the feel of his lips on mine.

'And for tonight, I'm sure I have all the ingredients I need to make pizza!'

Nico looks surprised but says nothing. What a wise guy he is!

After my fairly successful attempt at pizza making yesterday, it's Nico's turn to cook tonight. I'm chilling in the courtyard with a cold glass of white wine in my hand, eagerly waiting for him to join me. It's just after nine thirty in the evening, and a very early finish for him, but then Tuesdays are often a little quieter at the restaurant. It's the clearing up that takes the time and I'm sure they're still all back at the restaurant beavering away.

The fact that Nico is attempting what appears to be a tricky dish to impress me is heart-warming and when he eventually appears I try hard not to notice his flushed appearance. He looks decidedly hot and bothered.

'One of the side dishes ended up in the bin, I'm afraid,' Nico admits, looking sheepish. 'Luca would be mortified, but I think this *risotto ai frutti di mare* would have redeemed me. The clams, squid, shrimps and mussels are cooked to perfection – as is the rice. Regretfully, I got so caught up stressing over the seafood that I burnt the garlic bread.'

'Ah, but this smells heavenly. Let's eat, then I'll clear the plates away while you pop up to shower and cool down. Then we can linger over coffee.'

Even in the candlelight I can see the sparkle in his eyes. 'Great idea! And Giulia sent one of her desserts. It's in the fridge, but I haven't opened the box yet.'

I reach out to touch Nico's arm and give it a comforting squeeze, appreciative of the effort that he has put in.

He chatters away happily while we eat, bringing me up to date on the latest gossip. Dario and his father, Vittorio, have had another big bust-up and everyone is walking on eggshells around them. It strikes me that family arguments can get out of hand very quickly, more so with that fiery Italian temperament. And given what I now believe is going on between Giulia and Dario, I wonder if that is likely to cause even more problems in the not-too-distant future. Especially as Nico and Dario appear to be close friends as well as family.

'Is everything okay at home?' Nico narrows his eyes, focusing on my reaction and completely unaware of the fact that my thoughts are going off in entirely another direction. I was on the phone with Mum when he arrived home this evening and I suspect that he overheard a little of the conversation I had with her yesterday, too.

'Mum is in need of a listening ear. She has a lot going on and a few decisions to make. It doesn't help that things are a little tense between her and Guy right now.'

'I'm sorry to hear that, Marci. She must miss having you around.'

'Yes, you're right there. Oh, and I have more news

from Richard. Angel's family are expecting them to stay in Australia a little longer than they'd intended. They have all sorts of trips planned, apparently, and it might delay the date they were hoping to fly back to the UK. He has to sign the contract for the cottage Mum viewed on their behalf, but now he's going to do it electronically, without even having seen the place! Talk about trusting Mum, but at least she sent them some photos and a short video she took when she did the viewing.'

Nico's lips begin to twitch. 'You've got to admire that man. He looks conservative, but when he makes up his mind about something he doesn't stop to second-guess his gut instinct. That's quite something.'

My mouth goes dry. This is my chance.

'Was Richard like that when he approached Luca about becoming a partner in the business?'

I find myself holding my breath, worried that Nico will find my interest intrusive.

'I was a teenager at the time, so I wasn't really involved. As I said before, he was a customer for a while and like a lot of business deals, it happened late one night when Luca and Richard had a few drinks. At first, no one really thought it would come to anything, but it did – and rather quickly.'

I take my first forkful of risotto, and by the time I've finished complimenting him on his culinary skills it feels odd to rekindle that line of conversation, so instead I ask about Pietro and how long he's known him. Anything to do with boats immediately puts a smile on Nico's face.

As soon as we finish, Nico heads upstairs, leaving me

alone with my thoughts. This morning I found some loose bank statements from way back and when I opened one of the box files to place them inside, there was a tatty piece of paper taped to the inside of the lid. It caught my eye and I assumed it was some sort of index, but when I looked at it more closely it was a list of dates and payments going back almost twenty years, the last entry a little over a year ago. In total it came to 150,000 euros. I wonder if it's a record of money Richard has given to Luca.

And what was in that envelope from the bank that Richard asked me to surreptitiously hand over without Celia knowing? Is it a coincidence that it was so soon after Richard received the funds for the silver, which he told me he'd originally purchased from Hans?

My vivid imagination is going into overdrive. Has all that money gone into the business? Or maybe Luca is in some sort of trouble and because of their friendship, Richard is bailing him out.

I'm still puzzling over the unsigned painting; it's not illegal to copy a painting unless it's then sold on, but it has been on my mind. What is the chance of a painting passing through Richard's hands and being sold to a client in good faith without him realising it's a forgery? Maybe even a friend of Luca's? The likelihood of that happening is slim – Richard wouldn't be easily fooled, although he has been distracted recently. Besides, Richard would be straight onto the police as he's a man of principles. Which takes me full circle. What on earth could Luca possibly have to hide?

Luca asks after Richard every few days, so it's obvious they've had no direct contact and, clearly, they trust each other implicitly, no matter what's going on between them. *Paranoia is a terrible thing, Marci – let it go.* Is that my conscience talking, or that burning desire deep down inside of me that wants to believe everything is fine?

The sound of my phone ringing makes me jump and I scurry back into the kitchen to find it, desperately trying to shake off my unease. In my panic to get to it before it goes to answerphone, I don't even look at the caller ID.

'Marci, it's Everett.' Immediately I freeze. 'I hear you're in Italy. I sent you a text and I thought I'd check whether you received it.'

I listen out for the comforting sound of the shower running in the bathroom overhead and immediately walk back outside. Glancing up, the window directly above me is partially open, so I step over the low wall and wander down past the beautiful old olive tree. After Nico's hard work, the weathered stone path is now fully exposed.

'Yes, I did. I'm just rather tied up right now, Everett.'

'Not too busy to enjoy the wonderful Italian scenery, I hope?'

'I don't wish to sound rude, but I'm in the middle of dinner.'

'Oh, I forgot how late they eat over there. My apologies, Marci, but it's nice to hear your voice. Perhaps when you have five minutes you could give me a call and we'll . . . erm . . . catch up?'

'I don't know if that's going to be possible, I'm afraid, as I'm on a tight deadline. To be honest with you, I can't really see the point. Everything that we needed to say was said a long time ago.'

There's a stony silence. 'Oh. Right. Guy hasn't mentioned anything to you?'

'Guy? You've been speaking to him direct?'

'Obviously I've caught you at an inopportune time, Marci – my sincere apologies. You know what I'm like – a thought pops into my head and I have a tendency to act before I think. But I've been thinking about you a lot, lately. Anyway, it would be great if when you're back home, we could maybe go for a drink sometime?'

The cheek of this man. We've had no contact for what . . . fourteen months and now he wants to meet up?

'I don't think that's a good idea, Everett. Just so you know, if someone doesn't respond it usually means they don't want to talk to you,' I reply, my hand trembling. I'm getting angry now, and force myself to take a deep breath in. 'Perhaps it's time you deleted my number, Everett. Sometimes it's best not to rake up the past.'

Pressing end call, my fingers are busy blocking Everett when Nico calls out.

'Marci?' He wanders outside and I make my way over to join him. He's barefoot and only wearing a pair of shorts, as he towels his hair dry. 'Is everything all right?'

'It's all good. Just someone I haven't heard from in a long time. Now, I wonder what our surprise dessert is tonight?'

As I walk closer, Nico stops what he's doing to reach out, encircling an arm around my waist and pulling me into him.

I've never lived with a man before – not that this really counts, of course. But it doesn't feel as strange as I thought it might. And Nico seems fine with it, too. He looks down into my eyes, that easy smile of his lifting the corners of his mouth and making my heart flutter. And then I think, *why wouldn't it*? In the fading light, pressed up against a half-naked, incredibly attractive man, it's rather exciting. With the unmistakable smells of a balmy Italian night closing in around us – this is what dreams are made of. It's like a scene out of a romance novel and I'm living it!

July

24.

A Happy Ending to a Trying Day

The first week of July seems to fly by. Since Monday, Olivia and I have been hard at it and what a difference it's made.

It's a landmark day because it's Olivia's last one helping me at La Grotta. Her new translation project is about to kick off and while it's a sad occasion for us both, I can see how excited she is – not least because she's working with a new publishing house. Maybe that swimming pool will be achievable for next summer if everything goes well.

As she's about to leave, my phone rings.

'Guy, can you wait a minute or two?'

'Of course.'

I put him on hold while Olivia and I hug goodbye, and then turn to pick up the present I so carefully wrapped and hid behind the planter in the corner of the room.

'It's not really *arrivederci*, as we'll still see each other between now and when I leave. Although it is getting closer – a little over three weeks. But I want to thank you, Olivia, for all your hard work, your friendship, and some truly wonderful lunches.'

'Oh, Marci, you shouldn't have!' She's dewy-eyed as I press the gift into her hands.

'I wanted you to have a little memento to remind you of our time together.' I managed to get some wonderful old wine glasses in one of the little shops in Viale Pasitea. It just seemed like the perfect thing to give her, as both Olivia and Jack enjoy a glass of good wine. It always tastes a little better when it's drunk from something that is a thing of beauty and handmade.

It's several minutes until I get back to Guy and when I do, I hear the clatter of keys. He's at his PC and typing away on the keyboard.

'Sorry about that. It's Olivia's last day working alongside me.'

'Everything is all packed up?' He sounds shocked.

'No, but almost – I'm ninety-five per cent there. Olivia starts a new project tomorrow. Another few days and I'll be all done here. How's Mum doing?'

'Good and David is finally off my back. But I need you to do me a favour, a big one.' He sounds a tad hesitant and that isn't Guy's style, so I know it's not something I'm going to like.

'You'd better get it off your chest then.'

'Can you *please* unblock Everett? I know that he's the last person you want to talk to, but he wants to apologise.'

'For goodness' sake, Guy, why are you even talking to him? It's not like you're good friends – he always got on your nerves!'

'True, but this is business-related. His father is loaded, and he's always on the lookout for a little investment opportunity,' Guy admits, apologetically.

I can't believe it. 'You are joking – aren't you?'

'David and Stuart Berkeley are golfing buddies, you know that. Look, Marci, like it or not, Mum looks to David for advice, and she can sell her shares to anyone she wants given that neither of us are in a position to buy her out. Mum is doing this for *us*, Marci.'

My stomach is churning. 'Why are you so calm talking about this?'

'Ah, well.' He falters for a second, before continuing in a more robust fashion. 'Stuart called me out of the blue for an off-the-record chat. David told him that Mum is thinking of selling half of her shares. Now before you say anything – she's going to give us the proceeds to plough back into the business. This could be great news, Marci, with a cash injection *and* a new partner that would raise enough funds to give your plans the green light when you get back. Having someone of Stuart's calibre join us and be on hand to offer advice would be worth its weight in gold.'

'David clearly thinks that you're steering the business in the right direction but it's Mum's money, Guy.'

'Mum doesn't want us spending money we don't have, Marci – you know what she's like. And it's not as if she needs it. She says it's our inheritance anyway and one day it will all be ours.'

Oh Guy, that's not the point and you know it. Now my head is reeling.

'Why do I need to talk to Everett?'

'Just to clear the air, Marci – that's all, I promise. Let him say his piece so he can move on with no bad feelings. Nothing can go any further until you're back, anyway – you know that, but don't let your emotions cloud your judgement at this stage. There's a lot of talking to be done before a decision is made.'

'This is the last thing I was expecting, Guy. As for Everett, I'll think about it.'

'Please don't spend too long mulling it over, it's no big deal unless you turn it into one.'

'It was a big deal for me at the time – humiliating, actually.'

'Oh, Marci – Everett is a fool and if there was any other way to get around this, believe me, I wouldn't be asking for your help. Stuart knows it didn't end well between you and Everett, so I suspect he's had a word with him to clear up any loose ends. But the fact is that it will allow us to set the wheels in motion for much bigger things. If profits go up, the shares Mum has left will be worth more and we'll repay her in that way.'

Guy in persuasive mode is hard to argue with and I can't dispute the fact that an injection of capital would be handy. At least Stuart and I got on rather well and he is an astute businessman. It's just a pity Everett doesn't have the same backbone as his father.

'All right, but it won't be today. I have things to do.'

'I understand. And thanks, Marci. Mum's a lot happier and it shows. Did you know that she's volunteered to help down at the library? I'm not sure what that's all about, but Mum told me that she starts next week. David was a bit disappointed she didn't go for any of the options he offered her, but he's okay with it. Let me know when the deed is done, and I'll give Stuart a call.'

If this really is what Mum wants and it makes it easier

for her, then I can hardly cause a fuss over our potential new investment partner. Better someone we already know, rather than a total stranger who is unfamiliar with our business, I suppose. As for Everett – I'll unblock him, but I want to sleep on it before I make that phone call. It's time he learnt that the world doesn't revolve around him.

My next task is to have a go at making a dessert for tonight before I head back upstairs. I need to trawl through the remaining boxes of general bric-a-brac before I reach out to Richard's local contact again. He's happy to take whatever is left off our hands.

A couple of hours fly by and when my phone rings I assume it's Nico, giving me a heads-up so that I can get supper started. Towards the end of the week, he arrives back later and on Thursday evenings it's usually gone 10 p.m. at the earliest. However, it's Olivia's voice I hear, and it's obvious that something is wrong.

'Oh, Marci – are you alone? Nico isn't home yet?'

'No. He'll be another hour at least, I expect. What's up?'

'I've just come off a long and worrying call with Jack. He's had a really bad day and he was sat in his hotel room alone, drinking. That's not like him. He usually has a beer, or two at most, with some of the guys he's working with, then they grab a meal before he heads back to chill out. Tonight, though, he just wanted to talk.'

'About what?' It has obviously unsettled her, because the concern in Olivia's voice is very real.

'Nothing at all to do with work, as I expected. He kept jumping from subject to subject. Jack talked about when we first met, and he sounded nostalgic – that's when I realised that he was drinking. Then he got onto the subject of boats and how he'd like to sell the *Serpente di Mare* and get something bigger.' She sounds exasperated but people often witter on about nothing when they've drunk a little too much.

'Did he sound agitated?'

'Yes! Oh, Marci, that's exactly the right word, but I couldn't put my finger on it. His behaviour was a little bizarre. Like he was rambling at times. I just sat there listening to him going on and on, and when I did try to say something, it was as if he didn't hear me. In the end I made him promise that he'd make some strong coffee and then go straight to bed. Jack said he'd phone me in the morning, and that he was *sorry*. But for what?'

There is nothing Olivia can do, and I can sense her frustration. 'He was probably sorry for phoning you when he was too drunk to think straight. The fact he rang you, though, means something and you listened – which was all you can do given the situation. He'll make more sense when you speak to him tomorrow, I'm sure—'

'Oh – hang on, he's just sent me a text.'

The line goes quiet as she puts me on hold. I wait, anxiously, as the seconds pass.

'Ah . . . Jack said he didn't mean to worry me and to ignore him. He admits that too much alcohol doesn't help after a disastrous day but asked if we can talk about the boat.' She makes a little laugh, out of sheer relief, or perhaps his text was humorous. 'I texted him back suggesting he comes home for the weekend. It's a lot of travelling, but I think he needs a complete break and he agreed with me.'

'That's a great idea, Olivia. Try to get a good night's sleep. It will end up being a late one for you both tomorrow night, then, but I know you'll be relieved to have him back with you.'

Olivia's sigh is almost imperceptible, but it saddens me.

'Luna is unsettled, tonight, too, so we'll snuggle up together. That always helps. Thanks for listening, Marci – and for the reassurance. You really made an impression on Jack that day we were all together. I don't think I can recall him ever being that relaxed just chattering away with anyone. Even people he's known for a long time. Maybe you can pop over for lunch at the weekend to join us? It's a pity Nico won't be free, but it might be fun and help give Jack a lift.'

'That's a lovely thought, but why don't you wait and see if he's in the mood for company, first? You can call me any time – I never say no to a meal out if he's up for it.'

Poor Olivia. Tomorrow is her first day back at her desk and her mind is going to be all over the place until she can see for herself that Jack is okay.

'You made this all by yourself?' Nico stares at the plate I hand him, as a dribble of the rich tomato sauce and minced beef begins to ooze out from beneath the layers of pasta.

'I can't lie. It was a parting gift from Olivia. And the garlic bread is from Gianni's. But I did make my own version of a lemon tiramisu, using fruit from the garden.'

I found the recipe online and having had a quick look at it now that it's chilled, it looks pretty good if I say so myself.

'Well, this is served to perfection and I love tiramisu,' he grins at me. 'How was Olivia's last day?'

'We had a laugh and she left on a high, but uh . . . she rang about an hour ago and she's really worried about Jack.'

'He's okay, though – isn't he?'

'Yes, I think so. He had a little too much to drink and was rather maudlin. He's coming home for the weekend. They just miss each other, and I don't know how much longer he can hack the long spells away from Olivia and Luna.'

Nico stops eating and stares at me as if I've said something untoward.

'What?'

He puts his elbows on the table, cupping his hands together and leaning his chin on them. For a few moments the look in his eyes is distant.

'It's easy to lose sight of what really matters, isn't it?'

'What do you mean?'

'Oh, it's just an observation. I look at them and think they have everything, but it comes at a cost, doesn't it? It's easy to forget that. Anyway, so now that you're working on your own again, how long do you think it will take to finish off the job?'

Is it my imagination, or is Nico a bit unsettled tonight?

'I have plenty of time and I can finally slow down now that I'm on the home stretch.'

'Is that because you're running out of steam?' he muses.

'It's more that the pressure is off, and I can relax.'

'How about – and I'm just throwing this out there – you speed back up and then we head off on a sightseeing tour?'

I've just popped a huge forkful of lasagne into my mouth.

My taste buds are exploding as I look at him in surprise. I can see that he's being serious.

'A road trip?'

'Yes.'

'Not on a scooter?'

'No. I have a car. It's my pride and joy.'

'Really? So that little ride on the scooter could have been avoided?'

He grins back at me. 'I didn't realise it was that traumatic.'

Shaking my head at him, I raise my eyebrows in annoyance. 'Forgive my bluntness, but you drive like a fiery young Italian.'

'Ha! Ha! Ha! Naturally I do – but you were never in danger! You're just used to sitting patiently in long queues of traffic, rather than weaving in and out and getting to your destination super-fast. Richard said that in the UK it's either narrow country lanes, or motorways crawling along in the peak holiday season and one roundabout after another. You must get dizzy at times.' Nico seems to find that thought highly amusing.

'He was exaggerating. That's just his sense of humour.'

'I don't usually hang around the hotel on my days off and the few hours I get in between, it might surprise you to know. The scooter comes in handy for short journeys and it's easier to park. But uh, recently I've been a little distracted.'

Is he blaming me?

'Sorry, I didn't realise my presence was cramping your style,' I reply, teasing him softly.

'It's my pleasure, but it will be good to get the car out of the garage and spend some time cruising along.'

'We'd be travelling in style, then?'

As we banter back and forth, I can tell he's getting excited about the prospect.

'She's an Alfa Romeo Spider – 1992 was a good year and it's a great model. She's what they call an iconic roadster *cabrio* – all black, with a cream leather interior. I had her re-sprayed the year before last and she gleams.'

'A convertible? Hmm . . . so I'd get to feel the wind in my hair – it could be messy.'

'Anyway, don't change the subject – what do you think of my idea?'

'The two of us, just heading off to explore?'

'I can promise you a smooth drive and an experience of a lifetime.'

How can I resist that engaging smile, that haplessly curly, dark hair and the way he's looking so expectantly at me?

'Where would we stay?'

'It's not what you know, but who you know. There are always friends of friends who are happy to offer their spare room and it'll be fun. We could visit a vineyard and travel inland, leaving the tourists behind.'

My head is buzzing with excitement, but Nico can't just decide to take time off.

'I know that look,' he interrupts my thoughts. 'It was Mum's suggestion. The Romanos are a large family, and we cover for each other. All for one, and one for all!'

I'd love a road trip with Nico, but where do I draw the line?

'I'm taking your silence as a stunned and happy *yes*. You

can thank me later, when it sinks in. Can you get everything wrapped up in a week? It's the eighth today, so let's aim to set off on Thursday the fifteenth of July. I'll get you back by Monday the twenty-sixth, I promise. Remind me when the removal team arrive?'

'The twenty-eighth and I fly back on the thirty-first.' I cast around for some reason to turn him down, but I can't ignore the part of me that so desperately wants to go on this adventure with Nico.

'Perfect! You certainly won't want to spend the time mooching around and there's so much to see. Mum is going to be delighted and Luca, too. They both admire your work ethic, but think you take life a little too seriously. Richard wanted you to experience the real Italy and see how we live. It's my absolute pleasure to make sure I show you as many wonderful things as we can fit in. And I can introduce you to some of our wider network of friends and extended family.'

Extended? 'There are even more of them?'

He laughs. 'You have no idea. Now stop frowning – your work is almost done, and you've earnt this little trip. Leave everything up to me. You're in good hands.'

I know I am, but is that what I really want? To get drawn in even deeper to a life that just a couple of months ago was totally unknown to me is bewildering. Why are alarm bells going off in my head? I wonder.

Relax, Marci, I tell myself. *Richard wouldn't have encouraged you to come here if he thought it was going to be a huge mistake. He loves you way too much to do that to you and his intention was for you to have a good time and go back home refreshed. That's not a bad thing and it has put life into a bit of a different perspective for you, hasn't it?*

Seemingly out of nowhere, another thought jumps into my head unnerving me. What if it was a little reward for sweeping anything I might happen to stumble across under the carpet?

25.
Major Decisions

'Guy told me to wait until you called me, but I need to talk to you *now*, Marci. I made a huge mistake and I'm sorry, I really am.' In the entire time I was dating Everett, I never once heard him apologise to anyone.

It's only just after 9 a.m. and Nico is outside jet-washing the terrace before he heads down to the restaurant. I'm up in the workroom, trying to establish which books could be worth something, and which can be sold as a bundle.

Be nice, *Marci*, I tell myself. Guy told you that Everett has something to get off his chest. In fairness, the good times we had together were truly wonderful at the time. It wasn't until much later that I began to see how shallow his actions were, and that it was all about making the right impression – never about his true feelings. I'm not even sure he realises that about himself.

'Everett, now isn't the time . . . I . . . uh, I'm in the middle of something. Is this going to take long?'

Glancing at my watch, I know that Nico must leave here by ten thirty at the latest and he'll head in soon to shower and change. If Everett is quick, it should be fine.

'It's all over between Ingrid and me. It has been for a while but it's never easy to extricate oneself, is it?'

Extricate? From a relationship? He didn't have any qualms at disengaging himself from me.

'Poor you, that can't be easy.' I pop him on speakerphone and continue leafing through the tracing-paper-thin pages of the book in front of me. I note down the title and the author and look at the fly pages for any other relevant information I can glean to help identify its age and subject matter. I think it's in Latin.

'It's been hell, and my father wants me to straighten things out with you, Marci. But the thing is, I . . . I regret walking away and . . . well, I think I might actually be in love with you.'

Whoa – that grabs my attention and I stare down at my phone, unable to imagine his expression. Everett *thinks* he might be in love with me. Making an enormous effort to sound sympathetic, I choose my words very carefully.

'Oh, Everett, you are so sweet. Sadly, one thing I've learnt is that if something doesn't work out first time around, it's usually for a very good reason. But often, that's not apparent at the time because it's hard to break up with someone, isn't it? Going back to an old relationship isn't the answer, though.'

I'm holding my breath, hoping that he'll give up.

'But I mean it!' he replies, emphatically. 'My father now regards me as a total failure, he says I was a fool to let you go. And my mother is on at me every chance she gets about when I'm going to settle down. You must get the same,' he declares.

'No, I don't, and if I did, then I'd make it very clear that it's nobody's business but mine.'

'My father has asked me to step up into a new role, Marci, and I fear I've lost the only woman I can envisage helping me through an important stage in my life. And isn't your body clock ticking, Marci?'

I can't believe what I'm hearing and if I didn't find that remark so insulting, I'd actually laugh at his cheek.

'I think I've always been in love with you, Marci,' he continues, in earnest. 'I just didn't appreciate that until now.'

How convenient. Everett seems to be able to switch his affections off and on at will to suit his purpose, but I'm way past falling for it. *Remain calm, Marci*, I tell myself – *if you get angry then he's probably conceited enough to think you still care about him.*

'Well, I will admit that it's a bit of a surprise, Everett, because when we parted you didn't seem at all heartbroken.'

'I wasn't ready to commit, Marci. I panicked.'

And his natural reaction to that was to flirt with the first woman who batted her eyelashes at him.

'I'm just finishing up,' Nico calls up the stairs, startling me, and I quickly press mute on the phone to listen. 'I'll put everything away and then I'll get ready for work.'

'Good,' I reply, trying to keep my voice even. 'I was going to give you a shout as it's getting late.'

Grabbing the phone and putting it to my ear, I unmute it and come in on the end of what sounds like Everett having a moan.

'. . . and my father said the only woman I've ever dated with whom he felt he could have a meaningful conversation is you, Marci.'

Well, I suppose it's nice to know I have Stuart's approval, and he is a businessman worthy of my admiration, but going out with Everett is probably one of the biggest mistakes I ever made. It's just taken me a while to see what a pompous twit he really is.

'Yes, but I'm not in—' As I was about to say *in love with you*, he cuts me off.

'Let me stop you there, Marci. My father really wants to invest in Anvil & Anchor Antiques, and he told me straight that I need to mend fences with you.'

Mend fences? Everett has already said sorry, but now – out of the blue – he's trying to convince me that I'm the one for him. It's utterly ridiculous.

'I don't harbour any grudges, Everett, and you can tell Stuart I said that.'

'I know, I know! Just, please do this one thing for me.'

That little voice inside my head won't be stilled: *No, Everett, I'll do this one thing for Guy and then he'll owe me BIG time.*

'One drink. But I'll warn you now that I don't think it's a good idea. I've moved on, Everett. Anyway, I don't wish to be rude, but I really must go now.'

'Thank you for listening, Marci. You always were a good sort.'

How is it even possible that every single word Everett utters seems to wind me up on a whole new level? Was he this annoying before, but I simply didn't realise it?

'Bye, Everett.' Click.

Literally two minutes later Nico steps into the room, giving me one of his cheeky, laid-back grins.

'Sorry, I didn't realise you were on the phone – you should have said.'

'It wasn't important,' I reply, candidly. And in a way that statement feels empowering. It's good to realise that Everett no longer has any sway over my emotions, but I will let him say his piece and then be done with it for good.

'I don't suppose you fancy another shower, do you?' Nico offers, enticingly.

Now that's a tempting proposal which puts a silly smirk on my face and makes my heart skip a beat.

'No – sadly, these dusty, dilapidated books are getting me rather excited. I think Richard might have struck gold here!'

Nico looks downhearted as he yanks off his T-shirt. 'You're drooling over an old relic, and I can't even tempt you – something isn't right. You're a hard woman, Marci James – Richard has no idea how much he's in my debt for looking after you!'

It's hard not to give in and as Nico walks away from me, a smug little smile tugs at my lips as I get back to work. When the phone goes again, I snatch it up, ready to give Everett a piece of my mind.

'Marci, it's Olivia – I know you're head down working, but did you skip breakfast?'

'Yes, I just grabbed a coffee. Why?'

'If I drop by and pick you up, how about a leisurely brunch at the villa? It'll save you eating later, and I desperately need a listening ear. I feel that my head is going to explode if I don't talk to someone.'

'Of course. Give me an hour and I'll be ready and waiting.'

'Perfect. Thank you, my truly wonderful friend!'

I gently close the pages of the book lying on the desk in front of me and jump up. Unbuttoning my shirt, I call out to Nico.

'Don't turn the shower off. I'm going out and I need a quick freshen-up.'

Well, books are dusty, aren't they?

'Hey, Luna – *come stai?*' Her ears immediately perk up and finally I have it sussed. She prefers Italian to English. At that precise moment the little furry bundle unexpectedly jumps up into my arms and it's a miracle that I manage to catch her.

'Ahh . . . she's missed you!' Olivia croons, leaning in to smooth Luna's ears. 'Poor thing, what a start to the day.'

'Are you ready to tell me all about it?'

Olivia scans around. 'Mum's here. She's having lunch at her friend's house and offered to take Luna with her. It's a forty-five-minute walk and Mum loves the company. She doesn't know what's going on and I said I'd invited you over for brunch as a thank you for the gift.' She keeps her voice low, but there's no sign of Patricia.

However, Olivia points to the table down under an arbour on the first level, created from trelliswork over which a climbing rose and a grapevine have intertwined.

'Is that what your father cut back the other day? Last time I came I didn't even realise there was a seating area underneath all that foliage,' I remark, as we make our way down to it.

'I know – it's really opened it back up and we thought

it was probably too far gone. You get a different view out over the sea from here.'

What I love about this garden is the mix of informal evergreen shrubs and trees, and the long line of tall, slim Italian cypresses which stand erect, marking the edge of the garden on the far side as the tiers nestle against the limestone.

'Ah, there you both are. Just in time! Luna won't want to go for her walk now she has someone else to spoil her.'

Olivia and I exchange a smile as we turn and walk back up to the top patio.

'How are you, Patricia?' I set Luna down next to her and we watch as she jumps up onto her hind legs, her paws dangling as she dances around. 'I think you have your answer – she's ready to go by the look of it.'

'I'm fine, thank you, Marci and Luna certainly lets us know what she wants. Any news about when Richard will return to see us again?'

'No. He's in Australia right now and then he's due to go back to the UK. What his exact plans are is anyone's guess.'

'At least he's happy, that's all anyone can ask for, isn't it? It's time to go, Luna.'

Olivia takes the tray from her mum, leaning in to kiss her cheek.

'This is extremely kind of you, Patricia – you're spoiling us,' I say, following suit.

'It's my pleasure – I think my daughter needs a little time to chill this morning. It's never a good sign when she knits her brows together like that.'

'Oh, I'm fine. Go on, get off, the two of you – and not too many treats for Luna, Mum. You know how greedy she is!'

As Olivia wanders over to the steps down to the next level, Patricia glances across at me and it's obvious she knows something is up.

'Right, let's get ourselves settled, shall we?' Olivia calls out.

I hurry over to walk in front in case she needs help, but Olivia is so used to the trek up and back, that for her it's second nature.

'I should be working,' Olivia complains, sounding disappointed in herself. 'But Jack rang at six this morning and we talked for about two hours straight, so my stomach is in knots.'

As I help her decant the tray, it strikes me that I have never seen her this perturbed.

'Is it bad news?'

'Jack has quit his job and he's on his way home – for good!'

Even I draw in a sharp breath, and she looks at me, grimacing.

'It's scary, Marci, I will admit. But . . . well, let's sit and eat because I'm feeling light-headed. I haven't really eaten since yesterday lunchtime. Who would have thought this could be happening?'

Patricia has laid out a little feast for us, but we only pick at it, as Olivia recounts the highlights of her conversation with Jack.

'He wants to sell up and downsize, Marci.' Her voice

reflects her uncertainty. 'Jack says that if we reduce our mortgage, and live off our savings for a while, it will give us a bit of breathing space. In the meantime, he'll consider what his options are, given the circumstances. Obviously, it wouldn't have been as damaging if he'd simply handed in his notice and stayed to finish off the job he was working on. But I'm glad he had the courage to quit, because health comes first – there's always a way to earn a little money.'

'Is that do-able?' I venture to ask as Olivia seems a little distant as she talks.

'Yes. But obviously, it might take a while to sell the villa. I let him lay out his plan and just agreed with everything he said, because he was like an entirely different man when he was talking to me this morning. It's the old Jack, the man I originally married!'

Olivia picks up one of the paper napkins and wipes away a tear as it begins to trickle down her cheek.

'Oh . . . don't cry, Olivia. Jack told me that every day the two of you are apart, is one day less you have together and that is agony for him – I could see it reflected on his face.'

Now the tears are falling fast, and we sit in silence until she mops them all away and blows her nose.

'I knew it was bad, Marci – but thank you so much for sharing that with me because he wouldn't say that to my face. He just said that they've had so much trouble with faulty equipment and then delays getting replacements, that it's made the job hell.'

'That's probably true and it's what pushed him over the edge. But at least he's strong enough to know his limit, Olivia. Some people don't, and that's a sobering thought.'

'Let's cover this over and walk with me. I've been mulling over an idea of my own and I wanted to use you as a sounding board, if that's okay?'

'Certainly – that's what friends are for!'

We spread the remainder of the napkins out over the plates and make our way back up to the villa.

'A part of our long-term plan when we first bought this place was to renovate these buildings. This one isn't too bad; it looks shabby from the outside because it hasn't been painted in years but structurally it's in great shape.'

Olivia pulls a key from her pocket and inserts it into the lock of the single-storey building. It sits on the far corner of the property, beyond the main dwelling. Inside there's a small hallway and leading off there is a sitting room, two bedrooms, a shower room and toilet, and a kitchen-diner. The latter is very small indeed, and the dining bit is really a fold-down worktop hinged to the wall. When it's up there's barely enough space for two people to sit comfortably side by side.

'Jack's original idea was that we'd rent it out in the summer, but the drawback is that anyone staying here would have to use the main path, unless we made some major changes to the layout. We could create a separate little garden at the front by planting some shrubs and trees around it to give both properties a little privacy. That would help, but I wasn't convinced it was the right thing to do. Anyway, let's head back outside and I'll show you the outbuildings.'

Next door is an extension accessed from the front and with one window to the rear. It's a large open space and in the past I guess it was used as a storeroom. There's a spare fridge-freezer in here, a couple of bikes and a cavernous open space. Going back outside again, attached to that is a smaller room, which is used to store garden equipment and various odds and ends.

'Right, let's have another coffee and I'll spell out my idea.'

Olivia's mood has brightened and when we walk back to the villa to pop the kettle on, I insist on making the coffee. She is literally pacing around as she's talking, and I can see how important this is to her.

'Mum and Dad both spend a couple of mornings or afternoons here each week, generally helping out in the garden and taking care of Luna. They both love hanging around and pottering, and when I'm working, they take Luna for her walks. What if they sold up and came to live here permanently? Their house is wonderful, but they've spent so much time here that it's like their second home, anyway.'

'What a brilliant idea! Would they go for it?'

Olivia beams. 'They'd jump at it, Marci, and just between you and me, Mum and I have previously touched on the subject but that was a while ago. I don't know how Jack would feel about it, though. But if we were in a position to pay a lump sum off the mortgage, Jack wouldn't need to earn so much and maybe instead of being freelance, I could look for a permanent job with one of the companies I work for to make life even easier. And the bonus is that if we go away on holiday there's always someone to look after both places.'

As we make our way back down to the cosy little arbour, I'm imagining what I'd do to that cute little property.

'If your parents knocked through the wall into the extension on the side, imagine what a marvellous open-plan kitchen/diner that would make. And it would still leave the workshop on the end, for storage.'

'Yes, and if they installed bi-fold glass doors across the front, well – look at that view! But what if Jack doesn't relish having his in-laws living, quite literally, on his doorstep?'

As we start really tucking into the cheese and cold meat platter, I shrug my shoulders nonchalantly.

'You won't know until you ask, will you? But anything is better than what you've both been going through lately.'

'Should I do it tonight – when he gets home – or wait a day or two?' Olivia offers me a plate with thinly cut slices of what looks like rosemary bread.

My gut instinct is telling me that Jack is going to return home feeling that he has let Olivia down. 'Make him a strong coffee and bring him out here, then just launch straight into it. If he doesn't feel comfortable talking about it, I'm sure he'll make that clear. But having seen how you guys are around each other, being apart isn't worth the price you're paying. I'd give anything to have that sort of relationship with someone. And the fact that you both decided to settle here in Positano, so close to your parents, is telling. If there hasn't been a falling-out yet, I'd say that's a positive sign!'

And finally, I hear her laugh – a genuine from-the-gut laugh. 'They love him to bits, Marci. But I don't want Jack to feel he's being forced into anything. We only see his parents about three times a year, although they really look forward to staying with us.'

'Then say just that. Tell him it's simply another option to consider and then you can both sleep on it.'

'My goodness – day one on my new project and I haven't even turned on the PC. I'm not going to be able to settle to anything until Jack arrives back safely. Still, hopefully tomorrow will be easier all round and I can leave Jack to potter and think, while I get on with some work. And I've taken up most of your morning, too.'

I wave my hand in the air, brushing away her concerns as I munch away quite happily.

'Any reason to come visit is fine by me. And I have some surprising news to share with you.'

Olivia's eyes light up. 'About Nico?'

I nod. 'He wants to take me on a road trip. I'm not sure it's a good idea, though. It was Celia's suggestion – what do you think?'

'That's a wonderful idea! You must say *yes*, why wouldn't you? I bet Dario will love the chance to step into Nico's role while he's away and I'm sure there's someone else willing to cover for Dario. It's how people prove themselves and they all began that way.'

I guess I'd better go along with it as I don't want to upset anyone, do I?

26.
All Actions Have Consequences

I'm in high spirits when Olivia kindly drops me back at La Grotta. From the chat I had with Jack while we were lazing around on *La Fortuna*, I suspected big changes were coming. If I'd realised quite how close to the edge he was, it would have been hard for me not to take Olivia to one side and at least drop a hint. But I'm glad he had the courage to do the right thing and they have options, good ones.

To my surprise, Olivia didn't hesitate for one second when I told her about Nico's offer and if she can't see a problem with it, then neither can I. Oh, just a couple more days and my work will be done and then it will be a glorious end to my wonderful summer in Positano. One I'll always look back on with fondness.

Letting myself into La Grotta, I see there's no post for Richard again today which is a good sign. It feels as if the end is in sight at long last. Before too long, this building will have workmen crawling all over it. The work Nico has done in the garden, and the way Olivia and I have tidied it up inside, gives a tiny glimpse of what lies hidden and with Luca's vision it sounds like this will one day be a truly wonderful place to live. The only question is, who will be living here once it's done?

The day that Dario walked up here with a cool box from Celia, he was looking for reassurance that Richard wasn't gone for good. Albeit, he did his best to make it appear like a casual question. The fact that he went on to mention that Giulia's position wasn't clear if she didn't marry Nico told me everything I needed to know. While they might not be ready to tell the family how they feel about each other just yet, when they finally reveal their secret I can't see Nico moving out of the hotel to live here on his own. They do say that even the best-laid plans can go astray and isn't that the truth!

Heading back upstairs, I walk into the workroom and immediately my eye is drawn to the stack of books alongside the chair. How many times have I walked past them over the last couple of days and yet never noticed there's a bundle of papers in between two of them, about halfway down the pile? The books were lifted straight out of some tatty old boxes, and I'm puzzled. Enough to go straight over and gently ease them out.

Tucking the wodge of papers under my arm, I go downstairs to make myself a quick coffee, before heading outside to the patio area. It's been a rather disrupted first half of the day, what with Everett's call and the unexpected brunch invitation from Olivia.

After I sit down and make myself comfortable, I start leafing through. How on earth these old bank statements of Richard's ended up in among some dusty books, I have no idea. And then I see several folded documents held together with a large silver paperclip – I recognise it immediately.

I clearly remember the day Nico held them up, asking where to put them.

By the time I've gone through it all, it's obvious what's been going on and a chill runs through me. My coffee has gone cold, but I need the caffeine as a realisation hits me like a hammer. These weren't there when I sat down to begin working first thing. Nico must have done that as I was getting ready for Olivia to pick me up.

Have you ever experienced a moment when suddenly the bottom falls out of your world? Like the day some mean kid in the playground tells you Santa Claus isn't real. Well, this is one such moment and I feel totally, utterly broken to discover that Nico hasn't been here merely to help out – he has an entirely different motive and one he's chosen not to share with me.

'I'm not perfect and I never pretended to be!' Nico yells back at me, unable to refute my accusation as I wave the papers in front of him. Tonight, instead of the meal he was expecting to be laid out awaiting him on the patio, I'm sitting here with a grim look on my face.

'I wasn't expecting perfect, but I deserved honesty at the very least.'

'What do you mean, Marci?'

'You were searching for answers, Nico. Don't insult my intelligence by pretending otherwise.'

He hangs his head, and he can't even look me in the eyes.

'Was sifting through Richard's private financial records productive? This collection of old bank statements wasn't in the workroom this morning before Olivia picked me up.

You borrowed them, because you didn't want me walking in and catching you going through Richard's things. Is that the real reason why you've stayed close to me?'

'Look – it wasn't some sort of plan, please believe me. Dario and I got talking one morning, shortly after you arrived here. He asked me what will happen if Richard decides he needs his investment back to start his new life with Angel. I had no idea how much Richard has invested in the business, and I thought if I could find out . . .' He pauses, swallowing hard as a look of guilt begins to consume him. 'If Richard pulls out, Luca can't hand over the business to me when we have no idea if it's even possible to find another investor. It could be the end for Il Posto di Luca as a family concern. It started to make sense why Mum has backed off bringing Giulia's name into the conversation. Maybe she realises what Luca is failing to acknowledge – that without Richard's continuing goodwill everything hangs in the balance.'

Nico is clearly in shock at being confronted, but I can see from his reaction that he bitterly regrets not being honest with me. And in that split second, I know he's speaking his truth. We're like pawns in a game of chess – desperately trying to understand what's going on in case anyone gets hurt, but fearful of what we might find. We're talking about people we love and that makes it personal.

I stand, and as Nico steps closer, I launch myself into his arms. The emotions I'm feeling are so conflicted, I'm confused and yet a part of me deep down inside knows that Nico is a good man.

However, the sensation that courses through my entire

body is one of gutting disappointment, knowing I have let Richard down by not protecting his privacy. But it's more than that. It didn't take long for me to see that Nico was easy to love and would be hard to leave behind. But if family and business come first to the extent that he can lie to me without his conscience pricking him, nothing is what is seems. Why couldn't he simply be honest and talk about his worst fears? The fact that he couldn't confide in me hurts and I'm not sure I can let that go.

Neither of us can face the thought of eating and after several cups of coffee, we head upstairs. Wrapped in each other's arms we're both too emotionally drained to talk – words seem to make it even worse somehow. And yet here we are, clinging to each other – so close and yet in other ways so far apart. In my heart I know it's the beginning of the end.

The next morning the mood between us is subdued and as soon as Nico leaves for work I give Celia a call. She can tell something is wrong and she offers to come round so we can talk. When I ask her not to let anyone know where she's going, it obviously sets off alarm bells for her and less than an hour after Nico left, she's tapping on the front door.

Celia takes one look at my expression, and the colour drains from her face.

'I really appreciate you coming all the way up here, Celia. Please come through.'

As we step out into the courtyard, I ask if she would like a drink, but she shakes her head. I indicate for her to take a seat.

'I don't know how to broach this subject, Celia, as it's really nothing at all to do with me, but—'

Her shoulders sag and she takes a deep breath in.

'You've discovered just how heavily Richard has invested in the business. Is Nico aware?'

Walking around the table to sit opposite her, my stomach is in knots.

'He stumbled upon some documents, but I can't say for sure. It was enough for him to be worried about what might happen if Richard doesn't return and wants to sell his investment.'

'It's more than that, I can see it written all over your face, Marci.'

This is not the time to talk about my feelings, or my disappointments. 'Richard entrusted me with this task and it's my fault for not being more careful. I should have realised there would be things lying around that might . . . that might . . .' I cast around for the right words.

'Have wider implications?'

Celia looks down at her hands, cupping them together and raising them to her mouth as if in prayer. It takes her a little while before she begins speaking and I grow conscious of the sounds around us. The drone of a lorry in the distance, and a posse of birds fighting for the best branch in the recently pruned olive tree.

'Marci, is it wrong to try to bury the guilt of one single action that led our lives astray, to avoid hurting the innocent people who depend upon us? I've struggled with my conscience for a very long time, please believe that.'

Celia looks across at me, her eyes searching mine. For some reason it matters to her what I think. I can only assume that this is to do with Luca then, and while that's a relief in one way, it must be bad for Richard to get involved.

'That's quite a burden for you to carry, Celia.'

It's sad to think that she has had to sit quietly by, supporting her husband and a man who has become a good and trusted friend, and she's anguished by the effect it's had on their lives.

I have no idea what happened, and now I realise that I don't want to know. What is clear, is that Celia is concerned that others will stand in judgement of her, but unless they've walked in her shoes how can anyone possibly do that?

'I've caused you a problem – Richard put his trust in me, and I let him down. Nico and I have become close, but I had no idea what was at risk . . . and I never meant to come between him and Giulia – please believe that.'

She sighs, wringing her hands in agitation as I can see that troubles her.

'Nothing is straightforward, Marci. Giulia and Nico are friends and I know it can never be more than that. Nico has his suspicions about Dario and Giulia, but out of respect for Giulia he's not pressuring her. However, until Dario and Giulia decide what they are going to do, Luca remains totally in the dark. What really concerns me is that Nico doesn't want you to leave, Marci, and I don't think he knows what to do.'

And I've been pressing Nico to talk to Giulia, when he knew there was no point – he was simply waiting on her. It's a relief to know that Celia is aware of what's been going on and that's why it didn't faze her when Nico and I spent time together. And I can't help but wonder if Giulia's hesitancy to commit to Dario is because her goal was always to be the co-owner. If she truly loves him, then giving that dream up is the price she has to pay, but it can't be easy. As it won't be easy for Nico and me to say goodbye – the mere thought of it is tearing me apart right now.

'It would be unfair of me to stay and give Nico false hope, Celia.'

'If that's your wish . . . but Nico will take it hard because—'

I put up my hand to stop her going any further. 'My home isn't here, Celia, and Nico wouldn't be happy living in the UK and working for someone else, would he? It's an impossible situation and the longer I stay the worse it will be for us both.'

'I understand, Marci, and thank you for your discretion. What will you tell Nico?'

'That I'm needed at home. There are big changes happening for my mum and I know she's missing me. Nico and I both know my time is drawing to a close, I'll just be leaving a bit sooner than expected. It will only take me a couple of days to finalise things here.'

'Luca and Richard have safeguarded the future, but Nico might not approve of some of the decisions that were made in the past. That's something I need to tackle, as obviously Nico will now have questions he'd like answered and I understand that. In the meantime, what can I do to help you?'

'As I won't be here when the lorry arrives, I'll need

someone to be on site all day. They can phone me, and I'll give my instructions directly to the team. First of all, I need to see how soon I can get a flight home. And I think it would be best for Nico if I book a taxi to take me to the airport. Goodbyes are always tough, and I will miss you all.'

Celia can see how hard this is for me.

'If that makes it easier, Marci. You must do what's best for you.'

'I'm sorry I stumbled upon things I shouldn't have seen, and I'm devastated that I didn't do a better job of protecting Nico. If you're able to reassure him that the financial future of Il Posto di Luca is safe, that's his only concern. Family is everything to him.'

Celia stands and we embrace tearfully. When I leave, I know that a little piece of me will be left behind and there's nothing I can do, other than to accept it.

'Leave the arrangements for the flight and taxi with me, Marci – I can sort that for you. I will ask Dario to make sure your instructions are carried out when the removal men arrive, he won't let you down. You focus on what needs to be done here and know that I am so grateful to you for being so understanding. The problem with life is that every decision we make has a consequence we end up having to live with and sometimes it's nigh on impossible to look back and know for sure whether we've done the right thing.'

As I see her out, I remember what Jack said to me when we returned to the villa after that wonderful day onboard *La Fortuna*. He admitted that if he spent the time he has with Olivia counting down to his next departure, his life would be very miserable indeed. At least he had the courage to do something about it. I'm walking away because, in this case, there is no happy solution. Only acceptance and that takes courage, too.

27.

Sometimes Life Hurts

When Nico returns from work, the minute he steps into the kitchen I can see how stressed he is.

'Is there something you need to tell me?' His words are challenging and his tone bitter.

Is that fear I see in his eyes?

'As I was leaving Dario took me aside and told me something in confidence. Is it true – are you flying home early?'

I close my eyes for a moment. I wanted tonight to be relaxing and I should have warned Celia that Dario, too, is worried about his future at the restaurant. She obviously approached him about being here on the twenty-eighth and no doubt said not to tell anyone, but he's too close to Nico not to take him into his confidence.

'I'm sorry you should hear it from Dario first. I intended to sit you down quietly and tell you tonight. I'm needed back in the UK – there are big changes coming at work and both Mum and Guy need my support.'

'You told my mum and enlisted her help, but you thought you'd wait to tell me?'

'No, it wasn't like that. You know how quickly things happen and all it takes is one phone call to change everything. My head is all over the place and I didn't want to drag you back from work just to break the news. I knew how disappointed you'd be.'

'Disappointed? What about our road trip?'

'I'm so sorry how it's worked out, Nico, but it's for the best.'

'I was fooling myself thinking you were looking forward to it, then? Or is this a punishment for my indiscretion?'

He's angry and it saddens me to hear him lashing out with words I hope he doesn't even mean.

'Everything has become so complicated, Nico. When one's head says one thing and the heart another, this is what happens. And it's not about the upset yesterday. I understand why you did what you did. My mum is thinking of selling some of her shares in Anvil & Anchor Antiques to my ex-boyfriend's father. I need to be there to make sure that everyone is clear about where I stand.' It's the truth if I stop there. Nico can choose to interpret that any way it suits him, but he seems to shrug it off.

'I don't want you to go with things left unsaid between us—'

'If our friendship has meant anything at all to you, Nico, then please respect my decision, as it's the right thing to do.'

'But everything is coming together nicely for our road trip.' He's grasping at straws, and he knows it.

'My work here is done and if I stay it just muddies the water. You won't face up to the reality of your situation while I'm here – you're running from it.'

'Oh, so you aren't the one who is running away? It's

me. How convenient to turn it all around and simply walk away as if it doesn't matter.'

That is completely out of order and totally screwed up. 'It's been . . . wonderful, Nico – magical at times, because Positano is a very special place. But my real life awaits me and what's left of a familiar, showery UK summer. It's time for me to cool off.'

And then I recall something we said to each other on our first night together, here at La Grotta: 'I could let you grow on me, Nico,' I'd admitted to him, 'but I won't, because that's not what life has planned for us. It's rather sad, but true.'

Nico had pulled a face, but his words come back to haunt me as I understand now what he meant. 'We can pretend, can't we? At least for now, Marci. Don't let it spoil our time together.'

We were only ever living a fantasy that never was meant to last – and we both knew it.

To make matters worse, an hour later Celia texts to say she's managed to get a ticket for me the day after tomorrow, on one of those last-minute flight websites. Nico can tell by my expression I'm putting a brave face on it and that I'm as devastated as he is to be turning my back on Positano.

How angry can you be with each other when the raw pain begins to dull, and the inevitability of a situation begins to sink in? Our meal was pleasant, but understandably subdued, as we agree not to waste what little time we do have left together wishing things were different. Neither of us has done anything wrong, not really.

And now, as we lie in each other's arms, the only thought

on our minds is that the day after tomorrow I'll be up early and Nico will be packing his things and heading back to his old room.

'It all feels unreal, doesn't it?' His voice is low as his fingers gently graze my arm. 'You have goose bumps – are you cold?'

'No, my arm is catching the breeze from the window, that's all.' I exhale, a little louder than I'd realised, and it sounds like a sigh. 'I'm sorry, Nico, my brain is refusing to switch off tonight.'

'Same here. And I'm sorry for not being honest with you; sorrier than you can possibly know.'

I can't tell him about my conversation with Celia, he simply thinks I turned to her in a panic, not really knowing what to do first. With loose ends to tie up and the arrangements to fly home, it's believable. However, it hurts walking away like this. Nico doesn't mean anyone any harm, quite the reverse. Family stuff is never easy, I know that only too well. I'm doing things to pacify Guy, things that don't sit well with me. The truth is that I'd just like to tell Everett exactly what I think of him. But I won't because that would upset Stuart. I understand what it's like to be in the middle of something not of your making, with no easy way out. I hope Celia does sit down and talk to Nico, even if it's just to ease his mind about the future. Maybe it's best not to know about the past.

'I'm not ready to let you go, Marci. Is there anything I can do to persuade you to stay just a little longer?'

And how much worse will it be if I don't end this quickly?

'There's no point, Nico. My family relies upon me, as

your family relies upon you. And it would just be prolonging the inevitable.'

'Is this your way of ignoring the fact that you're walking out on me as if our time together means nothing at all?' It's a rebuke, but he's softening it with a little humour that doesn't ring true. It's also unfair.

'It was wonderful, Nico, but we both knew it was a transient thing. I need to sit down with my mum and check she really is making the right decision – not just for Guy and me, but for herself. And that's the truth of it.'

'It's not that you're running away from me, then?'

My eyes begin to well up, but I make a concerted effort not to lose it. Something inside of me suddenly switches off. *Make this as easy as you can*, *Marci*, *for both your sakes*, that inner voice tells me. And this time I listen.

28.
Hello . . . and Goodbye!

'It's true! You really are back at work, and two weeks ahead of time – that's good going, Marci. I can't thank you enough and I mean that from the bottom of my heart.' It's so good to hear Richard's voice.

'I know and it's lovely to be back,' I enthuse. 'Especially as I'm sitting at my smart new desk in my newly decorated office.'

'Ah, that would be Guy making sure you don't get itchy feet again. It's called bribery.'

'Me – get itchy feet? I didn't have them in the first place.' Having been at home for a week, after giving myself two days to wallow and a good talking to, I discovered that life goes on. Every morning you open your eyes and there's a new day stretching out before you – whether you're ready for it or not. After five days cleaning every inch of my house it gleams, and it gave me time to get my head straight. I'm ready to pick up my life again.

'And you really didn't need to pay for the wine rack.'

'It was a present for Nico, and it wouldn't be a gift from me if I hadn't, would it? He fell in love with it and given that he was so obliging, I thought it made a rather nice leaving present ready for when he takes on his new role. Celia arranged for some of the guys to take it apart and assemble it as a surprise. Jack distracted him with a boat ride, I hear.'

'You're still in close touch, then?'

'With Olivia, yes. I spoke to her twice last week. I don't know if you're aware, but Jack quit his job and hopes to set up his own business. She's so excited, as there are also big changes at the villa. Her parents are planning to renovate the guest house and outbuildings to live in and will be putting their own property up for sale.'

'Really – that's a surprise! I'll have to give Patricia and Aldo a ring to congratulate them on the news. I've always admired their home – great views, obviously, and the property is well laid out.'

I can almost hear the cogs inside his head turning, but he immediately changes the subject.

'Did you find love in Positano then, Marci? After all, it's full of handsome, tanned young men and sometimes a summer fling can blossom into something more meaningful.'

I burst out laughing – if he could see me now, I'm rolling my eyes.

'Yes, I did, Richard – the love of a group of people who were strangers to me when I arrived, but friends when I left.'

Would my parting have been as tearful all round if any of them had suspected what had really been going on between Nico and me? And how would Richard feel now if he knew that I'd left Celia with a problem, because I failed to protect his privacy?

'And that's all?' He sounds disappointed.

'What were you expecting?' My lip quivers and without warning, I'm close to tears. It wasn't a total stranger who touched my heart, but someone much closer to Richard and that's something I can't divulge.

'Take no notice of me – I'm an old romantic and I always will be. The outcome might not have been quite what I hoped for, but you sound happy.'

'I am, Richard. The memories I have, I will cherish forever.'

'That's what matters, Marci. And you made me proud. You stepped up for my second family and by all accounts, you helped Nico make a few tough decisions.'

Giulia has made her choice, then. And oh, how I wish I hadn't been a part of any of that, but Richard will never fully understand the price I paid for a summer affair that left a serious dent in my heart. I realise now that I didn't know what love was and, in a way, I wish that were still the case.

'When are you coming back to the UK?'

'We're still going from one relative to another. And they roped in friends, but they're all so welcoming and Angel is having a ball. I'm not sure when exactly we'll be able to book our flights. I'll let you know as soon as we do.'

'And I'll confirm when the container has been collected and it's on the way. Give my love to Angel and I miss you, Richard.'

'Same here, my lovely Marci.'

As I put the phone down the door opens and Guy's head appears.

'Are you still speaking to me after the weekend?'

'Yes, come in and take a seat. Perhaps you should shut the door.'

We exchange a grimace.

'Yesterday was the worst Sunday brunch ever, wasn't it?' Guy declares as he sinks down onto the chair opposite me. 'You could cut the atmosphere with a knife. I don't know which of us was the most uncomfortable, sitting around that table – Everett, or me. Several times I looked across at you and nearly burst out laughing, as you tried to make polite conversation.'

'Yes, well, if Mum and David hadn't been there, it would have been even worse.'

'But at least Stuart got the message when I kept shutting Everett down. I think Everett took it pretty well in the end.'

'Not before making a total ass of himself, though. Anyway, at least the deal is done. Stuart has already been on the phone this morning. He apologised and said it was a mistake letting Everett join us. In particular, he asked me to let you know that it wasn't his idea – it was Georgia's. Reading between the lines, I think she's now accepted that there is no chance at all of you and her son getting back together.'

I heave a massive sigh of relief. 'I did wonder if Stuart would have second thoughts after sleeping on it. But it's always best to tell the truth and I wanted to make my position very clear from the start.'

'Well, you succeeded in doing just that and it hasn't put our prospective new partner off. Mum's delighted, of course, because she'd been avoiding Georgia ever since you and Everett split up. Now they have a positive reason to rekindle their friendship. Anyway, what do you think of your new surroundings?'

Guy looks so pleased with himself and glad to have me back.

'You did a good job, and it was a huge surprise to walk into this morning.'

'And you're happy with Mum's decision?'

'I'm happy that it's *her* decision and no one else's.'

'When I called in to see you at the house on Thursday, you were spring cleaning. That's always a bad sign. Everything is all right, isn't it?'

'Oh, just a few cobwebs that needed my attention and a general freshening up. And the drop in temperature was a bit of shock to my system. It's taken me a few days to adjust but today it's lovely and sunny.'

'But not as *hot* as Positano?'

Guy is fishing. I didn't really say too much about my early return, only that the job was finished, and that I was missing everyone. I told Guy I needed the week off to get myself sorted and here I am today, eager to make a start. I want to get some firm figures together, so we can fix the budget before we move to the next stage of my project. Olivia said I should give Jack a ring as he has IT contacts everywhere. Maybe I will when I'm feeling . . . more like my old self.

There's a gentle tap on the door and I shout out, 'Come in.'

'Sorry to interrupt your meeting, but you have a visitor, Marci.' Briony looks a little flustered as she stands back.

The door opens a little wider and Nico steps over the threshold.

For several moments I sit here motionless, then gathering my wits together, I jump up.

'Guy, this is Nico Romano.'

My heart is thudding in my chest, and it was a mistake getting up so quickly, because now I'm feeling a little wobbly on my feet.

Fortunately, neither of them notices. Guy stands and Nico gives him a broad smile as they shake hands.

'What a surprise – Marci didn't let on that the house cleaning was because she was expecting a guest. We must all have dinner together, not least to thank you for looking after my sister so well. Richard certainly has a lot to answer for, as his little business wasn't quite as little as he led us to believe.'

'This isn't a holiday,' Nico replies firmly. 'I'm here to ask Marci to marry me.'

Guy is stunned and my reaction is to burst into tears.

Closing the front door behind me, Nico stands awkwardly in the hallway, and I indicate for him to step through into the sitting room.

'You can't just turn up like this, Nico. What were you thinking?'

'There's a time to think and a time to do, Marci. I've been frantically trying to get a plane ticket since the day after you left. I was laying up the tables in the restaurant the next morning and Mum appeared, her arms crossed and her eyes blazing. She said to me:

"For goodness' sake, Nico – if you're going to walk around looking like the end of the world is upon us, you're going to scare our customers away. You know what you need to do, so do it!" Then everyone else joined in. They said I was mad for letting you go in the first place.'

'Why not simply call me to talk?'

'If I'm going to be living in the UK at some point, hopefully soon, then I thought I'd better see what I'm about to let myself in for.'

We're standing here, looking at each other and neither of us knows what to do. My heart sinks a little. If we were in Positano we'd already be in each other's arms, but I see Nico's gaze wander around the room. I wonder if he's suddenly realising that he's made a mistake. A big mistake.

'It's lovely – very cosy. And it isn't raining – it's sunny.' When his eyes come back to rest on me, his smile is ginormous. It's like a beacon and he steps forward, throwing his arms around my waist and lifting me off the floor to twirl me around.

'I knew that the moment I held you in my arms I'd know for sure, because the heart doesn't lie. In hindsight, I'm pretty sure I fell in love with you that first night when we strolled along the beach together – I just didn't know what true love feels like. You can't deny it – I can feel it within you, too. You love me, Marci James.'

I can't argue with him. There's no point. But he's ignoring the elephant in the room – the one with a big sign on its back saying: *Marci, Nico isn't meant to be here. Luca and*

Celia are relying upon him to take the family business forward. Hopefully, with the errors of the past put to bed. What are YOU going to do about it?

'This is crazy, Nico,' I declare, as he lowers me gently to the floor. 'You don't know me, not the version of me on my home turf. A few weeks of fun in the sun is one thing, but it can be a little misleading. You're dreaming if you think you can just walk away from your life and your family, to follow me here. What we feel for each other is strong, but you'd end up being miserable and missing home – even love couldn't survive that sort of pressure.'

'That's where you're wrong, Marci. I do know you – I know a lot about you. I know that you're a good listener and you worry about the people who are close to you. You're loyal and you're loving. And you lie on your left side at night, with your right leg crooked up. You always end up lying corner to corner across the bed. That tells me you're not used to sleeping with someone else alongside you and that made me realise how special our nights together in Positano were. And the final giveaway was that even though you were sound asleep, when I leant over to sweep the stray hairs from your face, as my fingers touched your skin a contented sigh escaped your lips.'

'Oh, you fool!' I whisper, leaning my head against the side of his. 'You mad, lovesick fool. What are we going to do? It's an impossible dream, Nico. I can't let you break Celia and Luca's hearts.'

We linger for a few moments and then his lips are on mine and I know that I'm lost. Whatever happens now, we're both to blame, because I don't have the willpower to fight the man who captured my heart – truly, madly and forever.

'Mum, David – this is Nico Romano.'

Nico steps forward to greet Mum Italian-style and she loves it. Then he turns to David, and they shake hands.

'And this is Guy's wife, Selena.'

As Nico moves nervously from person to person, he's not sure how to greet our host, Selena, who is standing next to Guy. There's an awkward moment until he takes control and leans in to kiss her cheek, while taking the hand she had begun to hold out in front of her. They grin at each other and it breaks the ice.

'It's lovely to meet you, Nico. Anyway, don't stand on ceremony,' she encourages. 'Everyone, please take a seat around the table. Guy, I'll leave you to sort out the wine, while I pop into the kitchen – dinner is almost ready.'

'Thank you so much for the invite.' Nico engages Guy in conversation as he leads us through into the dining room. 'What a beautiful home you have.'

Guy and Selena's house is tastefully decorated, with lots of bold and vibrant colours reflected in the soft furnishings and the pieces of art displayed on the walls.

'It's kind of you both to arrange this dinner party,' I chime in. 'Selena is a much better cook than I am.' Everyone laughs except David.

'Have you been to the UK before, Nico?' Guy enquires, as he walks around the table filling glasses, a bottle of white wine in one hand and red in the other.

'I was born here but moved to Italy when I was almost three years old. I'm afraid I don't have any memories at all of living in the UK.'

'Oh, I didn't realise that. You're a lucky chap to be bilingual, though.'

I hope this idea that Guy came up with to get the introductions out of the way in one go, isn't going to turn into an awkward interrogation.

'You work in the hotel and catering industry, I gather, Nico?'

David's question only goes to show how out of the loop he is. Doesn't Mum ever talk to him about what's going on in her life, or does he only have ears for what affects him personally?

'Yes, David. It's a family business.'

'Richard has an antiques shop in Positano, doesn't he?' At least David is beginning to connect the dots, given that I was absent for six weeks.

I glance at Mum, and she glances at David. 'I talk to him all the time, Nico, but he probably only listens to about ten per cent of the conversation. Yes, dear,' she says, turning to face David. 'That's why Marci flew to Positano. Richard rented a little shop owned by Luca, Nico's father.'

David can see how frustrated Mum is with him for not paying attention, but Mum hasn't quite got it right, either. Luca was never Richard's landlord but, thankfully, that's what she's been led to believe.

'It's complicated,' Nico replies, rather graciously. 'In Italy, friends often become family in the nicest possible way.'

'Of course. And are you staying long?'

Now I'm getting anxious. 'Nico flew here to propose to me, David. Everything is a little up in the air right now.'

Mum really should have told him and if she did, he needs to start tuning in.

'And are you about to reveal your decision, Marci?' Guy asks, tentatively, as he takes his seat at the head of the table.

The silence is deafening. 'Well, it's *yes*, of course it is!' I turn to gaze at Nico, and he reaches out to grab my hand. 'We're not quite sure how it's going to work, though.'

Poor Mum – she's holding her breath by the look of it, hoping David remains silent. But it's Guy who jumps straight in.

'Well, it's obvious. You'll both fly back to break the news to Nico's family, and Anvil & Anchor Antiques will have an office in Positano.'

And just like that, my wonderful brother comes up with the solution, as if it's a no-brainer.

'I work remotely?'

Guy looks at me and it's clear nothing will stop him making this work, because my big brother loves me with all his heart.

'Naturally. I'd do anything to make you happy, Marci, because that's all that really matters to me. And you've more than proven working remotely is possibly on your trips abroad and the past few weeks. Once we have our new, state-of-the-art system and you're all trained up – you'll sort things from your end. And when you have time, you'll get to go on lots of buying trips to discover more wonderful Italian treasures for our discerning customers.'

I turn to look at Nico, and he's anxiously waiting to see my reaction. When I turn back around, I raise my glass and everyone else follows suit.

'It sounds like a perfect plan to me,' I reply. 'We should toast – to family and exciting times to come!'

After clinking glasses, hearing the raised voices, Selena rushes in to join us, as Mum, Guy, Nico and I jump up for a group hug. David is still sitting at the table staring around as if we've all gone mad.

'It's decided, then?' Selena asks and I nod my head.

'I'm so thrilled for you both – our dinner is now officially a celebration!'

As Guy heads off to help his wife in the kitchen, Mum leans in to explain in detail to David what this means for the future. Nico and I wander over to the window to look out over Selena and Guy's pretty little English garden.

Nico leans into me, throwing an arm around my waist and drawing me close.

'So, I will get to take you on that road trip after all,' he declares, unable to contain his delight. 'I saw the vision in my head. Driving along with the top down, your long hair flowing behind you and you're wearing the biggest smile. When I bought my prized car, I knew that she was waiting for a very special woman to sit beside me – and I've found her at last.'

'I can't wait for that day to come,' I reply, rendered a little breathless at the mere thought of what the future will hold.

The room behind us has gone quiet, but the only thing in my line of vision is the look on Nico's face. It's the look of love.

'I can't wait to take you back to Positano, but I guess I'd better get in some driving practice while I'm here, to prepare me for all those trips back to the UK.'

As Nico stoops to kiss me, I realise that love changes everything. Nothing else matters because you've found *the one* and suddenly anything is possible. Isn't life wonderful?

Epilogue

Richard Havrington

September in Positano – My Favourite Time of the Year!

There's only one other car parked up as we pull into the layby and you can tell that the peak season is over.

'We'll leave the luggage for now, Angel. There are plenty of strapping young men who will carry this lot down to the hotel, later. We're early and I want to surprise them all.'

My beautiful wife gives me the most dazzling of smiles. 'But you'll dig out the present, won't you?'

I extend my hand to grasp hers, as she eases herself out of the passenger seat of the hire car. The drone of an engine as the driver struggles to find the right gear makes me turn around. It's funny how it's the most innocuous things that bring the memories flooding back. My days of hiring a van and heading off to collect the latest acquisition and hairy moments, like dealing with a slipping clutch or a gearbox that fought every single change. It was all worth it, though, because the excitement of surrounding myself with treasures at La Grotta was a comfort – a crutch to keep me going.

Angel is standing in front of me, shaking her head. 'Remember: no regrets, Richie, you've moved on. This isn't an ending, it's a new beginning.'

'I know,' I reply, enthusiastically, pushing away all thoughts of how I'm going to feel when I visit La Grotta again. Angel slides her arms around my neck. 'And when we return to the UK, we can throw ourselves into making that little cottage of ours perfect.'

She puts her head back and the laughter as it falls from her lips makes my heart swell.

'It'll be fun, Angel.'

'Yes, but I don't think it will be long before you decide you're missing the sunshine, do you? Where you're concerned, Richie, nothing ever surprises me!'

A part of me will always belong here, and I know that Angel understands that. What if, during our stay, we just happen to stumble across the perfect place and fall in love with it – a place owned by some good friends of mine? We'd have the best of both worlds. Besides, there are a few loose ends I left behind that need tying up.

Angel looks deep into my eyes and words are unnecessary. She releases me with an artful grin, and I walk around to the back of the vehicle to open the boot. I gaze up at the noon-day sun overhead, then close my eyes for a brief second. Taking a deep breath in, I note that it smells of September here in Positano. Nature is welcoming the cooler days and nights, and the fragrances are subtly different.

'Angel, is it in a carrier bag? I can't see it.'

'No, honey, I popped it into the holdall.'

Thank goodness for that. I don't relish the thought of having to go through the suitcases. 'Yes, here it is!'

That's my wife – she can't visit anyone and arrive empty-handed.

'I'll take that – it's delicate.' She gives me a knowing look as I lock the car. 'Are you nervous or excited?'

'Both, in equal measure but I'm buzzing, Angel, simply buzzing.'

Walking hand in hand through the gated entrance to the hotel and restaurant, I spot one of Luca's easels with a printed sign on it, displayed in the middle of the courtyard. We head over to take a quick look.

'I so wish I could read that,' Angel declares. 'It's such a beautiful-looking language.'

'It says: *Welcome to Il Posto di Luca. The hotel is closed until 26 September as our family proudly celebrate the engagement of Nico and Marci. Ristorante Sul Mare remains open, and we invite our customers to join in our ongoing celebrations. Reservations for dinner are via our website only during this period. The Romano family would like to thank all our customers – old and new – for being a part of the journey.*'

'How sweetly put.'

'Richard!' Hearing Giulia shouting out my name as she rushes over to us, I know there's no hope of creeping in quietly now.

We hug and kiss. She looks happy and as I grasp her hands in mine, I stand back to look at her. She's wearing a floppy white chef's hat at a jaunty angle, instead of the usual bandana covering her hair. And in place of her double-breasted black jacket and black trousers, she's now wearing a crisp white chef's jacket and black-and-white houndstooth check trousers.

'Your dream has come true at last, and you wear that

hat with panache, Giulia!' I declare, as her smile lights up her entire face.

'It's more me, isn't it, than a tall pointy toque? Even Luca approves.'

'And when are you and Dario planning on announcing your news?'

'At Christmas. Uncle Luca has been wonderful and we are so grateful to him for understanding.'

'I'm delighted for you both, Giulia, and I know Nico is, too!'

'Richard!' Celia calls out, hurrying over and Luca is close on her heels. He's casually dressed and looking a good ten years younger than the last time we were together.

As Giulia and Angel hug excitedly, I walk towards my dear friends, feeling a tad emotional. Celia hugs me with tears in her eyes, and then Luca throws an arm around my shoulder.

'You 'ave been missed, Richard,' Luca states, brusquely. 'You 'ave been missed!'

The party is in full flow as the sky darkens around us. As usual, the diners eating here tonight feel very much a part of it, and that's what this Italian family is all about. It's the reason I stayed for so long and the reason I will never leave – not for good.

It was good to hear that Giulia now has a share in the restaurant. And Nico is the epitome of a *capocameriere* – the head waiter who keeps all the staff in line and ensures everything runs smoothly. As if my pride isn't already at bursting point, I'm standing next to my goddaughter, marvelling at the many blessings that life has been kind enough to bestow upon me.

'My darling Marci. I can't believe you're here and Positano is now your home. Here's to a wonderful future for you and Nico!' We chink glasses as we stare out to sea.

'Let's wander up to the pergola, Richard. It's quieter up there and I want to talk to you in private.'

'Lead the way, you'll know it well enough,' I chuckle away to myself. Nico and Marci are going to be married next spring and that impossible dream, the one I didn't even dare to utter out loud, has come true.

Marci is a very beautiful young woman, but she doesn't know it. Since the last time I saw her on a wet and windy day in January, at Gloucester Quays, she has blossomed. I have never seen her looking as relaxed and confident as she does tonight – it touches my heart.

As Marci goes ahead of me to climb the narrow steps up to the next level, she clasps the hem of her very chic-looking, floral, blue dress in one hand. She is going to be one stunning bride and when her mother, Evelyn, walks her down the aisle here in the grounds, she's going to be a tearfully proud woman.

When I join Marci at the top, she leans in, lowering her voice.

'Angel is every bit as special as I expected her to be. Is it unsettling, though, coming back, knowing that things are different now?'

'No, not at all. It's just a little strange not having a permanent base, but as we're here for two full weeks I'm sure something interesting will come up!'

Marci gives me one of her glittering smiles – she knows what I'm up to.

Stepping up onto the decking, I pull out a chair for Marci beneath the old wooden pergola, recollecting many a late-night discussion with Luca over a good bottle of wine.

'This was always my favourite spot,' I admit.

'Mine, too! It's where I first fell in love with Nico – I just didn't realise it at the time.' The way her eyes sparkle tells me more than words can ever convey. How can you describe that inner peace, the feeling of absolute contentment when you've found *the one*? The truth is that you can't, but you can see it reflected in the eyes.

'Ah, so you weren't trying to hide it from me, then?' I tease her.

'That's not my style, Richard, is it? I've always been totally honest with you. Even as an awkward teen, you were the only one I could tell my troubles to and know you wouldn't judge me.'

'As I hope you will not judge me, Marci. The truth has to come out sometime and that moment is upon us.'

Marci looks around nervously, even though we'd see anyone approaching long before they could overhear what we're saying.

'I'd hoped that Celia and Luca would have already sat down with Nico. Is the truth really that bad, that they couldn't face telling Nico until you were here too?'

'Partners in crime, Marci, partners in crime.'

She's visibly shocked and I'm surprised. I'd assumed that she'd guessed the truth.

'Hey, no one died. Some things aren't easy to hear, I grant

you that, but we all feel Nico will understand and forgive the decisions that were made in everyone's best interest.' I settle back in my seat to survey the garden in front of us.

Only my goddaughter could handle a situation she stumbled upon as delicately and as discreetly as she has, and we're all aware of that.

'Nico will understand that this is something that had to be done face to face, and we all wanted to be there to answer his questions,' I explain, hoping to reassure her.

It's a relief to be able to tell Marci the whole story. Even her mother, Evelyn, doesn't know about a part of my life that has remained hidden.

'As I went off to university all those years ago, I was totally unaware that one fateful night, when two young people sought comfort in each other and threw caution to the wind, would have repercussions that would bring me here to Positano well over a decade later.'

Marci hasn't moved a muscle – but the shock is very evident to see as the truth sinks in.

'Celia kept her secret from me and that was her decision entirely. The fact that she only reached out to me all those years later in sheer desperation, shows that she's not a woman who ever felt I owed her anything.'

Marci is stunned. '*You* are Nico's real father?'

'Yes. Celia wrote to me and told me the story of this place and the fact that Luca was about to lose every penny he'd invested. They were weeks away from having no roof over their heads, as the business was in dire trouble. Our son's happy life here and his future was under threat.' I stretch out my legs, tiredness beginning to kick in, but I'm not done yet.

'I wrote back giving Celia my number and she rang me a week or so later. In the meantime, she'd sent me some photos of Nico through the years. He was a teenager when I finally got to meet him. I'll never forget that moment. It was a rainy evening, and I was sitting inside the restaurant. It was the spot in the corner by that monster of an urn. Nico was waiting tables that night, but I had no idea he was going to serve me. When this young man suddenly appeared with my aperitif, I knew instantly he was my son.

'"I'm Nico," he said, proudly, thrusting his hand out to shake, like a real gentleman. "My mother said I should introduce myself."

'I felt an overwhelming sense of emotion sweep over me, as I stared at the confident young man I saw standing there. Of course, at that point Celia and I had already hatched our plan. I'd made it very clear that the money I gave her to tide them over was a gift. She named the sum, as it couldn't be too big. It had to appear to be her savings. Money means little to me and my aim was to help in an unobtrusive way.'

'And that's why you went on to become a partner in the business.'

'Yes. You look a little . . . relieved.'

Marci lifts her wine glass to her lips and takes a big gulp. 'You have no idea how happy I am to hear this, Richard. I can hardly take it in, but relief is putting it mildly.'

I exhale loudly, talking about this openly for the first time is releasing something inside of me. It's freeing to finally let go and know that the end is in sight. 'The money I put in isn't an investment for my future, it's Nico's legacy.'

Marci reaches over to put her hand on my arm, her eyes welling up as she can see how emotional this is for me. Tomorrow, Nico, too, will know the truth.

'It must have been a huge risk when Celia invited you here, Richard. For you and for her.'

And my darling Marci is right.

'It was, but Celia said it was only right that I should be a part of Nico's life going forward and at least have a chance of getting to know him as a friend of the family. I moved here, found somewhere to stay, and began eating at the restaurant. However, there is one thing Celia doesn't know. There was no way I could deceive Luca, a man I respect wholeheartedly, and who deserved my complete honesty. Even to honour Celia's wishes.'

'Luca knows?' Marci's eyes widen and I can understand why.

'He has always treated Nico like his own son and he has been a good father to him. One lie was enough to keep buried, two would have been unforgiveable. Luca understood I wasn't here to undermine him, as he will always be Nico's father. My role is different and it's one that Nico himself will determine.'

This is cathartic for me, but so very emotional for Marci, now that she knows everything.

'When I came here, the only sacrifice for me was seeing less of you and Guy – it was tough. And he rang a lot less frequently than you did, my darling! But at least he stayed in touch.'

That comment makes her smile.

'I was probably a bit of a pain at times, but I missed

you so much, Richard. If it weren't for your visits to the UK and my little buying trips to Italy allowing us to spend some time travelling around together having fun, I'd have been heartbroken.'

'And every call, every trip was precious, believe me, Marci.'

'But you never invited me here. Why?'

'Because I feared that if you saw me with Nico, you'd see the pride reflected in my eyes whenever I look at him. He takes after his mother, of course, with her mop of curly hair, but he has my nose and chin!' As she surveys my face for a moment, her eyes widen and she nods her head in agreement. 'Call it paranoia, Marci, but the secret wasn't mine to reveal.' It's not an easy admission to make, but it's the truth.

'Then why not talk Guy into coming here to clear out La Grotta?'

It's hard to suppress a smile as I look across at her.

'Because Guy would have focused on the antiques and probably thrown a lot of the paperwork away. In among that mess were things I couldn't let go of, not just yet anyway. And we all have our secrets, don't we? I knew you'd do a good job, but a thought kept popping into my head increasingly in those last few weeks I spent here. What if my goddaughter comes to Positano and finds true love with someone dear to my own heart?'

Marci lets out an explosive gasp. 'Richard! I can't believe you've just admitted that. I thought I was supposed to have a nice, relaxing summer while sorting out La Grotta?'

I give her a cheeky wink, and she bursts out laughing. 'It

was a huge job, and I knew it. But I also knew that you'd forgive me. Anyway, I'm an old romantic and if someone is going to fall in love, Positano is the perfect place to do just that, isn't it?'

And the rest, as they say, is history.

'Now let's get back to the others and have some fun!'

'Before we do . . . I have one more question. It's about the paintings in Celia and Luca's apartment. They're amazing.'

'I know what you're getting at. I gather you did look inside one of the crates. Some are mine, but one isn't.'

Marci looks a little embarrassed. 'I didn't go through them, but you'd said everything in the shop was for sale. When I managed to pull out one to take a quick peek, it wasn't signed.'

'You were, naturally, curious and a little concerned – and, in hindsight, rightly so. Luca painted it. His incredible artistry puts my dabbling to shame. But, oh my dear – now I can understand why you're relieved. I bet your mind was going off in all directions. Rest assured, everything connected to my financial affairs is above board.'

The look Marci gives me is apologetic. 'Luca? I will admit, that when Celia showed me around the apartment and I saw the incredible array of artwork displayed on the walls, I was surprised.'

I gaze at Marci, trying to see it from her perspective.

'Did you think they were frittering away my investment on paintings? Oh – don't tell me you thought I'd been caught up in some dodgy dealings?'

I can tell by her face that her thoughts were probably

in freefall at the time, wondering what on earth I'd got myself into.

'That particular painting is signed on the back and it's a near perfect representation. Luca's preference, though, is modern abstract and he paints for pleasure. You might not be aware, but he has completed many canvases – all originals, I hasten to add – over the years. I'm sure now that he's finally able to step back from his role, he'll be even more prolific. I've told him that it could be more than a hobby.'

Marci was worried for me and that touches my heart. As we stand, she suddenly throws her arms around me, kissing my cheek and I can feel her tears.

'Thank you for bringing me here to Positano and knowing me better than I know myself.'

'It's been good to get this off my chest and tomorrow is going to be a big day for us all, Marci. It changes very little, though, in reality. Nico will still be a Romano and he may prefer our secret to remain just that. But at least he will know the truth and that I've done the best I can for him in my own way.'

I watch as my beautiful goddaughter steps away, easing back her shoulders and drawing in a deep breath to shake off her worries. 'And I know he will be touched, Richard. You mean an awful lot to him as he sees you as both a friend and a mentor, which is rather special, don't you think?'

And that's the irony of life.

The moment I spotted her and Nico kissing earlier on, the chemistry between them made my heart soar. I knew then that my work was done.

As we find our way back to the vibrancy of the party that is in full swing on the terrace below, some words pop into my head.

'There is an old Italian saying, Marci: *Mangia bene, ridi spesso, ama molto*. Eat well, laugh often, love much.'

'Now that, my truly wonderful and eternally inspiring godfather, is exactly what Nico and I intend to do! And it's all because of YOU.'

Family first – always.

Lucy Coleman is a #1 bestselling author of contemporary romantic fiction. In 2013 she won the UK Festival of Romance: Innovation in Romantic Fiction Award. Originally from Bristol, she now lives in the Welsh Valleys with her husband, Lawrence and Bengal cat, Ziggy.

For Lucy, life is all about family, friends and writing. She is a self-confessed hopeless romantic and an eternal optimist. When Lucy is not writing, she spends time in the garden weeding or practising Tai Chi. And she is often found with a paintbrush in her hand indulging her passion for upcycling furniture.

Her novels have been translated into Italian, Czech and Croatian. She also writes as Linn B. Halton.

Lucy is represented by Sara Keane from the Keane Kataria Literary Agency.

About Embla Books

Embla Books is a digital-first publisher of standout commercial adult fiction. Passionate about storytelling, the team at Embla publish books that will make you 'laugh, love, look over your shoulder and lose sleep'. Launched by Bonnier Books UK in 2021, the imprint is named after the first woman from the creation myth in Norse mythology, who was carved by the gods from a tree trunk found on the seashore – an image of the kind of creative work and crafting that writers do, and a symbol of how stories shape our lives.

Find out about some of our other books and stay in touch:

Twitter, Facebook, Instagram: @emblabooks
Newsletter: https://bit.ly/emblanewsletter